THE MAGNES PROJECT

Gil didn't have a chance to reply before there was a flicker and flash of the floodlights bathing the entrance, and a rumbling vibration of the ground.

Corleski glanced around anxiously, weapon trembling in his tense grip. Somewhere in the distance a klaxon-like alarm began sounding.

Gil continued talking over its insistent bleat.

"Easy, detective, easy. You've known me for a while, Jeff, so I hope you can take some of this on trust. We have evidence that there's an illegal laboratory under this hospital. We know that there have been several murders there, and maybe a lot more. We don't know how many are involved, but it's more than a few. It's critical that we go down there before they get any further with something they call the Magnes Project."

Corleski looked nervously from person to person, his brow furrowed, then back at Beach.

"What's that alarm?" he finally asked.

"It's the hospital disaster alert," Michele answered. "It's part of our federal preparedness set-up. It only goes off to initiate the disaster plan. And from the ground movement we just felt, I don't think this is a drill!"

HAUTALA'S HORROR AND SUPERNATURAL SUSPENSE

GHOST LIGHT (4320, $4.99)
Alex Harris is searching for his kidnapped children, but only the ghost of their dead mother can save them from his murderous rage.

DARK SILENCE (3923, $5.99)
Dianne Fraser is trying desperately to keep her family—and her own sanity—from being pulled apart by the malevolent forces that haunt the abandoned mill on their property.

COLD WHISPER (3464, $5.95)
Tully can make Sarah's every wish come true, but Sarah lives in terror because Tully doesn't understand that some wishes aren't meant to come true.

LITTLE BROTHERS (4020, $4.50)
The "little brothers" have returned, and this time there will be no escape for the boy who saw them kill his mother.

NIGHT STONE (3681, $4.99)
Their new house was a place of darkness, shadows, long-buried secrets, and a force of unspeakable evil.

MOONBOG (3356, $4.95)
Someone—or something—is killing the children in the little town of Holland, Maine.

MOONDEATH (1844, $3.95)
When the full moon rises in Cooper Falls, a beast driven by bloodlust and savage evil stalks the night.

Available wherever paperbacks are sold, or order direct from the Publisher. Send cover price plus 50¢ per copy for mailing and handling to Penguin USA, P.O. Box 999, c/o Dept. 17109, Bergenfield, NJ 07621. Residents of New York and Tennessee must include sales tax. DO NOT SEND CASH.

DARK MEDICINE
BARRY T. HAWKINS

ZEBRA BOOKS
KENSINGTON PUBLISHING CORP.

ZEBRA BOOKS are published by

Kensington Publishing Corp.
850 Third Avenue
New York, NY 10022

Copyright © 1996 by Barry T. Hawkins

All rights reserved. No part of this book may be reproduced in any form or by any means without the prior written consent of the Publisher, excepting brief quotes used in reviews.

If you purchased this book without a cover, you should be aware that this book is stolen property. It was reported as "unsold and destroyed" to the Publisher and neither the Author nor the Publisher has received any payment for this "stripped book."

Zebra and the Z logo Reg. U.S. Pat. & TM Off.

First Printing: January, 1996

Printed in the United States of America

Disclaimer

Bellevue Hospital Center is a magnificent institution, with an incredible staff of dedicated medical and non-medical workers. It is necessary in a medical mystery thriller to create nasty characters and nefarious schemes within a setting. I hope my fiction will not be confused with fact, and that readers will understand that BHC continues to be an outstanding hospital center with a fine tradition of exemplary service to the community and those who come for healing. Conspiracies, prejudices, and negative attitudes that appear in the narrative are pure invention, and should not reflect on the actual institution or its people. Likewise, the fine officers of the Thirteenth Precinct, NYPD should never be compared to the characters described herein.

All events and characters of this book are fictional, and should not be confused with any actual events, or persons, living or dead. Descriptions of settings are accurate, except in certain instances, where minor modifications were made to serve the dramatic needs of the narrative, such as locating the specimen fixing lab next to the morgue.

Any inaccuracies are due to my failure as an observer or story teller, not to the fine people who aided me in my research. Errors or failures to accurately represent those institutions or professional groups that appear here, are my responsibility, not theirs.

Acknowledgments

A number of persons were helpful during research for this book. Particular thanks should go to Lucinda Klein, Office of Community Affairs, and Captain Thomas Moriarity, Bellevue Police, as well as their respective departments. Their assistance allowed me to see, first hand, the complexity and vitality of Bellevue. I shall never forget viewing the Emergency Department in action, or touring the lower depths of Bellevue's tunnel system.

Also invaluable in the research were previous books about Bellevue, including *Bellevue Is My Home*, by Salvatore Cutolo, M.D., *Bellevue: Documentary of a large metropolitan hospital*, by Don Gold, M.D., and *Emergency Doctor*, by Edward Ziegler, with Lewis Goldfrank, M.D.

Elements of the story were drawn from my own experiences working in acute care hospitals, and I could not enumerate the many who endured my ignorance and slow learning at St.Peters Hospital, Olympia, Washington, Lutheran General Hospital, Arlington Heights, Illinois, and Mercy Community Hospital, Port Jervis, N.Y. where I worked in positions ranging from orderly to administrator.

Thanks also to Mary Mullin, Bob Sullivan, Janet Wilkens Manus, and others who encouraged me before I ever published a word, my family who endured absence and obsession in the book's creation, to Lorraine, my earliest editor and perceptive critic, and Bill Wilson who made it possible for me to pursue my dreams. Engineers Al Pearson, Glen Schwenker, and Matt Coogan all contributed to my knowledge of their trade and the inner workings of a hospital. I also presumed on Rajan Gulati, M.D., Alan Vanderwald, M.D. and others for their kind technical advice. There are others who had their part in the creation of this piece of fiction. A novel is never the work of one person. To those who prefer to remain unnamed, or those I have forgotten, I offer my appreciation for their aid and apologize for anything I have omitted or gotten wrong.

It must now be understood that what has turned health care into a sick-making enterprise is the very intensity of an engineering endeavor that has translated human survival from the performance of organisms into the result of technical manipulation.
—Ivan Illich, *Medical Nemesis*

I sing the body electric
The armies of those I love engirth me and I engirth them
They will not let me off till I go with them, respond to them
And discorrupt them, and charge them full with the charge of the soul
—Walt Whitman, "I Sing the Body Electric"

One

This could be it. This could be the break.

Eddy Dorlander grabbed the old knit cap and held it up to the light, sticking a finger through one of several moth holes eaten into the drab fabric. He settled the worn cap on his head, pulling it down over hair mussed and greasy looking from a handful of lard he had applied to his longish locks for the occasion. Then he dumped the contents of an ashtray into one palm and rubbed it against his other hand to make a dirty paste of grime that he smudged onto his face and arms. His three-day stubble, naturally marked with patches of gray, helped create the look he was trying to achieve.

In a day or two, the contrived dirtiness would meld with the real thing, as he assumed the life of a homeless man on the filthy streets of the Bowery. Not that Eddy expected it to be too traumatic. He had carefully made emergency preparations which included money sewn into the lining of his worn jacket and stashes of food, cash, and booze in two secret locations near where he would be embarking on his little adventure. He didn't intend to get caught short. Naturally, he wouldn't mention that in the article. They don't give investigative reporting awards unless they believe the writer is some kind of adventurer, who places himself at risk to discover the truth.

Eddy had risked as much as he wanted to risk in his forty-seven years, and already knew enough truth to last a lifetime—truth about the world, truth about the city, truth about himself. But maybe this time he could fake it enough to get the big break. Maybe he could write a story about the homeless that would be his big break, make people forget some of his mistakes, win him some attention, maybe even a Pulitzer if he was lucky. He gave a dry laugh at the thought.

Edward Dorlander and luck had been real strangers lately, unless you count the bad kind. Once a halfway decent reporter for the *Post,* with a ranch house in the 'burbs, a good-looking wife, and a Corvette as his second car, recent years had not been as kind. Now he was a two-bit stringer for the *Eastside Evening Chronicle* and a couple of other forgettable weeklies, lived in a walk-up apartment in a bad neighborhood, didn't have any woman, even an ugly one, and borrowed his brother's ten-year old Dodge station wagon when he absolutely had to have wheels. Most of the time he put up with the buses, subways, and the riff-raff of the city that rode them. His ex-wife, Grace (now there was an example of a real poor choice of names), claimed the booze had something to do with it, but Eddy knew that was a pile of shit. For Eddy, booze was a solution, not a problem. It kept the world at bay.

He sat on his lumpy bed to put on his shoes, one of them slipping off his foot on the first try. After a couple of breaths and a swallow of whiskey, he tried again, and managed to get the thing on. The last drag on his cigarette had the bitter taste of a melting filter tip. He stubbed out the smoldering butt in a peeling coffee can on the scarred end table, almost tipping over the sand-filled container. He hawked and spit in the can. When he ambled over to look in the cracked mirror over the bureau, he was satisfied with the effect. Looking back at him was a believable Bowery bum. Maybe too believable.

Well, after this assignment, things would be different. Maybe he'd even try one of those A.A. meetings. Eddy took a long swallow from his pint of Jack Daniels. One of the nice things about playing the role of a down and out homeless bum was that he didn't have to worry, for a change, about how much he drank. No chance difficult editors or co-workers would poke their noses into his business and criticize him for his drinking. If he smelled like a brewery, so much the better. This was going to be a great investigative piece . . . a first person "smasheroo," as that idiot city editor put it. It would be better than "Black Like Me," the one written by a white guy who made himself look like a black man, and went around playing the part so he could get first hand experience of the life of minorities. Eddy sneered at the irony. That author had merely described the stuff black folks were saying all along, but got no notice until a white boy said the same thing. And the honky laughed all the way to the bank.

That's what Eddy planned to do. Spend a week on the street, write a great story, and break out of this rut where his life had gotten mired. Maybe it wouldn't even take a week. Five days ought to be enough. He could still call it a week. It was a workweek wasn't it? Eddy took another slug from the pint bottle. He figured he might as well finish it, since it was half empty anyway. Wouldn't hurt to start his adventure with a fresh bottle, just in case. He tossed the empty one into a trash can, grabbed another he had kept ready for such contingencies, and jamming it into his coat pocket, Ed took a deep breath, flicked off the bare-bulbed lamp, and locked the cheap room. It was a back-up place to crash, in case things didn't go well. He made his unsteady way down the stairs to the front entrance of the flea-bag hotel.

Eddy found out a couple of things about street life faster than he had planned. Half-crocked from the whiskey, he was weaving down lower Bowery Street in a pattern sure to attract human predators. Hardened youth on the prowl, they roamed in packs in lower Manhattan, that kept on the lookout for the weak and vulnerable . . . lone members of the herd, isolated and easy to take down. It didn't take them long to spot Dorlander and make their move.

After they were through with the reporter, he was missing four teeth and the contents of his pockets. He had a mild concussion and a broken hand, as well as several cracked ribs and a bruised kidney. He might have laid on the street for hours before someone noticed the difference between his bloodied form and the various other unconscious denizens of the Bowery, sprawled here and there along the street.

But luck was with him after all because a new storekeeper, not yet versed and schooled in the ways of the city streets, happened to see the assault. Unlike seasoned city residents, instead of pulling the shades he called the police. The dispatcher contacted the nearest available police car and EMS vehicle. In minutes the patrol car and an Emergency Medical Service ambulance arrived at the scene of Eddy's unfortunate introduction to the mean streets. The two EMTs that traveled with the vehicle quickly checked the groggy reporter's condition, determining that Eddy's life was probably not in danger. They strapped him onto a stretcher and loaded him into the ambulance. Fourteen minutes after he first hit the cement, Dorlander was on his way to the nearest hospital, Bellevue.

Two

In Holding Room #3 of the Bellevue Emergency Department, Dr. Michele Peters was having a tough time of it. Her patient had come to the ED instead of going to a doctor as was her custom, having no family doctor to treat her complaints. The presenting problem was stomach pains, a fairly common occurrence for the four-hundred-plus-pound woman. Only this time, Michele noted the woman's breasts were leaking colostrum, a thin yellow fluid secreted by the mammary gland around the time of parturition. A few other questions, and Dr. Peters confirmed that not only was the gargantuan woman pregnant, but that her stomach pains were symptoms of advanced labor. There wasn't time to transfer her to Obstetrics, and now the patient was in the process of giving birth to a full-term infant. Dr. Peters was trying to coax the baby into a position that would allow it to exit the large woman with as little damage as possible. It was quite a reach.

"Ain't that the damndest!" Aleesha, the patient, kept saying between groans, apparently unaware of her pregnancy until this moment.

"Goddamn Moe musta done it. Only man kept at it long enough. Ain't that the damndest!"

It had already been a tough sixteen-hour shift. Peters was assistant director of the Emergency Department. The director, Archibald Neely, actually directed both the

Bellevue and New York University Hospital E.D.s, as well as the New York Poison Control Center, while also serving on several other important boards and committees. As a result the assistant director handled much of the day to day management of the E.D. at Bellevue, as well as plenty of hands-on medical treatment. There were around a hundred-thousand cases seen in the unit annually, and Peters felt like most of them had come in during the last few hours. It was the week of the New York Marathon, and business was booming. But it wasn't the runners who came to the hospital. They went to private practitioners or more upscale medical facilities. During the Marathon each year, tens of thousands of athletes, relatives, and fans flooded the city. That meant several thousand people who spent most of their life living on the edges of New York civilization, were shoved out into the chaos and hostile environment of the city streets for a few days. Consequently they suffered additional diseases, exposure, and injuries. Sores festered, incipient diabetes flared up, strained cardiac muscles and circulatory systems shut down. Some desperate unfortunates even injured themselves on purpose, in order to get a place to stay the night—a place with clean sheets and hot meals.

Tonight was also October 31st. To some extent, every night at Bellevue was a bit like Halloween, but there were a few extra goodies on the real occasion. One woman was brought in with a serious bite on the neck from a guy who went a little too far with his Dracula impersonation. Another fellow had a severe allergic reaction to the red dye he used to coat his skin for a devil costume. He had added the dye to a tub of water and immersed himself, so certain sensitive portions of his anatomy were particularly affected. And there were also more than the usual number of knife and gunshot wounds, due to excessively realistic weapons carried by Halloween pirates, gangsters, cowboys, and knights of the round table.

Dr. Peters found her mind drifting, in spite of, or perhaps because of the bizarre circumstances, to thoughts of an administrative position in the medical world. Ira Wachman, the venerable medical director of this huge center, was nearing retirement. How close was anybody's guess, but plenty of folks were guessing. Other staff physicians were jockeying for the position, either hoping to succeed the aging patriarch or take the assistant medical director slot, should it be vacated in the process. That post was now held by Carl Troop, an excellent internist and viable candidate for the top job as far as Michele was concerned, but probably too nice a guy to get the position.

"Michele, are you okay?" a quiet voice interrupted her thoughts.

It was Elena Coogan, the assisting nurse. After hundreds of hours working together in crisis situations, they were on a first-name basis, and had shared many conversations about their work and the pitfalls of medicine. Peters realized she had been staring at the wall, oblivious to the messy scene in front of her.

"Oh. Yeah. Sorry," she said quietly, so the patient wouldn't hear. "I was just thinking about how it might be nice to have a job where you didn't have to work impossibly long shifts and get coated in bodily fluids several times a day."

"Not to mention having to worry about getting infected with Hepatitis or AIDS," Elena added in the same undertone.

There was nothing to do for a moment but wait while the woman worked to expel her baby. The doctor and nurse continued their conversation.

"Hmmm. True. I'd even settle for getting home at a reasonable hour."

"Well, if you want a job in administration, everybody knows that there's gonna be a spot or two available at the top, soon. You've got the right qualifications."

"If you mean the medical director slot, I might have the public qualifications, but there are others . . ."

"Oh, you mean . . . ?"

Peters nodded. They had discussed this before. Michele believed that one of the unspoken qualifications was that any director or assistant director had to be male. Apparently, Elena agreed.

"That pisses me off," the nurse responded. "Why don't you do something about it?"

"Well, as long as it's a secret criterion, it's hard to address. Some of them aren't even aware that they're prejudiced against women."

"So tell them!"

"Oh sure, and get labeled as a radical women's libber and malcontent!"

"But you aren't."

"I know," Michele agreed, "but I'm afraid that not everyone makes the distinction between a woman who asserts herself and one who's a fanatic."

Fanatics, Peters knew, didn't get top positions. She wondered what her chances were of obtaining the directorship or assistant spot. Though she wouldn't publicly admit it, she wanted nothing more than to try her hand at such a responsibility.

Peters continued to mull the issue in her mind, as Elena went to get some ice chips for the woman in labor. Michele suspected that for many in the medical establishment, woman physicians were just rather well-trained R.N.s—good for dirty work and assisting the real doctors. She wouldn't say that to Elena, as it might be interpreted as a put-down of nurses. But for centuries, that was the only role that a woman had open to her in the medical system.

Women had come a long way since she had been refused entrance to one medical school due to her attractive appearance. She was accepted elsewhere, but later learned why she had been refused at her first choice. The admissions committee felt she might be a distraction to the male students, and probably would become pregnant and drop out of school anyway. Not that they admitted it. She'd only learned of the prejudicial treatment, when having fought her way into the sacred ranks, she was told the truth in confidence by a physician who had been present at the admissions committee discussion years earlier.

Now almost a third of medical school students were women. But the power positions were still largely male-dominated and too often women seemed to find their way into pediatrics, anesthesia, and oncology rather than the glamour fields of surgery or emergency medicine. As usual, she was an exception to the rule, and in keeping with her pioneering career, she had her eye on an administrative job as her ultimate goal. Emergency medicine was not nearly as glamorous, as was underlined by the gush of blood and fluids that now sprayed over her arm, shoulder, and the side of a once white lab coat.

Along with the noxious fluids, however, came a squalling little tangle of limbs and lumps that she quickly identified as a healthy baby girl. As a waiting nurse swabbed off the worst of the birth coating, the infant opened its eyes and stopped crying. Big dark pupils stared out at a brand new world and seemed to be scanning her surroundings. As Elena checked off the APGAR score, the baby fixed its gaze on Dr. Peters. It had the expression of a wise old woman, silently monitoring, evaluating, noting. Michele found herself chuckling. But somehow, along with the laughter, moisture formed in her eyes. She didn't know if she was feeling good, or very sad.

Three

Eddy Dorlander was picked up by members of the East Village EMS division, ambulance number eleven. The hospital didn't send one of the extensively equipped and professionally staffed Mobile Emergency Rescue Vans, so there was no doctor in the vehicle, no heroic scene of anxiety laden telemetry transmissions and no dashing emergency rescue techniques. Maybe that was because the injuries didn't appear life-threatening, or maybe Bowery bums don't rate as much concern. Eddy had not taken any identification on his adventure, so that he wouldn't have it stolen, or be prematurely identified as the famous reporter he thought he was. So he was treated just like any other John Doe. Standard protocol covered most of this case, and they soon arrived at the Emergency Entrance of Bellevue on 29th Street, lights flashing only for show. As usual in Manhattan, most vehicles didn't pay attention anyway.

The ambulance rolled into the receiving bay with a loud screech of brakes by the driver, Roger Stamfer. It was one way to have a little fun with this job. Unlike his partner, Tony Pagano, who had just completed his EMT training, Roger had been at it for three years. He liked the job, but wanted some change and looked forward to qualifying as a paramedic—the next step up. He jumped out of the side door, walked to the rear, and opened the back. Tony was inside, next to the semiconscious figure. Together they slid the stretcher out onto the loading dock, the grimy reporter firmly strapped in place.

When they pushed through the scarred receiving doors of the Emergency Department, wheels clacking over cracks in the concrete, it was less like a scene from a dramatic TV medical show, than a Federal Express delivery. A few feet down the corridor, on the left, was the triage desk, occupied by a nurse that looked like she had seen everything.

"Sign here," she reminded them, shoving out a clipboard with rumpled pages of notations about "Patient Transport." Roger signed, and the two EMTs headed for the coffee shop.

"Hold it!" the nurse yelled, looking more like a prison guard than an angel of mercy.

"Move your friggin' vehicle before you go disappear to feed your faces. You think we got unlimited parking out there?"

"Okay, babe, okay," Roger placated her. "No need to panic. We'll move it."

While this interchange was taking place, a sharp-faced man in a white lab coat was looking at the man on the stretcher. He slipped a stethoscope onto Eddy's chest, prodded a few places, and glanced at the preliminary notes, including the classification "undomiciled," and the space for next of kin, which merely stated "none." He nodded, as if confirming something to himself.

"You can send him over to Radiology."

"But Dr. Wesley, he isn't even urgent," the nurse protested, "minor trauma, and AOB . . . John Doe from the Bowery."

The initials stood for "Alcohol On Breath," while the reference to where the man was found was another kind of code. It meant a hopeless indigent. It would be wrong to suggest that such people got less than excellent care from the medical personnel at Bellevue. But it would be just as wrong to suggest that no assumptions were ever made about this city's flotsam, or that it never made a difference in the speed of response.

The nurse's job was a sorting process, triage. Each case was first classified as "non-urgent," "urgent," or "emergent." This determined the order they would be treated. With hundreds of admissions a day, there had to be a screening procedure. Sometimes it meant someone with a broken finger might have to wait hours before they were seen, but it was either that or have patients with more serious injuries dying in the waiting room because they hadn't been moved to the head of the line.

The narrow-eyed man stared stonily at the nurse who was so presumptuous as to question a physician, then spoke in icy tones.

"A fractured rib can penetrate a lung, a concussion can begin a brain hemorrhage. There may be soft organ damage in the abdomen. Send him to Radiology!"

Mindy showed her disagreement in a tight-lipped pout, but said no more. She was a veteran of too many nurse-doctor conflicts where the physician pulled rank and won. She reached for the intercom to call one of the hospital volunteers that served as patient transporters, and nearly jumped when she found a huge form lurking inches from her back. It was "Buzz" Merkel, and only the fact that it would take at least a nuclear explosion or visit from an alien spacecraft to get a rise out of her kept the nurse from crying out. Mindy found the guy creepy, with his hulking weight-lifter's body gone to fat and heavy browed face wearing a perpetually sneering expression, but she especially hated it when he snuck up like that. What the radiology technician was doing in the E.D. she didn't know, but since he was there, Mindy told him to take the recent arrival down to X-ray, and she quickly turned to other duties. Buzz grabbed one end of the gurney and started moving down the hall.

The ride was a long one. Much longer than it should have been to take a stretcher the few yards down the main corridor and through the door on the right, connecting the Emergency Department with the neighboring Radiology unit. The main Radiology Department at Bellevue is located on the third floor, but the journey didn't go there either. There were several turns, and a lengthy wait, followed by a slow elevator trip downward, and another twisting trip that seemed to go on forever. A sensitive observer might have noticed many changes in the sound of the wheels, as they passed over wood, cement, tile and innumerable cracks, bumps, and dents. But Dorlander knew nothing of this. Between his injuries and copious intake of alcohol, he was not aware of much.

The reporter's first idea that something might be wrong was when excruciating pain flooded through his drugged brain, waking him from a semi-comatose state. He groggily opened his eyes and found himself in a dark room, where he lay strapped to a hard plastic table. Over him were several immense pieces of equipment, including two huge donut-shaped rings in molded plastic, reminding him of something from a science fiction movie. A dish-like thing with copper fittings pointed down at him as if aimed to fire, and it was surrounded by several large glass tubes with shiny metal wires, as well as elaborate circuit boards with numerous computer chips inside. Thick black, rubber-coated cables ran in a profusion overhead, connecting various pieces of apparatus. A deep humming sound was building to an ever higher pitch, and vibrations shook the entire floor, which appeared to be dirt.

The scene wavered before Dorlander's eyes, the result of something more than the booze, or even the pain, and that was intense. His whole head felt like it was exploding, and his body seemed to be on fire. Once, a couple of years ago, he had been seasick for eight straight hours on a drift-fishing expedition off of Cape May, but nothing could compare with the nausea he was feeling now. Dry heaves racked him and he felt as if his muscles were breaking apart. To some extent, he was correct in his analysis.

Four

As switches were thrown, knobs turned, and buttons pushed, power surged through the machinery. Massive electromagnets hummed into action, energy-emitting tubes glowed with power, and radioactive rods were drawn out of their protective cases. Intense waves of overlapping energy filled the room, and the man lying there. Generated fields of enormous strength bathed him in a silent storm of potent force.

At the cellular level, the basic building blocks of the body began to disintegrate. The ionization of the cell membranes, essential to their function and integrity, was disrupted. No longer able to maintain their integral qualities, the cell walls began leaking fluid into the spaces between tissues. Regulatory processes that control such insults to the body were also interrupted. Body temperature elevated, until blood and other vital fluids nearly boiled. In a brief time, Edward Dorlander's body went through much the same process as a slab of roast beef that has been "nuked" too long in a microwave oven. Only it didn't smell as good.

Eddy never saw The Doctor in the next room, watching through a shielded one-way glass window. The Doctor's furrowed brow and grumbling tone indicated displeasure, as an assistant scribbled dictated notes on a pad. It wasn't until several minutes after Ed died that The Doctor entered the experimental chamber and jabbed at the deteriorated flesh of his with a metal probe. Buzz Merkel stood ready for instructions, listening to the mumbled observations that made little sense to him.

"Still the wrong combination. But he lasted longer. And he seemed to gain an immense charge of energy there at the six-minute mark. Did you see him try to get up? The potential is definitely there. I just have to modify the ratios and find a way to increase the Odic force. That is clearly the element that's still missing."

Buzz nodded, without understanding. "You want I should take him away now, Doc?"

"Yes, yes, the usual."

The hulking man turned the cart and wheeled it away with its unmoving load to be swallowed by the darkness of a long and shadowed tunnel.

Five

Dr. Michele Peters was so tired she could hardly stand up any longer, but she knew that Darby Waterly needed help. Somehow Darby had managed to complete medical school and the requisite internship. However, Michele was convinced that it had to be a matter of preferential treatment. The man was ignorant and inept. Yet he was now a first year resident at Bellevue, and there could be no explanation other than politics. Waterly was the son and grandson of physicians—influential and wealthy physicians. The word was that it had taken an extra year for him to finish his work, even at the South American osteopathic medical school into which his family's money had reputedly bought admission. His residency at Bellevue, the rumors claimed, was an arrangement in respect to his father, a doctor of mediocre talent, but extensive political connections. Supposedly, Waterly the Second had been personal physician to J. Edgar Hoover, and knew where more skeletons were buried than the guide at Arlington National Cemetery. And some of those skeletons were to be found in the closet of a New York Assemblyman, an ambitious Borough President, not to mention various criminal justice officials.

But right now, Darby's father and money were useless to him. He was trying to perform a spinal puncture in trauma slot number two and was having a hell of a time with it. The patient had been admitted as the result of a motor vehicle accident, in which he had ran his motorcycle into a 3600 lb. luxury sedan. The man had been unconscious ever since the accident. Bruised brain tissue swells, and it was now imminently vital to determine if pressure was building inside the encased central nervous system. That could be done with a lumbar tap, the procedure Darby was now attempting.

Michele knew that the procedure was not without risk, though a relatively standard one that any emergency physician should be able to perform easily. But this wasn't any emergency physician, it was Darby Waterly. He had been jabbing away for almost half an hour on the poor patient. You had to say this for Waterly, he didn't give up easily. There were various puncture holes in the patient's back, as well as mangled needles lying bent and bloodied on the drape. Darby was dripping sweat, and had probably violated sterile procedure both with the drops of perspiration and the multiple attempts to accomplish his task without re-gloving.

Dr. Peters was alerted to Darby's problems by the assisting nurse, Carol Schmidt, who looked like she was ready to blow a cork. Michele understood the RN's frustration, but avoided any critical comment about Waterly. She didn't like him any better than Carol, but was determined to keep a professional attitude. After all, it was Waterly's case, whether she thought he could handle it or not.

Rather than rush to the scene, she stopped in the women's room long enough to splash some cold water on her face and run a brush through her hair. Among the reddish highlights, she caught sight of a strand of gray. It wasn't the first. Below fuzzy eyebrows that had been described as sexy, her deep brown eyes were ringed with dark circles of exhaustion. But Michele had learned long ago that she could keep going despite being bone weary. That was one of the first lessons of internship, and one which had served her well since. She patted her face dry with paper towels and tried on a cheerful expression. A little dimple formed in her cheek at the effort, but she didn't have the energy to maintain it for long. She sighed and strode quickly to where she was needed.

When Peters stepped into trauma slot two, she tried to act casual, announcing her presence in a cheery voice.

"How's it goin'?" It sounded like a cliché, but the question was in earnest. She raised her eyebrows and tilted her head in a way that suggested her concern. Waterly didn't answer directly, but his appearance was enough. He always had on a sort of droopy-eyed expression that seemed to go with his short, slump-shoulder posture. But this was the "I think I'm in over my head" expression, familiar to Michele Peters as one that often crossed the faces of many interns. However, the look wasn't supposed to be as common among residents like Waterly, especially when conducting such standard procedures. Fortunately, the patient wasn't conscious, so only the nurse and Peters saw the forlorn desperation and fear on the puppy-dog face.

Dr. Peters waved Carol over to the front of the patient, who was lying on his left side. She hooked the nurse's left arm behind the man's upper knee, and her right arm around the back of his neck, indicating that she should pull on both. This placed the patient into a fetal position that spread the spinal vertebrae, making it easier to insert a needle. Reaching across to feel the lumps of the projecting spinal processes, Peters saw from previous punctures that Waterly had correctly located the third and fourth lumbar vertebrae, but due to poor positioning he had been hitting bone instead of the intervertebral space.

She whispered a reminder to Waterly to keep the needle horizontal until it actually penetrated the spine, then slant it slightly towards the patient's head. He nodded, and with the vertebrae properly separated, finally managed to get the needle where it was supposed to go, a barely audible "pop" signaling that it had penetrated the tough membrane enclosing the subarachnoid space. A few drops of clear liquid escaped when he removed the inner cannula. Then he attached a gauge to the stopcock to check CSF pressure. The manometer registered a pressure of 11 millimeters of mercury, within normal limits. The sag of Waterly's shoulders told of his relief. It wasn't immediately clear whether that was because the pressure was good, or just that the test was completed. He filled three small glass tubes with small amounts of fluid for further testing, and then removed the tap.

Later Waterly acknowledged Peters' assistance.

"Thanks, Michele. That was stupid of me. It won't happen again. I appreciate your help, and . . . well, that you didn't embarrass me."

His sad-eyed remorse kept her from saying what she actually thought, that he had embarrassed himself. Waterly wasn't even an M.D. Unknown to most patients, there was another whole group of physicians that served internships and residencies at many hospitals. Doctors of Osteopathic Medicine, D.O.s, had once been completely snubbed by the medical establishment. An osteopathic physician was seen as a cross between a chiropractor and superstitious herbalist. Basically that meant a quack.

However, in recent years, both osteopathic medicine and the medical establishment had changed. Although trained in a more holistic theory of medicine than an M.D., a D.O. covered much of the same ground in med school, and in New York served their internship and residency alongside everyone else, which was partly why they could be fully licensed to practice medicine in the state. There was still plenty of prejudice, of course. Many D.O.s chose to establish their practices in small towns and hospitals rather than constantly deal with the resistance they got in the larger urban settings.

While it was unusual for a D.O. to be in residency at Bellevue, it was not unheard of. That could be another indication of Waterly's powerful connections. Michele wasn't sure how much her opinion of Darby had to do with his medical degree. She hoped that it wasn't just a prejudice. She had been on the receiving end of discrimination often enough that she didn't want to be guilty of it herself.

Seventeen hours after coming on duty, Dr. Michele Peters walked out of the Emergency Department entrance. Twelve minutes later, in her room at the staff quarters on the sixth floor, she fell into a troubled and restless sleep.

Six

Detective Sergeant Gil Beach was feeling lousy. He wondered if it was the donuts—a full half dozen that he had scarfed down since breakfast, or maybe he was just worn-out. He hadn't taken a vacation for over a year. Two days before, he had worked seventeen hours straight and only caught a few hours sleep on a cot in a back room of the precinct detective unit. His fitness workout the next day had taken more out of him than usual. Though he had been doing the same stair-climbing routine for years, he had limped home last night like an old man. He felt sixty years old instead of his actual forty-two. Even though he had gone to bed early, he hadn't slept well and awoke feeling tired and irritable. He tried doughnuts and coffee—cop vitamins.

But now, six cups of battery-acid strength Columbian and five assorted Dunkin' donuts later, he felt worse. When he rubbed his cheek he felt stubble, reminding him he hadn't shaved. He eased his body out of the chair and shuffled to the detective unit's bathroom where he kept an extra razor. The sink was ancient and must have been made for midgets. Gil was just under six feet, so he kept dripping water and shaving cream on his shirt. It was inevitable that he would also cut himself. It was one of those days.

So he wasn't in the best of moods when the call came

in from Lucille Sitra, city editor at the *Eastside Evening Chronicle,* New York City's only evening daily.

"Lucky Strike means fine woman," the voice said, when he picked up the receiver and punched the flashing button for line three. Lucille was a long-standing acquaintance, and years before he had christened her "Lucky Strike" because of her initials, L.S.

"Hiya, Lucille. What's up?"

"Look, I hate to bother you, Gil, but I'm beginning to wonder if it's open season on my people. Last year that creep killed Grady. You got the guy that did it, but it was still a real loss to us. A few months later Ellen Hefner gets run over by a friggin' horse-drawn carriage in Central Park because a hack didn't like the story she did on the treatment of animals in that business. Now one of my stringers is missing."

"What do you mean, missing?"

"Well, the guy is Ed Dorlander. You might remember him from the *Post.* He's had some good pieces over the years. He's got a problem or two, mostly with the bottle, but keeps trying. I don't know why I bother, but I feel kinda sorry for the guy. I told him he could do a story for me on the current status of services for the homeless. An exposé kind of piece, where he lives the life of a street person for a while and tells what it's like from the inside."

"Hasn't that been done?"

"Almost every story has been done, some way, somehow. The names and the places change, but people are always people, animals are always animals, and shit usually drops down the same direction. But a good writer can always come up with a new angle. Eddy used to be a good writer. I keep giving him chances."

"So what's the problem? He take off with your money?"

"No Gil, nothing like that. I'm worried. I don't need

to tell you that a week on the Bowery is no walk in the park. So I insisted that he keep to a schedule of call-ins, just to be on the safe side."

"He isn't keeping the schedule?"

"He never made the first call, Gil."

"You sure he started the assignment?"

"I think so. We talked about it just before he was to go out, and he seemed all set. When I didn't hear from him I sent Art Mellor, one of my best men, up to the room we rented for him near where he would start. The place is a dump, but it looked like he had gone on the assignment. He left all his regular stuff—wallet, credit cards, I.D., you know. I'm worried, Gil."

"You said he had a problem with the sauce. Maybe he just went out on a bender."

"I don't think so, Gil. This was a real important job for him. He talked like it was his chance to get back in the mainstream. He might have gotten drunk, but he'd call, he'd make excuses, he'd do something to keep this alive."

"Okay, Lucille, I believe you. So why don't you make out a missing person report, and . . ."

"Oh come on, Gil. You know that's not going to get any action. I was hoping you could do a little checking for me. I already did all the standard stuff, calling the morgue, hospitals, and all that. But he was using a fake name and wasn't carrying any I.D., so I could only do so much. Whadda ya say, big guy? The Bowery's your turf, isn't it?"

Beach sighed, ran his fingers through his hair, and swallowed the last cold coffee from the bottom of his mug before answering.

"All right," he grumbled. "When you get that tone in your voice, I know I'd better give in. I'll see what I can do."

An hour later Gil had checked the logs and tracked

down two emergency 911 responses that he thought might have had something to do with the missing reporter. The second sounded like he had hit pay dirt. Following it up he interviewed a kind-hearted storekeeper, who gave a description loosely matching Dorlander's for a bum that got mugged and taken to Bellevue. Technically, the hospital was located in the Thirteenth Precinct, but Beach was just after information at this point, so he didn't worry too much about boundaries. There was a lot of overlap at Bellevue anyway, with NYPD, Bellevue Hospital Police, and V.A. cops from the hospital next door, as well as visiting officers from a dozen other jurisdictions. There was even a full unit of corrections officers assigned to the hospital, with a special "Blue Room" just for holding waiting prisoners.

Bellevue was the designated hospital for various kinds of regional emergencies, including the place where the President of the United States would be taken, should he ever need emergency care while in the area. Several years before, Beach's partner Frank Terranova had been shot down and taken to Bellevue with a serious wound. Gil remembered the name of a physician who had been instrumental in pulling Frank through the crisis—it was Dr. Dan Holland. There was a Dr. Peters who had done the initial emergency stabilization, and a Dr. Whalen who had been the surgical wizard. But Holland had been the physician of record, the one who managed the overall progress of treatment, and the one who eventually discharged Terranova almost as good as new. Gil decided to give Holland a call.

After a frustrating series of delays, transfers, and incomprehensible instructions from the electronic voice mail system, he angrily slammed down the receiver. Gil hated the new mechanized answering systems. It seemed to him that machines and electronics were taking over, everywhere.

He gave himself a few minutes to calm down, and then called back. This time he immediately dialed "O" for the operator and waited until he got a human being on the other end of the line. She was surprised when he asked her name, but answered that it was Dottie. When Beach asked for Dr. Holland, Dottie apologized that the physician was no longer on the staff at Bellevue. So he asked for Whalen, who turned out to be in surgery and not available. Finally, he mentioned Dr. Peters. Dottie paged the emergency department physician, and after a short wait, Gil heard another woman's voice. It was a pleasant voice, suggesting warmth and humanity. But Gil had been through a lot of dead-ends and wrong numbers, so it took him a minute to realize he had finally reached the person he was seeking.

"Hello. Can I help you?"

"Damn. Uhh, look. I'm trying to reach a Dr. Peters."

"You've got her."

"Her? Oh . . ."

"Yes, the doctor is a woman. I hope that you're not too disappointed."

"Oh no . . . no. Not at all. I didn't mean anything. When my partner Frank Terranova got hit, I just heard that 'Dr. Peters' did a great job, and I, I . . . Oh shit . . . I guess I just did my usual thing and stuffed a number ten boot into my mouth."

There was silence on the line for a moment, then a small tinkle of laughter.

"Forget it. I remember your partner."

"You do?"

"Sure, the cop with the corny sense of humor. He comes into the E.D. half dead, missing so much blood we had to pump it in like water, and some nurse trying to be friendly asks him how he feels. 'With my hands, honey' he says, 'with my hands.' Can you believe it? A few minutes later he was telling dirty jokes."

"Sounds like Frank all right. I never thanked you for putting up with his awful jokes . . . or keepin' his butt out of a coffin."

"Temporarily, anyway. Even if he doesn't keep getting into gun battles somebody still might kill him on account of the jokes."

Gil was enjoying the conversation and had the feeling that this was a woman worth knowing. But when he started asking questions about recent John Doe admissions, unclaimed bodies, admitted indigents, and related matters, her tone changed. Instead of joking and sharing good-natured reflections, she became coolly professional, carefully evasive.

Beach was an experienced detective. He recognized the tone as one that people often acquired when they were not speaking openly. Most frequently it was a sign of fear. In addition to his curiosity about her evasiveness, he was interested in seeing the person behind the pleasant, yet assertive voice, so he asked if she could make time to see him. There was a long moment of hesitation. When Gil interjected that he would bring along Frank Terranova, the successfully recovered product of her earlier efforts, Dr. Peters agreed to meet with them.

Seven

When she hung up the phone, Michele Peters wasn't sure what she was feeling. The detective had been interesting to talk to, and it might be nice to meet him, along with the guy she had sewn up long ago. Despite her tongue-in-cheek criticism of his humor, she remembered the man as a real gutsy guy. Underneath his invariably cheerful attitude, he had shown the kind of mental toughness that few could claim.

One of the drawbacks to Emergency Medicine as a specialty, Michele reflected, was that after you did your thing, you seldom got a chance to see the end results. You made those crucial first decisions, took the initial steps, then turned the patient over to others. It was good to know that this one had turned out so well, and it would be nice to see for herself. It might be nice to see the person behind the voice of Detective Beach, too.

On the other hand, she felt uncomfortable about the questions the detective was asking. Or more accurately, Michele was uncomfortable with the answers she felt like giving. Standing at the nurses' station, where any number of people could hear the conversation, she was forced to fall back on stock answers and evasions. But she was troubled that she didn't really have good answers to some of the questions that she was posing to herself. The detective's queries were not really difficult by themselves, but they raised other, more disturbing issues—questions about the treatment of the disadvantaged, prejudices, values, and what made a death matter. Michele wondered if these doubts were better left unexamined, yet that raised still another issue—better for whom?

As these thoughts were bouncing around in her head, Michele walked along the corridor toward the rash room, where a case of dermatitis was waiting, possibly industrial chemical-induced. Lost in thought, she ran right into Theodore Jamison, the deputy chief administrator of the Medical Center. Ted was a busy man, and seldom missed an opportunity to let you know it.

The collision was minor, Michele's hundred and ten pounds lightly bouncing off the larger man, but Jamison still gave her an annoyed look.

"Oh hello, Ted. Sorry about that."

When there was no response other than an icy glare, Michele decided to move on, but the administrator stopped her.

"I've been wanting to speak to you, Dr. Peters. It concerns a procedural matter."

"Like what?"

"Well, it's these histories your people have been taking."

He was referring to the medical information taken as one of the first and most vital steps in arriving at a diagnosis.

"We've done a study," Jamison continued, "that indicates an average time of 9.96 minutes is being used to take a medical history. If that is multiplied by a hundred thousand admissions, we are talking about close to one million minutes, or sixteen thousand, six hundred hours, which adds up to some two thousand seventy-five eight hour shifts of medical personnel time."

"Tell me when you find a doctor that works eight-hour shifts around here," she interjected wryly. Jamison was not deterred.

"So in a year, we use the equivalent of almost six full-time equivalents just taking histories."

Michele knew that the time used taking medical background was well spent. Less than ten minutes per history was also a pretty efficient average, especially when she considered that certain physicians, like Darby Waterly, took a lot longer than that. It was obvious that the career administrator was thinking like an accountant rather than a doctor. But before making the mistake of saying that, she remembered that Jamison was, in fact, not a physician at all, though he had supposedly done some postgraduate research in allied fields. In truth, he was probably better trained in accounting than medicine.

"Are you asking me to push for quicker histories, Ted? Under ten minutes is really pretty brief, you know."

"Actually, I was thinking along other lines entirely, doctor. I have been looking into new computer-assisted assessment technology. With CAA, patients sit in front of a small monitor and respond to questions on the screen. By typing simple answers, or merely choosing options presented to them, they can give their entire medical history without anyone else being involved. By installing a CAA system, we could eliminate thousands of hours of unnecessary personnel involvement."

"You aren't serious, are you Ted? This is an Emergency Department. The people who come here are pretty sick."

"The greatest majority of our admissions, some seventy-five percent, are not truly life-threatening diagnoses. Even if we don't count urgents, that leaves almost half our admissions as non-urgent cases. A good many of them are just using the E.D. as their family doctor. They are able to sit on an examining table and answer questions—so why couldn't they do the same in front of a computer?"

Michele knew that part of what Ted was saying was true. Not all cases were emergencies. One of the sad realities of urban life was that there were few family physicians willing to treat uninsured or Medicaid-insured people, so they came to the E.D. for everything from ear aches and runny noses to boils and impetigo. Maybe some of these people with less severe problems could manage to follow the instructions of a computer, though she had her doubts about that, but there was a more important consideration.

"Ted, you don't really think a computer can have the insight of a doctor, do you?"

"Oh, no, not another believer in the mysteries of the medical mystique! Surely you know, Dr. Peters, that computers have evolved to such a degree they are making many human functions obsolete."

"Well, I'm sure you can't wait until that includes the role of the physician," she shot back at the administrator, "but until that day comes, you aren't going to find a box of electronics that can notice a tremor or pallor to the skin that suggests a question about exposure to certain industrial chemicals and suggest to a patient some possibilities he hadn't even considered, or sees a flinch in a man's eye when he speaks of how his father died, and guesses that there was a history of alcoholism, even when the patient denies it."

"You sound like the old anti-intellectuals, who refused to believe we would fly or reach the moon. Look, don't dismiss me as some kind of caricature here. I may not be a physician, but I'm not stupid."

Michele realized that he had nearly read her attitude. She was about to discount everything he said, because he wasn't a doctor. He was right about that, and Michele also knew the man was far from stupid.

"I'm not proposing to replace doctors," he went on. "I'm not even sure about supplementing our assessment procedures this way, but it's definitely worth investigating. Face it, Dr. Peters, technology is doing things now that your parents would have thought impossible, and in the decades ahead it will make your assumptions about human uniqueness seem like superstition."

"Well, maybe you're right, Ted. But I can only live in the present, not some fantasy of the future. And right now, a good doctor is most folks' best bet for finding medical answers."

Dr. Peters turned then, to head through the swinging doors, unhappy with herself for being so easy to aggravate, and wondering if perhaps she was more old-fashioned and rigid than she thought herself to be. Yet, one of the reasons she had applied to serve at Bellevue instead of many other hospitals was its emphasis on the skill of the physician. The center had many marvels of medical science available to diagnose and treat those that came crying to its doors. But Bellevue wasn't always the best when it came to state-of-the-art equipment or facilities. It wasn't technology that made it special.

What made this hospital the one where she and many thousands of other doctors had chosen to learn and refine their skills, was the reputation of BHC for making physicians use everything they had *inside* themselves. She believed this made the best doctors possible—not just glorified technicians who could choose tests and run machinery. And Dr. Michele Peters M.D., intended to be the very best doctor she could be. Even Darby Waterly shared one of her basic beliefs in that area—that the relationship between doctor and patient was essential to the healing process. Waterly carried it to extremes, of course, but Michele had to grudgingly admit that he had a way of establishing rapport with the patients that was a real plus. Because she treated each individual as a whole person, Michele believed that she was a better and more effective physician.

* * *

Another of the traits that made Michele Peters a good doctor, she believed, was her attitude about death. She was against it, not just theoretically or intellectually, but emotionally, viscerally opposed to it. Every time she saw a patient die, she felt a sense of frustration and failure, a feeling that someone—maybe even she—should have done better.

So a day later, halfway through her sixteen-hour shift, it didn't seem unusual for her to be curious about the covered cart that was waiting at the service elevator. It was a gurney with high rails which obscured the shape of anything, or anyone, being transported on it. She recognized that it was on its way to the morgue and thus was carrying a corpse. Efforts were usually taken to minimize the number of people who knew a dead body was being rolled to the cold room. Hospitals don't like to advertise the fact that some folks die there. It happened, but there was no use highlighting the fact.

Michele didn't recognize the attendant, a large bear of a man with an expression somewhat out of place for one transporting a human being's last remains. He looked almost like he was grinning. She couldn't make out the name on his I.D. badge, but it looked like he was from Radiology—an odd choice to be pushing cadavers to the Morgue. He was clearly startled when she grabbed the chart accompanying the body and flipped through it, but he kept silent. Apparently he knew better than to question a doctor, Michele thought, especially one in an administrative capacity. *Even if it is a middle tier position and the doctor is a woman,* her cynical side added.

The chart described the initial cause of death as a cardiac event. A final COD would await results of the postmortem. But the physician's name on the certification of death was a surprise, "Dr. Junghans." Michele hadn't seen Junghans around the hospital in months, except on rather well-publicized tours or lectures. Generally, he ran his rather lucrative radiologic practice out of his own well-equipped clinic. On the rare occasions that he did deign to honor the common hoard of resident physicians and less famous attendings with his august presence, Dr. Junghans was hardly likely to do a certification of death. The specialist did not bother himself with such messy and plebeian details. He was the reigning expert of nuclear medicine.

In any case, he was seldom anywhere in the vicinity of death, and never took responsibility for its occurrence or consequent red tape. So seeing this doctor's name on the C.O.D. was an incongruity sufficient to set off alarms in Michele's mind, a mind much more suspicious of motives and intents than ever before.

The incongruity was even more striking when she noticed that the corpse was a John Doe, nameless, homeless, and uninsured. The date and time of death for the nameless man under the sheet also coincided with a time that Michele had been on duty. Apparently the man had gone into arrest while being examined in the Radiology Department. Dr. Peotre Pretaska, resident radiology fellow and director of the unit, had co-signed most of the paperwork. She didn't remember a Code being called. When a patient went into cardiac arrest, it was standard procedure to call a "Code Ninety-nine." This was an overriding priority, that called designated personnel to drop everything and come running. Dr. Peters was always designated to respond to this code, so she couldn't imagine how someone had died of cardiac arrest in the Radiology Department, without a Code Ninety-nine being called. Curiouser and curiouser.

Eight

Gil Beach and Frank Terranova drove up to Bellevue near the main entrance at First Avenue and Twenty-seventh Street. A constant stream of people moved in and out of the opening in the ancient wrought iron fence. The side street was jammed with emergency vehicles, parked halfway onto the sidewalks and over curbs. In the midst of newer city architecture, the cluster of buildings looked like an anachronism, an eighteenth-century fortress in the middle of twentieth-century urban landscape.

To the uninitiated, the sprawling complex that covered several city blocks and housed both Bellevue and New York University Medical Centers might have been intimidating and confusing. But Beach and Terranova had been there many times, for both professional and personal reasons. Frank pulled the unmarked police car into a restricted-parking area a block away from the entrance by the Brookdale Center, he tossed an NYPD identification card on the dashboard. November wind slapped at their coats and ran cold fingers up their sleeves, making sure they didn't forget that winter was coming soon.

They cut through a small park with bare trees and a small three-tiered fountain drained for the winter, then passed the flaking iron fence and its gate that had "Bellevue" spelled out in metal letters. They turned down the blue awning-covered walkway and into the hub-bub of a long wide corridor lined with snack vendors, security and social service offices, and mobs of people in every possible garb, from turbans and dashikis to orange spike cuts and leather. As they approached the main lobby, they had to step around various sheets of cardboard laid out on the floor, the seats, beds, and territorial markers of many homeless that crowded the hallway. Some of the cardboard domains were occupied by scrubby figures, not always distinguishable as man or woman.

A large blue cloth banner, twelve or fifteen feet wide with the words, "Welcome to Bellevue" hung over the Information desk. The stylized flower border of the sign seemed at odds with the dirty ceiling tiles and cracked terrazzo floor. The men displayed their identification before walking down a hallway to the Emergency Department. When they reached the triage desk, the nurse was expecting them. She explained that Dr. Peters was presently in Resuscitation Room #7, but that they could wait for her next door at the Doctors' Station. They found the room indicated and went inside. White-coated men and women perched on the edge of chairs making chart notes, leafing through piles of lab slips, talking or arguing with each other, dictating into various receivers, and in one case, leafing through a huge red volume with the letters "PDR" on its thick binding.

The atmosphere was charged, the uniforms distinctive, and the language obscure. What was it, he wondered, that made both the Church and Medicine choose Latin to transmit their secret lore? There had to be some mystic commonality. Beach didn't feel comfortable entering this rarefied atmosphere, so he gestured to Frank and they moved down the hall. The next door was labeled as Resuscitation Room #6. Since Dr. Peters was supposed to be in #7, Gil moved to the next entrance and looked inside.

If the Doctors' Station was hectic, this room was chaotic. People were dashing here and there, often yelling instructions or requests. The space was small, yet it seemed a half-dozen white-uniformed figures were milling about, while every corner was jammed with strange equipment sprouting wires, tubes, and dials. The floor was spotted with bloodstains, empty paper wrappers, and various other discards of the furious process centering around a rumpled wheeled bed. Some of the tubes led to a human form, splayed out on a blanketless surface. An electronic monitor beeped from a platform at eye level, a snake-like tube ran from the man's face to a whooshing monster of a machine, and a woman leaned over him, looking directly into his eyes.

The man was obviously in distress, and the busy people were all doing things to try to alleviate it. But the guy on the bed looked like he was on a torture rack, hands gripping the edge of the mattress so tightly his fingers were white, arms and legs rigid. One doctor called for something called a "cut-down kit" and after jabbing the skin with a hypodermic, began slicing at the patient's ankle. Each of the white-gowned figures seemed occupied with a separate body part or piece of mechanical apparatus. Whether they were conscious of the person attached, was not clear. Except the woman, apparently a physician, who was staring directly into the fellow's face and speaking.

She was dark-haired and attractive, with slim wrists and delicate hands she clasped the patient's shoulders as she looked at him intently and spoke softly. The woman stayed by the man's side for a few more minutes, until she saw that he had closed his eyes. Then she threw out a flurry of instructions to the other personnel and turned to leave.

"You've gotta be Dr. Peters," Gil greeted her as she approached the door.

"Ahh—you are . . . Beach, isn't it? Detective Beach? Sorry to keep you waiting. And this . . ." her eyes swept over him to Terranova standing nearby, "this must be the Thirteenth Precinct's answer to Henny Youngman."

"Well, we're from the Ninth, ma'am," Frank answered, "but I guess I do have a reputation for coming up with jokes."

"Well from the looks of you, you got the last laugh on the joker that tried to kill you."

"Yes, ma'am!"

"If it's all the same to you guys, could we skip the ma'am stuff. The name's Peters, Michele Peters. I get called doctor so much that I respond to that like it was my first name, but Michele is fine, too. And I think we could talk better someplace else. How about a little less noise?"

Gil wasn't sure that he could bring himself to call the doctor by her first name. He had never managed that kind of intimacy with priests or doctors. Even the young cleric at St. Alphonsus who wanted the kids to call him Bob, had ended up "Father Bob" to Gil. But he liked the lack of arrogance it suggested on her part, and the air of informality it created. She smiled a pleasant smile that formed a small dimple on her left cheek. She had those attractive thick eyebrows like some of the models on the cover of *Cosmo*. When she raised them quizzically, Gil realized he had not answered her, and quickly agreed to a quieter spot for conversation.

She led them to the corner of a doctors' locker room, on the floor above. The atmosphere wasn't fancy, not much more than a large closet, with institutional green walls, matching metal lockers, and cloth bag carts for soiled scrubs. But they had three nondescript chairs and a little privacy. For the first few minutes, the conversation centered on Frank's recovery from his bullet wound. He even opened his shirt to display the puckered scar. As a side topic, they also got around to discussing his recovery from alcoholism. It had been several years since Terranova went on the wagon, and despite an effort at humility, he was proud to have gotten off the addictive merry-go-round.

"Not that I did it myself," he cautioned. "It was really A.A. that made the difference."

When the talk seemed to be veering off into a largely social vein, Gil brought it back to the subject that had led to their visit.

"It didn't seem like you could talk over the phone, but I'm still interested in whether you have any information that could help locate this guy, Dorlander."

"Well, we get a lot of indigents through these doors."

"From what I can see, you don't seem the type to classify everybody into one big lump."

Peters head came up quickly at that. "I guess detectives are paid to be observant."

"Yeah, and doctors are paid to heal people. I think you're probably very good at that. I also like the fact that you don't seem to forget there's a human being that connects all the parts."

"I think I'm being set-up for something here," she laughed. The two detectives laughed with her.

"Okay, so maybe I was laying it on a little thick," Gil agreed. "I'm not used to people that can spot it so quickly. Usually a few ego strokes help get better witness cooperation, and it gets to be a habit."

"Am I a witness?"

"I don't know," Gil replied, more seriously. "What have you seen going down around here?"

Michele was caught by surprise. The detective had asked her a question she hadn't really expected. It gave words to some uncomfortable feelings she wasn't even aware of having up until now. *What exactly was going on around here?* There had been some very odd occurrences lately. She had been so preoccupied with the frustration of her role and ambitions that she had ignored this other troubled feeling. She wasn't even sure what was bothering her. Her next reaction was a reflex. She didn't give away anything.

"Just a lot of good medical care."

It was partly true. There was a hell of a lot of fine medical practice going on at Bellevue. But it was also a cover. That's what you did when you were a doctor. You didn't unnecessarily expose the ugly underside of medicine. It wasn't the vast conspiracy that some people made it out to be, but most physicians weren't anxious to spill their guts about the mistakes that happen. Sharing the route through the tremendous hurdles necessary to become a physician, you felt a certain defensive fraternity . . . or sorority. People wanted their healers to be perfect. That was an impossible expectation, but there was no changing it. So together, the healers played the part they were asked to play, sharing only with each other the terrible imperfections with which they had to live, and providing a shield for each other against attack.

As all this raced through Michele Peters' head, the detective did his mind-reading act again.

"Dr. Peters, forgive me if I'm being presumptuous, but I get a funny feeling that you aren't telling me everything. Maybe I'm off-base here, but tell me. Is something going on at Bellevue that we ought to know about?"

She almost blurted out her uneasiness, but quickly thought better of it. Who was this cop anyway, and why should she bare her soul to him? His ability to read people's thoughts and motivations could be a problem if you had something to hide. And as far as she knew, Michele had nothing to hide. But that might not be true of some other people around Bellevue. The fingers of her right hand went to her head and twisted a lock of hair. For now, at least, she decided that she was certain of nothing. And that was exactly what she told Gil Beach and Frank Terranova.

Nine

Dr. Peters was troubled as she left the meeting with the two detectives. There weren't many occasions where she felt like she was inept, especially when the subject was medicine, but this had been one of them. The detective she had treated for a gunshot wound was pleasant and polite. It was the other one, Gil Beach, that had seemed to read thoughts she wasn't fully aware of. Not that he wasn't as pleasant as the younger man—he was actually quite nice, and rather attractive when you got down to it, with a strong face and a touch of distinguished gray around the temples. Though at this point in her bleak social life, she suspected that a fairly presentable orangutan would probably look attractive to her.

Dr. Peters' social life was lousy because she avoided mixing work and romance. There were plenty of available men around Bellevue, or at least available for certain types of relationships. But Michele had seen a lot of screwed-up careers, and had come close to messing up her own with an excruciatingly handsome, but married, cosmetic surgeon before deciding that she had to keep that part of her life separate. Unfortunately, as assistant director of the E.D., Michele found that work took up just about all her time, so there wasn't much "other part" to worry about.

Doctors like Ira Wachman, the medical director, didn't work sixteen-hour shifts, she reflected, and get called back for crises besides. Even Wachman's assistant could lead a more normal life. A twinge of annoyance tickled her belly as she thought of the lock men seemed to have on these and other non-medical positions of importance. Michele knew other women physicians, like Isabel Bourke, an excellent anesthesiologist and a good friend. But for the most part, it was the men that had the power. The grand mavens that students flocked to see—Hampton, Junghans, Walsh, and Doeppler . . . all men.

The only other woman that seemed to have serious influence was Joyce Castro, a leading oncologist who was a whiz at cancer treatment, but didn't take garbage from anyone. Of course that meant she inevitably wound up with the reputation of a bitch. Michele had overheard snide conversations referring to the woman as Joyce "Castrato." It was typical. Men were "assertive," while women with the same traits were "aggressive bitches." Men could be forceful, but woman were castrators. Women who didn't have tough exteriors and succeeded must have "slept their way to the top." It was a stacked deck. But that would change. It would have to change, and she was determined to do some of the changing. Of course, raising unfounded allegations about practices of treatment at BHC did not seem the way to work her way up. On the other hand, ignoring malpractice wasn't a particularly good start to an administrative career either. Dr. Michele Peters decided to do some research.

Dr. Peters wasn't the only one who left the meeting in a troubled frame of mind. Gil Beach was plagued by the mixed signals he had gotten from the physician. It was more than the missing reporter—Peters had promised her help there. But Gil was an expert at knowing when a person was concealing something. He had interrogated too many suspects, interviewed too many witnesses, and braced too many suspicious characters to be mistaken. At points in their conversation, Gil knew that Dr. Peters was dancing around some hidden spots. She was definitely not telling something. Detective Beach decided to do some investigation.

Politicians seek out people at the top for their inquiries. Cops know better. Gil started with Housekeeping. From a floor polisher, Gil learned that the lobby was crowded due to displaced homeless people during the week of the Marathon. A housekeeper named Violet explained how the EMS worked, proud that her husband was one of the paramedics. She even called him on the telephone to ask about the night they were investigating, but he had been working another section of the city. Violet, in turn, introduced Beach to Rafael Nunez, a member of the Bellevue Police security force who recalled being posted at the ambulance entrance the night Dorlander had disappeared. The officer remembered two admissions that could have matched Eddy's description. One had his stomach pumped and was discharged. Rafael remembered that one well, because the guy had done a discharge of his own, throwing-up all over the street on his way home. Nunez didn't remember seeing the other arrival again, and assumed the unconscious man had been admitted.

Meanwhile, Frank shamelessly flirted with a plain-looking admissions clerk with a name tag that read "L. Wapple," hoping he could gain a little extra cooperation. The woman reminded him of a mouse. But he figured there was nothing wrong with a little tease, and the plain little thing seemed pleased at the attention. He soon determined that the "L" on her name tag stood for the unlikely name of Lolita.

"I see you don't wear a wedding ring, Lolly."

"But you do, Officer . . . and I told you, my name is Lolita," the woman giggled, no longer the prim functionary.

"It's a good thing, Sweetcakes, 'cause if I was single, you wouldn't be safe for a minute. You don't mind if I give you a little nickname, do you Lollipop?"

Lolita's cheeks turned pink and she shifted in her seat. He then asked her about the records he wanted to see. With a wink of conspiratorial alliance she let him look at the computer screen she called up, listing admissions for the night in question. It showed no Edward Dorlander, and no John Doe.

"You want me to check the DOAs and so forth?"

"Gee, I didn't think of that. So you're smart, too. Boy, some guy is going to be a very lucky man. You sure there isn't somebody special?"

Obviously flustered, but just as obviously pleased, the woman didn't answer, but punched a few keys on her terminal and swung the screen around so he could see it. There were three DOAs that night, folks that arrived at the hospital too late for help. Two were female, and the other had a date of birth listed as 1909. All had names. But there was another listing that drew the detective's attention.

"What's this one, Lolly?"

"Um, let's see," she said craning to look at the turned screen and laying a hand on Frank's arm in the process. "Oh that one is coded confidential information."

"But it says John Doe, age forty-plus, white, undomiciled. What's confidential?"

"Well, I guess the diagnosis, cause of death, that sorta stuff, you know."

"Death?"

"Yeah, you can figure that out, if you know the codes like I do." She hadn't taken her hand off his sleeve. "Now don't tell a soul," she leaned close to him, and he tried to ignore her garlic breath. "But according to this, he died a couple of hours after getting here. Looks like a Code Ninety-nine. That's a heart attack," she whispered, proud of her knowledge. Her lips were a fraction of an inch from Frank's cheek, and her grasp on his arm was approaching the intensity of a death grip.

He was thinking of how to disengage tactfully, when Lolita jumped back. She swung the monitor back to its former position and began to tap furiously away at the keyboard. A severe-looking woman with eyeglasses dangling from a neck cord, clipboard in hand, came striding down the row of admissions desks. Apparently a supervisor, the woman ignored Lolita despite her reddened features and wildly tapping fingers, but Lolita had already retreated into her former identity as L. Wapple, prim, proper, and completely businesslike clerk. Frank thanked her for her help and left, looking for Gil, feeling a little guilty about the manipulation.

Gil was glad to get the information Frank had obtained—he had a strong feeling that the John Doe who had died of a heart attack was Eddy Dorlander. But if it was, there were new questions.

According to Dr. Peters, she had been working that night. How could a man die of a heart attack shortly after admission without her knowledge? It seemed an unlikely possibility. But if she knew, then she had been lying to him. He didn't want to believe that. Gil usually trusted his instincts. They had served him well over the years. More than once, he had regretted not listening to his inner responses to people. His gut response to Dr. Peters was one of attraction, admiration, and trust.

The attraction he acknowledged and dismissed. She was a very attractive woman, and he was a man with normal impulses. He had experienced that before, and knew that it didn't have to be acted on. Gil had a good marriage to a good woman, and he wasn't about to put it in jeopardy by entertaining such ideas.

The admiration was partly due to her status as a physician, though her intelligence and good humor didn't hurt either. Gil was impressed by anyone who mastered the incredibly complex field of medicine. For a woman to make it, was probably an even greater accomplishment, not to mention the elevation to Assistant Director of one of the world's largest and busiest Emergency Departments.

The trust part was much more of an intuitive response. And it flew in the face of the secretiveness that he also sensed in their recent interchange. If he had caught her in a lie, Gil would have to discount his own intuition, but he knew that he wasn't about to do that without more information. For the time being, he would assume that his instincts were correct, but the attractive, admirable and trustworthy Dr. Peters either had some very compelling reason to withhold the truth, or was being kept in the dark herself.

Ten

Michele Peters didn't like being in the dark, literally or figuratively. Since childhood Michele had been unable to entirely shake a fear of darkness that caused her to keep lights burning, even when she slept. It went back to when her alcoholic stepfather had shut her in an unlit closet to punish her for a minor infraction, forgot he had put her there, and left the terrified girl trapped for hours. There were no doors on her closets at home, now. She could handle a walk at night, if the neighborhood was relatively safe and street lights were in place, but any dark and enclosed space was still terrifying.

She wasn't disabled by her fear. She managed to operate quite effectively without the childhood trauma interfering in her life significantly. It was more embarrassing than anything else, but it did affect her choices at times.

She didn't like being in the dark figuratively any better. Michele had always possessed a natural inquisitiveness that sought to understand the world. This was combined with a purposefully trained and developed scientific curiosity that drove her to find answers to any puzzle that presented itself. But on top of that, she was a bit bullheaded. She didn't like the idea that anyone would keep important information from her. Nobody had the right to treat her like she was a child, only capable of handling certain things.

Thus she started in the Medical Records Department.

Computers were fine and stored tremendous amounts of vital information in a tiny space, but nothing could replace the basic patient chart for getting the feel of a case. Nursing notes, physicians' scribbled orders, vital sign tracking, lab slips—it was all there to see. A professional could learn plenty from a properly completed set of documents.

The chart record started the moment a patient stepped, or was wheeled into the hospital. If the person was brought by ambulance, the EMS report was the first medical information included, followed by admission vital signs, Nursing Assessment, E.D. Physicians Assessment, initial lab test values, and many other important pieces of data. If a person was never identified, the chart remained a John or Jane Doe record, but was coded with a patient I.D. number, admitting number, and date of admission.

Dr. Peters came to the Medical Records Office often, so she was well known there. Nancy Sager, the medical records director didn't raise an eyebrow when Michele searched through the files for the man she had only met on his way to the morgue. Medical Records were no mystery to Michele, so she didn't need any help, but she soon became convinced that the chart was missing. She checked the dates on either side, alternative spellings, even similar numbers in case the records had been misfiled. Nothing.

That left the computer files. She punched her access code into the terminal and reviewed by date and category. She found the nameless cardiac arrest and tried without much success to call up a screen that listed lab tests performed for the individual. Michele wasn't as familiar with this computer system as she would have liked to be. Her physician code allowed her almost unlimited access, but her knowledge of the data retrieval systems and codes was not complete. Support staff usually handled this end of things. She was tempted to ask Nancy Sager's help, but decided she would rather not reveal her purpose to anyone else.

After several tries, she found her error. She had been using the wrong admission date. That was puzzling, as she had been successful in finding the John Doe. Or had she? Checking back to the earlier screen, she found that the date was not the one she had been seeking. Yet there was a nameless, homeless, uninsured man listed, with a date of death matching exactly the date of admission. Cause of death was "cardiac arrest."

Michele moved forward in the hard plastic chair, and started the sequence again, only this time carefully entering the correct date. Incredibly, she saw almost the same information flash onto the screen. The only differences were minor—age given at around fifty instead of forty-plus. Small variances in estimated height and weight. She understood how she had made the error. As strange as it might seem, it appeared that two different John Doe's had been admitted and died within hours of admission, both from "cardiac arrest," on two successive nights. She tapped a few keys to work back through the records, day by day. It took a while, but in an hour she had found three more of them spread over the course of a six week period. They weren't all males, but they were all homeless, nameless indigents. And they were all dead.

She tried to get information from the billing screens, since she knew fiscal departments were often expert at tracking down information inaccessible to clinical staff. But despite her status, this only resulted in a message blinking on the screen, "Access Denied." It felt like someone was trying to keep her in the dark, and she didn't like it.

Michele jumped when she sensed someone standing behind her. Fortunately, it was her friend, Isabel.

"A little jumpy, aren't we?" the anesthesiologist laughed.

"Oh, hi, Izzie. Yeah, I guess I am. Too much work and not enough hours in a day, I guess."

"More like too much work and not enough play, if you ask me," the woman responded with a laugh.

She considered telling Isabel what she was seeking at the computer, but hesitated. First, because she was uncertain about what she was really looking for, and second, because she was so unsure about where it would lead. In fact it could lead to trouble. Michele decided to wait until she had a better idea of what this was all about. But her friend might know more about the computer system.

"Well, I'd probably have more time for play if I knew how to work this thing better. You got any ideas how to do a data search on the basis of diagnosis?"

Isabel gave a few hints on how to pursue the search, and an hour later Dr. Peters had exhausted the information the computer could give her, or at least as much as she knew how to get from it. The only new data was an odd link to Radiology-Nuclear Medicine. It appeared that several of the cases had either Dr. Junghans or Dr. Pretaska as physician of record. This was not usual for Pretaska, anymore than it was for Junghans. Junghans was difficult to contact, V.I.P. that he was, but Pretaska was much more accessible. As director of diagnostic radiology, his office was only a few yards down the hall from the E.D. She decided to talk to him.

Dr. Peotre Pretaska was one of those human beings that her friend Isabel described as just too gorgeous to be real. To some extent, Michele agreed. He was a native of what had once been Yugoslavia. With long dark hair, shadowed deep-set eyes, and a voice that fairly echoed Serbian sensuality, he was a remarkable specimen. When she found him in his office, Michele felt a shiver run through her and tried to remind herself that she was determined to keep work and romance separate. With Peotre, that could be a more difficult task than usual.

Pretaska quickly answered her questions and dismissed her concerns. The designation of himself and Junghans as physicians of record was merely a courtesy, he explained, so that other doctors did not have to explain excessive deaths on their caseloads at Quality Appraisal or Utilization Review meetings. Since the radiologists seldom had terminally ill patients assigned to them, an occasional death did not set off the quality measure triggers that it would for physicians in higher risk fields. He discussed this with a warm smile that made Michele feel peculiar inside.

As he sat casually draped on a counter, like a model for some men's fashion magazine, Pretaska reminded her that missing files were a common occurrence, especially those of deceased patients. Q.A. procedures required review of all in-hospital deaths, and the charts were undoubtedly pulled for precisely that purpose. A total of four deaths was hardly noteworthy, he suggested, despite some coincidental similarities.

There were faint alarms in Michele's logic center that seemed to tell her that the reasoning was flawed, the information incomplete, but all logic was drowned out by a rush of feeling as Peotre put one arm around her in an affectionate hug. She could feel a delicious warmth and hard muscles pressing her shoulders. If he had been less platonic and pulled her into his arms for a passionate embrace, she was certain she could not have resisted at that moment, no matter what resolutions she had made about romance in the work area.

Whether he sensed her reaction or not, she didn't know, but as she moved to leave his office, a little light seemed to glint from those marvelous eyes, an eyebrow raised in a suggestion of new interest, and he made the first move.

"If you want to pursue these matters further, I would be happy to assist you in any way you would like. Maybe we should discuss this another time, in a more relaxed atmosphere, perhaps over dinner and a glass of wine?"

Michele's stomach felt a little thrill that she tried to ignore. An invitation to dinner was hardly a seduction, but if she accepted, it seemed like she would be breaking her previous resolve. She could hardly imagine how she would react to this magnificent man in a private setting, much less with a little wine to numb her already wavering inhibitions. Unable to think clearly at the moment, she put off the decision.

"Perhaps . . . sometime," she temporized, and with a smile and little wave quickly left the office.

It was a long walk back to the staff quarters, thoughts of mystery and conspiracy competing for her attention with images of the handsome radiologist and romantic evenings. Pretaska was fairly new to the medical roster, brought in by Ted Jamison to replace the previous director who had moved on to a posh medical center in a suburb of L.A. Thus far, Pretaska had seemed effective and personable. Although he could easily have mowed through ranks of willing nurses like a scythe, the man did not have the reputation of a womanizer. He was not married, but seemed to keep his social life outside the hospital. Therefore, besides threatening to undo Dr. Peters' resolve along those lines, his invitation to dinner seemed out of character for him, as well. Perhaps it was just a friendly gesture, a courtesy that he hoped she would refuse. That would certainly make life simpler for everyone. So why did part of her wish it was more?

She unlocked the door to her small apartment, angrily kicking off her shoes at the entrance before padding to the kitchen for a glass of lemonade. She was mostly angry at herself for having such teenage reactions to a colleague. My God, she was thirty-eight years old! But as she looked around at her tiny living space, she wondered if that was partly why she was regressing emotionally.

The simple quarters were more often the province of nursing students. Occasionally a single resident took advantage of the relatively inexpensive and close lodging, but seldom was it the home of women physicians, especially those who were no longer learning their trade at the bottom of the medical totem pole. It was rather unusual for a mature woman doctor to be living there, much less the assistant E.D. director. Nevertheless, Michele had managed to reserve one of the efficiency apartments, actually little more than a furnished single room with one corner converted into a kitchenette, when she took the position of Emergency Department assistant director.

The promotion had coincided with her divorce from Randy DeVore, a marginally successful musician, who had turned Michele's head years before with songs he wrote for her. Unfortunately, Randy was much too insecure to withstand the pressures of her career. He was fine while she was still in school and he could pretend she was merely a student and he a well-known folk singer. But when she gained the magical title of "Doctor" and her career started making significant demands on her time, he balked. At first, it was just pouting immaturity and complaining. But then along with her greater achievements, came a campaign of derision, resistance, and downright sabotage that eventually destroyed the relationship. Finally they separated, and within a year he had found a teenage girlfriend that thought he was John Denver, John Cougar Mellencamp, and Prince, all rolled up into one. The new couple seemed quite happy together, and when Randy asked for a divorce to marry the child, Michele didn't object.

Michele took back her maiden name, Peters, and despite her position, moved into the staff quarters. The apartment gave her a new environment, it was extremely convenient to her work, and it was easy to maintain. But sometimes it made her feel like she was back in school. It was a good deal for the nursing students, but for Michele it seemed to emphasize the impression that she hadn't really established herself professionally. And the truth was, it got pretty lonely. The mattress said "twin" size, but there was no twin. It was alone, and just for one.

Within minutes, she was stretched out under the covers of the small bed. Well-practiced in the art of getting into the sack quickly, she had learned to maximize the amount of rest she could squeeze into the few hours usually available. But this time, perversely, sleep would not come.

Her mind and emotions seemed to be working their way through all the settings of a multi-speed blender. She daydreamed strange images. Ghastly visions of putrefying corpses wheeling past in wire shopping carts alternated with those of an Adonis-like Dr. Pretaska clasping her to his bare chest, while her ex-husband watched through a window. Thoughts of missing files and missing cadavers vied with questions about medical ethics, secrecy and boundaries.

She tried to focus on her determination to gain one of the coveted positions of power. Whatever else, she couldn't let go of that or she could end up like so many other women, trapped forever in a role of servitude. Wachman was ill and was sure to retire soon. What were her chances of taking his place, or at least the number two position? Was it the old situation of a woman having to be twice as good as a man to win, or was there no chance at all? *No good no good,* she told herself, *mustn't entertain the negativity.* She knew she could do it, she just had to have confidence in herself, and not let these extraneous matters confuse or distract her. Time and again she had succeeded when others doubted her. She would do it again.

Still, sleep would not come. Michele got up and drank a jelly glass full of Chablis. She knew that using alcohol to deal with emotions was dangerous. It could easily become a form of drug dependence, another easy trap for doctors. The accessibility of drugs for a physician was almost the same as liquor. But tonight she just said "to hell with it," and let the wine relax her tense muscles and knotted emotions. Eventually she drifted into a restless sleep colored with dreams of Peotre and passion.

Eleven

Gil didn't have Frank's easy way with women, but he suspected it wouldn't have mattered with this one anyway. Doctor Ira Wachman's secretary was a piece of work. Actually, "secretary" was the wrong term, because Ms. Shields was the director's administrative assistant. The type of woman you might call "handsome," the scuttlebutt Gil had gleaned from among low-level staff was that she backed up her mature, professional image with encyclopedic knowledge, superior skills, and force of personality. Gil believed it. The minute you walked into the room, you knew you were on her turf, and she would control what went down there. It didn't matter if you were a doctor or a cop, you had to get through Sue Shields if you wanted to see the medical director of Bellevue.

After working their way through the support staff, Beach and Terranova had a lot more information. But it still was mostly second or third hand, and there were some big gaps. Now it was time to see if they could get some support from the hospital administration in order to pursue a fuller investigation.

Gil wasn't having much success. Sue didn't care much for his vague response to her question as to the nature of his business with Dr. Wachman. She didn't like being called "Sue." This was Gil's third try for an appointment.

The first two times she wouldn't even admit that the Director was there.

"Dr. Wachman is under medical care," she explained, raising the eyeglasses she kept on a cord around her neck, "so he limits his office hours for utmost efficiency." Gil was sure he caught an implication that this did not include talking with stray detectives that couldn't explain their intent very well. He also wondered how much of Dr. Wachman's work was done by this rather formidable woman. He finally decided to stretch the truth a bit, hoping it would get some response.

"Okay, Miz Shields, I'll lay my cards on the table. We have reason to believe that a well-known news reporter came to Bellevue incognito. He probably died here, under suspicious circumstances. Furthermore, his body is missing. I don't think Dr. Wachman really wants the news media in question to run a big scandal story about this, without having a chance to investigate internally, or at least decide how to respond to the situation."

"Dr. Wachman is not in the habit of worrying about press coverage, whether it is accurate or not. His responsibility lies in assuring the smooth running of the clinical operations of this institution. It you wish to discuss public relations matters, perhaps you might like to talk with an administrator such as the C.E.O., Jim Hampton, or one of his assistants: Theodore Jamison, Richard Schwenker, and William Magwood. Ted Jamison is responsible for the units that would have any knowledge of this matter you describe, and Bill Magwood handles anything relating to personnel."

Beach could tell when he was licked. He thanked the woman and asked if she could direct him to the administrator's office. The directions took him to a door with the name, "Theodore A. Jamison, Ph.D., Assistant Administrator," lettered in gold on the glass. So Shields hadn't even sent him to the top dog! Beach was about to leave, when the door opened, and a wiry man in a precise, dark pin-stripe suit almost ran into him.

"Oh, hello. May I help you with something?"

"Ah, yes. Are you the assistant administrator?" Gil asked.

"Well, actually I'm the deputy chief administrator, but that isn't important. I'm Ted Jamison," the man answered, sticking out his hand, "and you are . . . ?"

"Detective Sergeant Gil Beach, NYPD. I wonder if I could ask you a few questions?"

"Well, let's see," Jamison hesitated, looking at his watch, into his office, and back at his watch again. "Well, yes, I suppose I could give you a few minutes. Schwenker can wait . . . all he cares about are utility bills and laundry procedures anyway." He gave a humorless little laugh. "He's the assistant administrator in charge of Building Operations, but they shouldn't really have him on the same level as those of us who deal with the more vital matters. But enough of my problems, come into my office and tell me what brings you here, Officer. Or am I making a blunder? Should it be Sergeant . . . or Detective?"

"Detective is fine, but I have the same problem. Should I call you doctor, or mister, or administrator, or what?"

"How about just 'Ted?' We limit the title doctor for physicians around here, and I don't much like to be called mister unless it's by somebody a lot younger—makes me feel too old."

As Jamison entered his inner office and settled in an elaborate chair that looked like it had more adjustments than a hospital bed, the lights automatically brightened and gentle background music began playing. There were no papers on the large desk, just a very complex telephone console and a separate panel of maybe two-dozen metal buttons and several toggle switches. One wall was bookshelves, filled with leather-bound volumes, many of them medical and science texts. On the opposite wall were several portraits. Gil recognized none of them, but one stern visage seemed like an older version of the administrator, and he assumed it was the man's father. Gil had always wondered what it was like to have your father staring over your shoulder every day. He didn't think he would care for it.

"Do you mind if I record our conversation?" Jamison asked. Without waiting for a response, the administrator flicked one of the toggles with practiced ease, and pushed a button on the bottom row of the panel, not even taking his eyes off the detective. To Beach, the man's manner seemed inconsistent with the earlier friendliness and invitation to use his first name.

"Well, I don't think there is any need for that," Gil noted, "but please yourself. I'm mainly here for information."

"And what information would you like, Detective Beach?"

Although Jamison gave the impression of more accessibility than Wachman, Gil ended up with no more information than he had before. There were promises that the matter would be "looked into," and guarantees of all the information the detective needed, "within the limits of medical ethics and confidentiality regulations" of course. But Gil walked out of the office fifteen minutes after entering it, hardly able to remember a word that Jamison had spoken. The detective strode away with a frown.

When Gil and Frank compared notes, they didn't have much to show for their efforts. Beach had been stonewalled by the administration, and Frank hadn't gotten anything beyond Lolita's first, and last, offering. When he went back to try again, she stared through him like he was a window. When he made reference to their earlier conversation, only her reddened neck belied the complete amnesia she effected. Everywhere they turned, they ran into regulations, computer codes, and bureaucracy. It contrasted sharply with Gil's memories of when he was hospitalized many years before, which though frightening, were very much memories of human touch and caring.

Gil was only eleven when the grandparents that raised him made an appointment with the family doctor to examine a slowly enlarging lump by his left ear. It was diagnosed as a possibly malignant tumor. Whether or not it was cancerous, it had to be taken out before it reached his eyes or other vital spots. Removing it would be tricky, since there was a high risk of damaging the nerve that controlled facial muscles in the area. Even a careful knife might not be able to prevent permanent paralysis to the whole left side of his face. As if it weren't enough for an eleven year old to deal with, Gil also had an acute allergic reaction to the anesthetics they used back then. After an unsuccessful attempt to use ether on the boy, they explained that the only way they could complete the operation was if he could endure the surgery with nothing other than local anesthesia—shots of novocaine in his temple that would reduce the pain, but not eliminate it. Since the tumor was next to his skull, and had invaded various soft tissues, it would be a challenge to the fortitude of a man, much less a small boy. But what choice did he have? So he told them he was ready, and did his best to hold on.

He hardly flinched when they stabbed his temple with injection after injection, and he calmly kept the surgeon informed of his distress level during the cutting, so additional anesthetic could be injected when the pain was too much to bear.

Gil remembered back to that day, so many years before, with a terrible clarity. But perhaps most of all, he remembered the kindness of the doctor, Tom Hazelrigg, and a nurse whose name he never knew. The surgeon talked to the boy the entire time, asking how he was doing, how he was holding up, and how brave he thought the lad was. Meanwhile, one of the scrub nurses stood beside him. And just when he thought he couldn't bear the pain any more, she reached out and squeezed his hand, a smile showing in her eyes over the green surgical mask. It might not seem much, but it made a difference—that little sign of care, that little squeeze of compassion. All the wonders of modern medicine mattered less than that one human touch.

Gil survived the operation, of course, and was fortunate enough to avoid the threatened paralysis. They got out all of the tumor, they said. They were wrong, but he wouldn't know that until years later when the lump reappeared. Another operation was necessary when he was nineteen that finally eliminated the growth. By then there was better anesthesia, and he was able to sleep through the surgery. But he would always remember the first operation and the importance of compassion and kindness.

Gil couldn't quite imagine that the world of medicine had changed so much as to eliminate that unique humanity, but right now he wasn't seeing much of it.

Clearly, they weren't going to penetrate the monolithic defenses of Bellevue and the medical fraternity from the outside. They were going to need a way inside. And unless they were prepared to spend a dozen or so years in medical training, that meant they needed a doctor as an ally. But was that a real possibility or a pipedream? Would any physician ally himself with those outside the profession? Gil reminded himself that he shouldn't necessarily use male pronouns when referring to doctors in general. Some of them were women. Some of them were very capable women.

He still trusted his hunch about Michele . . . Dr. Peters. He thought she knew more than she was telling, he also thought she was reachable. If they were going to have any inside help on this investigation, he had a feeling that she was their best hope.

Twelve

"There is no place in medicine for emotional weakness!" the speaker nearly shouted. "Fear masquerading as concern has interfered with the search for truth on too many occasions already."

Dr. Dietrich Rutger Junghans, renowned radiologist, theoretician, author, and lecturer, had his audience engaged. Love him, hate him, agree or disagree, you couldn't hear the man without getting excited. Despite advancing years, the grand old man of Nuclear Medicine, founder of the Junghans General Radiology Imaging and Treatment Clinic ("True G.R.I.T. clinic," as it was popularly called), author of the standard text on Magnetic Resonance Imaging techniques, and dominating member of the Bellevue Hospital Center Board of Directors, could still generate interest, not to mention a fair amount of controversy.

Michele Peters saw Isabel Bourke in a back row of the auditorium and slid into a seat next to her. Dr. Bourke had a new hairstyle. Michele smiled, but said nothing. She thought love was cute.

She scanned the audience, and saw most of the familiar faces. Richard Schwenker, Carl Troop, and Ted Jamison represented the administration. She never understood why non-physicians like Schwenker and Jamison attended these lectures, but apparently it was one of those requirements of the job they held. Darby Waterly sat near the front, furiously scribbling notes. She supposed that he had to be included in the category of physicians present, despite an alternative degree and skill level that made her wonder. Her boss, Archie Neely, was there for a change. He caught her eye and waved.

The big name present was Dr. John Malcolm, himself a renowned figure in his field of neurosurgery and frequent lecturer to the less knowledgeable. He and Junghans seemed to have a competitive thing going, vying for the unofficial title of "Great and Glorious Physician, Above All Other Medical Persons as well as the Common People." But for some reason Malcolm was in the audience instead of at the lectern. Knowing the man's enormous ego, Michele suspected that he wasn't present as an admiring sycophant. This might get very interesting!

"We know that introducing electrical current to the site accelerates bone growth and the knitting of fractures," Junghans was pontificating, "and we know that the greatest advance in imaging technique is due to the uniform response of the human cell to magnetic force. Yet we see that the startling potential for the use of magnetic and electric fields in such areas as Oncology, as well as proposals to extend our research seem to end up in the dark holes of space."

In the large audience, only Hampton seemed uninterested. He appeared distracted and uncomfortable, shifting constantly in his seat and whispering to the assistant seated next to him. Out of the corner of her eye, Michele detected movement. Several spectators milled near the upper entrances of the sloped theater. At one door, a group of several women and a bearded man stood huddled together. They were carrying bags, and small containers. Michele didn't recognize any individuals in the group, but Bellevue was a big place, and a lot of these lectures were open to the public, though generally only physicians had any interest in the topics presented.

She glanced at the other side of the auditorium, to see

if there were other visitors, and was surprised to see the detective to whom she had spoken earlier, Gil Beach. Isabel picked that moment to look at Michele. Noting the direction of her friend's eyes, she shoved an elbow into Peters' side and whispered.

"You like that stuff, Petey, my girl? Not too bad, not too bad. Maybe a little long in the tooth, but hey, go for it!"

Michele grinned and shoved back.

"For your information, that's a cop. I may be stupid sometimes, but I'm not so stupid as to fall for a cop!"

"Hey, ya fall for whoever ya fall for. You, however, seem to be unfallably set in cement, my unromantic friend."

Michele thought wryly of her amorous fantasies after seeing Peotre Pretaska the day before, but didn't reply. She just put a finger to her lips, in a shushing gesture, and turned back to the lecture.

"We must recognize our own lack of boldness," Junghans was emoting, "which has resulted in a failure to pursue one of the most provocative and promising areas of modern medicine. The effects of electrical and magnetic fields on human tissue is a study that is in its infancy. Yet no research monies are available to nurture this infant to maturity. Research is the key to progress!"

A yell went up at that statement. At first Michele thought it was just an audience reaction, since the oratorical style of the speaker would have been right at home in a revival tent or other venue where the audience was expected to respond with applause, cheers, amens, or whatever. But then as dozens of heads swiveled to look at the back of the theater, she realized that the shouting was localized in the area she had been watching before. The group that had appeared disinterested in the lecture before, were now very much focused on the podium. It was their cries that she heard, but they were not cheers. Far from appreciation, the loud noise now revealed itself as protest. Michele tried to figure out what they were shouting.

"No animals for research!" they hollered shrilly. "Stop animal torture!" They marched down the aisle toward a flustered and monumentally offended Dr. Junghans, banging on coffee cans, rattling jars of marbles, tossing leaflets, and generally creating a scene. They carried signs with odd slogans, like "Animals are SAKRED," and "We die a little with every kitty's death."

"Get those assholes the hell outta here!" Junghans shouted, the lectern microphone allowing him to be heard over their racket.

Peters was close enough to Dr. John Malcolm to hear his candid reaction and confirm her suspicions concerning his presence at the lecture.

"Damn busybodies. Won't have question and answers now—I won't get a chance to poke holes in the old tart's stupid gibberish. Well, at least he won't get to finish."

The only people who did respond to the demonstrators were Carl Troop, the acting assistant medical director, who intercepted the raucous group of protestors faster than the Bellevue security force could, and Ted Jamison, who jumped up to the podium to surreptitiously turn off the microphone, then calm Dr. Junghans with deft ego stroking. It wasn't until he left the stage that Junghans' withered leg became apparent. The doctor usually made arrangements to minimize the number of people who saw his disability. The unplanned end to his lecture disrupted those preparations.

Michele assumed the protestors were basically loonytuners, and therefore considered it a minor miracle when Carl Troop managed not only to quiet the group down, but engage them in a semblance of dialogue. In a few minutes he was ushering them out of the auditorium, his tactical success marked by the expression of one obese protestor in an orange polka dot muumuu, who actually looked pleased, if only in a rather self-righteous way. Carl had a way with groups of people. He was one of those nice guys who had the rare ability to allow others to see his niceness, without being contrived or phoney about it. While acknowledged as a respectable physician, Troop also seemed such a genuine person that the only enemies he made were such nasty characters, it was to his credit rather than detriment that they opposed him.

Carl wasn't the Mel Gibson, Kevin Costner, knock-em-off-their-feet-with-sex-appeal-and-charisma type by any means. He had a medium build with a hint of spare tire, was nice-looking, without being terribly handsome, wore glasses, had a fun laugh and was generally just a pleasant person. Despite his lack of dramatic qualities, Michele could understand how such a man could be attractive to the right kind of woman. For some reason he wasn't married, and she wondered if he was divorced. She also wondered why she was sizing up every available man like a judge at a cattle sale. Isabel whispered in her ear and zipped out of the row of seats, up the aisle toward an exit.

"See ya hon," her friend had murmured "go sic 'em."

Michele didn't understand what she meant until she turned to find the detective, Gil Beach, standing a few seats away, looking at her with a grin.

"Nice entertainment you got here," he laughed, "and I was beginning to think you guys just came to these things for education."

"Well, today I guess we learned we need better security. Say, you're a cop. Why didn't you do something?" she teased.

"Like what? Pull out a gun and start shooting? Aww, I got in my kill quota this week," he chuckled. "Actually, I thought it was kinda fun. By the way, how true is that stuff Doctor Big was saying about electricity healing bones and all?"

She smiled at the "Doctor Big" reference, but answered his question seriously.

"Oh there's some truth there. It has to do with a Piezoelectric effect and collagen formation. The government sponsored some research in the V.A. hospitals that definitely proved long bone fractures heal better when exposed to certain electrical stimuli. But as far as electrical and magnetic field effects are concerned, he's not on such solid ground. And when he gets into cancer cures, Dr. Junghans is definitely on thin ice."

"Unsolid ground, thin ice . . . He sounds like the unsteady man for all seasons," the policeman laughed. "I thought he was the big know-it-all in this field. The program flyer makes him sound only a couple of steps removed from God."

"Oh he's a specialist alright, and don't get me wrong—he has made important contributions to his field. He's no lightweight by any means."

"I guess that's another reason he shouldn't do much skating on thin ice," Beach interjected drolly.

"Okay, so you don't like my metaphors. But a lot of this stuff just hasn't been proven—one way or another. I agree with him on that part of it. There hasn't been enough research. There's a good book on it for laymen, if you're interested. It's by Becker and Selden."

"It'd have to be pretty simple for a layman like me," Beach said, raising his eyebrows.

"I didn't mean that negatively. It's just that some research texts are impossibly obtuse. They put me to sleep. The Becker and Selden one describes their research without boring you to tears."

She wondered if she had offended him.

"Speaking of research, I'm not doing too good with

mine," he added, apparently unruffled. "Any chance you could give me a hand?"

Michele found herself looking around to see who might overhear. Except for the two of them, the auditorium was now empty. She felt an urge to leave, before someone turned out the lights. Her old childhood fear wouldn't even allow her to enjoy being caught alone in a dark room with an attractive man.

"Oh, I can't imagine you needing help with much of anything, Detective. If you don't find anything, maybe it's just because there isn't anything to find." She mentally kicked herself, even as she said it. What had started out as a compliment to make up for her earlier comment, somehow turned into a defensive-sounding statement. Besides, she wasn't sure that she didn't need his help as much as he needed hers. But the damage was done. He nodded, unspoken responses running across his face like the electronic scoreboard at Giant stadium. Michele opened her mouth, to retract, or at least explain her words, but he had already assumed his policeman's role. He thanked her courteously, told her to call him if she changed her mind, and handed her a slightly dog-eared business card that looked like it had spent a lot of long days in his wallet.

Thirteen

Manfred Sullivan had spent a lot of long days and nights on the streets of the Bowery, and looked pretty dog-eared, too. Of course, nobody knew him by his real name. On Houston Street, where he lived most of the time, near the Salvation Army shelter where he could crash if the weather got too cold, he was known as "Sully." He hadn't used a full name for years. You didn't need a last name to live on the street. You just needed a spot. His favorite place was on a grating under the building overhang of the Saint Theresa's Community Center. There was a loose collection of men that hung out there who formed a "bottle club." Whoever had a nickel or could get a hand-out chipped in for the next bottle of cheap wine, which was then shared with whichever members of the club happened to be present and conscious at the time.

At Bellevue, they didn't even know Sully's street name; they simply referred to the regular E.D. visitor as "Old Joe." He was a regular sight at BHC, and the dedicated staff were so clear about their mission to the people nobody else would touch, that he seldom failed to receive compassionate and timely medical treatment. He averaged forty or fifty admissions annually. Today he came in for an eruption of seborrheic dermatitis. It was hardly a new problem, but Joe had let it go, even exacerbating the outbreaks by scratching at them, in the hope of gaining admission to the general hospital wards, where he would have a bed and good food for a few days.

Old Joe only waited a few hours before the nurse called him. That wasn't bad. And Joe couldn't care less anyway, since a corner of the heated waiting room was at least as comfortable as his grating. He even got a "hello" from that Dr. Castro, the one that seemed tough, but never had an unkind word for folks in the E.D. waiting area.

When his number was called, Joe limped to the desk on ulcerated feet that often provided a back-up reason for admission. The nurse was Ginger Harris today, and she greeted him like an old acquaintance, which in fact, he was.

"Hi Joe, what's bothering you today?"

He described his oozing scalp, though the nurse could see it for herself.

"My feet ain't been feelin' too good, either," he added, just to make sure he covered the bases that might get him into a ward for the night.

"Okay, Joe. The doctor will see you down in room four. If he admits you, you aren't gonna give us a hard time with the shower, are you?"

That was the part Joe hated . . . the delousing and clean-up that was required whenever he got in. Sometimes he fought them about it, especially when he was having one of his spells with the voices and all, but he assured Ginger that it wouldn't happen again. No use screwing up his chances for "three hots and a cot" his belly told him, grumbling its protest at a diet of nothing but Gallo Thunderbird for the last three days.

While he sat on the edge of the examination table in room four, there was a parade of important visitors. He didn't know any of them, but he could tell they were V.I.Ps by the way the nurses hovered and offered help. First some guy they called Doctor "Young Hands" was ushered in the room by another guy he only referred to as "Ted." Joe thought he was going to be examined by "Young Hands," who looked too old to have "young" anything. He started to unbutton his grimy shirt for the doctor, but apparently it was more like what they called "granny rounds," or maybe a guided tour. The guy called "Ted" patted Joe on the shoulder, and said stupid things to the VIP about getting bums off the street. He didn't say "bums," he said something else, like "indians" or "indigens," but Joe knew what he meant. Joe noticed that when the big man doctor left, Ted paused to scrub his hands vigorously at the sink. Later, that foxy lady, Dr. Peters stopped in for a moment, but seemed to be checking something about the room instead of doing any treating. At least she smiled and waved when he called out to her.

Finally ol' Weasel Wesley appeared and started the actual exam. Joe didn't care for Wesley, though he only called him "Weasel" in private. Dr. Wesley was about the only doctor that seemed to dislike Joe, and acted kind of angry every time he came in. It was bad luck, because Weasel hardly ever had him admitted. But to Joe's surprise, the physician was almost friendly this time. After a cursory examination, he made a couple of notes on the chart and told the nurse to call Radiology. The woman looked puzzled, but did what the doctor ordered, and soon a great big lug arrived with a rolling cart. Joe's eyes weren't good enough to read the name tag on the big man's jacket, but he looked familiar, and Joe thought he remembered a name like "Bud" or "Buzz." That wasn't so good, 'cause this was the guy that dropped Joe off the X-ray table last spring, fracturing a wrist, and then laughed instead of apologizing. In fact, it seemed like the huge ox managed to have an accident every time he transported Joe somewhere. The old man didn't often require an X-ray, but it had happened often enough that Joe saw a pattern to the big man's accidents. Somehow his hand would get caught in the wheelchair locking lever, one of the heavy X-ray plates would happen to fall on Joe's sore feet, or the guy would miss a high speed turn with the cart, giving the rider a hard jolt against a doorframe or wall.

Joe was so much on guard for one of these deliberate mishaps, that he didn't notice until much later that the ride was too long for the short distance to X-ray. By the time he sensed something was wrong, he was pushed into a dank room off of a long dark tunnel he had never seen before. A familiar person appeared, dressed in white, a stethoscope peeking out of a side pocket.

"Doc, I think Old Joe here needs a little something to relax him," the big attendant said.

So it was a doctor, Joe thought. That was okay. There was something strange about this, but the doctor's presence kept him from resisting the needle that was shoved into his arm. Very quickly, the medication affected his vision, giving everything an even more fuzzy out-of-focus appearance than his failing eyes usually saw. The last thing Joe saw, was an odd smile on the face of the doctor who had given the injection.

Fourteen

"You see, Buzz, there is the absolute possibility here of regeneration—renewal of the body, even the possibility of unlimited longevity . . . we are finding the key to eternal life!"

The big attendant nodded at the right times, though he had little idea of what the Doctor was saying, and didn't really care. All he knew was that he was being paid well, got a chance to play around a little with the patients, and had to cooperate if he didn't want his little pastime of fucking the retards at the handicap center to get out. The one last night had been the best in months. Definitely better than the girl two nights before. Merkel smiled, remembering the mute girl's cowering surrender; secure in the knowledge that the Doc would protect him from any trouble as long as he did his part for the Doc's crazy experiments. So he tried to look as if he was interested, and could understand the scientific gobbledygook that was being thrown at him.

"Our tests confirm the inverse relationship of cancer and regenerative potential. The more a species like the lizard is able to regenerate lost parts, the less the incidence of malignancy. The fields we are generating should allow us to induce unequaled regenerative activity . . . not just bones, but soft tissue, nerves, even organs. So I expect we are in the process of finding the cure for cancer, as a simple side-effect of our ability to regenerate lost tissue. Most of the MDs here haven't a clue to the new world I am charting."

Merkel didn't get the technical stuff. He didn't even get a lot of the non-technical stuff. He wasn't really a radiology technician at all. He had dropped out of school after the sixth grade, and was barely able to read comic books. But when The Doctor decided to use him for the project, Buzz was given fake credentials. From what he could figure out, the Doctor was talking about curing everything and making people live forever. He felt like asking why everybody they had used for the experiments just ended up dead, but figured it was probably just a dumb question and would get him in trouble. Besides, the more subjects they used, the more fun he had—some of it before they died, and more afterward.

As they stood in the musty room deep beneath Bellevue, Old Joe lay on the cart in front of them. The Doctor was doing an external examination, while lecturing to the fraudulent technician about things he could not understand. The exam completed, Buzz responded to a waved directive by rolling the gurney further into the hospital's shadowy recesses, through dark passages with wet pipes overhead, past moldering storage rooms filled with ancient accumulations of trash and treasure. Finally, he slid up a plywood panel, like a garage door, to push the cart down a hidden side tunnel, into a room filled with monstrous machines and power lines, the Doctor following carefully a few feet behind.

Pain must have penetrated Old Joe's drugged mind when Merkel unloaded him roughly onto a polished formica table. As he restrained his limbs with heavy leather straps, the old man stirred, whimpering aloud in hurt and despair.

"Heeeelp me Doc!"

It was the wrong place to seek aid. The Doctor stepped through a shielded door, and began pushing buttons, dialing knobs, flicking levers. Machinery started to hum, as invisible forces of magnetic energy and nuclear particles were gathered and channeled toward the rather pitiful lump of human flesh and blood on the table. As the mechanical whine climbed to a piercing pitch, Old Joe's eyes fluttered and his nicotine stained fingers scrabbled desperately, as if trying to find something to hold onto as he felt himself descend into chaos. As they had done during most of his life, Old Joe's hands closed on emptiness.

Fifteen

Michele Peters had just assisted in the gastric lavage of a teenage drug overdose. The patient was a petite Hispanic girl, about sixteen, named Rosalinda Alvarez. She came in cyanotic and unconscious, with extremely depressed vital signs. She was also poikilothermic, her temperature fluctuating radically—often a sign of exposure. The girl's aunt had found her niece passed out on the back porch, an empty pill bottle still clutched in her hand.

They put in an endotracheal tube so the girl could breathe, while they pumped over eight liters of sterile water in and back out again, to recover the unabsorbed pills. It wasn't the case of a hophead, but a pitiful suicide attempt, using a mixture of barbiturates and assorted tranquilizers borrowed from her absent mother. Dr. Peters recognized Librium, Valium, and Xanax in the mix that they sucked out of her stomach. They gave her intravenous Naloxone in D5W to counteract the drugs that had already been absorbed, and added B_1 to the I.V. drip for good measure. Finally, they gave her activated charcoal to pick up any chemicals floating around her G.I. tract.

A psychiatric consult was standard in these cases, and Dr. Paul Gordon had been called. But as Michele supervised the emergency care, Rosalinda had regained consciousness, reached out and grabbed her hand. For most of the critical moments, they had stayed locked together.

There was some deep level of need and wanting in the slight girl, who was really nothing more than a child. Michele could feel it extending through the need of the moment, a hunger far beyond that momentary reaching out for the nearest hand. What terrible hurts or deprivations would lead a child to this extreme measure was a mystery that perhaps Dr. Gordon could solve.

By the time Rosalinda had been turned over to Dr. Gordon, it was almost two hours past the end of Michele's shift. Instead of heading for the staff quarters, she caught an elevator going down. She had decided to visit the Pathology Department where she might be able to gain more information about the dead or missing John and Jane Does. Some of them must have had postmortems completed. Perhaps she could find a pathologist who had done some of the autopsies.

The Pathology Department at Bellevue did not appear to be a well-planned or organized space, a source of complaint by the staff for many years. Some of the work was done in a basement area adjacent to the morgue. A secretary with coke-bottle eyeglasses directed Michele through the cluttered area to the fixing room, where Dr. Sal Roncali was doing a frozen section. She passed rows of stainless steel drawers, numbered consecutively. Michele had never bothered to count the total number of refrigerated body receptacles, but she saw the numbers 87 and 88 on the end of one long row. And this morgue was only for patients who died at Bellevue in the normal course of events. Two blocks away, at 30th and First Avenue was also the City Morgue, with additional rows of steel drawers to receive even more bodies spit out by a hostile city.

In the fixing room, Dr. Roncali nodded to acknowledge her presence, but neither of them spoke. A frozen section was a "stat" procedure, usually done while a patient was still on the operating table. The results helped

DARK MEDICINE

the waiting surgeons decide whether to begin the often massively invasive procedures appropriate to a malignancy or the less traumatic steps necessary if the sample in question was benign. When Roncali finished his examination, he stepped to the phone and dialed the number for surgery from memory.

"George? It's Sal. It's a bad one. Tell Ghandi he'll probably want to do the radical. Goodbye happy honker."

Michele shivered at his words. They meant some poor woman who went to sleep with two breasts, would wake up with only one. No matter what anyone said, a great deal of a woman's self-image was tied up with her mammary glands. There were cosmetic options that could create less than perfect substitutes, but for a very long time, this would color some woman's entire outlook on life.

"To what do I owe the pleasure of a visit from the best-looking doctor at Bellevue?" the pathologist asked.

At least the guy was consistent, she thought. Try as he might, Roncali was about as biased as anyone she had ever met that managed to make it through medical school. To him, anyone from a country near India was a "Ghandi," blacks were "Hersheys," and a woman was a sex object, physician or not. He tried to keep his marked prejudices discreet, not using the worst terms to peoples' faces, but everyone knew anyway, and assumed that this was one reason he had chosen pathology as a specialty. Lumps of tissue and cadavers weren't easily offended.

Michele ignored his comments, asking instead about a patient who had recently been brought to the Emergency Department D.O.A. from an auto crash. It was a ploy . . . an attempt at misdirection. She didn't want to be too obvious as she asked her questions. She situated herself on the opposite side of a formica counter from the pathologist, remembering the last time she had been alone with him and how he managed to repeatedly find ways to "accidentally" touch her. Roncali had a curled leer frozen in place, apparently his version of a smile, and she wondered it he really thought it was attractive. Actually, the man wouldn't be considered bad looking, but his personality and behavior made anything more than professional contact a disgusting prospect.

Roncali wasn't much help. He had no record or memory of the people she mentioned. When his leer started to change into a suspicious frown, she stopped asking questions. Until she knew more, the fewer people who knew of her real concerns, the better.

"Well, thanks Sal. I suppose I could have just called, but I have to get out of the pressure cooker once in a while."

"Hey, come down and visit anytime," the pathologist responded, the leer quickly reappearing. "If there's anything I can do to you . . . I mean for you . . . well, you just ask, and I'll be happy to accommodate you."

Michele didn't even smile. She understood his message, and he knew it. He should also know that she wasn't interested at all in his games, though in her experience Roncali's type never seemed to accept a negative response anyway.

She turned and headed out through the morgue. Several carts were arranged along the hall. One gurney held a lumpy form, covered with a bloody sheet. That would be the leftovers from an autopsy recently completed, she assumed. Another cart with a veiled corpse was against the wall. A fetid odor hung about the area. Without much forethought, mostly just out of a passing curiosity, she paused and lifted the drape. It took a moment before she recognized the face of Old Joe. It was a bit of a shock, since Joe seemed a permanent institution at BHC. He was one of those sights you always expected to see, but in the E.D. not the morgue. In fact she seemed to remember seeing him just hours before, when she was cruising rooms for an acuity check. She hadn't recognized Joe's body at first, because his skin was a bright red color, as if burned. Peeling layers of flesh matched that impression. She pushed at the deltoid muscle of his shoulder with a pen from her pocket. The flesh gave and parted, like cooked meat.

Such deteriorated remains were not upsetting to Dr. Peters. She had seen too many burn, trauma, and disease victims to be shocked by rotten flesh. But she was puzzled. How did Old Joe get into this condition? When she had seen him, only hours before, she didn't remember anything like this. Not that he would have been sitting up on an exam table if he had been in this condition. This looked like the condition of a severe burn victim, perhaps a fire fatality, except for the lack of charring. Could he have been treated, released, and then had some awful accident? With homeless people, such deaths were not uncommon, from mattress fires when they passed out in an alcoholic stupor with lit cigarettes in hand to room fires when unsafe heaters or hot plates started a blaze. But this looked more like a scalding, or some non-flame heat damage.

Michele replaced the drape and stopped at the clerk's desk to request the chart. The flustered woman couldn't provide it.

"I think it was sent up to Medical Records," she stammered.

"Why would that be the case," Michele asked, "when the postmortem hasn't even been completed?"

"Well, I, I . . . I'm not sure. Maybe Dr. Roncali took it, or Dr. Pearsall. He's the head of the department, you know, and . . ."

"Yes I know Jack, but you must have some documentation of the case."

The woman hemmed and hawed, obviously at a loss, and Michele realized it wouldn't accomplish much to press the issue. The clerk was only able to show her the written order for a post-mortem. In the spaces requesting permission from next-of-kin, the word "none" had been written in, and the form was signed by "J. Wesley, M.D." Preliminary C.O.D. was "cardiac arrest." More strangeness. Old Joe had just about every ailment *except* heart disease, as she recalled. And here he was, looking like a parboiled red snapper, and that wasn't mentioned on the form.

Michele began to feel worried. Here was another one—a homeless derelict with no relatives; a strange, unexpected death, listed as "cardiac arrest" despite no apparent history of heart disease, and a missing chart. Her anxiety increased when a few minutes later, she used an available computer terminal to check the files, but found no record of Old Joe's admission. The list of his visits was lengthy, but the last entry was dated two weeks before. Admissions were entered from the moment a person came into the E.D. She knew Joe had been there today. It was possible, but extremely unlikely that there had been an error of omission . . . procedures were too uniform, too automatic, too much built into regular operations. The more likely, and much more frightening possibility was that the information had somehow been removed. She tapped a few keys, working her way to the data fields she had reviewed before, and confirmed her fears. None of the cases she had previously discovered were any longer a part of the computer record. Someone had been alerted to her inquiries—someone that didn't want her to learn anything.

The implications ballooned. If someone was expunging records of deaths, there was something seriously wrong going on. And a person of importance had to be involved, or they would not have the capability or access necessary either to be involved in all these cases or to alter the computer files. Furthermore, her investigation of the matter had led to an immediate response. Whoever had deleted the files knew that someone was asking too many questions, probably knew it was her, and had already demonstrated willingness to go to extreme lengths, including clearly illegal acts, to prevent this coming to light.

Michele felt like *Alice Through the Looking Glass,* only the strange world she had stepped into was more like one from a novel by Robin Cook. Despite constructing some rather bizarre and unrealistic plots, that author had been a favorite of hers, and she had enjoyed his tales of medical mystery. But she had never confused such fantastic ideas with real life. However, this was real, and it had a disturbing similarity to the strange happenings in those books. Maybe she had read too many of them, because the logical step in one of those plots would be for the "bad guys" to go after the naïve young woman doctor who had stumbled onto their plot. Michele wasn't naive, and she wasn't all that young anymore. But if someone was hiding serious wrong-doings, it was not totally paranoid of her to think that she could be in danger.

Michele quickly logged off the computer. She searched through the voluminous pockets in her white coat that allowed her to avoid carrying a purse, though she sometimes felt like a pony express rider with bulging saddlebags. In a moment she located it—a crumpled and worn business card. "Detective Sergeant Gil Beach" was written on the card, "Ninth Precinct, New York City Police Department."

Sixteen

Beach had just filled a coffeepot from the ancient water cooler when Dr. Peters' call came in. He was carefully examining the clear carafe, a recent habit from when he had picked up a full pot of hot coffee, only to have it crack apart in his hands and spray steaming liquid all over his shoes, pants, and a stack of reports. Despite the minor burns he had experienced, the worse suffering was when he had had to retype the entire sheaf of documents. Few things could pain him as much as paperwork.

He was emptying the pot into the stained old coffeemaker with one hand, while mopping up a mixture of scattered sugar crystals, congealing milk, dirty brown smears, and coffee grinds with a rag in his other hand. Rose Sena, the civilian employee who handled phone calls, approached and told him there was some woman on line two that refused to give her name. He finished pouring, flicked the brewing switch on, and dropped the filthy rag into the garbage. It was only a few feet to his cluttered desk and the phone. He moved a pile of papers, slumped heavily into the creaking office chair, and swung his feet up onto the desk before he punched the blinking button, and answered.

"Ninth Precinct, Detective Unit."

"Uhh . . . I was trying to reach Detective Sergeant Beach."

"Speaking."

"Oh, Hi. I didn't recognize your voice at first. This is Michele Peters, you remember? Dr. Peters from Bellevue."

"Oh yes . . . Dr. Peters. Of course I remember! Nice to hear from you. How can I help?"

There was a moment of silence.

"Hello, Dr. Peters. Are you okay?"

"Umm, yes. Thanks for asking. I guess I have to apologize for my reticence before. I'm beginning to think there is something going on. I'd prefer not to discuss it over the telephone."

"Are you at the hospital?"

"Yes, but I think I'd like to meet somewhere else."

"Well, you could come here. Or if you prefer, there's a coffee shop two blocks over from the hospital on Third Avenue, at Twenty Eighth. We could meet there."

"The coffee shop sounds good. Is that the Constantinople?"

"That's the one. Usually most folks at Bellevue don't know about anything outside the hospital cafeteria."

"Yeah, well most folks don't live here, like I do. When could you meet me?"

"I could be there in ten minutes."

Peters told him that would be fine, and Gil hung up the receiver, wondering what she meant by "living" at the hospital. Was it just a figure of speech because she worked so hard, or did she mean it? He shrugged into his coat and automatically checked for his wallet, weapon, and notebook. Then he remembered that be had promised to meet with Helen Joseph at the Youth Bureau about a series of drug-related gang fights. He dialed her number, apologized, and asked if they could meet later in the day. Helen sounded a little annoyed, but agreed to the new time. Nine minutes later he was sitting in a booth at the rear of the Constantinople Coffee Shop. A ceiling fan turned slowly, mixing aromas of cigarette smoke, fried foods, and strong coffee. He ordered coffee and warmed his hands around the cup, as he sipped the strong black liquid.

Dr. Peters arrived a couple of minutes later, slid into the booth, and asked for a Diet Pepsi when the waiter followed her to the table for her order. He may have been following for another reason, as she walked to the rear of the restaurant with the self-possessed stride of a model on a fashion show runway, her finely rounded hips moving smoothly in close-fitting slacks, long graceful neck set off by the ruffled collar of a designer blouse and deep auburn hair in a short cut of bouncy soft curls.

She said nothing until the soda was served, keeping her eyes directed everywhere except at the detective. Gil waited, giving her the chance to choose her opening. He took in her finely formed face, with its high cheekbones and large eyes, framed by bushy eyebrows. She absently twisted a lock of shiny hair in the fingers of her right hand.

"Okay, here it is. There is something wrong. I didn't want to go to you before because nothing seemed very certain. I know you probably think we have a code of secrecy—in a way, you're right. It's not a nasty conspiracy or a desire to cover up lousy medicine. But we're human, and as much as we try to avoid it, it just isn't possible to learn without making errors. Nobody is perfect, but you can't even be close when you're starting out. Unfortunately, most people can understand the need to learn from mistakes in computer programming, car mechanics, or even hair styling better than in medicine. They think somehow we can learn the most complex systems, incorporate massive amounts of data, and develop fine-tuned skills of diagnosis to find our way through millions of potential possibilities without ever making a mistake. And you know, of course, that any damaging outcome—death, disfigurement, disability—is seen as a golden opportunity for a lawsuit, even though those awful results are inevitable in some cases. With the way people file a suit at every hangnail, thinking they will grab the brass ring at a rich doctor's expense, no physician could hope to survive, if every error or case of less than perfect judgement was made public."

"I'm not so sure I like the idea that doctors aren't as perfect as I thought they were."

"Exactly. We're supposed to be infallible. Sometimes that myth is even helpful to the patient. They can heal better if they have confidence in us. So it's better that the public doesn't know every little thing."

"But aren't you telling me that the public's confidence isn't justified?"

"No I'm not," she responded quickly, eyes direct now. "For the most part, we have the finest physicians and the best medical delivery system in history. But that doesn't mean it's without flaws."

"So it must be more than one of those 'slight flaws' that led you to break Omerta."

"Omerta?"

"Sorry, that's like the Code of Silence. I mean the uhh . . . habit of not telling everything that goes on."

"That's an understatement. I think something very nasty is going on. I really don't know too much about it yet, but I'm worried. The truth is, I'm a little scared."

As she went on to tell him about some of the things she had discovered, Gil knew he was talking to a very intelligent and talented woman, a woman who had risen to a position of importance in one of the toughest possible environments. Despite the rather charming nervous habit of twisting a strand of hair between her fingers, the anxiety in her expression was not that of a helpless school girl, but the honest well-placed fear of an extremely capable professional.

"Why don't you think anyone has noticed these cases before?"

"Well, I hate to say it, Detective . . ."

"Please," he interjected, "call me Gil."

"Oh, well, yes. Michele is okay for me, too. I hate to say it . . . Gil, but there is a certain prejudice when it comes to the homeless, the indigent. I think most medical people still try to do their best, but the number of indigents, the extent of their problems, and the way they just seem to work against our efforts for them . . . well, sometimes they just aren't seen as being quite so important as other folks. It's easy to start thinking about them as a type instead of individuals—as something a little less than human. And when you don't see people as human and valuable, it's a lot easier to forget about them, to put them at the end of the waiting line, not put yourself out for them. So masses of them get shoved through, over and over. If one disappears now and then, or the records aren't available, who even notices?"

"Obviously you don't feel that way."

"Damn right I don't feel that way!" she declared, fire in her eyes now. "Every person we treat is a human being that deserves the finest care, and the best efforts we can give them. I know that sounds like a hospital P.R. flyer, but I believe it, Gil!"

And Gil believed her as well. He asked more questions, and they began making plans as to how they might penetrate the mystery at Bellevue. In the course of their conversation, he got a much better sense of who this doctor really was. He liked the person he saw behind the white coat and felt she could be trusted. As she talked, her concern for the poor and mistreated came through, as did her extensive knowledge and skills.

"You sound like you really love working in the trenches," he observed. She got a funny, sort of puzzled look on her face when he said that.

"Well, not always, really. It can be pretty draining, and dirty. As a matter of fact, I hope someday to get out of the tempest and settle down into a nice cushy administrator's job."

"Oh really?" Gil answered, "You seem more of the caring, direct help kind of person to me."

Apparently it was the wrong thing to say.

"So you think women are only good for nurturing."

"Hey, wait a minute. I didn't say anything about women or nurturing. I just saw your eyes light up when you talked about saving that guy in ana . . . anafol . . . whatever you call that big allergic reaction. And the guy with both legs chopped off . . . and the little girl who O.D.'d. And I saw you myself, with that guy in the trauma room, talking him down, when everybody else forgot he was more than a hunk of organs."

The hardness went out of her expression.

"Sorry, I guess I'm a little oversensitive. I've seen so much prejudice in my life that sometimes I react to it, even when it's not there."

Gil nodded.

"I saw my mother's life wasted because of the rigid ideas of gender roles. She was a marvel of intelligence and capability, but an insecure and controlling man made sure that she never fulfilled any of her potential."

"Your father?"

"Stepfather. My father wasn't like that, but he died very young and mom was so devastated she fell into a bad relationship to save herself from despair."

"And traded one kind of pain for another."

"Well, aren't you the psychologist. I don't know why I'm telling you all this. I thought you were a detective."

"Oh I'm a cop alright. But cops learn to be good listeners, too. You can't learn anything if you're doing all the talking."

"It's more than that, Gil. There's something about you that makes a woman feel comfortable . . . safe."

There was a hint of moisture in the woman's eyes. It made them sparkle. She looked so directly at him that Gil began to feel uncomfortable. When she reached across the table and touched his hand, he realized what was happening.

"Uhh, my wife is a psychologist, though. I guess I can't help picking up a few things from her. She's a pretty special woman."

Peters blinked twice. She looked down at his hand, as if noticing his wedding ring for the first time. Gil thought he detected a tiny drop of her shoulders. She took a deep breath and gave his hand a squeeze, then pulled hers back to her lap.

"I'll bet she is. Anyway, I guess I feel strongly about the way women have been treated, but I'm not anxious to be seen as a fanatic either."

"Yeah, I understand. You don't seem like that to me. By the way, speaking of fanatics, you have any idea what ever happened to those animal rights . . . activists?"

"I see you know the politically correct titles. Actually, I don't have a problem with most animal rights people. I don't agree with 'em, but I don't think they're nuts either. But as for this particular group, *SAKRED*, I don't know."

"Oh, that's their name? I saw it on a couple of their signs, but I thought they just misspelled it."

"I think *SAKRED* is some kind of acronym—Stop Animal Killing . . . and Research Death—or something like that. I don't remember exactly. Seems like a couple of real flakos in charge of that bunch. Carl Troop settled 'em down a little—he's a great guy with that sort of thing. He took them on a tour of the hospital, to show that no animals were being mistreated. Actually, there isn't much animal research going on at all, but what little is conducted follows all the humane guidelines for that kind of thing."

"So he satisfied them."

"No, that's what I mean about them being a little wacko. They didn't believe it. They stormed out in a huff, insisting that he hid portions of the hospital from them, and they just knew that animal torture was being conducted in secret labs. I guess there's no convincing a paranoid that there isn't a conspiracy."

"Present company excluded, I assume," Gil teased.

"Well, I may be paranoid," she laughed, "but that doesn't mean I'm not being followed. Seriously, Gil, I would be very happy if I were proven wrong, and nothing bad was going on. But so far, I'm finding it harder and harder to dismiss."

"Okay, let's see what we can find out. Is there anyone else that we need to involve in this?"

"Ummm. Well, there is a radiologist named Pretaska. I don't know if he would want to help, but he's department head, so he would be in a good place to find out if this possible common thread of radiological referral has any substance to it. I could see if he'd be interested, without giving too much away."

Gil noticed an odd expression on Peters' face when she mentioned the other doctor. Was that a little flush on her neck? He wondered whether the interest she wanted to determine in Dr. Pretaska had more to do with this mystery or with the mystery of human attraction.

Michele found Peotre in the film developing area. She started with small talk, but when she began broaching the mysterious demise of indigents, he seemed uninterested. He kept turning the conversation back to her, and the discussion became increasingly personal, as Peotre seemed fascinated with her life and family history.

"I want you to see something," he said, and pulled an X-ray film from a drawer, snapping it in place on the glowing white viewer where she could see it.

"Look at this one," he suggested, putting a hand across her shoulders and drawing her toward the screen. His touch was again like an electric shock, sending thrills up and down her back and tickling her insides. This time he didn't remove the hand from her as he pointed out a subtle shadow in the film. She honestly didn't hear a word he was saying, but was excruciatingly aware of the hand and its movement to the back of her neck, where it soon began to gently caress and knead her skin.

"Oh my God," she thought to herself, "it's happening." Her secret fantasy of having Peotre attracted to her was coming true. Then he reached out to turn her toward him, and she raised her eyes to look directly into his dark piercing gaze. She had felt before that it would be impossible to resist him, and felt no different now. Only now, there was something real to resist. The controlling part of her heart, gut, or whatever was being whirled around in an emotional centrifuge she didn't want to resist at all.

They stared into each others' eyes for an interminable moment, until the tension was too much to bear. She wasn't sure who moved first, who responded. But then their lips touched. There was no obvious transition from a simple kiss to a clawing desperate passion, but that's what it soon became for her. Hands searched and squeezed as their lips moved and tongues explored. It went on until she had to come up for breath, at the same time realizing that his hands were hungrily massaging her buttocks and a hard lump was pushing out from his hip area, thrusting against her, low on her belly.

The film developing area was relatively private, but not enough for this. Michele spoke out more loudly than she intended.

"Stop!"

He paused and looked curiously at her. She couldn't answer the question in his eyes. Did her demand mean she didn't want this at all, or that it was just the wrong place and time. Was she calling a permanent halt, or just a temporary pause, until it could be continued elsewhere. Her mind was far too muddled to answer such questions for herself, much less Peotre, who was breathing heavily in front of her.

"I . . . I . . . I'll talk to you," she blurted out, and dashed from the room.

Seventeen

By lunchtime the next day, Michele had settled down a little. At twelve-thirty, she was even able to sit at a cafeteria table to eat a bowl of watery vegetable soup. While she slurped down the thin broth, she took inventory of herself. She wasn't sure how much she was operating from her head, or how much from her emotions, but she had decided that her "Stop!" to Peotre in the developing room had not meant "No, Never!" If Pretaska still felt something for her, and didn't either regret the intimacy or resent her for backing off the day before, she was ready to take a chance. Life was full of risks, she told herself. There were worse ones than finding out if a handsome fellow physician was worth a lasting relationship.

Her lingering fear was that a "lasting relationship" might be a foreign concept to Peotre. Was his continuing bachelor status a case of not having found the right woman, or an inability to sustain long-term relationships? She realized that she really knew very little about the man, other than his nationality and smoldering good looks. But then she rationalized that all relationships have to start somewhere. Most of the time, they start from the outside and work their way in. She had to admit, there were a couple of ways that she would particularly like Dr. Peotre Pretaska to work his way into her.

A voice interrupted her libidinous thoughts, asking

"Are you alone?" She almost gave a sharp retort to the speaker when she saw it was Richard Schwenker, the assistant administrator for operations. Of course she was alone. That was obvious! But the little man's perfect manners made her feel guilty for almost telling him to get lost. She made up for it by inviting him to sit at the table, and soon he was gabbing away about his latest petty problem.

Schwenker was nearing retirement age, which was probably the only reason the hospital hadn't fired him by now. He didn't seem to have much influence or real responsibility. His biggest job seemed to be that of "official worrier."

Bellevue was an enormous operation, with annual resource utilization figures that would astound most people. There were 26,000 annual inpatients, around 100,000 E.D. visits, and close to a half a million outpatient and ambulatory surgery visits. Schwenker's current concern was the power bill. The figures didn't mean much to Michele, but apparently the electrical usage was running at an all-time high. The inventory of departmental demands did not explain the total usage.

"Not that every kilowatt can be counted," the graying and plump administrator acknowledged. "This old monstrosity can never be totally quantified." He shook his head in frustration. "But this goes beyond nickel and dime stuff. There's only a few possibilities." He ticked them off on his fingers.

"One: someone has made a big accounting error. If that is true, I know it's not me. But it could be one of the high usage departments.

"Two: it's Con Ed's fault. They've screwed up the metering or the billing. It's happened before, but I doubt it, since I really chewed them out last month.

"Three," he went on, "there's some serious theft of services going on."

It was hard for Michele to appreciate the man's concerns in light of her personal crisis and the frightening mystery she was attempting to solve that could be counted in terms of human lives, rather than kilowatts. But she tried to be polite. After all, he was an assistant administrator, even if he wasn't a very formidable one. Even a figurehead deserved some respect.

"Have you discussed this with other administrators?"

"Well, uhh . . . yes, I have. Actually, I brought it up in the Safety Committee meeting yesterday. That's the proper venue for anything impinging on the safety of patients or personnel, risk factors, and such."

"You think this presents a risk?"

"Well, probably mostly to the budget," he chuckled. "But theoretically, until we know where all that power is going, there's a chance that it could be malfunctioning equipment or something that would create a risk factor. Some people have been badly hurt when such things got ignored. You can read about incidents all the time in *Risk Management Quarterly*."

Michele regretted her earlier discounting of the man and his concerns. He might not be photogenic, or have a lot of political power, but he had a pleasant manner, a good sense of humor, and ultimately some of the same goals she had—the best interests of people, especially the patients and staff at BHC.

"What kind of response did you get?"

"Oh you know that committee—a bunch of hard-noses."

Michele didn't really know the membership, except that its chairman was James Hampton, the hospital's chief administrator, who seldom actually attended, preferring to turn the unglamorous duty over to one of his assistants.

"Ted was chairing," Schwenker said with a slight frown. "I don't know why. Seems like the head of operations is the logical chairperson in the absence of Hampton, don't you think?"

Michele noted the implied rivalry, and the signs of Schwenker's extremely limited influence. They were emphasized even more by his next comments.

"Anyway, he never listens to anything I say. Wachman was there for a change, but unless something is clinical, he doesn't get very involved. Joyce Castro asked some good questions, but I don't think she really understood the magnitude of the problem. Most of the others were absent or not paying attention. Pretaska was the only one who seemed interested, and he offered to form an investigative committee. I had to leave—for another meeting—so I don't know if that actually happened, the committee thing I mean . . . or not. The agenda was so packed, I understand they needed more than one session. I think they plan to meet again . . . maybe today. I have to check with Ted."

At the mention of Pretaska, Michele's ears perked up, and she found herself scanning the cafeteria for a sign of the infuriatingly interesting man. There was still no sign of him. Before she could ask directly about the one person she wanted to discuss, the insistent beeping of her remote pager broke into their conversation. This was one of those undependable voice transmitters, that might or might not work. She held it to her ear and switched to "receive." As usual, other faint conversations could be heard on the line, but despite the background whisper of some technician explaining a lab test to someone else, she made out the operator's voice telling her to come to the E.D.—STAT. She asked Schwenker to dump her tray in the kitchen for her and headed for home turf.

When she arrived, she was directed to Trauma Room Three where a child was lying gasping, with a hugely distended belly, arms and legs like toothpicks, and a skeletal head. Her age was hard to determine, probably somewhere between ten and twelve. It only took a quick examination to see the problem. Michele stepped out of the small room to confront the resident in charge.

"Are you telling me you can't diagnose an advanced carcinoma like that?" she almost shouted at Soon Twa Quan, the first-year resident who had paged her.

"Yes, I can, Dr. Peters. But there is another matter I wanted your help with." He nodded to a pair of gangly people standing in the corridor. The man was in heavy coveralls, a long sleeved faded pink tee-shirt, and work boots the color of soil. The woman wore threadbare jeans and a dull checkered flannel shirt. Her sneakers were cheap and laced with pieces of string.

"Those people are her parents. Would you please talk with them. Apparently they have kept her from getting treatment."

"I see," Michele said, looking over at the couple, who seemed normal, if poverty-stricken in appearance. She walked over to them, trying to think of what to say without blowing up.

"That's your daughter in there?" she asked. They nodded. "Why hasn't she been treated?"

"Well, we did take her to the doctor a while back," the woman began, glancing hesitantly at the man, who nodded, but kept silent. "He said it were too late to do much, on account of the cancer. That was about three-four months ago."

"But didn't he explain that even inoperable cancers can be treated with radiation or chemotherapy to extend the patient's life span? This is your child!"

"We love our child, Doctor. You might not believe that, or understand, but we thought it would be just too much for little Tina to handle, knowing that she was going to die, an' all. We could have started all that fancy treatment, and she might have lived a few months longer. But she's still gonna die, right?"

"Well . . . I . . . perhaps, but . . ."

"From what we heard, some of those treatments are almost worse than dying. Your hair falls out, you get so sick you don't much care about living anyhow. So we could have given her a few extra months of suffering, and even worse suffering in her heart, knowing she's gonna die. Now Doctor, who's to say it's not better that we don't even let her know."

There were tears running down the woman's face, and forming in the man's eyes, too. Michele realized the poor parents had a certain point. They loved their daughter in their way, and she should be slower to judge them so harshly. But she disagreed with them, nonetheless.

"Don't you think she knows now?" Michele asked the pair, who stood straight, despite the moisture in their eyes, willing to stand up for their beliefs and actions, trying to be strong for their child. "She doesn't have long, you must realize."

"Not long?" the man asked, a catch in his voice.

"No. She doesn't seem to know," the woman answered, sobbing now, perhaps at the doctor's assessment. "She talks about being sick, sometimes, but like a bad bellyache, or a cold, or something. We got pain-killers that seem to take care of it. And as long as she don't know, we don't want nobody puttin' ideas in her head. See if you can make her feel better, so's she can breathe and all. But you start all that cancer stuff, she's gonna find out, and you're gonna break our little girl's heart."

Michele wondered whose heart was most in danger of breaking, but she stopped arguing with the woman and returned to the trauma room. The child seemed to be breathing a little easier, staring up at her with big dark eyes, huge in her shrunken features.

"Hi Tina. I'm Dr. Peters. How are you doing?"

"Well, I expect I'm dyin', don't you think?"

The statement almost floored Michele.

"You think you're dying, Tina?"

"Might not be tonight, but I don't have a long time."

"How long have you known, sweetheart?"

"Oh for ages now. I saw this TV show about four months ago about cancer, and then after we went to Dr. Higgins, and my belly started swelling up so I figured what was going on."

"You're very brave. Your folks would be proud, if they knew how brave you are."

"Yeah, well don't you go and say anything to them, Doc. They don't know I'm dying, and I want to keep it that way."

Michele shook her head, not sure it she heard right.

"You don't think they know?"

"No. They act like everything's okay. They wouldn't do that if they thought I was dying! Honest Doc, I don't think momma could take it. Daddy might hold on, but I think momma would just curl up and die herself if she knew."

"I don't know, Tina. They seem like pretty strong folks to me. Maybe you ought to tell them."

"No. I love momma and daddy, and I don't want to see them hurt. Let's just keep this between you and me Doc."

The child weakly lifted her arm to extend a hand. Michele took the emaciated little fingers in her own for a moment, feeling completely inadequate. After a while, the child dozed off and Michele left, marveling at the strength that could lead a dying child to be more concerned about her parents than herself. She put in a call to Psychiatry, to send someone down that might have a better idea how to deal with this strange and remarkable family, then walked out the ambulance entrance and down the street. Her own eyes were wet as she set off down First Avenue.

As she walked, she became aware of someone walking

close behind. She was getting spooked, ready to run, when a familiar voice called out. It was Carl Troop, the acting assistant medical director. She breathed a sigh of relief when she saw his pleasant, smiling face.

"Hi," she said, "just trying to get some fresh air."

"Won't find any of that in Manhattan," he laughed. "I hope I'm not being presumptuous to say so, but you look like you just got a hit in the left emotional hemisphere."

"Is it that obvious?"

"Well, you're always such a strong one, it's a little strange to see you looking vulnerable."

"How come you didn't go into psychiatry?" she asked, wondering whether she preferred the image of vulnerability to that of constant strength, "You're a natural."

"Look, am I being too nosey? If I'm out of line, just say so. But then, you're probably too nice to do that. I should know better than to butt in without an invitation. I'll head back to the hospital."

"No, no. Don't be silly, Carl. It's nice that you're interested. I think I want to let a few things simmer in my brain before I burden anyone else, but it'd be nice to have company. I'm going to walk down to the V.A. and back. Why don't you come along?" He smiled and nodded.

They cut through Bellevue South Park and Phipps Plaza, coming out at 27th Street, then turned south for several blocks and back east to the Veterans Administration Hospital. During the walk, they had a nice chat about other subjects. Troop was a pleasant person to talk with—he didn't compete with her, dismiss her, or come on to her, the most frequent reactions she had been getting lately. She discovered that his wife had died of a ruptured cerebral aneurism several years before, and he had immersed himself in work ever since. He only revealed this with hesitation, and there was no hint that he was suggesting she fill the gap in his love life. If Michele hadn't been so interested in Peotre, she might have thought more about that, but it didn't seem relevant. Carl was nice as a friend. They even seemed to have some common ideas about social values and the need to keep a sense of humor.

Along the way she marveled as usual at the Theodore Roszak sculpture, "Sentinel," across from the hospital at the Public Health Labs Building, and Carl remarked that it resembled some kind of futuristic crossbow aimed at the sky to hold off the plagues. They smiled at the signs engraved in the stone facade of the recreation center which still labeled it as the Public Baths it had once been, grumbled together at the numerous empty liquor bottles deposited here and there, and generally had a good time. When twenty minutes later they got back to the E.D., Michele felt refreshed and a little lighter.

That evening, Michele felt like she was floating on a magic carpet. Peotre had called her later in the day and asked if he could see her. They had a wonderful dinner together at Tavern on the Green, followed by a romantic stroll in Central Park. Now they had returned to her room at the hospital and were sampling a bottle of Beaujolais he had purchased on the way.

A little careful after the surge of passion that was unleashed by a single kiss in the hospital, she had avoided rushing into physical intimacy. But the wine was making her giddy and melting her inhibitions. Peotre sat next to her on an overstuffed couch, dressed in perfectly fitting wool slacks and a light Jacquard sweater over a white-on-white dress shirt. She almost felt embarrassed that such a picture of fashion and suavity should be seated on her lumpy furniture in the stark surroundings of the staff quarters. But when he put his arm around her shoulder, she put her insecurity aside and moved against him, snuggling into his side and laying her head against his shoulder. The warmth of his body seemed like an instant stimulant, spreading an aura of warmth and excitement into hers.

They had been discussing art and technology for the last few minutes. He had described computer-generated artworks, and she was expressing her belief that no machine could ever imitate the human's creative spirit. She was using a Chagall print she had hung on the opposite wall as an example. But he remained silent, and she ran down like a wind-up toy, feeling the expectancy of the moment.

Finally, he took the wineglass from her hand, set it on the end table, and touching her chin with one hand, turned her face to his. Michele felt the blood drain from her head, as he again stared into her eyes, with that smoldering, dark gaze that would have made flowers wilt. She felt weak as she stared back, yet was also conscious of a building rush of adrenaline, pooling somewhere in her midsection.

When he pressed his mouth to hers, there was no hesitation on her part. The ambivalence of yesterday was gone. Eagerly, she moved into the kiss and his arms. They hung together, moving in rhythms of heartbeats and sensation, until his gentle hands slipped down from her face and neck to unbutton her top. The blouse slipped from her shoulders, and in an accommodating movement she also shrugged off the straps of her bra. His lips never left hers, while his hands found the hook and released her breasts. Then his kisses moved down her face and throat to her chest. She shuddered in arousal as his mouth found her nipples. Her back arched instinctively, pushing into the feeling; eyes closed as she was transported by the torrent of stimulation.

Moments later, they lay on her small bed, his firm,

muscular body on top of hers. It didn't seem to matter that there wasn't room to lie side-by-side. She spread her legs and cried out when he entered her. She was as intoxicated by her emotions as by the wine, but together they drugged her with a potent combination that lifted her to wondrous heights. It had been so long since she had felt anything like this, so long since she had felt a man inside her, that she had no ability to separate the gratification of her long and intense deprivation from her feelings for this particular man. But she knew that right now, it felt like a fantasy come true. It felt like love.

After he climaxed, she waited, hoping that he would want to fulfill her as well. She was pleased, when after a few minutes of rest, he began to stir again, and touched her in new and wonderful ways. She wanted to be on top this time, but for some reason he seemed to resist that. Michele didn't have much time to consider this. A clutch of panic gripped her heart, as the lights blinked out, and they were plunged into darkness. She gave a small yelp of terror as she fought to keep from screaming. The darkness seemed like something viscous, oozing around and over her. She felt Peotre pulling away.

"N-n-no," she gasped, "don't leave me!"

"It's just a power outage," Peotre laughed, jumping up from the bed. "If it doesn't get restored in a few seconds the emergency generators should kick in."

Michele curled into a fetal ball, angry at Pretaska for abandoning her, terrorized by the heavy darkness, and desperately trying to hang on to her composure. She prayed that he was right about the brevity of a black-out, and shivered for a seemingly endless minute or two until there was a yellowish blinking, and then brightness again flooded the room.

"A bit slow. Schwenker will be having fits. But no sweat, girl," he told her. "Jesus, grow up. You aren't still afraid of the dark, are you?"

It was like a bucket of ice-water being poured on her, and she couldn't bring herself to answer his insensitive question. When he made a move to return to bed, she turned away, facing toward the wall.

"What's the matter, Sweetie? Didn't you like it?"

Michele lay quietly, mortified at Pretaska's words. He sounded like a jerk, and she wondered if she had made a big mistake. Had she been so blinded by her lust and loneliness, that she didn't see this man for the oaf he sounded like, or was she so neurotic that she was overreacting to a normal response on his part. But had he really called her "Sweetie?" And could he actually have asked her if she "liked it" in that self-assured, almost arrogant tone? Could she really have been so blind?

"I think I want to get dressed," she said, wrapping a sheet around her as she got up from the bed.

"Damn, I never know what to expect from you," he complained, shaking his head. "What? Did I say something that offended you?"

"I don't know. I don't think I want to talk about it. Look, let's just cool off for a little while and talk later."

"I don't think you need to cool off, lady. You seem like pure ice already," he countered, then he strode into the other room, slipped on his clothes, and left.

Michele sat on the edge of the rumpled bed, sobbing. She couldn't sort out her feelings or even her memory of what had happened. Had she distorted his words and attitude because of her insecurity? She fell back on the small cot and covered her red-rimmed eyes.

Eighteen

"This has got to be one of the more colossal screw-ups in current memory!" Ted Jamison shook his head in amazement, staring at the report from Engineering. "We spend over $50,000 on new ventilation for the T.B. unit and they route the exhaust ducts into the main hospital air supply?"

Paul Albarino, the Engineering Department representative filling in for Chief Pearson, looked at the floor.

"We just followed the plans. It's not our job to approve design. We just put in the duct work the way the plan read."

"Thank God we didn't activate the system," Carl Troop commented. "T.B.'s already on the upswing, we don't need to expose an entire hospital population!"

Almost twenty minutes of wrangling followed, mostly with everyone trying to assign blame to someone else. Finally, Joyce Castro interrupted.

"Look, we can spend all day trying to find out who's at fault, but we still have to come up with some sort of recommendation. Screw the blame, what's the solution?"

As usual, her comment cut to the heart of the matter and the discussion moved forward more productively, though there were a few annoyed glances in her direction. After another hour spent listening to the squabbling, she gathered her papers and walked out of the room, obviously frustrated with the committee process. One by one, several others took her cue and made excuses so they could leave.

There were only five of them left. One was an obvious leader, who looked around at the remaining members. It was not an accident that these remained. A new subject was raised now that the others were gone.

"We have some serious problems with information leaks and security of the . . . Project."

"It's that woman, Peters, again, isn't it?"

"Yes, it seems she is becoming a problem. I am fairly certain that she has been talking to the police. But I'm also concerned about Schwenker. I fear that the recent problem with switching power to our facility has put him on a crusade."

"I thought you had something in mind for her."

"Oh yes. Actually, it's already in operation. But we can't expect immediate results."

"How dangerous is she?" The weasel-faced one asked, furtive glances adding to his ferret-like appearance. The leader swiveled to face him.

"I don't think she has much to go on. We sterilized the computer files, so she has nothing solid. As long as we all keep our mouths shut, she will come off as a typical hysterical woman until it is too late and she is out of the picture."

"But Schwenker is director of operations. He's a fool and hardly worth anything, yet he has the authority and access to find out too much."

"Yes, you are correct. I think Mr. Schwenker is going to have to be taken care of."

After a moment of heavy silence, the discussion moved on to the procurement of isotopes. The radiologist expressed some concern about the amount of radioactive material that was being used, and how it was accounted for. He hinted that he might not go along with the secret arrangements any longer.

"This stuff is under federal jurisdiction," he complained. "I can get a federal rap if this ever comes out."

The leader of the group gave him an icy stare. "You will do whatever you are asked to do, Doctor. Or should I say, 'nearly a Doctor' for accuracy sake?"

"Come on, you can't keep holding that over my head. Look, I've done everything you've asked me to do. For God's sake, I even screwed that damned woman so I could find out what she had learned. It disgusted me. But we're talking the U.S. Nuclear Regulatory Commission here!"

"No, we are talking loyalty, here, sweetheart," the leader said smoothly, walking over and laying a hand on the radiologist's shoulder, rubbing his neck with a sensual stroke. "All of you owe me a great deal of loyalty, even if you have no commitment to this project which will change modern medicine . . . will change life as we know it. And I expect you to abide by that loyalty!"

The protestor dropped his head. The others stared at the floor, table, anywhere but at the head of the table. There was no further discussion, and the subdued group shuffled from the conference room.

Nineteen

Deep under the conference room, in a dim tunnel, Richard Schwenker took off his horn-rimmed glasses and cleaned them with a handkerchief. The basement passages were poorly lit, and despite his large flashlight he was having trouble seeing into the nooks and crannies of the catacombs. That was what he thought of whenever he came down here . . . the old catacombs of ancient Rome, where fugitives lived and died hiding from the mighty Roman authorities. Someone could easily do that here. In fact, few could forget the lunatic who had done just that, living in a machine room and posing as a staff member, until he murdered one of the pathologists in a highly publicized incident in 1989. People who didn't know the complexity of Bellevue's enormous facility didn't understand how that could happen. But threading his way through a small part of the warren of tunnels connecting the numerous buildings, subterranean storage areas, and utility service rooms, Richard could only wonder how many lunatics had wandered or camped out in this underground world.

A few years back, he recalled, in connection with the 250th anniversary of BHC, the hospital archivist, Lorinda Klein, and her associate, Susan Marsden, had explored some of the maze of underground areas, looking for interesting illustrations of the institution's history. They found some remarkable things, including ancient medical instruments and fragments of hair and bone taken from President Lincoln's fatal bullet wound. There was apparently quite a little political scuffle between rival medical leaders about the accuracy of the autopsy, and the treatment of the dying President. Most of the dark corners down there contained less interesting refuse.

Schwenker was not underground for historical research though. He was trying to find out what was going on with the power. First, there was the evidence of enormous over usage, then a power failure that should never have happened. Power was restored in minutes, but even that was a problem, because the emergency generators never kicked in. They should have been triggered in the first fifteen seconds at most. Instead, the blackout had lasted for over two minutes before the main system was restored.

Al Pearson, the chief engineer, hadn't been able to explain it. He mentioned the possibility of something called a "grounded break," but said they would have to see if a rainy day made any difference. He kept yelling at subordinates, and Schwenker wondered if he was looking for a scapegoat. Richard didn't want a sacrificial lamb, he wanted a solution. While Pearson investigated the normal avenues, Schwenker decided to trace some of the major power trunk lines which no one ever checked, just in case something out of the ordinary was going on.

He tracked electric supply lines for what seemed like miles in the semidarkness, constantly referring to the intricate diagrams in his hand. His pants' legs were wet from wading through flooded rooms, and pasty mud clung to his shoes and cuffs from the dirt and clay oozing here and there in the dank catacombs. He had been searching for over two hours before he found something.

He estimated that he was probably more than a block from the nearest vertical access at this point, and at least two stories underground. He had been following a main trunk line that ran from the main building out toward the School of Medicine. The line was ancient, encased in a faded and pock-marked rubber housing, coated in places with lime, mold, and other evidence of its long history and undisturbed life in the tunnels. Then he stopped at an unexpected juncture, holding the light steady on the overhead conduit. A heavy feeder line branched off the cable at this point. But unlike the rest of the lines, this one was coated in a shiny new case of silvery insulation.

He was examining the secondary line, trying to figure out from his diagrams where it could run, when he thought he heard a slapping sound in the dim tunnel behind him, like footsteps. Schwenker stopped and listened, even directing his flashlight back in the direction he had come, but the sound ceased. He followed the silvery track to an apparent dead end at a wall lined with moldering cartons and discarded pieces of plywood. He had just discovered that the debris covered a hinged plywood door which opened to a side corridor, when he heard the footsteps again.

"Hello!" he called out. "Is someone there?" But he received no answer from the darkness, only the sound of his own voice echoing eerily down the tunnel.

The door swung open smoothly. Additional lights lined the corridor here, illuminating a cleaner path that seemed to suggest regular use. The diagrams he held were useless at this point, because they showed nothing beyond the main tunnel. They didn't even show the side corridor. Whatever this area held, it was recently installed, as the shiny brackets and modern couplings of the cable demonstrated. He shook his head in puzzlement. As assistant administrator in charge of operations he should have known about this, whatever it was.

Schwenker stepped through another door to view a

shocking array of modern equipment and new machinery. He was so surprised that he put out a hand to steady himself, jerking his arm away in dismay when he touched a mushy form lying on a stretcher against the wall. A peeling, reddened cadaver stared up from the cart, and Schwenker felt his stomach do a flip-flop. He instinctively stepped back a few paces into the adjoining tunnel. A sound behind him made him turn in time to see a figure slip through the second door he had entered a moment before.

"Oh, it's you!" he stammered. "What the hell is going on here? Is this your work? You have no authority . . ."

Schwenker's words were cut short by a clanking sound. He swiveled to see a heavy metal gate drop in front of him from a recess in the ceiling. He was barred from further progress into the large room ahead. Another bang brought him around again, to see a second gate swing shut behind, effectively imprisoning him in a small six-foot section of corridor. Only then did he notice that this part of the floor was different, layered in a dull metallic plate. A section overhead with similar plating and round inserts contained glowing elements, like those of an electric range, but without any noticeable heat.

"What the hell do you think you're doing?" he broke into a rare use of profanity. "You realize I'm going to report this to Hampton immediately." The unchanged icy expression that returned his challenge made him shiver. He began to wonder if such a massive operation might not already have the C.E.O.'s knowledge and approval.

"Look, just tell me what's going on, okay? If it's none of my business, fine. But I am operations director. It's only right that I know where it all fits in."

The only response to his words was the sound of mechanical humming and a high electronic squeal that was being generated above and below him. The air became charged, and he felt his hair literally standing out from his head. The furry ring effect that his balding tonsure produced might have seemed humorous, if he weren't so terrified. The whine increased and he felt strange waves of heat and cold run across his skin. There was a feeling of intense pressure building in his skull, like it was going to explode. His heart began a heavy pounding rhythm that mimicked the throbbing of machinery around him. Then he felt a tremendous slamming pain in his chest, and as he clutched at his shirt, he fell heavily to the floor.

Dr. J had left the Safety/Risk Management Committee Meeting in a state of simmering rage. If Peotre wasn't a protege he would have been more of a recipient of that fury. The gall of those ingrates! They had the nerve not only to whine and complain, but even to challenge the need for continuation of the Magnes Project!

Nevertheless, as long as they needed to preserve their dirty secrets, they would not dare back out or betray the Project. Magnes required their loyalty, Magnes required their very lives if it should become necessary. And he would see to it that they didn't forget. A few minutes later, deep within the earth where Magnes was being born, the Doctor had to make an example of Richard Schwenker, who was a valueless cipher, except as a warning to those who might not understand the stakes of this undertaking. Unless silenced, Schwenker could only be a piece of sand in the grinding cogs of fate . . . a puny and destructive foreign object in the beautiful workings of a new technology that would usher in a new age of healing and regeneration. Cancer had done its worst, but would now be vanquished. Indeed, death would finally lose its sting.

Twenty

"We are talking DEATH, here!" Regina Allistair screamed in her high-pitched voice. "Little helpless animals being KILLED!"

The small group sitting in a semicircle before her seemed accustomed to her shrieks, like folks who lived next to a subway line and hardly noticed the screeching roar of its passage, when others would have been startled out of their skins.

"We can no longer sit back and let this CARNAGE continue!" she went on, her pitch lifting a register to emphasize key words. At each elevated squeal, the heads of the assembled listeners nodded in unison, as if all were attached to an invisible puppeteer overhead.

Regina was not a natural leader, but she had a certain charisma, an ability to overwhelm lesser souls with her rigid certainty and unswerving focus. Perhaps that was why she dared not admit the possibility that Bellevue had no animal research worth protesting. That would be tantamount to a halt in her march forward, and her hold was too tenuous for that. There could be no pause, no delay in the mission that would allow her small group a chance to look around for another goal or another leader. As long as she kept their eyes on the enemy, they would follow her into battle.

"We have been LIED to," she insisted, "and we must take steps to STOP the SLAUGHTER of innocent living things! This is a sacred mission! It is the mission of SAKRED!"

As the moving force behind SAKRED, "*S*top *A*nimal-*K*illing *R*esearch and *E*xperimental *D*eath," Regina knew she had to find something to unite her followers. She was convinced that the hospital was hiding horrible secrets, secrets that would not only provide a proper target, but propel SAKRED into the public spotlight that would bring new members and resources to their small operation. It was an opportunity too good to waste.

Regina had done her research and knew that there was much hidden in the medical center. A 1986 article in the *New Yorker* entitled "The Lower Depths" suggested a maze of underground facilities relatively unknown to the public and even to many of Bellevue's own staff. She was sure that was where they would find nasty goings-on. She had a mind to call in the press and the police, but decided that she and her followers could expose the matter themselves. All it took was determination. The police would be no help anyway. Most of the time, they only harassed them and interfered with their demonstrations. This time, Regina and her SAKRED group would be the true arms of the people, defenders of justice, and guarantors of rights for those poor creatures who could not defend themselves.

A half mile away, in the Ninth Precinct Detective Unit, Gil Beach dropped into his squeaky old office chair and swung his legs up onto the crowded desk, displacing a small pile of papers that in turn knocked an empty coffee container off the edge. In a rare instance of efficiency, the cup fell straight into a waste basket below. The refuse container was brimming full, so the cup should have ended up on the floor anyway, but in some strange instance of cosmic favor, it wobbled on top of the brimming collection of forms, food wrappers, and other assorted detritus of Gil's day-to-day work, and stopped, balanced at the top of the mounded garbage. Gil watched it all with a weary expression.

"Damn," he reflected, "first thing that went right today."

It had been another seemingly endless day of hard and thankless footwork, and his feet felt like boiled sausages. He had four open homicides on his caseload, only one less than two weeks old. Like every detective, Beach knew that the longer a case went on, the less likely it was to be solved. Most of his open cases were at the stage of laborious, slow and mostly fruitless door-to-door interviews, or innumerable calls to a list of businesses that might have sold a potential weapon. Today he had been trying to track down the owner of a late-model Mercury Marquis which had been seen at the site of a drug-related homicide. With no license plate to go on and no good description of the driver, it was a nearly hopeless task, but unless something better came along, it was the only clue they had. He had visited no less than nine homes, six garages, and three junkyards.

The business at Bellevue was hardly on his official caseload at all, but he kept reviewing it in his mind. Lieutenant Shannon had grudgingly given him the okay to stay with it, even though the hospital was in the Thirteenth Precinct, as long as he didn't drop any of his present cases and carefully kept the other unit informed of what he was doing. A quick call to Mike Thomas, who headed the Thirteenth, took care of that.

"Be my guest," was his response to Gil's request.

But he also said he would be sending over a detective to work alongside Beach—Jeff Corleski, detective first grade, whom Gil remembered from a task force they had served on together a year ago. The man had always seemed a bit high-strung, but other than that had left little impression.

Having permission to investigate and having any success at it, were two different things. So far, all Gil had discovered was that doctors weren't the paragons of excellence he had always assumed them to be. A part of him had always said, nobody's perfect. But in truth he didn't apply that idea equally. Certain groups, like priests and physicians, were not supposed to be imperfect in the same way as he expected lawyers or hack drivers to be. Maybe he didn't expect absolute perfection, but whatever he did expect, it was a lot higher standard than he had for most other folks.

Gil was startled when the telephone rang, interrupting his quiet contemplation. The call was from his wife, Pilar.

"How's it going?" she asked, but didn't wait for his answer. She was conditioned to his habit of keeping work as distant as possible from his home life, not even telling her about current cases. Early in their marriage, she had thought it was a personal shortcoming on his part, but some frightening and hurtful incidents of the past, some of which were inadvertantly started by her involvement in his work, convinced her that he was only being reasonably protective. So she didn't really expect him to tell her what was going on anymore, and only asked out of habit.

"You know when you're going to get home? I got some great shrimp at the fish market and thought you might like them in a stir-fry."

Gil was actually more of a red meat and potatoes kind of guy, but had expanded his menu greatly since his marriage to a part Spanish, part Irish whirlwind and cosmopolitan cook who happened to be an excellent professional psychologist as well.

"Sure," he agreed, looking at his watch. "Let's see,

it's after five and I'm pooped. I'll catch the ferry about six and be home, say, around six-thirty."

"Haven't seen you much lately, you big lunk. How about a little date after supper?"

"You mean a date, or a DATE," he chuckled.

"Come home and find out, lover."

"You got it, my lady."

Unfortunately, it didn't work out the way they planned. That was another thing cops' wives got used to. Or at least they tolerated, if they wanted to stay wives of cops.

Twenty-one

Billy Breen swore to himself. He was having a devil of a time loading the overweight woman onto the chair lift. Bellevue was a very old facility, and despite renovations, it still had a couple of places dating back centuries that were wheelchair accessible only through the installation of clumsy power lifts. This was one of them. Few patients had to be taken through the administrative offices, but Nora Van Ness was having unusually complex problems with billing and insurance payment. Nora was supposed to meet with a representative of the Billing Department, a compensation lawyer, a social services worker, and a few others. The meeting had to take place near the Fiscal Department so computer data could be referenced and accessed. That meant getting Nora through several narrow doorways, up a very steep ramp, and a four-foot vertical trip on the chair-lift.

That's the obstacle they were now negotiating. Billy wished the woman was a little smaller, so he could physically lift her up the eight stairs that stood between her and the next level. But Nora was very heavy and they had to use the inefficient mechanical lift. Just to make the trip more frustrating, Nora's robe caught in the wheels twice, the safety bar wouldn't engage during the first half dozen tries, and after a futile round of button pushing, circuit-breaker flipping, and sailor cussing,

Billy found that the power cord for the lift was not plugged in.

Finally, when he noticed the plug halfway out of its socket, he pushed it in, stabbed at the start button, and was rewarded with a smooth hum as the lift rose tediously up to the next level. That is to say, it *almost* reached the next level. As the mechanism sluggishly raised the metal platform to within a couple of inches of the offload dock, Billy and Nora were plunged into semi-darkness. Another power failure! A small reinforced window nearby only admitted enough light to see dimly, but it was enough for Billy to watch with an expression of disbelief as the mechanical platform began a slow but inexorable descent back down to where it had started.

The consequences of the power failure were more serious for Emma Gentile. A former cigarette smoker, chronic asthmatic, and victim of the ravages of emphysema, Emma suffered from Chronic Obstructive Pulmonary Disease. She had been admitted two weeks earlier to the Pulmonary Care Unit, specifically designed for people in respiratory distress. In Emma's unit, there was always a characteristic background noise of respirators and oxygenators whooshing and swishing. Most of the patients there were dependent on some sort of mechanical assistance to keep them from suffocating. When the power went out, a few pieces of apparatus had back-up batteries that kept them operating temporarily, but most were too large for that, and depended on main power.

The sound level in the unit dropped dramatically. It was soon replaced by coughs and wheezing gasps of desperate people. Emma began thrashing on her bed, suffocating from a lack of oxygen that her fibrous and narrowed respiratory passages could not provide. There was an average of one nursing staff per patient on the unit, but that included respiratory/pulmonary technicians and therapists. It didn't actually result in one-on-one care, and emergency CPR technique required two. That was the only emergency procedure that could be mounted in response to the power failure. But even for this temporary measure, there just weren't enough trained staff to go around. For whatever reasons, somebody made the decision to help the young asthmatic in the next cubicle first. Meanwhile, Emma's gasps slowed and quieted until she joined the stillness of the machines.

Dr. Lloyd Manners had been performing surgery for thirty years. As a young battlefield surgeon in the Marine Corps, he had even operated by flashlight when no other light was available. But this wasn't a battlefield. It was Surgical Suite #3 at Bellevue Hospital Center, a maze of technological wonders that all depended on uninterrupted electrical energy. When the power failed, he expected emergency generators to kick in. Flashlights don't run cardiac monitors or heart-lung machines. Thus when the lights went out, Dr. Manners merely paused, waiting for the momentary darkness to pass and resumption of illumination to allow him and his team to proceed with the open heart surgery he was conducting. Long moments passed before he realized that something was seriously wrong and that the emergency back-up system was not going to engage. The inhalator had ceased its breathy cycle, bright green monitors blinked and collapsed to tiny points of light that held the center of the screen for long moments before dimming to nothing, the "on" light of the cauterization machine slowly faded from bright red, to deep ruby, and finally to black. But most important, the heart-lung machine rumbled to a stop. The patient, a fifty-six-year-old dentist from Chelsea, had no operational heart in his chest. The machine, though basically just an oxygenator, had taken over for him during the time when the team had sliced into his cardiac muscle to enter and repair a malfunctioning mitral valve. Unless the power came up, he had only minutes to live.

Isabel Bourke, the anesthesiologist, began manually inhalating the patient as the team darted looks of amazement, confusion, even panic toward each other in the minimal light of the overhead skylight. Manners' colleague, Dr. David Twilling reminded them of a feature of the heart-lung machine that was seldom noticed. It had a simple hand-crank that is used during the cleaning process. It couldn't fully operate the machine as intended, but Twilling suggested that turning it would restore some circulation of blood, at least extending the time before the level of oxygenation decreased to the point of causing brain damage in the patient.

"Go for it," Manners agreed.

Twilling dropped his surgical tools and moved over to the apparatus. In moments he was cranking away, slowly moving dark red liquid through the baffles, which gave Manners time to speedily abort his procedure and close the chest. The dentist would have to undergo surgery again, two weeks later. But, for now, he lived.

Not every patient was as fortunate. In the first five minutes of the blackout, three people died. During the seven minutes and twenty-two seconds before power was restored, two others died, and one additional man suffered permanent brain damage from a lack of oxygen supply to his starving brain cells. There were dozens of injuries, mostly falls and collisions, including a tumble down a full flight of stairs that broke one man's back, and put him on disability for the rest of his life. The cost in supplies, machinery, and lost computer data was hard to determine, but later was estimated in tens of thousands of dollars. The human cost was much higher.

Michele Peters was helping control an individual with a case of the DTs when it happened. The alcohol dependent man was a regular, but not welcome, patient. Bud

Bowers was fine when he was sober, but that was a rare occasion. When he went into withdrawal, Bud's delirium tremens were something to behold.

He was just nodding off into drugged sleep, attendants and security guards hanging on each arm and leg, when darkness enveloped the windowless room. Michele felt a desperate cramping in her stomach, but held stationary for a moment, hoping the emergency generators would quickly remedy the situation. In a voice elevated a full octave by her anxiety, she squeaked out a face-saving excuse.

"I think he's under now. Take over Indiri, I'm . . . going to see who else needs help."

Actually, it was Michele Peters who needed a lot of help at that moment. She stepped toward where the door should be, arms outstretched, and gasped when her hand touched the back of a person. She jerked back, hitting her shoulder against a wall. Panting in anxiety, she felt her way to the door, and out into a corridor into which a small amount of light leaked through the windows in the swinging doors leading to the ambulance entrance. Michele moved toward the light, feeling so dizzy she had to keep a hand on the wall to prevent herself from falling. Only then did she notice her shallow hyperventilation and the perspiration which drenched her shirt. Shame-faced, she pushed through the doors and stood on the receiving platform, hungrily sucking in the outdoor air, which seemed fresh and cleansing despite the urban smog.

It didn't help that she had seemed to be fighting off a case of some virus that had kept her dizzy and nauseous much of the last day. She didn't have her usual energy and was burdened with a continual headache. But she couldn't use that as an excuse. She had never let little illnesses stop her before. Her biggest problem wasn't physical, it was emotional.

After long minutes of internal struggle she went to an EMT vehicle which sat empty in a nearby slot, rummaged about inside until she found a flashlight, and with a deep breath walked back into the darkened building. Two minutes later, before Michele had found any way to help, the lights came on. She was both relieved and frustrated. The return of power was vital and removed the source of her fear. But she also knew she had just started to face that fear. The frustration was that it had taken her so long to climb over the obstacle of her own dread, she had not been there for others who needed her.

Twenty-two

Half an hour later, Gil Beach received a telephone call from Dr. Peters. Her voice sounded shaky and troubled.

"Please come quickly, I think we need you."

When he walked into the main lobby of Bellevue a few minutes later, he immediately sensed a changed atmosphere. It was hard to put a finger on what was different, but faces seemed more tense, uniforms more rumpled, voices more controlled. Dr. Peters was waiting, and quickly ushered him to a side office where a tall, distinguished looking man greeted him.

"Hello, Detective. I'm James Hampton," he said, clearly assuming that Beach would know who he was. In this case, he was correct, but Gil found it an interesting assumption of self-importance.

Michele, not as certain of Hampton's universal recognition, added to the man's self-introduction. "Mr. Hampton is Bellevue's President and C.E.O."

Gil was tempted to mention he knew the name from a scandal of several years earlier, but he said nothing. Beach didn't need to build his own ego at someone else's expense. Besides the man apparently needed help now or he wouldn't have asked for Gil. So instead of saying anything, the detective just nodded.

"We've got a problem," Hampton continued. "You've been doing some investigation here, I understand?"

Gil nodded again.

"Uhh-huh," the Administrator spoke as if slightly annoyed at Gil's nonverbal response. "Well, I don't know what you think you were investigating, but there's no need for anyone else to get involved."

Gil wasn't sure yet what the man was getting at, but he saw a cover-up at work. They called him, rather than someone at the Thirteenth Precinct, so there would be fewer people involved. Maybe Hampton remembered the discretion of certain members of the Ninth after all—or maybe that's just where he happened to have more political clout. What was he trying to finesse this time?

"Al, why don't you explain," Hampton tossed the hot potato to someone else. "Al is our chief engineer."

Apparently, Gil reflected, tradespeople didn't have last names. The man looked uncomfortable serving as spokesman, but he followed orders.

"Oh. Well, yeah. You see, we've been having some problems with overloads. Today we had a big break in service, on account of the back-up generators not kicking in. We got main power back in a little over seven minutes, but when I checked out the emergency equipment, I found . . . something," He glanced quickly back and forth at the other hospital management.

Gil figured the guy as someone who wasn't as comfortable in a coat and tie as in work clothes, and not as comfortable in an office as in a basement full of pipes and machinery. At the C.E.O.'s suggestion, that was where they now headed.

The Main Power Plant was a massive operation. Most of the Engineering Department was located on the thirteenth floor of the new building, occupying over an acre of space. The Engineer kept up a steady stream of facts and statistics about the system as they walked. Gil wondered if it was an attempt to delay explaining their purpose in coming, or just to cover the man's nervousness.

"Bellevue's one of the three largest medical centers in

the country," he said, like he was leading a travel tour, "and the largest in Manhattan. The entire complex of hospitals and clinics covers ten city blocks, contains fifteen buildings, and seventy-five separate entrances. We have a staff of over twelve hundred doctors, and six thousand other personnel, including a thousand nurses. We have twelve hundred medical beds, and see more than four hundred thousand outpatients a year. That means we need a tremendous amount of power. We don't usually use the term, but the electrical usage alone could be calculated in terms of gigawatts, rather than kilowatts. Our heat is all New York City steam."

Finally, the small group arrived at the emergency generators, two burnished metallic structures resembling halves of giant spark plugs, in a room adjacent to the central switching/monitoring area. Hampton had not accompanied them, claiming he was needed for other "vital duties." The engineer pointed to an area between the two dynamos. Lying across a series of exposed cables was a rigid form, a man with contracted limbs, singed hair, and protruding eyes. He was dead. He looked like he had been electrocuted.

"I don't know what he was doing here," the engineer said, shaking his head, "But I know he was all upset about something to do with the power demands."

"It's Richard Schwenker," Michele Peters offered weakly, "He's . . . I mean, he was, deputy assistant for operations."

"Terrible accident," interjected Ted Jamison, who Hampton had appointed his representative on the grisly tour. "Just terrible."

"You think it was an accident?" Beach questioned.

"Well, uhh . . . yes, of course. What else? I mean, I know you're a homicide detective and all, but really, this is quite clear cut, don't you think?"

"I don't know enough to answer that, Mr. Jamison."

"Well, what is there to know? The man was snooping around, looking for trouble, and tragically he found it. This area is completely off-limits. He should never have stepped in there in the first place."

Jamison straightened his tie, the only one in the group whose appearance remained impeccable. Seeing the detective's dubious expression, he apparently realized how he was sounding, and did a little backstepping.

"I mean, it's a tragedy, of course. We'll have to make arrangements for a commemorative service, perhaps some lasting memorial . . . a plaque, or an office in his name . . ." Jamison's voice ran down. "But surely there would be no reason to expect foul play, would there?"

"That's something we'll have to determine, isn't it? Tell me, again, what you think led him to step into this dangerous area?"

"Well, Richard was kind of a . . . well, let's just say, he was always looking around, searching for problems, inefficiency, waste, that sort of thing. When we got some rather high power bills, he had some silly ideas about the possible cause. He thought the power could be leaking somewhere . . ."

"Or was being siphoned off, or stolen somehow . . ." interjected the engineer.

Jamison gave him a withering glare for his attempt to be helpful.

"I just got a call from Con Edison," he reasserted his control of the conversation, "that suggests it's a simple matter of computer error, but in the meantime, Richard has been crawling all over the hospital, from the roof to the tunnels, looking for some imaginary power drain."

"Tunnels?"

"Oh, I was just using that as a term. You know, there's a maze of connecting corridors under the hospital complex, linking various buildings and so forth. But it looks like he went too far, right here. He was probably eyeballing the set-up when the back-up system was triggered. That would explain the failure of the emergency generators to cycle properly."

"I see. Well, I'll probably have more questions later, but let's get the boys in here to take care of Mr. Schwenker's body. You think we could get a sheet or something to cover him?"

The others looked embarrassed that they hadn't thought of that, and someone went scurrying off for a cover. A few minutes later he returned with a green surgical drape and a uniformed police officer, who was directed to wait with the body so that the integrity of a potential crime scene would be preserved. The rest of the group slowly dispersed.

Gil felt a hand grab his sleeve, as Dr. Peters stumbled and nearly fell. She apologized and excused herself, claiming to be feeling ill. Gil waved to her, then positioned himself so that he was with Al, the Chief Stationary Engineer, separated a few steps away from the others. Gil glanced at the man's I.D. tag.

"Tell me . . . Mr. Pearson, why that cable was unshielded."

"Oh, yeah, that was no good. The usual insulation isn't in place because we've been running tests. But it should have been covered with the temporary shield. I don't know what that was doing off. Maybe somebody forgot to cover it, or maybe Schwenker was screwing around."

"How likely would it be that the shielding was inadvertently left off? Or how likely that Schwenker removed it?"

The engineer shrugged.

"He could have done it," Pearson said, but his expression, his shrug, his stance all suggested doubt.

Twenty-three

The small group had gathered in a conference room adjacent to the Department of Psychiatry offices on the eighteenth floor. The psychiatric wards occupied this and the next four levels. Gil wondered if the location was significant—something crazy certainly seemed to be going on.

Frank sat in the corner, his shoulders against the wall, straight chair tilted back, and his feet swinging free. He was whispering with Helen Joseph and Jeff Corleski, who stood next to him. A combined unit had now been formed between the Ninth and Thirteenth Precincts to investigate the situation, and Jeff was the detective from the Thirteenth that would be working with them. Helen usually worked with the Youth Bureau, but had been on operations with Beach and Terranova before. In Frank's case, she was more than a colleague or even a friend; she was his live-in companion.

The Director of Security, Donald Scarletti, stood off to the side. He oversaw the Bellevue Police unit, a security force of the Health and Hospitals Corp. that approached the size of a city police precinct in personnel. For political reasons the Bellevue Police had to be involved, but would play only a supportive role.

Seated in chairs at the large conference table were Doctors Peters and Troop. After additional conversations with Michele, and his own interview with Troop, Gil decided to include him as their liaison to the administrative echelons. The man seemed intelligent, concerned, and discreet. Doctor Pretaska entered the room, sat at the opposite end of the table from the other physicians, and appeared to be avoiding eye contact with Michele. She'd kept her head down, and shifted in her chair as the radiologist walked in; a pink tinge creeping up her neck. Beach wondered at this development. Was it a sign that they had the hots for each other and were having a hard time handling it, or was something wrong? The only reason he had invited Pretaska was because of Michele's earlier suggestion to include the man.

"Okay, we're all here now," he began, "so let's talk about what we know, and where we're going."

The talk was restrained, providing little new information. Michele believed that Schwenker's death was intentional, Pretaska thought it an accident, and Troop said he was keeping an open mind. Gil always kept an open mind, but he already had preliminary autopsy results which suggested certain conclusions. His friend Anton Krispnick had done a post-mortem two blocks away at the City Morgue, sharing his impressions with Gil by telephone. The forensic pathologist felt certain that there had been foul play. Although the death was consistent in some ways with electrical shock, there were some anomalies that made the pathologist doubt that it was caused by contact with the cables on which the body was found. Schwenker's heart had apparently been stopped by external means other than trauma or chemicals, but the characteristic muscle tears usually found in shock death were missing. Most significantly, Anton estimated the time of death hours prior to the power failure. Now Shig Higawa was at work in the crime lab, examining minute particles and invisible traces that might tell where death had occurred. Gil decided not to share any of this information with anyone yet. Instead, he intervened in a heated exchange between Michele and Peotre Pretaska.

"He had no business being there in the first place. No wonder he got zapped," Pretaska was saying. "If a stupid electric bill is that important, there's something wrong."

"Then you better *zap* me, too," Peters shot back. "Because my electric bill has been sky high, too, and it's bothering the hell out of me."

She was acting flustered, her reasoning obviously less important to her than a quick and aggressive comeback.

"For the time being, we will proceed with the assumption that the death was a homicide," Beach told the group, watching various expressions change at his statement. "We also need to pursue the disappearance of Ed Dorlander, the newsman who may have been admitted as a John Doe, and some other issues that need clarification. So now we should look at ways to get more information. It seems likely that Schwenker uncovered something he wasn't supposed to find, and whoever we're dealing with here stopped him."

"Which means we'd better watch our tails, too," Terranova quickly added.

Gil nodded, and went on.

"We've determined that a number of unexplained deaths have also occurred among patients. Those cases have been systematically hidden, the computer files erased. I think we should assume that this isn't the work of a single person. That's why the confidentiality of this meeting is of utmost importance."

At that point Dr. Troop jumped in with a question, and Pretaska followed with several of his own. A lively discussion ensued about whether a conspiracy was believable, and if so, what it might be and who might be involved.

"Those missing records—they aren't just any patients," Corleski pointed out, "they are undomiciled patients, with no families or other ties."

"What significance do you think that has?" asked Scarletti, the Security Director.

"I think someone has been counting on us to overlook that kind of person," Michele jumped in, her voice becoming more forceful, "somebody that thinks they don't count."

"Oh come on, Michele," Pretaska countered, "don't be so predictable. You see discrimination everywhere you look. You aren't seriously suggesting that someone is letting patients die just because they don't have homes or families, are you?"

Her response was fierce, and Gil was sure that something more than Pretaska's comment was responsible for the intensity of her reply.

"No, Dr. Pretaska, I don't think that," she said, her excessively formal tone an obvious rebuke, "although your naïveté is remarkable if you don't think different types of people get different kinds of treatment here."

Cords stood out in her neck as she spoke, eyes flashing danger signals.

"But I don't think they were left to die, Dr. Pretaska. I think they were KILLED!"

A shouting match ensued that only quieted when Gil intervened again. Then Peters and Pretaska settled back in their chairs, each looking like they had competed in a hundred-yard dash and was sure the other had cheated at the start. Peters looked drained, but still threw a parting shot at the handsome doctor.

"If you were in their place for a while, you'd see. You wouldn't be a star, you'd learn what it was like to be a non-person."

At this comment, Helen Joseph chimed in.

"Well, what about it? What if I dress up and come in

like one of 'em? I can do a pretty good bag-lady routine."

The others seemed surprised at the suggestion. Gil was the first to react.

"That might not be a bad idea, Helen. Whoever is behind the stuff going on isn't going to let on much to suits and uniforms."

"They aren't going to say much to somebody that looks like a homeless woman, either," Pretaska objected.

"But she would be in a position to hear and see things that we might not," Peters countered, predictably taking the opposite tack from the radiologist. Gil wondered what exactly was going on between these two.

"But how are we gonna back her up?" Frank asked, protective of his companion.

"I could wear a wire, or carry a communicator," Helen answered.

"That's only good if we've got somebody nearby," Terranova went on. "Look, Mr. Scarletti, is there any way you could put me in the power plant, or get me a maintenance job?"

There was another half hour of discussion before it was agreed that between Administration and Security they would find a way to get Frank into the Engineering Department, and Helen would go undercover as an indigent street dweller.

"Just remember, Helen," Gil reminded her, "that we haven't heard back from the last guy who tried that."

"Ahh, he was just a reporter," she laughed, "I'm a cop. And I got my stripes working undercover in Vice." She glanced at Michele Peters, an unspoken bond of understanding in the weary smile she got in return.

Beach didn't respond to the implied criticism. Instead, he reviewed the meeting for the group, as well as the various responsibilities of those present. They promised to keep details of their plans secret for now.

Michele Peters was one of the first out of the room, a hand on the arm of Carl Troop for support; the others drifted out more slowly. Gil noticed that Pretaska was talking privately to Helen Joseph. As the doctor spoke to her in an apparently confidential manner, he draped an arm around her shoulder, leaning his head close to hers. Frank noticed too, shifting uncomfortably and staring with a frown. Helen, however, looked animated, and made no move to disengage from the close embrace until Terranova stepped over and took her arm, asking to talk to her as he pulled her away from the handsome radiologist.

Gil noticed the tensely whispered conversation between Helen and Frank, wondering how he would react if Pilar were the one being so closely attended to by a man as alluring as Pretaska. The allure included the fact that he was not only attractive, and casually seductive, but also carried the mystique and powerful aura of a physician . . . brilliant man of science, successful and wealthy professional, dedicated healer. It was a powerful combination, even without his good looks. And power, they say, is the greatest aphrodisiac.

Twenty-four

Helen giggled to herself, as she slipped on a shapeless housedress over several layers of other grimy clothes retrieved from a thrift shop's worst offerings. Although she had stood up to Frank's jealous questioning, telling him she could take care of herself, she thought his anxiety was kind of cute. Not that he really had anything to worry about. The fancy pants doctor was a real Casanova of course, and it was kind of fun to see him come on to her, but he was definitely not her type. Helen had known a few of these fashion plates that oozed sexuality. She had even gotten married to one a few years ago. Good ol' Max had turned out to be more in love with himself than anyone else, and was a lot less sexy than he appeared when it came time to actually do the deed. He was mostly show, and ended up running off with a lover that was willing to act like Max was the only thing in the world that counted. Max, of course, agreed with the lover's assessment of his importance.

On the other hand, Frank was the kind of man you could get close to. He had plenty of imperfections, but he was real. Helen knew she had her own weaknesses, and she liked the idea of somebody on the same plane of existence. Still, she sort of enjoyed the fact that he was a little insecure, and she wasn't anxious to completely relieve his jealous worry. Might as well keep the big lug on his toes, she thought merrily.

The knee-high nylons slipped on next, and Helen rolled the tops down to mid-calf. She donned a pair of threadbare cotton socks over these, letting the stretched out tops hang loosely below the nylon donut rolls. Her hair could have been longer for the role, as length made it easier to give a tangled, unkempt appearance. A wig was out of the question, in case she was given a medical exam, so she just avoided washing her hair, and skipped the weekly tint job that usually covered a sprinkle of gray. She tied a kerchief around her head, and rubbed dirt into her face. It would play havoc with her complexion, probably, but even that would be a short-term advantage in appearing as a street dweller. "Not to worry, Frankie-babe," she laughed, speaking to her image in the mirror. "Mr. hot-shot lady-killer doctor would not find me very attractive in this get-up!"

She practiced walking in a waddling shuffle, then gathered several shopping bags and plastic sacks and ambled out toward the street. With one hand, she patted a lumpy thigh, where she felt the hard shape of a police-band transceiver. It was the only thing that felt comfortable about her whole costume. The comfort was in the link it provided to help. Helen could handle a hell of a lot, she assured herself, but it was nice to have the radio just the same.

Frank Terranova looked at the small transceiver he carried, a twin of the one in some inner layer of Helen's bag-lady disguise. He shoved it into an inside pocket of the heavy canvas vest he wore over a dull gray poplin work shirt and pants. The heavy steel-toed boots were comfortable, despite their weight. He hadn't needed to fake the wear that had been etched on them, as he had worn the boots while moonlighting on a highway maintenance gang during the months he was on suspension, trying to kick a booze habit. That seemed a long time ago, now, though it had only been three years that he had stayed sober. Dried mud was still caked in the crease between the uppers and the sole.

Frank was a little uncomfortable with how many people knew of his masquerade as an employee in the hospital Engineering Department. It was decided that Al Pearson had to know, in order for Frank to be accepted as a legitimate employee. Although the chief engineer had been sworn to secrecy, it added one more person to the list of those who could let something slip, even if it was unintentional. They had settled on the Engineering Department, because it involved locations throughout the facility, allowing him to be as accessible as possible to any place Helen might be taken. There also seemed some potential relationship between Schwenker's death and his interest in power usage, so Frank might be able to pick up valuable information in the power plant, while he was waiting around to provide back-up for his friend.

"Friend!" he snorted to himself, thinking of the way he had felt when he saw that groping doctor laying his paws all over her. Friend, lover, companion . . . none of the terms seemed to cover it. She was as close to being a spouse as any of those words—he even wore a ring to avoid explanations. But he had been leery of making it legal due to a previous bad experience with marriage. They shared a walk-up apartment in the Bronx, even though she hadn't given up her own place entirely. That was just her way of saying she wasn't dependent on him. She hardly ever used her little flat on Tremont Avenue, but kept some personal things stored there, and occasionally spent a night, when he was working a long shift.

The truth was, he loved everything about Helen, from her athletic frame to her husky voice and tough woman act. She had a heart as big as Long Island, and when she wasn't helping out runaways, strays, or abused women, she shared that big heart with him. He knew she loved him, but it was pretty tough to not feel insecure when a guy straight out of most women's fantasies decided to hit on his lady. Or at least that's what it looked like. Helen had pooh-poohed the whole thing. But if Frank found out that the guy so much as copped a feel from her, he would . . .

His macho meanderings were interrupted by a buzzing vibration from his side. It was the radio. This model came without a beep or ring that could alert the wrong people that you were wearing a communicator. Instead, it simply vibrated. Frank pulled out the small transceiver, remembered that they had not yet settled on codes, and answered with a "Yeah . . . that you, Helen?"

"Yup, it's me, Sweetcakes," the voice answered tinnily from a miniature speaker, "who else sends little vibes up and down your bod?"

"Hmmmm," he responded.

"C'mon sweetie, don't pout. I wanted to test the radio and after this, I think we're gonna have to be all official and use codes, don't you think?"

"Yeah, so what did you have in mind?"

"Well, let's see. Okay, you remember that time we went away to the Poconos, and got the place with the heart-shaped tub?"

"Yeah, I remember."

"Well there was this real neat thing you did after we had that bottle of sparkling cider."

"You mean . . ."

"With a little oil?"

"Uh, how could I forget? You found some pretty good uses for that oil, yourself, as I remember it."

"Ummmm, yes. I get all excited just thinking about it. So how about I call you Crisco?"

"Jeez!" he laughed, a little embarrassed. "What about you?"

"You can call me Cider."

"I can't believe you, woman! You're outrageous!"

"You better believe it, Frankie. And after this little operation, I just might prove it to you. Bye for now . . . Crisco! Ten-Four."

Frank smiled in spite of himself, replaced the radio in his pocket, and headed out of the precinct. A few minutes later he was at Bellevue. He checked in with security, and followed their directions through the medical center maze. By the time he got to where he would be working, a basement engineering shop, he had descended several levels, walked along corridors lined with huge conduits, past massive tanks, through humming banks of dials and levers. He had worked his way into the guts of the hospital, the vital organs and systems that kept it going.

Since he had some experience in duct-work, Terranova was put to work doing simple metal fabricating. Also it was easier to start him with a separate project, than as a part of the regular crew. As he got started, notching and creasing the galvanized metal to form sections of heating duct, he noticed a huge, heavily muscled black man sneaking glances at him. They weren't friendly looks. When he tried smiling in return, the giant just glared.

"What you lookin' at, man?"

"I'm looking at the room, the wall, and you. I'm new—just came over from the Bronx. My name's Frank, Frank Delissio." He knew that he might be asking for a confrontation, but also knew that he couldn't start off like a weak sister, or the guys would probably walk all over him.

"Who the fuck cares yo name?" the huge man sneered. "I call you scum. You call me Mistuh Weems."

"I call bosses *mister*, and figure they need that, because they're stuck-up assholes. Now you don't look like that to me at all, so I don't think you want that either."

The big man paused. There was almost a smile at the corner of his mouth, but he didn't let it out.

"Don't think you can get away with anything around here, cause you can talk good, white-boy. I ain't no boss, but you ain't mine neither. For now, you can call me 'Monk,' but that don't mean we're friends . . . and it don't mean I'm going to trust you any farther than I can throw you."

Frank wondered what he had done to set Weems off, other than being new and white. Of course he couldn't ask directly, as that didn't fit the unspoken rules of man-talk in the trades. It would come out in time, and he would gain acceptance, or he would be gone. As long as it didn't escalate into real conflict, it didn't matter much, since as soon as he and Helen found out what they needed to know, he was outta there.

He almost said "goodbye" permanently an hour later, when he swung a section of duct over his shoulder, hit a barrel on a raised platform, and saw the heavy metal container tilt off the edge. No one had been around when he called for help with the ungainly duct pipe, but they appeared from nowhere to gape and laugh at the mess the toppled barrel created. The fact that he could have been seriously injured didn't seem to bother the tough-looking group.

Later, in a private moment with Al, he learned that recent cut-backs had made most of the men nervous about their jobs. Pearson apologized for not working things out a little more carefully and speaking with the workers before Frank started, but the need for secrecy had made him uncertain of what to do. Part of the problem seemed to be that stationary engineers weren't normally involved in metal fabrication. It wasn't unusual to put together a single piece of duct-work, but anything more than that was potentially a union problem. Pearson promised to put Frank on more routine duties as soon as possible.

While he was in the more private setting of Al's office, Frank used the opportunity to test his radio by calling Helen. There was a long period with no response, and he was about to assume she was in a position where she couldn't answer, when the speaker came to life.

"Roger, Crisco, this is Cider. What's up? Over."

"Just testing the wire, Cider," he said, grinning a little, glad no one else could understand the meaning behind their choice of code names. "It took a long time to get you. Over."

"I read you clear, Crisco. I just didn't notice the jiggle, at first. All these layers! You know there's something kinda funky about you vibrating me on the thigh. Over."

"Uh, we're on police band, Cider. Just let me know if you need anything. Over and out."

"Roger, Crisco. Will do. Out."

Despite the fact that Helen was mumbling into her hand and grinning, while seated on the floor in a corner of the public waiting area of Bellevue's Adult Outpatient clinic, no one seemed to notice. Strange mutterings to oneself was fairly standard behavior in this setting. A grimy skeleton of a man only a few yards away was speaking to the ceiling, muttering curses and angry threats at invisible antagonists.

Helen had been waiting for over two hours. There was nothing to indicate she was any closer to being called than before. She looked around at the great variety of people crowding the room. Some looked very sick, others seemed fine.

From her vantage point, Helen watched people waiting their turn to get quizzed by admission clerks, who fed the information into computers. No one was allowed to see a doctor in the Outpatient Department until they had passed this hurdle.

The old clock by the information desk indicated that three hours had passed since she first gave her name and asked to be examined. That was ridiculous. She wasn't even sure this was the way to go, since Dorlander had purportedly been brought in by the emergency route, not as a standard outpatient. An alternate plan began hatching in her mind. After a few minutes, she got up and shuffled out of the lobby, through the entrance doors, to the street.

Helen had remembered an old scam used by Sonny Santana, a two-bit con man she had busted when she worked Vice. The man would stand behind a parked car and wait for an unwary driver to pass. Usually he picked an elderly woman, who he figured would be a less secure driver, personally unassertive, and potentially soft-hearted. Sonny stepped out, just as the vehicle passed, gave a whack to the side of the car with the briefcase he carried just for this purpose, let out a horrible wail of pain, and fell to the street, faking unconsciousness. Sonny then worked the scam one of two ways.

If he needed cash fast, and the driver looked like an easy mark, he would appear to woozily regain consciousness and put on an act of being hurt, but not vindictive. If the shocked and guilty driver would just give him money to cover the cost of his visit to the local clinic, he assured her that a few elastic bandages and painkillers would take care of the problem. If he was looking for a bigger score, Sonny could go another route, maintaining his unconscious act until an ambulance arrived, which would take him to the nearest hospital emergency room, where he accurately mimicked the symptoms of whiplash, backsprain, joint dislocation, or whatever was necessary to get fitted out with a neck brace or crutches. Then Sonny could really put the bite on the sucker who had happened to drive by when the con-man was lying in wait. Eventually, Helen had collared him in the act, but it was a tough scam to disprove. However, it was an automatic trip to the emergency room if you were looking for one. That was exactly what Helen was seeking, and she decided to use it for her own purposes.

Helen walked over on Twenty-seventh Street, not willing to risk the speed and recklessness of drivers on First Avenue. On the side streets, unloading trucks, double parked and illegally parked vehicles added to the congestion, and tended to slow the traffic to a series of short bursts of relatively limited speed. She ambled over to the middle of the block and peered down the street, until she spotted a compact Chevy sedan working its way toward her. The small car had Pennsylvania plates and a woman driver who looked like she was already in shock from trying to negotiate the chaotic city streets. It seemed about right. Helen felt a stab of guilt, but it wouldn't take long for the ruse to be played out, and there would be no actual injury, no insurance claim, no litigation, or any of the real consequences that an accident could produce. The woman would probably feel so relieved later, when everything turned out alright, that she would hardly mind the scare. Besides, lives were at stake.

Helen tensed, as she timed her move to catch the side of the passing car.

Twenty-five

While Helen Joseph was preparing to move, another woman was getting ready for daring action as well. Regina Allistair handed out white garments to the small band of stalwart SAKRED members who were going to take part in her plan. Then she clipped a laminated plastic tag on the lapel of each. The I.D. badges would not stand up to close inspection, but she was counting on the fact that a person dressed appropriately, with an official looking photo I.D. tag, would never be questioned in the crowded and rushing atmosphere of the medical center.

When the group was all appropriately garbed and tagged, she viewed the results with pleasure. At first glance, no one would have taken them for anything but a group of official medical personnel, especially when she added a couple of details, like a red smear of food coloring here and there to imitate bloodstains, and a stethoscope from her home blood-pressure kit, which she casually hung from a pocket.

Too bad she couldn't do as well with their behavior.

"If you act confident, it will be your best disguise," she reminded them. "That's why doctors get away with so much, anyway. They act like they know everything, and people believe it's true. Remember, our cause is just, and our mission righteous! Now walk and act like you believe it. Animal lives are at stake!"

One of the members provided transportation in her mini-van, dropping them off a block from the hospital. The white-coated impostors fanned out to approach different entrances.

Once in the hospital, Regina fiddled with the walkie-talkie she had borrowed from her nephew Jimmy. He had insisted that it could transmit more than a block away, but all Regina could get out of it were squawks and screeches. She worked her way down two levels, until she reached a deserted passage, exactly like what she had expected, except for the fact that it was clean and well-lighted. After a few twists and turns, the corridor took on a look more akin to her dark imaginings, with dim lights at long intervals, walls darkened with rusty water stains and chalky lime deposits. A side door revealed piles of twisted and rusting hospital beds of a long outmoded style, sitting in a pool of dirty red water several inches deep. Further on she passed a pile of crumbling and damaged air-conditioning units.

When it still refused to work, she gave up on the walkie-talkie and stuck it in her bag. She wished she had brought a flashlight, as she moved hurriedly down the hall, anxious to find the cages and torture devices she was sure the animal killers had hidden somewhere.

Regina gave out a whoop of fright, when she turned a corner quickly and ran right into a tall bony man. It took a moment to get her breath back, then she saw it was just the SAKRED member Maury, searching for the same evidence. He still wasn't acting like a doctor.

"Where's Gretchen?" he asked nervously. "And Paula?"

"Paula is going for the administrative office files. She's upstairs somewhere. I haven't seen Gretchen," she answered, a bit testily, "but she's a big girl and I'll bet she's not standing in a mucky tunnel asking stupid questions. Have you found anything worthwhile, yet?"

DARK MEDICINE

He hadn't, so she agreed to let him stay with her. She bemoaned his lack of guts to strike out by himself, but didn't mention that she actually felt safer with someone else at her side, even if it was Maury.

Only a few yards away from Regina and Maury, but separated by several feet of tiled concrete wall and rocky earth, Gretchen Fancher, too, was wishing she had company. She reached to her throat and grasped the animal rights medallion she wore as a necklace. She had been massaging it like an amulet for hours. The tiny cat's face imprinted on its front was polished to a silvery sheen. Now she replaced it in her ample shirt front and moved forward down the dim corridor.

Minutes earlier, Gretchen had found a dark and abandoned office in the subterranean maze. Besides dusty discarded furniture and boxes of outdated medical books, the office held files, labeled with such titles as "Dissection" and "Animal Specimens." It looked like she had hit pay dirt, and she would have been sorely disappointed if she had known that her treasure was merely a medical student's old notes, that had been moldering in the ancient file cabinet for twenty years or more. Unfortunately, she didn't get a chance to carefully review the old folders.

She was now hopelessly lost in the underground labyrinth, and was feeling the first waves of panic. She tried to follow a tunnel that seemed to slope upward, but soon came to a dead-end, where the way appeared to have been bricked up. There was even less light in this cul-de-sac, and her small penlight only revealed the corpse of a large swollen rat decomposing on the floor. That was when she heard the shuffling sound of footsteps behind her. She spun to face a large, hulking figure who seemed to appear from nowhere. The handful of damming papers slipped from her perspiring hand and fell in disarray on the dirty floor.

With trembling hands, she raised the small flashlight she carried, and directed its light over the man. He wore a white coat similar to hers and a photo I.D. tag. A hospital employee. He certainly didn't look like a doctor, with his ratty sneakers, punk haircut and creepy smile, but his uniform reassured her that it wasn't a monster or a psych unit escapee in front of her. She fought to quell her primal fear, and tried to proceed on Regina's theory that a confident act would get someone through any obstacle.

"Well, I'm glad you showed up," she announced in as forceful a voice as she could muster. "I'm Dr. Miller. Who are you? Are you an orderly?"

"I'm Buzz," was all the man replied.

"Well, yes . . . I seem to have taken a wrong turn. Maybe you can direct me to the lab."

The imposing figure said nothing, his unsettling grin unchanged. He looked down at the scattered papers, then reached out with a huge paw to look at her name tag. Gretchen tried to think of something she could say, to distract the man, or explain herself. Maybe in the dim light the tag would pass muster by a slow-minded orderly. But before she could come up with anything, he snatched her light to examine the badge more closely. Now she knew she was in trouble, especially when his grin seemed to change into an evil leer.

"You ain't no doctor," he whispered.

Gretchen was acutely aware of how isolated they were, and her anxiety quickly evolved into terror when the man reached out again, toward her neck.

She pulled back, thinking he was going to choke her, but his hand caught the top of her clothing, and with a tremendous yank, ripped away the entire front of her shirt. Gretchen knew she should fight back, scream, or do something, but instead she froze. The immense bulk of the man, looming over her, the nightmarish surroundings, the frightening realization that not only was she trapped, but that he was going to hurt her, the numbing force of his ripping hand, all contributed to a complete inertia on her part. She couldn't even raise her hands in defense, but stood trembling and immobile as he moved in closer, forcing her back against the moldy brick wall.

"I'm gonna take you to the Doctor An' you're gonna get all fixed up," growled the giant who called himself Buzz. "But not until I get a little piece of ass. So let's see whatcha got."

As she was thrown to the filthy floor strewn with muddy papers and discarded refuse, an enormous weight slammed down on top of her. Gasping for air, as the weight compressed her chest and lungs, Gretchen turned her head to the side, away from the stinking breath and leering face of her attacker. She felt a tearing penetration and searing pain shot through her body from her groin.

As the pain and horror dragged on, Gretchen's mind broke free of the nightmare that she was living and drifted away to a happier place. It was a safe place, and a peaceful place. She liked it so much better than the place her body lay being attacked, she decided never to come back.

Ira Wachman was horrified, and he was angry. The stupid animal rights group had mostly been rounded up, though one or two were missing and had apparently gotten away. But they had created a great deal of trouble, and some of them had gotten into files they shouldn't have. Papers were gone that could spell real trouble for Wachman, and his colleagues. The documents had nothing to do with animal experimentation. But the weird little fanatics might do damage with them anyway. Then there was this business with that woman, Peters—not to mention the tremendous screw-up of Schwenker's death.

Wachman took a bottle of black and green Librium capsules from his desk drawer and popped two into his mouth. Ten milligrams wasn't enough anymore, he needed twenty. He knew he was in very bad shape. But he would never give up. There were options that he could pursue—even if some of them were beyond the pale of current medicine and FDA approvals.

But he would be able to do nothing if he was tied up in this Peters woman's tangled web, his secrets revealed for anyone to see. He decided that tougher measures were called for. The fanatics would have to be stopped. And Peters had to be taken care of as well.

Twenty-six

The medical director's conference room was richly appointed in dark wood panels and mahogany furniture. The meeting table was a deep burnished hue, with polished red highlights and an inlaid border of teak and ivory. There was silence in the room except for the sound of breathing, and an occasional squeak of leather, as one of the meeting participants shifted in the calfskin upholstered chairs. The members of the Ethics and Professional Standards Committee were waiting for the object of their discussions to appear before them.

Dr. Wachman glanced impatiently at his Rolex. Ted Jamison was still as a statue, staring at his reflection in the tabletop. Jim Hampton was habitually impatient, and squirmed in his leather seat, while Dietrich Junghans sat impassively, a picture of self-possession. Dr. John Malcolm scribbled notes on a yellow pad, and Lloyd Manners cleaned his fingernails with a dissecting scalpel. Archibald Neely stood looking through a barred window at the street outside.

Finally, the large door swung open, and Dr. Peters stepped into the room. Her mouth was tight, and despite dark circles under her eyes, they flashed with anger. She wasn't expecting anything good. You don't get called before the Ethics Committee to be praised. She stepped to the head of the table and steadied herself against the back of a large chair.

"Dr. Peters," Wachman began, "I'm sure you know why we have asked you to appear before this committee."

"No, Dr. Wachman, I do not. I have received no notification of any charges, hearings, or complaints. And frankly, I am offended that I have not been informed of any problem prior to your summons."

"This is not a court of law, Dr. Peters, nor are we under the same constraints as such bodies. Due to the confidential nature of the matters we discuss, it is preferable this way."

Michele started to respond, but thought better of it, and clamped her teeth together to avoid saying some of the things she was thinking. Perhaps this was something minor.

"We have clear indication, Dr. Peters, that you have revealed sensitive information, including patient records and other confidential matters, to persons outside the medical center."

"If you are referring to the police, they were invited into our facility by a member of this very committee." She glared at the chief executive officer, who avoided her gaze.

"That has little to do with the nature of the information you chose to disclose, Dr. Peters. You have clearly violated federal confidentiality regulations, as well as our own rules in this matter."

"Do I get to address these charges?"

"Of course you do, Dr. Peters, and that is why you are here. Do you have anything else to say in your defense?"

"I haven't said anything yet in my defense. But if this isn't a court, and the intent is a sensitive and confidential inquiry, your use of such a term as 'my defense' is rather odd, don't you think?"

"I do not think anything about the terms or the proceedings, Dr. Peters, other than that you are a bit presumptuous to question a tradition and process that has served us well for a hundred years."

"That's exactly why there is a problem, *Gentlemen*. I use that term advisedly, to recognize the fact that all members of this committee are male, not necessarily as a description of character." Her sarcasm was not lost on the group, but it only seemed to make them more rigid, if that were possible.

"All of this is irrelevant to the issue at hand," Wachman continued coldly. "We have come to a consensus that you have violated both ethics and commonly accepted professional standards. As this is a first offense, and it would not benefit the Hospital Center to make public charges, we have decided to use our internal powers, and impose a temporary suspension . . ."

"A what?" Michele interrupted, "Why, you can't . . ."

". . . of your staff privileges," the medical director continued, as if she hadn't spoken. "You will be reinstated after a period of sixty days, subject to this committee's review, and no further indication of unacceptable behavior."

Two months—one-sixth of her entire annual salary! But most important, it would completely ruin her chances of a promotion. A negative mark like this on her record and she could forget about advancement. In one simple stroke, they had determined that her career would never go further. And there wasn't a damn thing she could do about it.

Michele felt an awful lethargy. She was so tired, she couldn't even bring herself to protest. She hadn't been able to shake the virus that had been attacking her, and continued to experience waves of nausea and weakness. Whether it was the strain of her long work hours, or the stress of recent events, her immune system didn't seem to be doing its usually efficient job, and she had been dragging. It was not like her. She had always been the sort to keep going when others wore out. But the last few days had been different. Every step seemed an effort, every procedure a demanding task, every day a monumental obstacle to overcome. At the same time as she felt waves of resentment, frustration, anger and helplessness, a part of her wondered if two months off might not be beneficial.

What am I thinking? she asked herself. *These high and mighty assholes ruin my career without giving me so much as a chance to prepare a defense, and here I am thinking it would be a good vacation!*

Yet she realized that there would be no sympathetic hearing from the group this day. Determined to find recourse, but stumped for alternatives at the moment, she decided to detach; to get out of the situation. However, she couldn't leave without tossing out a final comment.

"This is a travesty, of course. I was tried, judged, and convicted before I even knew anything about your concerns. This isn't a hundred years ago, Gentlemen. You cannot do such vile things and expect that no one will challenge them. And if you think that I will meekly accept your will, because I am a woman, you are very much mistaken."

It took every bit of energy she had, to stalk out of the room, down the hall, and into the nearest doctor's lounge, where finally she collapsed on a couch, bursting into tears and deep sobs of helpless frustration.

Gil Beach noticed the red-rimmed eyes of the woman across his desk. Michele Peters had looked better. Besides the evidence of tears, she sat in a slumped posture that spoke of great weariness. Her hair hung limp and lifeless, her skin was sallow and dry looking. When she spoke, her voice rasped, and she took shallow breaths between words. If he had known she was in such bad shape, he wouldn't have agreed to have her come all the way down to the precinct.

"Look, I'm no doctor," he told her, "but you look sick to me. Is something wrong?"

"Yeah there's plenty wrong, but it isn't me, it's that bunch of horses' asses that control the hospital."

"You think it's part of the conspiracy?"

"I know this sounds weird, but I hope so. I'd hate to think that this was just male chauvinism and power politics. I sure know it isn't straight pool."

Gil nodded his understanding. The telephone on his desk gave a warble, and excusing himself, he lifted the receiver. The caller was Shig Higawa at the lab. Gil put him on hold, while he made his apologies to Michele. She told him to go ahead and talk to the technician, as she was so exhausted she needed to go home and get some rest. Gil promised to talk to her the next day, and waved goodbye as he got Shig back on the line.

"What ya got for me, Shig?"

"Well, there are some very strange things here, Gil. I can't get out of the lab, but maybe you want to drop by and take a look-see."

Higawa had worked with Beach for years, and knew that he couldn't resist a chance to see some of the forensics magic first-hand. Therefore, he wasn't surprised when Gil not only agreed to look, but was at the lab less than an hour later. Higawa took him to the area of the lab where he had been working. There were several types of microscopes, assay machines, and other paraphernalia in view.

"We got some interesting chemicals from the body—on the clothes, vapors in the lungs, and so forth."

"Like what?"

"The chemicals we got here are photographic chemicals. Developer, toner . . . that kind of stuff."

"Got any ideas?"

"A photography lab maybe? But what would that have to do with a hospital?"

"How about X-rays? Do they use that kind of chemical?"

"Well, sure. But only in very controlled environments, generally. This stuff is contaminated with a lot of filth—dirt, mold, and so forth. I haven't had a chance to do an analysis on the soil, yet, but I'd say the environment had to be dirt or at least an earthen floor. Not too many X-ray departments like that. Maybe in Old Doc Schweitzer's place in Lamborene or such, but not in a modern hospital."

"Something's contaminated, that's for sure."

"That ain't half of it, my man."

"What, there's more?"

"You might say. Take a look at this." Higawa moved a small metal box over to the table. It had various switches and a couple of dials on it. There was a cord leading out of the box to a small metal tube, which he moved over one of the glass vials. The box gave off a low hum, and one of the dials twitched slightly.

"I'd like to take credit for great insight, but actually, I was just playing around with the counter, when it started registering, and this turned out to be the source."

"Source of what?"

"Radioactivity," Shig replied, and pointed to another gadget that looked like a metal thermos, with a vice as a lid. "This is a scintillian well counter. It's sort of what you would call a geiger counter, but built with a central well where you can place samples. After I got a slight reaction from the large crystal probe, I tossed a sample in here. We practically got the thing to waltz." He pointed to one of the dials on the device and threw a switch. The needle started jumping around like a nervous dog at a cat show.

"This guy was transported from a place where there was a major set-up for photography or some kind of film with a dirt floor and a lot of radioactive material lying around."

"That sounds like an X-ray department doesn't it?"

"Well not really. First, it's called radiology these days, since they do more than X-rays, and its nuclear medicine, when it's radioactive material that's involved. But I can't imagine it would be any legitimate hospital department. There are all kinds of rules and safeguards in the certified places. It's not just good practice, it's governed by all sorts of federal regulations. You don't just leave radioactive materials lying around loose for somebody to sit in."

"So what are you saying Shig?"

"I dunno, Gil . . . you're the detective. But I got a feeling this was an intentional dosing, and somebody is doing something that is definitely not kosher."

"Says my favorite Jewish friend."

"Ha ha! Anyhow, I'll call you, once I get the soil samples percolated. But before you leave, take a look at this," Higawa nodded toward a binocular stage microscope.

"Okay, what is it?" Gil asked, after staring at the mysterious slides.

"That's a tissue section from Schwenker's leg. It's a cross section of his skin and fascia, from the thigh. Krispnick thought it looked odd, and took a slice for analysis. It you look carefully, you'll see a tiny particle at the end of each of those lines."

Gil looked again, and did recognize little dots and squiggles of various size at the end of the lines. He nodded to indicate that he had located the details.

"The lines are actually tissue trauma. They are literally holes drilled through the epidermis, dermis, and subcutaneous layers by the little particles."

"So what are they—worms, parasites?"

"Not at all. They aren't even living things. I was able to separate a few of them for finer analysis. They are just tiny irregular slivers of metal . . . the kind most guys have in their pocket, from coins rubbing together, pocket knives, money clips, or whatever . . . metal filings you could call 'em. You don't usually see them, because they're microscopic, and accumulate over a long period of time, deep in a pocket, ground into the seams. Even washing or cleaning doesn't get 'em all out."

"What could have made them burrow into his skin that way?"

"Well, my guess is a powerful electric or magnetic field. Only metal fragments were involved, even though there's usually a lot of other tiny particles deposited in clothes the same way. It's just a guess, but a potent magnetic field could make 'em not only migrate, but vibrate and rotate as they go, effectively creating little buzz-saws, or microscopic drills. Is that weird, or what?"

Twenty-seven

Michele Peters' head felt like it was being attacked with a dentist's drill. She had only intended to stop in her room for a few minutes. Except for the ticking of her wall clock, and the whining hum of her ancient refrigerator, the place was silent and empty. She thought rinsing off in the shower would make her feel more relaxed, but when she dried herself in front of the mirror, she was shocked by her appearance. Then, as she drew a brush through her hair, she was startled to see large clumps of hair come free. She grabbed a lock near her temple and gave a tug. A patch came off in her fingers. She had yanked out a few strands in the past, with her nervous habit of pulling on her hair, but this was much more serious.

As a doctor she knew she was sick. As a smart doctor, she knew that she couldn't heal herself. During medical training, her instructors had repeated ad infinitum: "The physician who treats himself, has a fool for a patient." And despite the masculine pronouns, she knew it was wise advice. It wasn't as easy to act on, in the present instance, because she had never gotten around to selecting a personal physician.

She reviewed the attendings she knew, and the house staff that might be called on to help. Either she was too close to feel comfortable, too suspicious, or too critical to come up with anyone she felt like calling. But this couldn't wait.

Finally, she settled on Carl Troop. He didn't have a private practice, but he was accessible. She felt his participation in the conspiracy investigation had demonstrated his common sense and intelligence. And when she was around him, she felt comfortable. He was a little close to home, but this was no time to get too finicky. She needed help, and she needed it soon. He seemed like someone she could trust.

Soon she was sitting in an examination room, putting her clothes back on after he had completed a thorough and competent exam, a nurse remaining in the room to assist. Michele also appreciated his respect for her modesty, finding ways to conduct the exam that required little exposure of her body, and minimal indignity to her ego. The whole issue of men doctors prying into women's bodies was sensitive enough, but especially when the man in question was a colleague. It was with the warmth of a friend that he returned to discuss his impressions.

"Well, you're right, Michele. Something is definitely going on. It could be a histaminic event, an allergic tornado. I'd have to keep open the possibility of a toxic reaction, some poisonous substance getting into your system. In some ways, it is even consistent with exposure to ionizing radiation, though that seems a little far out unless you've been spending nights at Three Mile Island without telling anybody. Seriously, Michele, I'll be able to tell more after we run some tests. I'd like an MRI done tomorrow, and some fasting blood work. In the meantime, avoid any unusual food or activity; go home and get some rest."

"This sounds like a fair approximation of 'take two aspirin and call me in the morning.' "

He chuckled, and handed her forms in triplicate to take to the lab for additional tests. "Yeah, I suppose that's about as good as I can do until I have more information. An analgesic might actually help you sleep, and we won't know much more today, so we can talk tomorrow." He placed a hand firmly on her shoulder and looked her straight in the eye.

"Don't let this get to you, Michele. I'll keep on it, and we'll get to the bottom of whatever's causing these symptoms. I know it's a cliché, but . . . trust me."

The funny thing was, she did.

Twenty-eight

Deep in the bowels of the hospital, in a secret laboratory financed and fed unknowingly by a siphoned tithe from the vast stores, systems, and energy of the enormous hospital center above, The Doctor lectured to a deserted classroom. The only thing listening was a tape recorder, set up to retain his pearls of wisdom being cast into the empty room.

"Project Magnes! Our bold exploration will use fields of energy and magnetic force to pull the staff of power out of the hands of the entrenched hollow-minded frauds that sit at the head of the medical and scientific establishments."

The voice echoed from bare stone and concrete.

"We have proven that various cells and even organisms propagate more effectively within a field of energy. We have demonstrated that magnetic fields can exert either life-preserving, or fatal force on living things, including man. It is only a matter of time before we will create a machine able to heal our loved ones, and with the flick of a switch, to annihilate our enemies.

Through a glass wall panel, the Doctor saw Buzz Merkcl wheeling a loaded gurney into the applications area. A dark-haired woman was stretched out naked on the cart. The Doctor pushed the pause button of the recorder, opened the side door halfway, and called to the big attendant.

"Is that a potential specimen?" Merkel stopped, looking confused and something else. It was his sneaky expression, the Doctor thought, but knew that it was part of the moronic giant's natural personality.

"What is her status?"

"Kinda messed up, I guess. She had an accident. She was nosing around the east tunnel."

"Is she someone we have to worry about?"

"Only if she blabbed, an' I don't think she's gonna do that. She might be a spy. She was pretending to be a doc, but she ain't. She ain't nobody important."

After a pause, the Doctor nodded.

"Alright, then, you can prepare her for the Magnetofield rejuvenator. We will be using a setting of 325 on the alpha LET and 600 on the beta LET."

At the quizzical expression of the attendant, the Doctor added, "The big red and blue dials. Never mind, I'll show you later.

"Buzz, I don't want you to do anything to this one before we treat her. Afterwards, if she terminates on us, I'm not as concerned, but your games can alter our experimental data. And Buzz . . ."

The hulking figure looked up at his mentor and keeper, a silly grin now on his face. The Doctor would have expected more of a resentful sneer given the limits he was imposing.

"Cover her up. Let's show proper respect to our specimens. Their lives will save many in the future. They may even save yours and mine. Put her legs back up on the gurney and cover her immediately."

The big man looked back impassively. He took a drape from the lower shelf of the cart, whipped it in the air to open its full width, then let it settle over the unconscious form. As he lifted her legs and tucked the drape along the edges, his back to the Doctor, a hand went under the cloth, to slide over the breasts and flanks of the woman a final time.

The Doctor was upset moments later, to find that the woman on the gurney was already dead. It helped explain the idiot's attitude and lack of resistance, but made the experiment useless. Eventually, the procedures might well restore life to the dead, but that was in the future. For now, the experiments required living tissue for proper data and result analysis.

"What have you done, Buzz?"

"I didn't do nothin' doc. I told ya. She was nosing around and got herself where she shouldn't a been. Then she had an accident. Fell down a shaft, on some boxes and stuff. I gave her CPR and all, but it didn't do no good."

It was obvious from the woman's injuries that Buzz was lying. The Doctor glared at Merkel, but said nothing. If the woman was spying, it was best that she be eliminated, anyway. It was a shame to lose a specimen, but there were always plenty of those available. It galled the Doctor that this sorry excuse for a human being could get away with such abominations, but sometimes it was necessary to ignore the brute's deviant pleasures. He came in handy for the dirty work, and would remain loyal as long as he was given opportunities to sate his perverted desires. Anyway it was too late now for this woman.

There was one factor Helen had not considered in her little pedestrian accident scam. She was correct that the driver was a nervous out-of-towner. Alma Benedict was practically terrorized by the combination of noise, congested traffic, and unfamiliar territory. What Helen had forgotten was that for his version of the scam, Sonny had dressed the part of a respectable businessman, while she was in the disguise of an addled street dweller. Even in his more socially mainstream costume, Sonny also hid behind an intervening vehicle, so he could dart out abruptly, not allowing the driver a chance to see him and react one way or another.

Helen stood in the middle of the block, in relatively plain sight. Despite efforts to appear a part of the scenery, she was like a red flag to the nervous out-of-towner. Having a decent self-image, it never dawned on Helen that Alma would sight her from far away and be scared. The woman detective was only playing a role, and didn't realize the impact of her appearance on a sheltered and shy visitor to the mean streets of New York.

Miss Benedict knew little about city ways. With no information to go on other than gossip, she assumed that all city street people were crazy, and all crazy people are dangerous. Who knew what a crazy person might do? She had heard stories about women dragged from their cars when they paused in city traffic. So instead of ignoring the dumpy figure, or taking special care, Alma slammed her foot down on the accelerator, hoping to get past the creature. Her sudden acceleration coincided with Helen's move to step forward and simulate contact with the vehicle's fender.

Before Helen realized that she had seriously miscalculated the auto's speed, she had stepped too far out to avoid the veering path of the fast moving vehicle. There was an all too real whump of metal against flesh, and Helen's body was spun around before being thrown against a parked delivery truck. Her head made slamming contact with the truck's side, and she fell heavily to the asphalt. There was no need to feign unconsciousness. The EMS vehicle that arrived minutes later loaded her senseless form onto a stretcher, and took her where she had intended to go, but not in the state she had anticipated.

Twenty-nine

Michele had asked Gil to come to her apartment. It wasn't a come-on, she assured him, she was simply too sick to go out. When he saw her, he understood. Dark bags hung under her normally lively eyes, which now looked dull and unfocused. Her skin was dry and flaking, hanging on her like a loose wrapper. Despite a bandanna over her hair, Gil could see patches of bare skin showing through, where the once lustrous tresses had been pulled or fallen out, the remaining strands now looking lifeless and drab. She huddled on a kitchen chair, in a colorful robe that only seemed to emphasize her lackluster appearance. Shoulders slumped, she spoke in a weary monotone that he could hardly hear over the whine and hum of an old refrigerator stuck in the corner of the room that served as a kitchenette.

"Something is . . . seriously wrong, Gil. Carl is checking me out, but I don't know if he's going to find something in time."

She paused, taking several deep breaths, as if she needed to gather energy before she could continue.

"I'm sure you'll be okay, Michele. Troop has a good reputation, doesn't he?"

"Yes, but it may not be enough."

"Don't talk like you're dying or something. This might not be anything too serious."

"Look, Gil, I'm a doctor. I know this is serious . . .

and whatever it is, the progression is fast. There's a good bet I'm not gonna make it. I'm bleeding, Gil—in the wrong places. My heart feels like it's close to giving up. It's giving me serious warnings in the form of tachycardia and chest pain."

"My God, why are you wasting time, talking to me? You should be checked into the hospital!"

"Yes, that's where I'm going now. But only because I have no alternative. I don't think they are going to be able to help. I think this is happening to me purposely, Gil. I think that whoever has been making patients disappear, and killed Richard . . . I think they are somehow poisoning me. But I don't know how. And they're here in the hospital, Gil. I know it sounds paranoid, but I figure that if I'm helpless in a hospital bed, they'll be able to get to me . . . even easier than now. I haven't eaten or drunk anything but bottled water, but I keep getting worse. That's why I called you. I think somebody is trying to kill me, Gil . . . and . . . and I think they're gonna succeed."

Tears coursed down her face as her shoulders shook with silent sobs. He put an arm around her, and she slumped limply against him.

"Okay, Michele. I don't think you're being paranoid. There's definitely a conspiracy going on here. They are killing people, and you are a logical target. But we aren't gonna just let them do it. Tell me everything you can about the last few weeks—changes in schedule, new exposures, drugs, treatments, or anything that might have created an opportunity for something to be introduced."

"Believe me, Gil, I've thought about all that. My boss, Archie Neely, is a Toxicology specialist, and he gave me a lot of insight into possibilities you might not ever think of. Hell, I even tried to think like Agatha Christie, or somebody. Like considering the possibility of DMSO or something as an agent."

"DMSO?"

"Di-methyl-sulfoxide. It's a controversial drug that some folks claim has its own healing powers, but it also has a quality that makes it an excellent vehicle for introducing other chemicals cutaneously."

"That's through the skin?"

"Yes. You can mix a substance like, say, caffeine with DMSO, and smear it on the outer skin and presto, you have caffeine in your system without drinking a single cup of coffee."

"So, I suppose poisons could be introduced the same way."

"Right. Smear a solution of Thallium and DMSO on a steering wheel, and the person who grabs it could get a fatal dose through his hands."

"Sounds kind of James Bond-ish."

"Yes, but it could work in the right situation. Still, I haven't been able to come up with anything to which I could give a high degree of possibility, much less probability. I even feel worse after lying in bed all night."

"No new bedding, anything like that?"

"No, nothing."

"Do you sleep soundly?"

"You mean, could somebody sneak in and spray me, or something? Not that soundly! Between my noisy fridge and a few personal worries, I tend to be a little restless."

Gil got a contemplative look on his face, and rubbed his temples with his fingers, as if trying to massage a thought out of his skull.

"What is it?" Michele asked, childish in her pleading tone and look of hope, "did you think of something?"

"Well, that problem with money . . . bills. It made me think of something you said the other day."

"Like what?"

"Maybe you just meant it as a wisecrack, but didn't you say something to Pretaska about your electric bill?"

She looked even more uncomfortable, if that was possible.

"Oh shit, I don't know what I said. I was just mad and wanted to yell at him."

"But did you mean it . . . about your bill being high?"

"Oh, hell yes."

"So you pay your own utilities? I thought it would just be covered by the general building supply."

"Fat chance. No, each efficiency has a separate meter. I think mine's broken. It makes it look like my usage is triple what it should be."

"Unless something is going on, that you don't know about."

"Like?"

"Well, forgive me if I'm way off base here. Most of this stuff is for you doctors and scientists, but I heard some stuff at the lecture the other day."

"Junghans's show?"

"Yes. Didn't he say some stuff about the harm from being exposed to electric fields?"

"Uh huh. But that's like living under big power lines, or something."

"Maybe, and pardon my layman's approach to this. But didn't I read somewhere that they are warning folks about exposure to hair-dryers, and electric blankets."

"Yes, that's true. There seems to be special danger to children that are exposed for prolonged periods of time."

"Well, what if somebody wanted to hurt somebody else? Couldn't they set up some kind of a field like that?"

"Well . . . it's not totally out of the question, though the technical aspects are a lot more complicated than you make them sound. If you're talking about any distance, or focusing, it becomes rather complicated, and the amount of power involved is pretty impressive."

"Like maybe triple your usual, and a noticeable increase in the hospital center's usage? And I gotta tell you, Michele. Since I've been sitting here talking to you, I've had a very queasy feeling start up in my stomach, and I can't seem to focus my eyes as well as usual."

"You mean, you really think there might be something here, in my place?" Michele pushed back from the table, darting worried glances around the area.

Gil got up, and walked the perimeter of the small apartment, examining walls, ceiling, and floor. He found nothing.

"You got anything decent to drink?" he asked, returning to the table, "I'm getting dry in the mouth."

"There's some beer in the refrig, if you're allowed to have some while on duty. You are on duty, aren't you?"

He smiled and nodded, but stepped to the old refrigerator, opened the door and removed a bottle.

"Jeez, it sounds like this old thing doesn't want to keep working," he laughed, as the refrigerator whined and hummed its usual weary tune.

Gil pivoted to return to the table, but then his eyes narrowed, and he turned back to the appliance. He set down the bottle, grabbed the refrigerator, and eased it out from the wall with effort. He took the now exposed electric cord in his hand and pulled, disconnecting it from the socket.

"Shit. Listen to that," he said to Michelle, whose jaw fell open in surprise. Because with the refrigerator completely disconnected, the whine and buzz that she had blamed on the aged appliance, kept right on going.

"It isn't from the refrigerator at all!" she observed, unnecessarily.

Gil pulled the old machine farther away from the wall. A gray plastic panel was behind it, which came off with the help of a kitchen knife. In a deep recess, a strange apparatus was hidden. Its hum and whine were louder now that it had been uncovered, and could not be confused with that of a normal household appliance. Heavy copper buss bars connected it to silver-colored cables that disappeared into the walls and ceiling. Gil took a kitchen chair, and climbed up to pull off several of the interlocking panels that formed the drop-ceiling. A mat of metal strands was revealed, woven into a mesh sheet that appeared to line the entire ceiling, since the woven material extended beyond the area exposed by the missing ceiling tiles. Gil swayed dizzily as he stood with his face near the coppery mat, and nearly fell off the chair.

"Let's get out of here!" he barked. "You don't need to be in the hospital, you need to be as far away from this place as you can get!"

The only place he could think to take Michele was his home on Staten Island, where his wife Pilar could help the ill physician. Just finding out the cause of her deterioration seemed to rejuvenate Michele a bit. As they climbed into his car, she spoke in a more animated voice.

"You know, Gil, there is such an immense difference between having some hope or not. I feel better, just knowing there's a reason for this, and maybe a way out. Are you sure your wife won't mind?"

"Pilar is special, you'll see," he assured her.

"Yes, you said that before. She's Spanish?"

"Half Puerto Rican. The other half is Irish. She said the kids used to call her the 'Mick-Spick.' Mean, but she overcame it . . . and a lot more. I think you'll like her."

"I'm sure I will. I hope she likes me too. You two are lucky to have each other."

"You sure this thing with what's-his-name isn't going to work itself out?"

"Peotre?" She bristled, even in her depleted condition. "Not on your life. Or mine. In fact, I noticed something about that generator, or transformer, or whatever it was at my place."

"Having to do with that guy?"

"Yes, indirectly. There was a tag on that machine, Gil. It's an official inspection and maintenance tag, that only gets attached to equipment belonging to Bellevue. That means it came in through official channels, Gil. And the receipt for installation was initialed."

"Not by who I think it was?"

"Yes. It was initialed by Peotre as department head."

"Well, it's possible the initials were forged, but it would explain why we haven't been getting anywhere. Maybe they had a man inside our team."

"Well, I have to take responsibility for that, I'm afraid. I was as smitten as a schoolgirl over the guy for a while. The initials look authentic to me. They'd be hard to imitate. I can accept the blame for having him in our group. But as for the part about him being a man . . . well, I'll reserve judgement."

Thirty

Pilar was glad to help out with Dr. Peters. She said that she looked forward to talking to the woman physician. As a psychologist, Gil's wife spent most of her time with troubled patients, and seldom had an opportunity to converse intimately or at length with a fellow professional like Michele.

First, though, she needed rest. Pilar quickly packed her upstairs to the bedroom, and made the weak woman comfortable before rejoining her husband.

"She looks pretty sick," Pilar observed.

"Yeah, but I think she'll bounce back now. Thanks for being so flexible."

"Well, there are limits to my understanding, big guy. We missed our date, you know."

"Yeah, I'm afraid things got a little complicated. And now I have a message that I'm supposed to see the lieutenant, as soon as possible."

"Well, okay. But you owe me one, buster."

"No problem, mon," he said in his best imitation of a Jamaican accent, "and I intend to repay my debt, with interest."

She laughed and kissed him a warm goodbye.

When Gil returned to the precinct, the lieutenant was at lunch, so he made some call-backs from the pile of message forms stacked on his disorderly desk. Despite the mess, the desk had a system of organization that Gil understood. Like his mind, it gave an outward appearance of casual disarray, but was actually a highly organized, if eccentric, system that held an amazing amount of valuable information. Beach had a reputation as one of the best homicide detectives in the city, and would have been bounced up to increasingly higher positions of administration, until he was completely removed from what he did well, except that he refused to move or accept promotion. With the combined salaries of a detective sergeant and a psychologist, he and Pilar didn't really require more money for their simple needs. And his ego didn't need the boost of a high-sounding job title either. There were times, like everyone, that he hated parts of his job. He even had moments he wondered why he'd gotten into police work. But mostly he felt he was doing what he did best. And in the simplest terms, what he did best was to catch killers.

Unfortunately, his ability to do the job well was sometimes curtailed by others. In this case it was Lieutenant Philip Shannon that stepped in to make things difficult. The message Gil had gotten earlier just read "See Lou," referring to the officer's rank rather than name. When the lieutenant returned, he called Gil into the office. Only the man's superior status prevented Gil from exploding when he heard what the commander had to say.

"You're telling me that the influence of these pill-pushers is more important than finding the truth? I'm supposed to ignore one clear-cut homicide and a potential of many others, so that the medical bigwigs can save face?"

"I'm not saying that at all, detective," Lieutenant Shannon objected. The formal tone was a clue to the nature of the meeting. It wasn't conversation, it wasn't discussion—it was orders. "This is a case that was never really in our jurisdiction to begin with. The facts will be ferreted out. But it will be done with all appropriate tact and sensitivity. And it will not be done by you. Like it or not, Beach, your reputation is more like a bull in a china shop than a politician."

"Thank God," Gil blurted, "I wouldn't have it any other way. But if you ask me, all the 'Bull' is coming from someplace else, and it stinks like hell!"

A few minutes later Gil walked out of the commander's office with a red face and a stride energized by unused adrenalin.

"Bad news?" asked Rose, the civilian employee who handled phone-cover and general clerk/secretarial duties.

"Politics!" Beach spat out the nasty word like it was a mouthful of rotten food. "Well, if they think I'm going to stay out of this, with Frank and Helen inside, they can shit in their hats and use 'em for lunch."

For Gil, this was more than normal annoyance at interference from the brass. It wasn't the first time that the word had come down from high places to back off from a case. But it was more blatant than usual. Not that he had ever been good at such games, but his sense of rightness was particularly offended by the idea of pulling out when his partner and his partner's companion were inserted on an undercover operation and depending on support.

"Fuck'em!" he mumbled. The secretary was used to such displays. His exclamation and similar curses from other officers, often followed their visits to the brass. She waved goodbye to his departing back, slipped earphones over her head, and resumed typing.

Shortly thereafter, Gil sat in the office of the hospital center's acting assistant medical director. He didn't describe the meeting with Shannon. Until someone informed the hospital administration of the decision to pull him out, he intended to gather as much information as he could.

Troop leaned over to slide a small pile of papers across the desk toward the detective.

"This is the stuff we found on Richard Schwenker's desk, plus the notebook he had with him. Maybe you can find something useful in it."

"Thanks," Gil accepted the papers with a nod.

"You know, detective, I'm really worried about Dr. Peters. I've been doing a work-up on her, and she appears to be very sick."

Gil was about to explain recent events and his efforts to remove the woman from danger, but Dr. Troop sped on, his words rushing out.

"She isn't well, and . . . and this whole thing has a feeling of some kind of conspiracy that could place her at risk. I think we need to take steps to protect her . . . and . . ."

"Whoa, there!" Gil finally interrupted, "I agree with you, and I can assure you that she is safe for the time being."

"But the tests I'm doing . . . I have to see her to discuss the results, and . . ."

As his words finally trailed off, the doctor's distressed expression made Gil wonder if Troop's concern was entirely professional. It sounded more heartfelt. He told the administrator about his visit to the staff quarters, and what he and Michele had found. However, he didn't reveal her present location. The discovery of Petraska's connection to the conspiracy had made him extra leery about information getting leaked to the wrong people. Troop didn't question him further, though Gil thought he noticed an extra furrow of the doctor's brow.

"That's fine. Thank God she's safe, wherever she is. But please tell her to call me if her symptoms don't immediately start improving. I tried to be positive with her, but I'll admit to you, Gil, that . . . well, I was very worried."

Beach noticed Troop's use of his first name, which was accompanied by a more relaxed posture and a move to loosen his tie. The doctor was obviously relieved, and probably feeling more like an ally to Gil as he shared the detective's desire to protect Michele. Gil's instincts about people were seldom far off the mark, and he responded to the informality and openness. Troop seemed like a nice guy, and he had a hunch that the doctor could be a good friend to somebody.

Troop apologized when his beeper went off, and insisted on stepping into an adjoining room to answer the call. He told Gil to stay in the meantime and use his office. Beach wondered if the doctor would be as helpful if he knew the precinct had called him off the case, but decided to let that remain a secret a little longer. There were so many secrets going on in this place, what was one more?

He spread Schwenker's papers out on the desk, quickly skimming most of them and seeing little of importance. In fact, the small collection made him view Schwenker as a rather insignificant cog in the Hospital Center's operations. From years of piecing together profiles from limited data, Beach had developed a finely tuned ability to image a person from their notes, papers, and daily tasks. The more he examined the papers and put them together with people's comments and what he knew of the administrator's last days, the more he got an impression of someone who was a peripheral figurehead—a tolerated, but disrespected extranumerary. The man's last papers were a catalogue of pointless tasks and busywork. Memos to him were never formal, but used his first name, or omitted it entirely. Messages from Hampton, Jamison, and others were more like commands to an inconsequential person, than communications to a respected colleague. He may have had an official title as "Director of Operations," but it appeared from the papers that more often than not, those who were theoretically his subordinates told him what to do, rather than vice versa.

"As a non-physician . . ." one note began, "you will not have familiarity with these matters." It appeared to be a denial of his request for participation in some committee or decision-making body. The note was unsigned, but a couple of words were scrawled at the bottom in handwriting that matched Schwenker's. It looked like he had used the note as a scratch pad for a list of other items he wanted to remember. One of the words looked like a scientific abbreviation for a chemical or element—Manganese or Magnesium, Gil couldn't remember his periodic table from high school chemistry well enough to be sure. The word "Project" was there also, and something illegible, that looked like "Tel," or "Til." Beach then leafed through a small notebook that Schwenker had carried with him, apparently to aid his memory. It was filled with lists of supplies, meeting dates, names of vendors that dealt with the hospital, and notes to himself that were not particularly enlightening to the detective . . .

"The Doctor is a doctor is not a Doctor is a doctor is not a Doctor." Under the line was written "Dr. J.," underlined several times.

Maybe Schwenker wasn't playing with a full deck. But without the man present to interpret his strange records and scribbles, it could easily be genius or insanity. Most likely it was nothing. Schwenker was beginning to look like he had been little more than a high level gofer. But even gofers didn't deserve to be murdered.

"Finding anything useful?" Dr. Troop asked from the doorway. "That was a little committee from the NRC. These days, it seems like all we see are irate supply vendors or government inspectors. I fobbed them off on Jamison."

Beach looked up from the utility bills and spreadsheets he had pulled from a large manila envelope.

"I guess you've got enough to worry about."

"You can say that again. But is there any way I could help with this investigation?"

"I'd appreciate your help interpreting some of this," Gil said. "If you have time to take a look, maybe you would notice something I might miss. You docs seem to use a lot of Latin and stuff, that I don't get at all."

Troop laughed. "Yeah that's part of the trick. That way people think we actually know what we're doing."

"You don't?"

"I'm joking Gil. But come on. Surely, you know that just because somebody's a physician, it doesn't mean that he or she stops being human. There's probably more that we don't know than what we do know. And we all make mistakes. But if you write in Latin, most folks have no idea what you're saying!"

This time Gil chuckled with him.

"If you have a few minutes, take a look at that notebook. It was Schwenker's daily log, journal, or whatever. There are some odd entries that maybe you can figure out. I'd be interested to know if anything in there looks important to you.

Carl Troop nodded and took the book. For several minutes he paged through the pad, occasionally staring at a single entry, other times quickly leafing past several sheets.

"Well, it's kinda cryptic. But these last entries ought to be important. Better chance that they had to do with what he was working on at the end. I wonder who Dr. J is supposed to be."

"To me, it's a basketball player."

Troop grinned and rolled his eyes.

"Well, of course there's Doctor Jaspers over in the Pediatric Outpatient Clinic," he suggested, "but that's no help."

"What about Junghans?" Gil asked. "He has the Radiology connection, and from what I've seen of the guy, he's got an ego the size of Long Island."

"I don't know. It seems pretty farfetched. Junghans is so well-established and has so much to lose from something this crazy that I can't imagine him being involved. But then again, I'm having a hard time imagining any physician involved. I mean, it's true what I said about doctors being human, but this isn't an easy field to enter. Anybody that sticks it out through all the difficulties usually has a real commitment to the values of healing. I could believe it more easily about a non-physician. But I suppose this 'Dr. J.' reference limits the choices."

"If it has anything at all to do with this mess," Gil cautioned. "Besides, who knows if it's a last name?"

"Oh Man," Troop shook his head, "that could make it almost impossible to figure out, but I guess you're right. I had a couple of kids call me 'Doctor C.' once. Let me see . . . well, there's Jim Hampton, John Malcolm, Jerry Wesley . . . even Joyce Castro."

"Any of them seem like they could be involved in some kind of illegal conspiracy?"

"Wesley is a nerd. He wouldn't have the balls to run any kind of big operation. Sometimes I wonder how he even passed the Boards. Hampton and Malcolm seem too peripheral to hospital operations, though I can see a couple of possible connections. I can't imagine Joyce Castro involved in anything sleazy, but I guess her work in oncology would put her in some of the right places."

Troop got a thoughtful look on his face, and reached over to a bookshelf. He pushed aside several loose-leaf folders to pull free a paper-covered volume titled "BHC

Administrative Directory." He leafed through it, quickly finding what he wanted.

"You can check the physician's directory, here in section one. But I don't know. After all, we've got about twelve hundred physicians on staff. That's a lot of potential Dr. Js. Section two lists the administrative staff, and in section three you can find out committee assignments, and so forth. You might find that interesting. Committees are the key to power in the medical center. Sometimes they tell you more than official lines of authority."

Thirty-one

Nurse Madge Speer was deferring to authority. She wasn't comfortable yet at the triage desk. It was an intense and daunting responsibility. After years of experience doing intensive care nursing, she had decided to make a change and had applied for a vacancy in the E.D. It almost came as a surprise when she was chosen to fill the position, since emergency medicine would be a new field for her. But her critical care background provided much of the knowledge needed for the job, and besides keeping a wider scope by occasionally covering shifts as a "floater," Madge had kept up her skills through volunteer work with an EMT team in Westchester County where she lived. Still, the variety of maladies was intimidating, and she did more checking with the residents and interns than she might after she was more acclimated to the unit. She envied Mindy Osbourne, who seemed so at home here.

Madge never thought to question Jerry Wesley, when he pulled the bag lady out of line, and made his own decision about her place in the priorities. Even if the nervous little doctor was not following procedure to the letter, his opinion wasn't terribly different from Madge's own . . . and, after all, he was a doctor.

The derelict woman just admitted was unconscious, and Madge wondered if she might be suffering intra-cranial bleeding besides other trauma from her collision with an auto. Curiously, Dr. Wesley seemed less interested in the woman's injuries than the admission data in her chart. Wesley picked up the desk phone, made a brief call, then directed the nurse to have the patient taken to Radiology. Apparently, the call had been to that department, because Madge didn't even have to call a transporter. Within seconds, a burly technician appeared with a gurney in hand. The derelict, who looked like she might be relatively young and healthy under the grime and threadbare layers of clothing, was quickly loaded onto the cart and trundled off. As Madge watched the big man move off down the hallway, she gave a little shiver. She hadn't been around this area for long, but already knew the technician, Merkel, by sight. She didn't know if it was his silent stares, his enormous bulk, or that sneering, smirking expression, but the man gave her the creeps.

After passing through the swinging doors, Buzz didn't turn right to the X-ray suites, but instead moved quickly to the bank of elevators and pressed the button to go down. Glancing around, he saw no one in sight, and slipped a big paw under the woman's clothing. He felt a trim and well-muscled leg, instead of the flabby limb he was expecting. His hand traveled higher, and contacted with smooth firm thighs. He was bringing a thick finger even higher, when a loud bell sounded from the elevator, signaling an arriving car. When the doors opened, he pulled his hand away, and looked impassively at the maintenance man and cleaning woman who waited inside. He shoved the cart over a raised lip of metal onto the elevator, and positioned himself behind the gurney.

Merkel cursed to himself when moments after finally leaving behind the maintenance workers, he was interrupted and prevented from taking the unconscious woman to his hidden place. He had just gotten to a more deserted section of tunnel where he could make his detour, when he ran into Doctor J. He stood right there in front of him, and examined the woman on the cart.

"Strange . . . apparently a street woman, but in excellent health other than the trauma she's suffered," the doctor remarked. "Even clean under the clothing. Looks like a fracture of the femur, some soft tissue bruising in the pelvic region, but no apparent major damage. Can't tell about the head—could be some intra-cranial bleeding, subdural hematoma, maybe transtentorial herniation, but I suspect not. We can do a diagnostic in our lab, but she should make a good specimen, regardless. If we can regenerate brain tissue, we will have gone beyond our expectations, but it's worth a try. I don't like the looks of her get-up. I wonder if it might be a costume and she's some sort of spy . . . like the one you . . . you . . ."

The doctor searched for words, but finding none adequate to describe Merkel's handiwork, settled for giving orders.

"Anyway, I don't want a repeat of that, do you hear?"

The sullen man didn't respond, but the Doctor took his lack of response as compliance.

"Take her to the I.R. Chamber, and I will be along shortly to do the prepping. Don't get difficult with me, boy, or you will quickly find yourself in a prison cell."

Merkel scowled at the threat, but gave one half-nod of understanding, and pushed past his mentor and controller.

Helen had been left alone on the cart for some time when she began to regain consciousness. Her eyelids fluttered, and she raised them enough to see strange surroundings. She had little memory of the accident, but figured that she had been taken to the hospital, since the only other place that would ever look like this was a modern electronics factory, or other futuristic manufacturing plant. No human presence softened the scene of heavy machines, metal and plastic surfaces, looping bundles of power cables, and banks of dials, levers, and buttons.

As she woke up, and her head started clearing, there was a fogginess she couldn't entirely shake, but she wasn't so groggy she didn't realize something was wrong. It went beyond the pain she felt, though the terrible hurt she experienced when trying to shift positions, told her those signals were not to be disregarded either. Her whole pelvis felt numb, but searing pain shot up from her left leg anyway. There were other sore spots, including the entire right side of her head, which hurt even where it touched the stretcher pad. She couldn't move her arms much, because of the straps that held her down. That was the first real hint that something was wrong. Injured people had straps put across them to prevent them from falling off the cart, but not like this. A series of heavy leather bands were positioned to not only limit movement, but to fasten her limbs in place as well.

The second wrong note was the lack of supervision. In these days of medical malpractice litigation, it didn't seem possible that an accident victim, untreated, would lie untended for long periods of time. When someone finally showed up, an inner voice told Helen to continue feigning unconsciousness just in case something strange was really going on. When she felt doughy fingers start to slide under her skirts, she was going to yell, regardless of the danger. But just as the outrage began, it stopped again in response to a distant voice.

"Buzz," the voice called out, "Get away from there! I warned you about that."

Helen began to think that this might be a legitimate setting after all, until she heard the next words.

"You can . . . have her, after the procedures. That will have to satisfy you. Now come out here and finish the set-up. As soon as I enter the final computer codes, I will prep the specimen myself."

Prep for what? Helen wondered, fearfully. The permission to "have her" after whatever procedures were planned sounded bizarre, and being referred to as a "specimen" confirmed her fear that something inhuman was about to be done . . . with her body as the object.

It sounded like she had a few moments before she was to be "prepped." The blood that had oozed from a scraped wrist and forearm made her right hand slippery enough to pull out of the bindings. Helen gritted her teeth to keep from crying out in pain, as she shifted her shattered leg in the process of reaching for her transceiver. Thankful that Frank was somewhere nearby, she located the communicator and with great effort managed to get it out of the clothing and up to her mouth.

Helen hadn't noticed the subtle hum and whine that permeated the chamber where she was tethered. But now, as she pushed the signal button to get Frank on the line, and switched to the "listen" mode to hear his response, an electronic squeal issued out of the small speaker that resonated in harmony with the background tone. She rotated the tiny squelch and gain dials, but heard only static, crackling, and the same constant whine that seeped from the apparatus around her. She punched the signal button again and again, waiting in desperate hope for a voice to answer, but hearing only the mating call of electronic entities. The call did, however, draw the attention of others.

Thirty-two

Frank stood only a block away and some twenty feet above Helen's position. He was facing Monk Weems, who had a crowbar in his hand and a vicious expression on his face.

"Okay, man!" the big black man was yelling, "we knows what you all about now!"

The transceiver in Frank's hand was giving out warbles, shrieks, and buzzes. He had barely felt the signal vibration that alerted him to a call, and voice transmission was being drowned out by some electronic interference.

"You dealers don't belong here . . . and we don't want you here," Monk growled. Two of the big man's friends stood beside him, mimicking his expression of rage, and wielding their own makeshift weapons. One of them Frank knew as Garcia, and the other as Turk.

"What the fuck are you talkin' about?" Frank asked honestly, since he was at a loss about what was going down. Helen was trying to reach him, and he felt unnerved by his inability to respond. Weems must have heard his attempts to make the transceiver work, and made some kind of conclusion about it.

"What's a dealer?" he asked out loud, trying to stall for time, as he sought understanding.

"Don't try to bullshit us, man. We been around too long, to believe that bullshit. We know a dealer when we see one. Ain't nobody else around here struts around with no BEEPER!"

"Beeper?" Frank thought desperately, looking down at the transceiver Monk indicated. Then it started to make sense.

"No—no, Monk, you're wrong. This isn't a beeper, and I'm not a drug dealer."

"I tol you . . . don't jive us, man. Who else gonna be getting called on one a them things. We know—we got 'em all over the South Bronx. You cocksukkas think you big shits 'cause you carry dem toys, but you ain't nothing but trouble. We ain't stupid, we knows how you use that thing to get your orders and call back from a pay phone, so the screws can't track you. Well, that don't make you nothin' in my book, but a cocksukka that's taking the bread outta childrin's hands and stuffin poison into their mouths instead. You ain't gonna bring that shit into this hospital, man."

Frank had very mixed feelings. On the one hand, he was scared, but on the other, he was pleased to hear the man's anger and opposition to drug selling. Now it all made sense—the anger and the suspicion he had been facing. He had not thought to hide his gadget, instead keeping it on his belt so he wouldn't miss a call from Helen. Now he remembered that it was a favorite technique of drug dealers these days, to use beepers to get their users' calls, and not be tied down to a single location where they could be tracked and busted.

He had to make a quick decision. If these were bad guys, the revelation that he was a cop would not be received well. It might be the worst thing he could do. But the look in Monk's eyes when he talked about drugs and what it was doing to the city, made him think it might be worth the risk. The hate Frank had thought was aimed at him was really for the scum who traded lives for money in the drug business. Frank shared that anger. So with a lump in his throat, a tremble in his fingers, and an aching tension across his shoulders, Terranova pulled his badge out of a back pocket and flipped it out to be seen.

"I'm a police officer."

There was no response from the glaring men.

"I'm part of an investigation that has nothing to do with you. I'm sorry I couldn't let you guys know," he explained, "but there are some lives at stake, and I didn't know who I could trust. This isn't a drug case, but if you are against that shit as much as you say, I think we got a lot in common, and I oughta let you in on what's going down here."

The three men didn't attack, but suspicion stayed in their stances and expressions. Weems stepped closer, crowbar still in hand, but hanging at his side now.

"Investigation of what?"

"We don't know a whole lot yet, but we think some doctor or doctors are mistreating homeless folks—maybe using them somehow for improper purposes."

"That ain't nothin new," Weems said cynically. He stepped close enough to look carefully at the gold shield and plastic laminated I.D. before relaxing.

"Well, shit, man. Why'nt you say you was a cop?"

"I guess, I didn't know you well enough to be sure you weren't somebody on the wrong side of things, Monk."

"Heh, heh, heh," the big man laughed, the first time Frank had seen him smile, "Well, I guess none a' us is saints, that's for sure! But nobody got nothing big to hide, neither. Not unless you plan on going after a guy for drinking too much booze or diddlin the wrong woman! Heh, heh, heh."

He gave a sly glance at Garcia, who looked sheepish, but started chuckling, too.

"Shit man," Frank agreed, now laughing along with

the others, "I probably spilled more booze than most of you ever drank, and I expect that whatever woman you're diddlin is most likely getting just what she wants!"

The relaxation of the previously extreme tension probably contributed to the humor of anything said at this point. Frank was so relieved, he almost forgot the reason he had been exposed in the first place. When he started filling in the three men about why he was trying to pass himself off as an employee, he remembered the earlier call, and the communicator's malfunction.

"Look, guys, there's another cop somewhere in this place, and she's my lady." That got a couple of hoots and raised eyebrows, but his expression told them it was time to get serious.

"I don't think she'd call me, unless she needs help. Something is interfering with the transmission, so I can't tell where she is, or what's going down. Got any ideas?"

So a group of men that had been close to beating each other to pulp minutes before, now knelt down on the dirty floor and talked about how they could work together.

Thirty-three

Dr. Wachman stood looking at the female form in front of him. Before beginning the procedure, he had to sterilize her abdomen. It was not usually his function to prep a patient, but it was late, he was upset with his support staff, and doing it himself would save time. He took large swabs and painted the Betadine solution over her chest. For a street person, she had decent musculature, and her skin was surprisingly free of boils, scars, rashes, and dermatitis, breasts firm and clear. The resiliency of some of these people was amazing, he thought. Take a typical person and throw them out on the street, and in days they would be suffering exposure, near starvation, massively infected and probably beyond functioning. But some of these people survived, some practically thrived, until a catastrophic medical problem intervened.

Wachman hadn't been doing much direct clinical work, but since he knew of his limited options and abbreviated life-expectancy, he had become more actively involved again. The woman who lay before him, the file stated was nameless and homeless. So it was a less personalized body that was stretched out under his gaze. It was almost like the cadavers they had dissected in med school, without name or identity. Not so much a human being as a specimen.

Of course this one was alive. Or at least she was alive for the moment. Wachman was all too aware of the complexity of the organism he was dealing with. He knew how little it took to throw all the systems into disarray—a few milligrams of some innocuous metal in the blood, like Magnesium—harmless in the correct quantity, but lethal in a minutely different balance, a change in electrical activity for a millisecond interrupting the heart's built-in trigger system, a single hormone ceasing to be secreted in sufficient quantity to carry out its designated and precisely defined work.

When he was finished with the woman in front of him, she might no longer function. It would be his responsibility in a sense, but in another, it was always beyond his control. Wachman thought cynically about how little control he had over life and death, including his own. It he could prolong his struggle, perhaps the answers would be found, the secrets of rejuvenation for this tired old body. But he sensed that his time was short.

He glanced up at the clock on the wall, and noticed out of the corner of his eye that imbecile Buzz Merkel staring through a glass window set in the door. With a glare and impatient wave of his hand, Wachman shooed the hulking oaf away. He had no need of help from such idiots.

The doctor finished prepping the woman, and moved away. From outside the door, where the gurney had been stashed after delivering the woman, he thought he heard a buzzing and screeching noise, like the sound of a poorly adjusted hearing aid, or malfunctioning beeper.

Thirty-four

"Remember, I told you that the body had some significant dirt deposits—smudges, dust and fragments in cuffs, and so forth," Shigura Higawa explained.

He sat perched on a counter, swinging his legs, looking like a precocious college student even though he was in his thirties. Gil leaned on the same counter, a bag lunch spread out in front of beakers, test tubes, and microscopes. At Shig's suggestion, he had brought his lunch to the lab and was munching away between sentences. Gil claimed that he brought lunch from home as often as possible to balance the greasy fast food meals he was forced to eat when he was on the move. Shig suspected it was more the idea of Gil's wife, than the detective. Today's lunch was clearly low fat, low cholesterol, low taste. Each man sipped from sodas Gil had pulled from the vending machine outside Higawa's office.

"Enough to tell anything?" Beach asked between bites.

"Oh yes . . . tons. Or at least the equivalent of tons in microscopic terms. There must have been several grams in the shoes alone." He pointed to a row of glass vials, several of which contained reddish-tinted solutions. "I ran it for color, density, particle size, and presence of plants. We have primarily a reddish color clay, which relates to the presence of iron in the forms of hematite and limonite. I've got a density gradient column for comparison purposes . . ."

"What's that?"

"Well, we mix a series of solutions from bromoform and bromobenzene in different densities. We arrange them in a tube, and drop soil samples into the top. The various particles settle into different levels, depending on their specific gravity."

"What does that tell you?" Gil asked, quickly swallowing the last mouthful of his sandwich.

"Well it indicates the soil composition, which isn't a lot by itself. But it provides a good comparison measure. If you have another specimen to run, we can tell if it's from the same place, with a pretty high degree of accuracy."

"But since I don't have anything to compare it with . . ."

"Hold on, don't get too disappointed, until you get the full report. There were some other materials in the samples, too."

"Like what?"

"Well, under the stereoscope, I found a ton of mold spores, and other fungus. No chlorophyll plant material at all."

"Is that unusual?"

"Depends. It would be strange for any place that had light, but normal for a cave, tunnel, or other underground place."

"That it?"

"No, there were also traces of cement, lime, and other stuff that suggests concrete walls . . . old ones. The natural material is consistent with the soil composition of Midtown Manhattan, deep down, like where the subways were built. So put those things together, and you got a sub-basement setting in the middle of Manhattan."

"Like the lower levels of Bellevue."

"That would be consistent."

"What I'm having trouble with is the other stuff you told me. I can't imagine an X-ray . . . I mean a radiology set-up, from that. This latest data says a tunnel or sub-basement setting with dirt all over the floor . . ."

"Or even a dirt floor."

"Yeah. Either way, it doesn't seem to go with a medical or laboratory kind of place. So probably, the body was taken from place to place. I mean you science guys are not known for a lotta dirt laying around."

"True. Well, Gil, there is one more piece that I can add."

"So, what is it?"

"You can thank Anton for it, really. He may be a bit of a ghoul, but he's thorough as hell. I didn't even check the swabs, till later, because I wouldn't have thought of it."

"Wouldn't have thought what?"

"That there would be evidence of sexual molestation."

"Of Schwenker?"

"Yup. Anton did oral and anal swipes for analysis, even though it isn't standard procedure. I just checked them. The anal swipe shows sperm."

"Are we talking some kind of homosexual murder, then?"

"No particular reason to think that. I called Anton and we compared notes. It would appear that the sperm was deposited post-mortem."

"There's a fancy name for that, isn't there?"

"You mean psych-wise? I guess so. I never had any psych beyond 101, so I couldn't tell you. Around the morgue, they see this kinda thing every now and then, and of course joke a lot about staff doing it."

"Really?"

"Oh, I don't think it really happens much. It's one of those jokes that certain jobs always get. But you hear it, and end up using their words. They call it 'stiffing the stiffs.' "

"Yeah, well that's not quite what I had in mind. It's something like necro . . . necromol . . . oh, I remember now—necromancy. Yeah, that's it, necromancy."

"Like romance with the dead, eh?"

"Uh-huh. Only, there ain't nothing romantic about it."

Gil tried not to think about sex with corpses on his way home to Staten Island. The ferry ride was always a tonic to him, and he rode on the upper deck, facing the breeze, despite a chill in the air. The air and water of New York might be polluted, the streets dangerous, and the taxes high, but from his vantage point high above the harbor, it looked like a picture postcard. He breathed in the cool salt air, and let some of the tension drop from his shoulders. Off in the distance, the Statue of Liberty stood in regal beauty, too secure and wise to react to momentary troubles and petty issues. Gil often thought of her when shit hit the fan, and tried to take her long-term perspective.

The trip was an optimum twenty minutes or so, since there was no fog or rain today. Beach walked from the ferry station in St. George, up the steep grade of Victory Boulevard, taking a jog to the left at the little vest-pocket park where a large boulder was the local kids' equivalent of play-equipment. With legs hardened by his regular stair-climbing workouts, he pushed quickly up Howard Avenue the last two blocks to his house, and finally mounted the steep driveway that he had to salt in the winter in order to have any chance of getting the Plymouth into. The walk was like a mini-workout itself, and he grabbed a soda from the refrigerator, before sitting down at the kitchen table with his wife and their recent houseguest.

Pilar pointed out how much better Dr. Peters was looking. Michele did look remarkably improved. She still wore a kerchief to cover the bald spots where her hair had come out, but she held herself with a new energy, her eyes had regained their brightness, and the bags under them were no worse than the kind you get from a late night and too little sleep.

Gil filled the doctor in on what he had so far. Pilar listened, and was able to add some insight from her perspective as a psychologist.

"That's disgusting!" Peters responded to the information about semen found on Schwenker's corpse. "I've seen just about everything in the E.D., but when it's somebody you know . . . and he's dead . . . well, you know."

"It's not common, but not awfully rare, either," Pilar noted. "Besides catching an occasional mortician that takes advantage of his work setting, we get a killer every now and then that has sex with his victim after death. It goes with the picture of a socially dysfunctional type—unable to deal with the complexity in real relationships, they can get some satisfaction in a setting where they have complete control. They aren't usually as sick as you might think, but terribly inadequate."

"Well you call it whatever you want, I still think it's sick!" Gil said with a wry expression.

"Well, yes, of course," Pilar modified her earlier words, "I don't mean it isn't pathological. I just mean it isn't an indication that somebody is a bona fide paranoid schizophrenic, or anything. As often as not, it's the mousy little cart-pusher who lives alone and has no friends, instead of some dramatic axe-murderer."

"Speaking of paranoid," Michele interjected, "I might be way off base, but there's a couple of weirdos at Bellevue that might fit that picture. I can think of one in particular—this radiology tech that must have bought his certificate, since he doesn't seem to have the brains of a pea-pod. He acts very strange, he's always transporting patients and cadavers, even though that isn't usually a tech's job, and, well . . . he's got this leer . . ."

"Well, a leer isn't a lot to go on, or I'd have to arrest my partner, but it sounds like your guy does have access to the right kind of places."

The mention of his partner, made Gil realize he hadn't heard from Frank . . . or Helen either. He made a mental note to call the precinct and find out if either of the two had reported in through regular channels. Also, Dr. Troop might know how they were doing, since he had been included in the undercover operation, and was Frank and Helen's on-site contact.

"Yes, and . . . well, I didn't report it, because it was too brief and hard to prove, but one time I swear I saw him touching an unconscious patient in an inappropriate way."

"You didn't report your suspicions?"

"Look, it wasn't that clear, if you know what I mean. I just happened to be there when the elevator doors opened, and thought I saw him pull his hand out from under the sheet."

"Well, couldn't you just mention it confidentially to his supervisor, so they keep an eye on him?"

Michele looked down at the table, and a pink blush appeared on her neck. Gil put two and two together.

"He's a radiology tech, you said. So his supervisor would be . . . oh, that would be Dr. Pretaska. I see." He quickly moved on to other matters.

"I can have the guy checked out. But let's get back to the forensics report. Is there any kind of laboratory or radiology set-up in the sub-basement area?"

"No, not at all. We have an X-ray unit next to the E.D., but most of the Radiology Department is way up on three, along with Nuclear Medicine."

"I feel handicapped, trying to make sense of Bellevue. It's such a huge place, and so chaotic."

"Yes, but it's a grand old place, too. Don't let all this craziness make you think it isn't a fantastic institution. In fact, this whole situation gets my dander up. All the wonderful services that go on at Bellevue, and this kind of thing can give a completely wrong impression. It's a vital and important institution. There are a huge number of people that would be lost without it."

"Yeah, well most of the time, I'm lost IN it!"

"Maybe I could go with you now. I'm feeling a lot better."

"Well, maybe. If you really think you're up to it. But this isn't a game, Michele. You, of all people, should realize that now. There's some real danger in this situation. People are dying, and not by accident. You were almost one of them."

"I know. That's why I have to help. I have an inside view of it. I think that I have a better chance of getting to the bottom of this than almost anyone. I feel a responsibility, Gil. Those poor homeless people aren't going to have a chance, unless we do something."

"Well, I'm game if you are."

"I feel like such a mess," Michele apologized, "I have to clean up. Can I have a half hour to get myself presentable?"

"Take your time," he said.

Once Michele had disappeared upstairs, Gil and Pilar moved into the living room, where he sat on the couch, rubbing his temples with his fingers. She stepped behind her husband and began massaging his shoulders.

"Do you know what it's like for me, darling," she asked, "waiting and wondering as you go off and get involved in another dangerous job?"

He didn't respond quickly. The pause was an indication that he was taking her question seriously, thinking it over.

"Yeah. I think I do."

She kept massaging him. With one hand, she also reached up and slid fingers through his hair. Then she leaned over and kissed him on the neck. He turned and kissed her hungrily, soon grabbing her and pulling her down onto the couch.

"What if Dr. Peters comes down?" she asked breathlessly.

"Oh, she'll be a while, I'm sure. Remember, you explained to me that women are different than men . . .

"And so they are!" he exclaimed, as he freed her breasts, leaning down to kiss them.

"Ummmm, vive la différence!" she agreed, and moved a hand to touch him as well.

Knowing each other's needs and pleasures, they quickly moved together with a rush of familiar passion, spiced with a subtle recognition of their need for each other in the face of the danger inherent in his job.

After the rush of passion slowed, Gil and Pilar replaced their clothing, to avoid being caught in an embarrassing state, but continued to cuddle on the couch, sharing a moment of tenderness and mutual satisfaction.

When Michele descended the stairs, minutes later, Gil thought he saw moisture in her eyes, and wondered if she had heard more than they intended, or if it was just the sight of them curled together on the couch that made her sad. Then again, it could have nothing to do with them. But Gil's sixth sense told him that this was a woman that hungered for a close relationship.

When the telephone rang, Pilar answered, listened for a moment, and covering the receiver with her hand, spoke to the two others.

"It's a Doctor. Dr. Carl Troop."

Michele glanced at Gil in surprise. He shook his head, and leaned over to whisper.

"I didn't tell him you were here. But I gave him my home phone, in case something came up."

"It's okay . . . even if you told him," Michele reassured him. "I . . . well, I know I haven't had a perfect track record in the character analysis department lately, but . . . well, I think you can trust him."

Gil nodded, and took the receiver from his wife.

"Hello, Dr. Troop . . . uh, yes, okay . . . Carl. Anything from Frank or Helen yet? Jeez, I don't know. Yeah, I'm kinda concerned, too." Gil glanced at Michele and Pilar, who had questioning looks of concern. He raised a finger, signaling that he would explain in a minute.

"What? Yeah, I know he's your boss. No, I understand . . . Is that dangerous? A Jane Doe . . . and you think it might be Helen . . . Radiology is involved? Look . . . Carl, can you delay things at all? I couldn't get there in much less than an hour. See if you can find Frank, and do whatever you can. I've got Michele with me. If she's up to it, I'll bring her along. We'll get there as soon as possible."

He slammed down the phone and turned to the two women.

"Okay, you probably got the meat of it from what you heard on my end," Gil explained. "It looks like the Medical Director, Wachman, might be our man. Troop says he's acting strange, and has scheduled some unusual procedure for a nameless patient—in the middle of the night, practically. The guy isn't acting like he's too tightly wrapped, and he's got Radiology involved. Nobody's heard from Helen in the last twelve hours, and it seems she might be the one Wachman is about to put under. Troop says he has other evidence, too."

"I can't believe it would be Wachman," Michele said

thoughtfully. "He can be a jerk, but it's hard to imagine him as a murderer."

"Didn't you say he was in poor health?"

"Yes, the scuttlebutt is that he has cancer and doesn't have a lot of time."

"Maybe he thinks he can save himself by testing some radical treatments on people who don't count."

"Maybe, but it's hard to fit that with my image of Wachman. He has such unwavering standards, and is such a stickler for ethics."

"In my business, we see plenty of that," Gil answered. "It doesn't always make the news, but plenty of times its the loudest voice of protest that's doing the thing he condemns—in his closet or the dark corners of the city."

"I guess you could be right. But I'll have to see it to believe it. Is Carl going to delay things for us?"

"Well, as much as he can. You said you were willing to go back to the hospital. Do you feel strong enough for a real fast ride? At this hour I can take the car and get there quicker than public transportation. But I'll be moving at warp speed."

"Yes, of course. I feel pretty good now. Except for being a little weak, and having a funky hairdo, I'm fine."

"Go ahead," Pilar answered her husband's questioning look. "I know you have to go." She gave him a gentle kiss.

Minutes later Gil was speeding across the Verranzano Narrows Bridge, Michele in the seat next to him, a flashing light stuck on the roof, the accelerator to the floor. He crossed into Manhattan, sliding into the ambulance parking area less than forty-five minutes after leaving the house.

Troop was waiting and had located Frank, who was worried about Helen's lack of contact since the afternoon. Though he was obviously pleased to see Michele and gave her a big hug, the acting assistant medical director was looking uncomfortable and spoke in a tense tone.

"I didn't tell you everything over the phone," he said, "but I overheard something. There are a couple of kinds of beepers we use around here—some just call you to a house phone, others are actual voice transmitters. They're kind of temperamental—you get interference, crossed frequencies, all sort of weird stuff. I had one of those today, and like a couple of other times, I accidentally tuned in on somebody else's call. I heard somebody talking about some kind of experimental procedures. I swear that I heard 'em say that whatever they were doing, killed specimens. No matter what those animal rights folks say, we don't do that here. Not to animals, and especially not to humans. But that is what it sounded like. There was one part I heard pretty clearly about some derelict woman scheduled for a procedure and something about her being a spy or something.

"I was beginning to think I'd gone crazy, but just for the hell of it, I check the E.D. and it looks like maybe they admitted your woman colleague this afternoon, as an accident victim. All the physical information fits.

"Then I found out that Wachman has a procedure 'scheduled' for the middle of the night. I ask myself, 'Am I just being paranoid? Or am I just ready to believe the worst about my boss?' Then I notice the entry. Usually, the O.R. schedule describes the operation to be performed, but this one has a blank there. I called the O.R. and asked the charge nurse a couple of questions. What I get is that Wachman is doing an experimental procedure this time."

"On Helen?"

"Well, she didn't use her name when she went undercover, so all I know, is that it's a homeless woman who was just admitted. But I can't think of any other explanation. I'm afraid your colleague is about to become a guinea pig for something." He had perspiration on his forehead and kept clasping and unclasping his fingers.

Gil realized the risk the man was taking, especially since he had found out that it was his boss doing the procedure. So Gil told him to stay in his office. There was nothing he could do to help, and fingering his superior could unnecessarily make him look bad, even if he were right. It was also important to have a contact in reserve. Michele insisted on going along, and the group of three dashed to the elevators, anxious to reach the 11th floor operating suites in case Troop's delaying tactics had not been successful.

Thirty-five

Dr. Wachman drew on the thin latex surgical gloves with such a forceful tug that they split. He snapped them off, and threw the offending pieces across the room, where they hit with a soggy slap. He was frustrated by the delays, and he was beginning to have doubts about his acting assistant, Carl Troop. When Wachman stepped down from his position as medical director, Troop was one of the most promising candidates to succeed him, except for the lack of a political killer instinct. That was no small requirement for the job, and it was also why Troop had not been admitted to Wachman's inner circle—those who knew all the secrets. Troop's advantages were his skill and knowledge as a physician, coupled with a personality that seemed to charm most people. But this evening's series of stupid questions, requests, and unnecessary delays, had eroded Wachman's confidence in the man. Finally, the medical director had stopped answering calls, and went ahead with the procedure. Now he stood with the blade poised, and contemplated the human form before him. An excellent female specimen, it was a wonder that she could have ended up living on the streets.

She might die during the procedure, or his creative approach might save her, and in addition give some validity to a radical and aggressive approach that could save many lives. He inserted the blade at the sternal notch, and sliced downward through layers of skin, blood welling to the surface as capillaries were severed. Though not as long, the slash into her thorax reminded him of the descending cut that made up the traditional "Y" incision of an autopsy.

Nearby, at the Doctor's signal, a radiology technician flicked switches and turned dials. The apparatus gave a thin whine as it built up energy to deliver the ionizing radiation Wachman intended to direct at the woman's viscera. The anesthesiologist looked at Wachman with a worried frown. The patient's vital signs were not holding up well. There was some question, the other doctor suggested, that the patient could survive the procedure. Wachman glared back and went ahead. The anesthesiologist gazed intently at a cardiac monitor, which showed a weak heart rhythm, with increasingly frequent arrhythmias, irregularities of beat that could presage a complete cardiac arrest.

When the door burst open, allowing Beach, Terranova, and Peters to enter the operating suite, the patient lay exposed, like a carcass of beef, with the chest cavity open and bloody.

"What the hell?" Wachman erupted, "Get out of here. You haven't even scrubbed!"

The medical director's self-assured demand stopped them for a moment, but Michele walked to the shrouded form on the operating table and pulled off the drape hiding her face. Underneath was a dark-haired woman of apparent Hispanic ethnic origins. Michele swallowed, and looked helplessly at her colleagues.

"If you have finished destroying our sterile environment, doctor," Wachman hissed at Peters, "You can take your partners in crime out of here. And don't come back. You were already on suspension, but as far as I am concerned, you are now terminated from the staff of this hospital center. You can expect charges to be filed against you, and these people—that's Beach isn't it? He was also told to stay away and didn't listen. Well, you have both just flushed your careers down a very deep toilet."

"But what are you doing?" Michele made a last ditch effort. "And why are you doing it in the middle of the night?"

"Not that it is any of your business, Dr. Peters, but I am hopefully saving the life of this woman, who has a malignancy that is interrupting vital blood flow. This combination of surgery and radiation therapy delivered directly to the site of the cancer may not be familiar to you, but I assure you, it is the only chance this poor woman has. That urgency is one reason for scheduling the operation as quickly as possible. The other, is that medical directors don't have a lot of time during the day, because they are busy with stupid problems caused by nutcakes—like paranoid women doctors who spend their time on cloak-and-dagger fantasy instead of medicine. Now, I demand that you leave this instant!"

Looking dumbstruck, Michele nodded, and the group moved out of the operating suite, Gil rubbing his temples, and Frank shaking his head in amazement. They were so lost in thought and numb disbelief, that none of the would-be rescuers noticed the lurking form of Buzz Merkel, peering from a distant hallway. He pulled back, out of sight, and moved as quickly as his cumbersome body could go to a back stairwell, where he headed down to the bowels of the medical center.

Buzz knew that other procedures were in progress in a different part of the hospital. Somehow the cops had been alerted, but they had walked into the wrong place, and accused the wrong people. That should keep them out of the Doc's hair for quite a while, but it would be important news to carry to the deep levels where the spy was going to get cooked.

He had overheard some of the conversation by the group outside the operating room, before they made their stupid entrance. Their comments made him understand that the woman in the chamber many levels below was a cop. Buzz had never screwed a cop before. He had never killed one either. But who knew what the night might hold?

More than a dozen floors below, The Doctor watched, as assistants did their work. Pretaska finished setting the apparatus for a new combination of fields. The unconscious woman lay on the platform, almost ready for the procedure. Earlier, they had noticed movement and had had to sedate her. She was either a typical crazy bag lady, which the Doctor doubted, or some kind of spy, because she had been trying to use a radio or pager of some sort. It would be useless, of course, with the surrounding equipment and magnetic fields, but if she was trying to call for help, she wasn't the homeless Jane Doe she had pretended to be. In any case, the radio or whatever it was now lay smashed into a hundred fragments, and the woman was lying passive, dumbly awaiting her fate.

Pretaska joined Doctor J in the adjoining control room, where he was setting the instruments at the correct frequency.

The door suddenly burst open, and a breathless Buzz Merkel came in.

"Doc . . . that woman . . . I mean that specimen, there. She's a cop! I heard 'em talkin'. Peters has got Troop and some other guys helping or something. A bunch of them and some cops just busted in on Wachman in surgery, and I think they was lookin' for this one."

The two others in the room glanced at each other.

"I don't like this, I don't like this at all," Pretaska whined. "I'm getting inspection notices from the AEC and the NRC, Schwenker is getting treated as a murder, and now this. Let's skip this one, and just get her the hell outta here."

"For once, you might have a logical thought, Peotre. I think I agree. We were right that she is a spy, but a police officer? And with others actively seeking her? I think that disposing of the body in the usual way would not be the best course. Up to now, there is nothing that would implicate us. However, another disappearance might be a problem, especially since she's a policewoman and they are looking for her. I think I might have a better idea, anyway."

A few minutes later, Helen was on her way back to the E.D., still unconscious, and with a carefully prepared set of orders attached to her chart. Pretaska had written them, but he had carefully forged the name of Ira Wachman, just as he had imitated others on various documents, like the name of Junghans on a few death certificates. Pretaska wrote a note, with the Medical Director's signature, asking Darby Waterly to take personal charge of the case, and give certain specified medications. The medicines were fairly normal, despite rather high dosages. What Waterly wouldn't know, was that the unconscious woman had already been injected with maximum doses of the same or similar drugs. Neither the first injections, nor the second ones ordered were large enough alone to cause death, but the two together would certainly prove fatal.

Waterly already had a reputation as a mediocre physician at best. The fatal overdose would be interpreted as another screw-up by the fair-haired young doctor, for he wouldn't be sharp enough to either question the orders, or know what was going on, until it was too late. In fact, Pretaska had laughed, the fool would probably accept the blame, since he wouldn't have the smarts to figure out what really happened or the confidence to believe he hadn't made an error. The autopsy would show death by overdose, Wachman would deny any part in the process, Waterly would be blamed, and the cop would be out of their hair forever. According to Merkel's report of what he saw in the operating suite, Wachman was already angry at the police and others who had made accusations. This would go even further in distracting attention that had been focused on the side-effects and by-products of the Magnes Project. Thus they sent the woman off to her fate.

Buzz got a little extra benefit. On the way back up through the tunnels, he had time to take one of his little detours. In a dark side passage he took his pleasure, before delivering her to the hallway outside Trauma Room #3, where Dr. Waterly was working. Who would know? Merkel stood by the gurney, subtly stroking the woman's thigh, until the previous case in room #3 was finished, then wheeled the stretcher in and quickly departed. No one even noticed that he had been there.

Thirty-six

Dr. Waterly knew he was spending too much time on the old man, but speed had never been his strong suit. Despite criticism from some other residents who moved through admissions like they were on an assembly line, Darby feared that he would miss something important if he didn't complete a thorough examination. Actually, conversation with the former Merchant Marine captain had been so interesting, he wasn't anxious to rush things. Nils "Salty Dog" Johnsen was suffering from an acute episode of hypersensitivity pneumonitis. He was shivering with chills, and Darby could hear respiratory rales when he pressed a stethoscope to the man's puny chest.

Weighing in at no more than ninety-five pounds, the feisty little Norwegian had most of the symptoms of chronic exposure to an antigen. This was a recurring case of occupationally-induced pathology, as Darby had diagnosed months ago. It was an instance where extensive history-taking had provided the necessary clues. Nils had apparently contracted Bagassosis, a type of occupationally induced pneumonia caused by microorganisms found in sugar cane waste. For years the cause had been missed, since it was normally a disease only contracted by sugar cane workers. But Darby had taken time to listen to the old man's stories. During one conversation, he heard Johnson brag about "naps on the cane," as a means of avoiding unpleasant work. With additional questioning, he learned that Nils spent years on a garbage trawler, hauling the waste product, Bagasse, from a sugar processing plant to a distant factory where it was converted into hog feed and mattress stuffing. "Salty Dog" would habitually sneak afternoon siestas in the hold, on top of the cane waste, not realizing he was exposing himself to the T. vulgaris and M. faeni antigens that created his lung disease.

Waterly wrote out a scrip for sixty milligrams of Prednisone QID, to last two weeks and sent the man off to his next exposure and next adventure, warning him that the corticosteroid could have behavioral affects. Salty Dog just laughed at that idea.

Shaking his head at the complete unwillingness of some folks to do what was healthy for them, and still thinking about the old man's story of a month stranded on a Tahitian island frolicking in the surf with naked native women, Darby hardly noticed Buzz Merkel rolling a gurney into the room with the next patient. This one was unconscious, so he didn't begin the verbal routine he normally used to lower the patient's anxiety and get to know them better. Nils Johnsen was only one example of the important information he often gained for the medical history while he was talking with a person. But not this time. He was going to have to rely on whatever he saw directly or could get from tests.

Distractedly, he grabbed the chart from the cart and opened it. He was surprised to find orders already there, addressed to him and signed by Dr. Wachman. Why was Wachman involved? And why was the patient here if the medical director had already examined her?

Darby swallowed. He decided it must be some kind of test. Wachman was checking up on him, to see if he could follow orders and proper procedures. The prescribed medications didn't seem unusual or tricky—although he didn't think the Demerol was necessary for an unconscious patient. Maybe it was a prophylactic measure to prevent some potential pain response. The synthetic narcotic was common for analgesia, and it looked like this woman had had some nasty lumps, though apparently not life-threatening. The other meds seemed straightforward enough. He told Carol, the assisting nurse, to get them all, including the Demerol. Darby wasn't about to contradict or modify the orders of the medical director. He was going to have trouble enough just getting through his residency, without creating powerful enemies as well. He decided to give the woman an external exam, just in case Wachman had purposely left something for him to find that wasn't covered by the previous orders. Then he would pop her full of the drugs listed, and be home free.

Carol returned with two syringes and an I.V. bag. Waterly let the nurse set the I.V., while he went over the woman's body, marking off a mental checklist as he worked. The nurse noted the label on the first syringe, and held it out to him. Waterly stepped over to the PDR and checked the dosages, just to make sure that Wachman hadn't written an overdose order. Might he have done that, just in order to test the young resident's knowledge or thoroughness? The amounts seemed within normal ranges, if a bit on the heavy side. Besides, Darby was sure Wachman wouldn't take the chance of a slip-up. If there were an overdose, the senior physician's orders would be responsible, even if Waterly shared the blame. As he returned to the exam, he ignored the RN's impatient expression. He had to be careful, even if the nurse was being pushy.

Darby knew he wasn't a superstar. He would never win the award for Most Brilliant Mind of the Century, but if he took his time, he could usually do a decent job. Most patients were glad for the time he spent with them, no matter what the fast-paced Emergency Department staff thought. He knew emergency medicine was not going to be his field, despite the residency he was serving here. Part of the reason he worked so hard to get placed in this program was that he knew it would challenge him—perhaps even beyond his abilities. But he planned to be a good doctor, no matter what the others thought about him, or how he got there. He knew the rumors, but couldn't counter them, since they never came out in the open.

The truth was, he had worked his tail off to get through med school, and had even refused offers by his family to exert their influence. This was something he had done on his own. One day, he hoped he would be able to practice humane medicine someplace where a doctor who treated his patients with respect, courtesy, and a little time, was appreciated. But first he had to survive this year, the E.D. pressure cooker, and this snake pit of a hospital. He would give Wachman's patient as much medicine as the old fart wanted him to, and get through one more day.

Beach was meeting with Michele Peters and Carl Troop in an office nearby. Troop was sitting in a chair to the side of his desk, again leafing thoughtfully through Richard Schwenker's notebook, while Gil and Michele moved chairs over to him, so they could compare notes.

"I appreciate your help," Gil said, "I know you'd be in a lot of trouble, if anyone saw us here."

"I'm already in a lot of trouble," Troop replied with a shrug. "That surprise visit to Wachman's operation is going to get dropped in my lap very shortly, I'm sure."

"Is there anything we can do?" Michele asked, guiltily.

"Yeah, get to the bottom of this!" Carl laughed. "I still believe something very wrong is going on here.

Maybe if you can prove that, I might not end up in such a tight spot."

"I dunno, Carl. I'm not seeing much new. Does anything in that notebook look different on another pass?"

"Well, I keep coming back to this 'Dr. J' thing."

"I wonder if Pretaska changed his name from something that started with a J?" Michele suggested.

"Yeah, like 'Jerk-off,' maybe?" Gil asked.

"Right," she laughed, "but there's the radiology connection again. That has to be part of this."

"Speaking of radiology," Troop commented, "take a look at this!" He held out an official looking envelope toward Gil. It had a government seal.

"Save me the trouble of demonstrating my ignorance, and tell me what it is."

"It's from the Atomic Energy Commission. They issue our Title 10 license for handling radioactive materials. The AEC is the watchdog agency that makes sure we do it all correctly. They make sure we are in compliance with the Federal Code of Regulations we have to follow for all our radiopharmaceuticals, radioisotopes, and other radioactive materials. They're supposed to see that there isn't any misuse, improper disposal, or that kind of thing. They work closely with the Nuclear Regulatory Commission. We had a little delegation from them the other day. Remember, I was meeting with you when they showed up?"

"Was that the group you passed off to Jamison?"

"Yes. But they didn't tell me their real concerns. It seemed like a routine visit at the time. Now we have this inspection report that says they weren't satisfied at all."

"What's the problem?"

"Well, in the simplest terms, there's a lot of radioactive material unaccounted for. This report includes a notice that we are about to be investigated for a significant disparity in the amount of materials we're licensed to use, and the amount we are actually getting. If their figures are correct, it's either an enormous error, or a prosecutable offense. And if it isn't an error, there is a big stockpile hidden somewhere because our disposal records don't match the purchase amounts either."

"Are you telling me that someone at Bellevue is running a separate nuclear medicine operation?" Michele questioned.

"Unless this is all botched paperwork, it would have to be something like that, at the least. But given the type of material supposedly coming in and the quantities involved, it could be even more serious than that. This unaccounted inventory represents a significant accumulation of radioactive material . . . a potentially dangerous amount."

"You can't be serious," Michele protested. "Aren't we usually talking microscopic quantities for radiologic procedures?"

"Yes, usually we're limited to relatively small amounts, though in an operation as big as we are, that can add up to a substantial quantity. But this isn't even the usual amount. It isn't usual at all. If this was another time and another country, I might be wondering if somebody was making bombs."

"Wait a second, this isn't fissionable material, is it?"

"No, but that isn't the only kind of bomb. Other kinds are possible that would be just as deadly. In this quantity, somebody could have enough stuff to create dirty tactical weapons."

"Dirty weapons?"

"Yeah, you know, conventional explosives, but a shell of radioactive material that disperses in the blast. Not such a big bang as a purely nuclear device, but you could probably kill almost as many—just a little slower, with the lasting effects of the radiation."

"I'm surprised a doctor would think of such things," Gil said, looking at Troop.

"Well, I got my nasty ideas in the armed forces of the old U.S. of A. I was trained in treatment of radiation exposure as part of my military service. In fact I was involved in a few things I'm not even supposed to talk about . . . classified stuff. Some of it I wish I'd never heard about. That's why I didn't stay. I didn't like what was going on behind the scenes. The reason I became a physician was to help and heal . . . not to be an advisor for death and destruction."

Michele looked at Carl as if she hadn't seen him before. He was showing himself as a man of greater depth than he usually let on. She smiled, apparently liking what she saw. Troop noticed her look and lowered his eyes to the desk, a rosy shade creeping up his neck.

"That might be another connection with Junghans," Gil picked up the conversation. "But we better be careful jumping to conclusions. We already made ourselves look pretty stupid that way, when we stormed the operating room. We're all pretty much on the shit list now. I think we'd better come up with something pretty quick, or we aren't going to get another chance."

"Maybe we ought to be looking at the doctors that have first names starting with J., like we were talking about the other day," Troop suggested.

"What's that?" Michele asked.

"Oh, Gil and I were talking the other day about how maybe this 'J' referred to a first name, instead of a last name. Like maybe Jerry Wesley, or John Malcolm. I also thought of Joyce Castro, who has a lot of involvement with radiation, because of her oncology work."

"You still have that big roster book?" Beach asked.

Troop pulled open a desk drawer and withdrew the BHC Administrative Directory. He slid it across the desk to Beach, who opened the volume to the third section.

"Look at this committee list," he said, pointing at one page. "If you compare the Ethics Committee and the Safety Committee, aren't there some dual memberships?"

Michele looked at the proffered listings.

"I don't know," she mumbled, "some of 'em are the same, but others are different. All these people couldn't be involved."

"Let me see this, again," Beach said. The others sat quietly, as he pored over the names. Then Gil sat up straighter. "That notebook Schwenker carried," he exclaimed.

"What?"

"That poem, or whatever . . . right there before the 'Dr. J.' reference. Give it to me," he insisted, grabbing the notebook and flipping through it.

"Here it is," he said, finding the page. "The Doctor is a doctor is not a Doctor, is a doctor is not a Doctor."

"Okay, what's the significance?" Troop asked.

"When is a Doctor not a doctor?" Gil asked intently.

"When he's asleep . . . when he's unethical . . . when he's a husband?"

"No, no," Gil shook his head, and held up the book. "Look, this manual has everybody's titles after their name. 'Michele Peters, M.D., Carl Troop, M.D., Darby Waterly, D.O.' But not everybody here is a doctor. Look at Schwenker, he's listed as Richard Schwenker, M.A."

"Yes, Master of Arts. He was an administrator, not a physician, so what?"

"So what about this one—Theodore Jamison, Ph.D.?"

"What about it?"

"So what do you call a Ph.D. around here?"

"Well, he doesn't use the title 'Doctor' if that's what you mean," Troop responded. "In fact, I think it's kind of a sore point with him. But the board made it a matter of policy that patients shouldn't be confused by us calling a Ph.D. 'Doctor' in a medical setting."

"It might also be a bit of medical elitism," Michele suggested. "We physicians are rather jealous of our prerogatives and status. I'm sure that over time the board got the message."

"Whatever," Gil went on, "but doesn't that mean that Jamison is a Doctor who isn't a doctor, but is a doctor even if he isn't a Doctor?"

"Jamison . . . Dr. J., it could fit," Troop agreed. "I've noticed a little sarcasm from him once in a while, aimed at those who hide behind the M.D. degree."

"Not without some justification," Michele added. "But I agree, there's always been some jealousy or something there. He's always putting himself in places you would normally see a doctor. I notice him at all the inservices and grand rounds, and he takes pains to show off, anytime he thinks he might know some medical fact that one of us doesn't. Truth is, sometimes he's right."

"Do you have any idea of what his Ph.D. was in?" Gil asked.

"I just assumed it was Hospital Administration."

Troop went to the bookcase again, scanning the shelves for something. As he looked, he chuckled.

"I don't think I've used anything on these shelves for a year, and now they have just what we need. Probably be years before anything is touched again. But somewhere, I remember an awards dinner, where the administrative officers were honored. I think the program book gave bios on each one. Yes, here it is."

He found a thin volume, and opened it to a section of biographical sketches.

"Okay. Theodore M. Jamison, Ph.D. Born in Utah, attended college at Brigham Young . . . here it is. Damn! It says here that he got his Masters from Arizona State in Bio-engineering, and would you believe, his Ph.D. from the U. of Pennsylvania in Nuclear Engineering."

"Nuclear engineering? Are we talking about splitting atoms . . . inventing nuclear weapons?" Michele asked.

"Well, there's a lot of stuff that has nothing to do with weapons, like power generation, metallurgy, medical technology, all sorts of stuff. But it is quite a coincidence that Jamison has that kind of background."

"I don't believe in coincidences," Beach remarked drolly. "Nine times outta ten, you can figure it out, if you don't let assumptions get in the way. For instance, when there's a lot of missing radioactive material in a hospital where the administrator happens to have a background in nuclear and bio-engineering . . . maybe he has something to do with it. And with all the other things that are happening. This is the guy who apparently didn't give the NRC boys what they needed, or they wouldn't have sent that report."

"According to this, he went back for another Master's in Health Services Administration after working for Gentech Research Corporation a few years," Troop read on, "and held administrative posts at a couple of other medical centers in Vermont and New York before coming here in '87. Oh wait, he was also an administrative officer at the Corellos Medical School in the Malvinas for a while. I guess that's the Falklands now."

"This is just too weird," said Michele, paging through some of the papers she had examined earlier from Richard Schwenker's effects. She found one slip and passed it to Beach.

"This note indicates that Richard was getting rejected from some committee. The words are a put-down, dismissing him as a non-physician, but the handwriting looks like Jamison's. And look at the notes at the bottom."

"Yes, I saw this before," Gil nodded, "but didn't make much sense of it."

"Well it looks like Richard wrote Ted's name underneath."

"Oh that's 'Ted?' I couldn't tell what the letters were."

"Yes, I think so. And there's also a note about something called the 'Magnes Project.' "

"What'd you call it—Magnes? I thought that was the abbreviation for Magnesium or something."

"No, I'm afraid not. It's the same name as I found on another page of Richard's book, and . . . and on the tag we found that Peotre had signed and attached to that generator we uncovered behind my wall."

"That means Pretaska is part of this, too."

Michele just nodded her head, eyes downward, lips tight.

"Let me see that committee list again."

Thirty-seven

The Committee was in danger of falling apart. Pretaska was openly defiant and the others were resisting. Jamison rapped his polished teak gavel for attention.

"Gentlemen, I think we have had enough of this. The Magnes Project will continue, and the earth-shaking advances it represents will make all of this furor seem irrelevant."

"Look, Jamison . . ." Roncali began, but stopped when he saw the cold stare that the man directed his way at this use of his proper name. "I . . . I mean . . . Dr. J."

"Your lack of respect is noted," Jamison interrupted. "Without my intellect and favor, none of you would carry that inflated title of which you are so proud. Because of me, you receive society's honor and respect, but don't ever forget that without this inconsequential, low-status little Ph.D., none of you would have anything!"

It was an old refrain, but a powerful one. All of the physicians gathered around the table carried the burden and secret of Jamison's role in achieving their M.D. status. Most had rationalizations for their inability to succeed without his help. For Wesley it was a criminal conviction that would have kept him out of the ranks of the medical elite. He, of course, claimed he had been innocent of the drug selling charge. Pretaska blamed prejudice against his sexuality for not getting through med school, though he never explained how that made him flunk computer-scored tests. Roncali was the only one who admitted he never would have made it without Jamison's creative modification of records. Since all had eventually completed residencies and passed the Medical Boards, there was increasing resentment at his blackmail, yet none of them would have received the Corellos medical degree without his trickery. Even the Boards had been easier for some of them, after he made available copies of original exams.

Jamison seldom pulled hard on the invisible chain, but when he made suggestions they each felt the tug. That is why they came here to Bellevue, for the most part. And in some cases he had added weight to the debt, as he protected them by hiding errors or falsifying documents to assure their safety from malpractice litigation. Eventually he had gotten them on the Safety Committee as well. A few others filled out the committee membership, but once they left the room for other business, the gatherings became secret meetings of the Magnes Project.

"Look, Dr. J," Jerry Wesley whined. "This was supposed to bring the hospital money and make you a big name in research. But nobody's gonna get nothing but grief if things keep going like this. I saw those guys from the NRC. That's the feds we're talking about."

"How dare you challenge me! You owe me your phony degree, your career, your life!"

"So what good is that gonna do me in prison, anyway? I been there once, and I ain't going back. Not for you, not for anybody."

Jamison was losing his composure now. His high forehead was mottled with rage; veins pulsed at his temple.

"You vile little ingrate! What makes you think you have a choice in the matter?"

"Screw you, Jamison! Screw you, and your magnets and your crazy theories. You try anything on me, and I'll squeal like a rat in a wringer. You got more to hide than I do. All I did was get some grades changed. You'd face murder charges."

Dr. Theodore Jamison, Ph.D. stiffened, stood up straighter, and stared at Wesley with a look of pure venom. He seemed ready to explode, but held his position, trembling with rage. Then his eyes narrowed as he seemed to make a decision. He slowly raised a hand, and nodded his head as he moved his arm, fist closed in a tight ball, hammering downward. In response, there was a spitting puff of sound from the opposite end of the room, and blood shot out of a hole in Doctor Wesley's chest. The wiry man was shoved forward, catching himself with his hands splayed out on the table. He looked down in disbelief at his life fluid pumping out onto the polished surface, then raised his eyes in disbelief to the man at the head of the table. There was another puff, and the front of Wesley's head popped open like a grotesque egg hatching. He pitched forward onto the table where a bubbling wheeze and several twitches marked the end of his life.

The others had been frozen in their places, but now jumped away from the table. Together, they swung their eyes toward the door behind Wesley's chair, where the ominous figure of Buzz Merkel stood with a dull black pistol clenched in his hand. It was fitted with a long silencer, from which a curl of smoke slowly rose toward the ceiling.

Meanwhile, in Trauma room #3, Darby Waterly, D.O., hardly looked at the computer print-out that had just been handed to him. He was feeling tired and depressed after more than twenty hours on duty. But it was more than the long hours that had him down.

He was tired of being treated like a moron and a burden. In his weary state, he was beginning to think they were right—that he wasn't really cut out to be a doctor. In his stronger moments, Darby knew they were wrong. In fact, he sometimes wondered if it wasn't the other way around, the osteopathic courses even more stringent to overcompensate for the lack of respect they received. But this wasn't one of his better times, and he was filled with self-doubt. He questioned his knowledge, training, skills, and abilities—which finally led him to question his entire vocation. Why put himself through all this? Why spend life justifying himself?

Yet despite the nurse's impatience, the implied authority of orders from the medical director, and his depressingly negative thoughts, Darby did not vary from his slow and careful examination of Jane Doe. He knew he wasn't a whiz kid, but that made him even more careful and thorough in his work. When he saw the sticky exudate from the perineal area, he made a meticulous inspection and felt sure that he was seeing male seminal fluid. Bloody discharge was mixed with the semen in a manner consistent with forcible penetration. All evidence led him toward the conclusion that this woman had been raped. Nothing in the chart gave an indication of such an event, however it appeared to be recent.

He looked at the woman's slack expression. Her face had been cleaned up a bit, and she no longer really looked like a bag lady. She looked like a normal person . . . somebody's mother, wife, daughter. Somehow she had gotten on the receiving end of a terrible list of bad things. And now he thought, mired in self-criticism, she didn't even have the luck to get a good doctor.

It was all so confusing. Rape, auto accident, dilated pupils, depressed respirations . . . it didn't add up. Or rather, it added up to something that didn't justify the orders he was preparing to carry out. There was every indication of depressed CNS function, and even Darby knew the last thing that called for was the additional depressant effect of narcotics.

The weary doctor thought about the reaction Wachman might have if he found his orders ignored or countermanded by a two-bit D.O. resident. It was a scary thought. But for that moment, looking at the woman, completely helpless, completely dependent on him and his small bit of expertise, he decided it was even more scary to think that someone would die because they had to place their trust in him.

"I want a full chem screen on this woman," he ordered. "And I want it stat!"

The nurse huffily drew the blood as directed. The order was quickly executed by the lab, which then sent the results electronically to the E.D. printer. Immersed as he was in self-doubt and weariness, at first he only glanced at the curled computer paper Carol handed him with its rows of numbers and codes. But when he saw the values, he looked more closely. The tests indicated that his patient was already stuffed to the gills with a drug chemically similar to Demerol, as well as two or three other medicines near the limits of tolerance. No wonder her respirations were so depressed. He couldn't believe what he was reading. It meant that Dr. Wachman's orders would have been an automatic death sentence for the nameless woman lying unconscious on the cart.

"I don't know how to say this," Carl mumbled, without looking directly at Michele.

They were sharing a cup of coffee in his office. He had seemed uncomfortable despite the relaxed setting, and now seemed to have found the courage to explain what was bothering him. Michele kept silent, letting him take his time, though his introductory phrase made her nervous. It didn't usually mark the start of a pleasant conversation.

"I'm sure you know Henry Walsh . . . he's got a great reputation for diagnostics."

"Of course."

"Yes, yes, of course. I've seen you at several of his lectures. Not that I'm checking up on you, or anything. I . . . I mean, in the sense of following you, or anything. I mean, of course I did your last series of checkups and all, but . . . I wasn't spying on you, or evaluating your professional development . . ."

"Are you trying to get to something, Carl?"

"Ahh, well, yes. I mean I've been giving it some thought, and I just thought maybe it would be better if . . . Or let me put it another way. I think Walsh would be a good person for you to consult about your personal medical needs . . ."

"Are you telling me you don't want to be my personal physician anymore?"

Michele saw the red that had been creeping up Carl's neck flood his cheeks and tint his ears a bright rose color. He turned toward her, looking extremely self-conscious.

"Ahh, well, I guess that's the problem. I hope this doesn't offend you or anything. But, you see, I've come to think of you as . . . as a friend. Maybe it just seems too 'personal' for me to be your personal physician."

Seeing this important administrator and skilled physician so tongue-tied, was somehow touching. Michele felt her heart melt, as she realized what was behind his words, and how difficult it was for him to say them aloud. She rose from her chair and walked over to him.

"Oh, Carl . . ." she laughed, and hugged him.

He put his arms around her, too. For a long minute they held each other close.

"I was so worried about you, Michele!"

She pulled far enough away to look straight into his

eyes. Impulsively, she pressed her lips to his. He responded eagerly, but then stepped back, out of her arms.

"Gosh, I'm sorry," he apologized. "I guess I let myself get carried away."

Michele was ready to claim responsibility for the embrace, but found herself confused. What had begun as a sympathetic hug, had become much more. Like Carl, she felt like backing away from the intimacy, but not because it had been inappropriate. Part of her wanted to respond to this kind and honest man. There was no absence of passion, either. He was attractive in a pleasant, down-to-earth way. She felt her heart thudding in her chest with enthusiasm.

Michele felt like running into his arms. But her ego-deflating experience with Peotre was still too fresh. She was too raw to give in to an impulse with such potentially far-reaching consequences. Instead she made light of the situation.

"You don't need to apologize, Carl. What's a little kiss between friends?"

She smiled and gave a little wave as she left the office. In her mind's eye she observed herself, and realized that even as she distanced herself, she was acting coy as hell. She had never been a flirt, yet she found herself adding a wink to her words, and could not help a little extra swing to her hips as she walked away, conscious that he was watching her departure.

Thirty-eight

Everything was beginning to fall apart. Dr. J knew that the die was cast now. Wesley's body would soon be found, and the idiot Merkel had brought news of the police meeting with the acting assistant medical director. Now as he listened to tapes from the hidden microphones in Troop's office, he saw that his plans were seriously compromised. The group that was meeting there was well on the way to completely exposing him.

Jamison dialed a combination on his office safe, swung the door open, and removed a thin metal box. Twenty centimeters long and eight wide, it was about the size of a checkbook and almost as thin. Arranged on the top of the box were a row of four white buttons, and a red switch, as well as a small LED display. Each button was programmed to set off an explosive device. The first two were connected to standard explosives, hidden in strategic parts of the hospital. One button was wired to charges near the Emergency Department. One was attached to explosives situated along a section of the tunnels leading to his laboratory and treatment module. The other two were designed to produce more massive and permanent effects. They would be the last resorts, but if necessary, he could make most of mid-town Manhattan uninhabitable for generations to come. He was sure that the idiots would back-off. He believed that the threat of such destruction would be too great for anyone to call his hand. Yet, he knew it was no bluff. If they didn't understand that much, he would finally have to accept failure, if not defeat. They might force him to destroy his achievement and ignore his genius, but not without serious consequences.

Jamison knew he could have been an M.D. just as easily as anyone, if life had been fair. Certainly as easily as his arrogant and disdainful father. But life had been very unfair. Part of the inequity was due to his parentage. Dr. Clarkson Heidel had achieved notoriety because of his murderous tendencies rather than his healing skills. He poisoned no less than seven relatives to gain an inheritance, killing three before he aroused suspicions. His illegitimate son, James, had to carry not only the stigma of being a bastard, but also the burden of being the son of an acknowledged, if unconvicted murderer. He had been forced to move on repeatedly, as rumors of his parentage followed him. Eventually, he had been forced to change his name. He used his first name, James, and turned it into his last name, Jamison. Finally, he could begin to construct a new life, as he ceased to live under the perpetual cloud of his father. Not that he was really free. The old man had used his money for a series of appeals that finally wore out the prosecution. Despite the general acceptance of his guilt in a double poisoning, the old man was let loose. Yet even after the loss of reputation and status, he refused to "lower himself" sufficiently to accept James. In Clarkson Heidel's mind, the boy was without value or honor.

In time, James completed his education and began to accumulate power. He had proven his superior intellect repeatedly . . . to everyone except his father. Dozens of physicians owed their careers to his favor, and hundreds to his largesse. If they would only let him be, he could show them that the most profound advances in science and medicine could come from a *mere* Ph.D.! But once again, they were uniting forces to defeat him; to exclude him because he wasn't a member of their pretentious club, his father's arrogant fraternity. But they would not triumph. They would only succeed in bringing destruction down upon their heads. Technology always had the upper hand.

Of course, he expected that no one would believe his warnings. Life had taught him that he would never be treated with the importance and respect he deserved, anymore than his father had ever recognized him as the brilliant young man he was. They would only understand if they actually experienced his power. Even that had not worked with his father. The terrible old man died when Jamison injected a lethal dose of insulin into his vein. But even as the hormone was rushing into his body, knowing he was about to die at the hands of the one he had discounted, the evil old reprobate had spit into his bastard son's face.

Jamison didn't know if he could expect that kind of unrepentant resistance from the functionaries and slaves of the system. He had prepared a message outlining his "arrangements." They constituted a threat, but only if his warning was ignored. He had left the details in an envelope addressed to the policeman who had caused so much of this trouble, along with the woman, Peters. But the message would undoubtedly be ignored, unless accompanied by a demonstration. It was unfortunate that it had to come to that, but it was necessary.

Jamison held the control box in hands which were trembling slightly with anticipation. He flicked the switch on one end of the slim controller, activating the device. The computer chip inside was programmed for a three minute delay. This time gap between completing one of the four circuits and the actual detonation was to give him time to distance himself from the area. That would not be necessary for this explosion. The first charges were hidden in the developing room of the Radiology Unit, near the Emergency Department and the Main Lobby. He was two floors and almost a block away . . . almost at the limits of the detonator's broadcast range. The tiny LED screen confirmed that the device was operational, displaying a row of small circles to represent the four explosive charges. That meant all were armed and within range of the transmitter. He took two deep breaths, exhaling slowly to calm himself, then firmly and resolutely reached out to press the first button. The letters next to the first symbol on the LED display changed from "act" for "activated" to "det" for "detonated," and the tiny box blinked out of existence.

Thirty-nine

Gil looked up and was surprised to see a black giant standing in front of him. Then he saw Frank in the shadow of the man, and realized it was Monk Weems, the stationary engineer that had offered to help search the immense hospital center for Helen. He and Terranova seemed to be getting along well together.

"Whatcha got?" he asked the pair.

"Don't know if it's important," Frank said, "But Monk found something in one of the tunnels. Didn't you say that group of animal rights weirdos were missing somebody?" Frank asked.

"Yeah, but I haven't seen them since that day."

"Well, Monk and his guys know the tunnels under Bellevue pretty good. In one real outta-the-way place he found this." Frank held out a brown paper bag. "It was too dark to get a good look, Gil, but he says it looked like there had been a struggle."

Gil dumped the contents on top of the other debris covering his desk. There were several pieces of crumpled paper that looked like old student notes, and some torn clothing, including the ripped halves of a woman's brassiere. It was shiny white material, with little edgings of lace and quite large. The men avoided each other's eyes as Gil examined it.

"Are they missing anybody that's . . . uh, kinda . . . big?" Frank mumbled.

"They didn't say anything about that," Gil shook his head, "Maybe it was somebody else. Don't they get homeless people hiding out down there once in a while?" He looked at the Bellevue engineer.

"Oh Yeah," Weems replied, "lotsa times. But they don't wear no fancy clothes like that. An' I foun' this, too."

The big man stepped forward and dropped something on Gil's desk. It looked like a necklace. Gil picked it up to examine the piece of jewelry. It was actually a medallion on a chain. The metal piece had an animal face on its front, rubbed shiny from handling, and the letters SAKRED printed on the reverse.

"Tunnels . . ." Gil spoke almost to himself, "with lime and mold and fungus." He looked up now, at Monk and Frank. "That has to be where Schwenker was killed."

"In the tunnels?"

"There's something down there," he said, nodding at them, "And it isn't just tunnels. There's something else. I think we'd better find it before somebody else gets killed."

"That somebody else better not be Helen, or I'm gonna get the bastards that did it, and they'll end up at the bottom of tunnel six feet underground," Frank growled.

"Speaking of underground, are there any maps, or diagrams of these tunnels?" Gil asked, looking at Weems.

"Naw, at least not any worth a damn. They been tearing down and building up for so long, they don't know what all's underneath anymore. But I know them pretty well. I can take you down there."

"Thanks for your offer," Beach held up his hand, "But we can't take that risk. You could get hurt down there, and . . ."

The big man's face slowly spread into a grin, and

Frank scrunched his face into a wry expression. Gil stopped, looked again at the giant of a man, and nodded.

". . . Yeah. I guess that doesn't make much sense, does it? Well, I tell you what. You can take us part way. But if there's any trouble, you stay out of it. This is our job. You can show us the way, but that's it."

The others continued to smile, but agreed to Gil's conditions.

"I'm going too!" a voice announced from the doorway. The men turned to see Michele Peters standing there, looking better than she had in days. The kerchief on her head was smaller now and only covered a small part of her hair, like a stylish headband. Her skin color had improved, and she stood with a posture that suggested energy as well as challenge.

Gil started to protest, but never got the first syllable spoken. Peters spewed out a torrent of words describing the logic of her participation, the sexist prejudice that refusal would represent, the capabilities and skills she would bring to the task, and the right she felt to be there that could not be denied. When she ran down, several minutes later, Gil and the others stood in silent awe, mouths slightly agape.

Despite his misgivings, Gil agreed when Michele added a final point about the advantage of having a doctor along, for Helen's sake. He weakly tried to save face by assailing her with the same warnings and conditions he had given Monk and the others. He felt like the group was humoring him when he got no disagreement, but let it go. They agreed to meet at a service entrance of the Hospital Center, where they wouldn't be seen by those who had already forbidden them entry.

As soon as the others left, Gil checked his weapon, a nine millimeter automatic, and put it in his belt holster. He also slipped a .25 caliber auto pistol into his ankle holster for insurance. It was small, under five inches long and weighing less than a pound, but had a six shot magazine and could do the job if he lost his main weapon. He didn't expect violence, but believed in being prepared. When backed into a corner, even rabbits were known to attack.

Apparently, he wasn't the only one who believed in being prepared. When he met the small group at the service entrance, Frank was carrying a twelve-gauge shotgun, as well as his usual weapon, a Glock 17 nine millimeter automatic. Monk Weems even carried a huge monkey wrench that must have weighed five pounds.

"Just in case anything needs fixing," he said with a sly grin, hefting the tool like a battle axe.

When a loud voice sounded, Michele nearly jumped an inch off the ground, and Frank wrenched his neck, jerking around to see where the sound was coming from.

"Hold it right there! Don't anybody move!"

A figure stood a few yards away, braced in textbook police firing stance, a big black automatic pistol held in a two-handed grip pointed right toward them. It looked like a Springfield, but Gil couldn't tell from that distance. However, he could tell by a slight trembling of the barrel that the man holding it was jittery.

"What in the hell do you think you are doing?"

It was Jeff Corleski, the detective from the Thirteenth Precinct who had been assigned to work with them, prior to things going awry.

"You know you aren't even supposed to be here, Beach."

"I know Jeff, but things have changed."

"I guess so. The body of a Dr. Wesley was just dumped out a second-story window. He was dead from bullet wounds before he took the dive. You look like you're ready to take on the Medellin drug cartel. I can't let you in, you know."

"The truth is, Jeff, you couldn't stop us if it came to

that. But I'd rather you understood, 'cause I think you'd back us up, if you knew what was going down."

The other detective looked from one member of the group to the other. Besides the bristle of weapons, he saw a look in their eyes that was hard and unyielding. There was a long tense moment before he spoke. He kept his weapon trained on them.

"Okay, so convince me. What's happening?"

Gil didn't have a chance to reply, before there was a flicker and flash of the floodlights bathing the entrance, and a rumbling vibration of the ground. Corleski glanced around anxiously, weapon trembling in his tense grip. Somewhere in the distance a klaxon-like alarm began sounding. Gil continued talking over its insistent bleat.

"Easy, Detective, easy. You've known me for a while, Jeff, so I hope you can take some of this on trust. We have evidence that there's an illegal laboratory under this hospital. We know that there have been several murders there, and maybe a lot more. We don't know how many are involved, but it's more than a few. From the way they've been operating so far, Jeff, life doesn't seem very important to them. Which means it's critical that we go down there before they get any further with something they call the Magnes Project."

Corleski looked nervously from person to person, his brow furrowed, then back at Beach.

"What's that alarm?" he finally asked.

"It's the hospital disaster alert," Michele answered. "It's part of our federal preparedness set-up. It only goes off to initiate the disaster plan. And from the ground movement we just felt, I don't think this is a drill."

It wasn't a drill. There was good reason for a disaster plan. The blast had been centered in the Radiology Department's first-floor developing room, where a potent chemical bomb had been wired inside the housing of the film developer. The force of the explosion was hardly weakened by the hollow wall construction that partitioned off the unit. The surge of fire blew sheetrock walls away like paper, maintaining its force to collapse the first heavily solid structure it encountered, which happened to be the entire front side of the main lobby. Two clerks and a receptionist in attached cubicles died immediately, along with five of the derelicts that had taken up places along the wall. Fifteen others were injured. Some of them would not live out the day. In the smoking debris, a small plastic name tag lay bent and melted. It read "L. Wapple—Admissions."

The explosion also moved through the opposite walls, snuffing the life from three patients waiting in the hallway, a radiology technician, and a teenage candystriper named Piper, who had the misfortune of delivering lab slips at just the wrong time. Five others avoided immediate death, but were simultaneously slammed down by the force of the blast and doused in a caustic solution of chemicals from the developing tanks, spit out at them by the explosion. It was like being hit with a hurricane of acid. The harsh screams from those whose flesh was burning and peeling, mixed with the soft moans and death rattles of others buried in the rubble.

Forty

Detective Corleski shifted from one foot to the other, like he was standing on hot coals. He swung his weapon slowly from side to side, as if trying to decide who would be the first target. Just then, a figure in a grime-coated suit appeared by the door. It was Carl Troop. Now Corleski was even more confused. He started to swing the gun toward Troop, but quickly brought it back to bear on the armed group before him.

"Carl! What happened?" Michele blurted out.

For a moment the acting assistant medical director said nothing, just shaking his head from side to side, new lines etched in his forehead and around his eyes.

"Whatever we guessed, I think it's worse," he finally said, holding out a manila envelope toward Beach. "He blew up half the building already, and he left this for you."

Gil looked at the proffered envelope, and then at Corleski.

"What's it gonna be, Jeff?"

The other man looked like he was going to pop a blood vessel. Then he took a deep breath and the tension began to ease from his stance. Finally he shrugged.

"Oh screw it."

As he lowered his gun, there were audible sighs of relief from the assembled group.

Gil took the envelope and removed a folded piece of

paper from inside. There was a message printed carefully in a perfectly regular, almost machine-like hand, every letter squared, exact and precisely drawn. He stared at it for some time, then slowly crumpled the paper in his hand.

"The lab boys aren't going to like you doing that to a piece of evidence, my man," Frank commented wryly.

"If we don't get this guy quick, it isn't going to matter."

"What does the thing say?" Michele asked.

"It's a warning."

"From Jamison?"

Gil nodded.

"The explosion, it wasn't the only one he has rigged, is it?" Troop asked, but it was more of a statement than a question.

"I'm afraid it's even worse than that."

"Oh God, not the nuclear material?"

Again, Gil nodded.

"But he said he's only interested in the good of mankind. He said he doesn't want to hurt anybody," Troop offered.

"What do you think?" Michele asked, looking at Beach.

"I think he's a lunatic."

"Maybe he means it," Troop suggested, "maybe he doesn't want to hurt anybody. After all, he thinks he's a doctor. You know, the Hippocratic Oath and all that?"

"Yeah. That's probably why he says he might release a blast of radioactive shit that will make most of Manhattan uninhabitable for the next ten generations. The fruitcake says he'll do it, if we don't let him go. Otherwise, New York City is gonna be sort of a 'Chernobyl West.' Sound normal to you?"

"Right. I guess there isn't a way to know for sure what he might do."

"But if this is as big as you say, maybe you need help," Corleski said with a grimace.

"Thanks Jeff. I think it's big, alright, but once we get to the guy, I don't expect much direct resistance. If he doesn't blow us all to hell before we get him, we shouldn't need a SWAT team to take him."

"What you can do, though," Michele suggested, "is alert the authorities to start evacuation procedures."

"Is there somebody official to call?" he asked.

"Better contact the Federal Emergency Management Administration," Michele suggested, referring to the process that was designed to initiate disaster preparedness procedures.

"Look, I can take care of that," Carl Troop offered. "Although from the sound of that alarm, somebody may have already done it. That's usually only activated from the Emergency Operations Center, which only goes into action once the process is already started."

"Look, Gil, don't make me feel like the last kid chosen for the sandlot baseball game," Corleski complained.

"Okay, Jeff," Beach finally agreed. "We might be able to use another cop. There are several potential accomplices in this deal. And I might need somebody to keep this other crazy doctor off my back!"

Michele Peters made a wry face, and smirked at him. Then her expression became more serious as she turned to Troop. The expression on his face telegraphed his feelings.

"I . . . I wish you wouldn't go, Michele."

She stepped closer to him, took his hand in hers, and pulled him far enough away from the others to speak privately. She stared into his eyes, an intimacy in the intensity of her gaze.

"I have to go, Carl. And don't worry, I'll be okay. I've got a whole group of big strong men to watch out for me."

There was a hint of sarcasm in the last phrase.

"Maybe that's what worries me," he smiled.

"Not to worry. Look, Carl, I'm afraid I've been a little coy with you. That isn't my usual way. I'm not sure how to say this, but I hope that after I get back, we can spend some time together. I . . . I like you, Carl. I . . ."

Now she was the one who seemed tongue-tied. As for Carl, he was beaming. He raised his index finger and touched it to her lips, stopping her words.

"Enough said," he laughed. Then, more seriously, "Just be careful, okay? I'll do what I can from here."

She heard one of the group call to her, that they had to get moving. She squeezed his hand and rejoined the others, turning her head to offer one more suggestion.

"Carl, make sure they know about the radiation hazard. That involves a lot of steps that might not be required in other disaster scenarios."

Forty-one

The disaster was not merely a scenario. Now it was reality. Dr. J watched the panic and confusion displayed on a monitor that received its signal from a security camera mounted high on one of the undamaged walls of the main lobby. The picture was black and white and carried no sound, so he didn't hear the screams and calls for help of the injured, the shouts and orders of those trying desperately to help, the sobs and moans of the devastated and the dying. He watched as dust turned the air to a hazy purgatory of destruction, pain, and dying.

He was not moved. Most of the victims were mere rabble, hardly worth interest, much less compassion. They came, they clogged the system, and they eventually died—often rather ugly and painful deaths. His actions had caused little change, except to make their disgusting existences a trifle shorter. If a few medical personnel were taken along with the riffraff, so much the better. Some of them were probably the same scum that had turned up their noses at him, because he wasn't an M.D. . . . just like Father. If they died, it would be no loss. In fact, the idea gave him a little tickle of pleasure.

Those who would hunt him and destroy the works of his genius needed a clear message and an unmistakable warning. If they persisted, the message would be still more dramatic and exact an even greater cost. His monitoring room had tapped the security feeder line, so he could see everything they could see in their fifteen screen security center, and several additional areas where he had installed his own cameras. He flipped switches to access other camera views of the hospital center, looking for signs that his warning had not been properly heeded. His hand went into a pocket of his coat, to caress the remote triggering device. Strange as it might seem, part of him almost hoped that they would keep coming.

Forty-two

"We have to keep going," Gil told the others. He saw readiness in his partner Frank, and the engineer Monk. Jeff looked keyed up on emotion, pounding one fist into another repeatedly. Gil didn't know the Thirteenth Precinct detective as well as his fellow personnel in the Ninth, and hoped he wouldn't act like a cowboy or worse, someone who choked under pressure. Michele was clearly determined, but a couple of times, when she thought no one was watching, he saw her give a little shiver and swallow. It was probably the normal fear of someone not used to going in on police raids.

"You sure you want to be in on this?" he asked again. "I'd be just as happy if you waited."

"We covered that," she said firmly. "I'm going."

He knew arguing was fruitless, so he turned to lead the group into the building, where they separated from Dr. Troop at the elevators. He gave a squeeze to Michele's hand, then headed for a telephone, while the others piled in the first car to arrive. Riding in it was a dietary aide who was so unnerved by the sight of their weapons that she ran off down the hall, leaving her food-laden snack cart on the elevator. Frank lifted a corner of the cloth covering the cart's goods, removed a piece of chocolate cake and munched on it as the doors closed. His expression was so innocent, that Gil saw Michele fighting to quell a giggle. He recognized it as another sign of nerves. Was it the radiation threat, he wondered, or something she wasn't telling?

They gathered together at the second basement, following Monk's lead through passageways narrow and lined with huge bundles of pipes and cables. Some of the thick ends hung down, like predators waiting for victims. There was a dank and moldy smell.

During his service in the Marine Corps, Gil had occasionally been shipped out on a sea-going vessel. He had never liked the idea of riding below the water-line, and he had a similar uncomfortable feeling as they worked their way deeper into the roots of the great hospital center, many feet underground, far from any natural light or air. Sounds were magnified by the concrete walls and narrow spaces, including the whoosh of forced air coming from irregularly spaced air vents in overhead duct work. Wire-caged bulbs provided adequate lighting for a few yards, then seemed to fade away a short distance further on, so that there were shadowy reaches in between. Holes were punched in walls, large sheets of paint peeling, and cryptic notations scrawled here and there, arcane graffiti of decades past. Doorways to unused areas looked like dark mouths ready to suck in the unwary. One hall was painted with strange dark murals of jungle beasts and foliage, the colors faded and worn by time. In places there was brackish standing water, wood pallets serving as makeshift walkways, even dark pools of unknown depth where water had filled a previously excavated hole. It was easy to let imagination run wild.

Eventually, there was a spot where the lights had burned out, and they had to go a few yards in near-darkness. When Gil looked back, he noticed Michele had stopped, and stood with a hand supporting herself against the wall.

Gil moved back to where she stood. He noticed that she was breathing rapidly, and looked pale and sweaty.

"What's the matter? Are you okay?"

"Yes, yes. I'm okay. My health is fine."

"You don't look it. Is there something else?"

She looked at him more closely. Her eyes searched his face, and seemed to accept what they saw. She took a deep breath.

"I'm sorry, Gil. You're right, I shouldn't leave you wondering. Look, I know this sounds ridiculous, but ever since I was a kid, I have this unreasonable fear . . . of the dark."

When Gil didn't laugh at her confession, she seemed encouraged to go on.

"It's a phobia, I guess. It's embarrassing, but dark places absolutely terrify me. I suppose you think I'm a complete child."

"Actually, I think you are a pretty neat woman. I don't exactly understand this phobia thing, but I've had a couple of things that scared the shit out of me, that most people wouldn't understand at all."

Gil wasn't about to bare his soul to the woman, but he felt a shiver of memory at his own words. Certain things and places still had that power over him. They might not be phobias, but he could understand a gut reaction to certain objects of fear that went far beyond what might be considered rational, or even normal. Apparently the few words he had already spoken were enough. Or maybe what he hadn't said was just as important.

"Thanks, I think I'll be okay now. I guess it helps, just that somebody else might understand."

She stood up, set her shoulders, and marched into the dark passageway. Gil followed.

"Look at this," Weems said when they rejoined the group. He was in a squatting position, staring at the floor under one of the lights. Gil bent down to look, and saw faint footprints in the fine dust of the seldom-traveled tunnel. There were too many impressions to have been made by one person.

"Light's a little dim, but I can tell these are new."

"Didn't you say that homeless folks sometimes got in down here?" Frank asked.

"Yeah, but I don't figure this is any o' them. Look's like new shoes to me."

"What are you, an Indian tracker?" Frank chuckled.

"Don't be too quick to laugh, Mister Deee-tective. I know you white folks think all us people of color are the same, but I happen to be a quarter Iroquois . . . for a fact! I have a lot of friends that are full-blooded Indian, and they taught me a thing or two, believe it!"

"Can you figure out how many people made these?"

"Yeah, I figure at least three. But two of em's either got awful little feet, or they're women."

Gil looked toward Michele Peters. Her expression was unreadable, but she hadn't missed the man's words. As for Gil, his mind was doing its standard sort and file process. If the footprints were those of their quarry, Jamison might have a female accomplice or two. Gil thought about his earlier list of suspects, and once again came to the name of Dr. Joyce Castro. He knew Michele wouldn't like that, but he had to stay objective, and no one could be beyond suspicion.

"It looks like we're on the right track," Corleski said.

"Maybe, maybe not," Gil cautioned, and moved ahead.

Monk now produced a large flashlight seemingly out of nowhere. Gil wondered what else the giant man had hidden in the huge pockets of his coveralls, but was glad for the engineer's foresight, as well as his keen eye. They walked on in silence, Monk leading the way now, and descended another level into the subterranean maze. Then the footprints disappeared.

"No more tracks," Monk said, straightening.

"What did they do, just disappear?" Frank asked, looking a little spooked by the development.

"Nothin' magic," Weems replied calmly, "Just no more dust. So no more tracks."

"Is this an area that gets used regularly, then?"

"Looks that way, Mr. Beach," Monk answered. "But no regular use is supposed to be going on down here. Nothing regular happened down here for years."

Gil stepped ahead, and led the group farther. The light was better here, and Michele walked behind him, apparently handling her fears better now.

They came to a series of four doors off the main corridor, two on each side. The detectives unholstered their sidearms, and inched along the wall to the first set of doors. There were no windows to reveal what was on the other side. Frank took the door on the left, pulling it open to reveal a small room filled with large pipes and valves—the wet heat indicating that it was some kind of transfer station for the steam pipe system that ran throughout the hospital center.

Gil reviewed his crew's status again. Monk was unruffled. Michele seemed alright, and well back from the action. Frank was in that determined, single-minded mode that many cops assume during a raid. Every door they approached set the tension level a notch higher. Jeff looked less settled than some of the others, and kept looking around at the walls, like he was trapped. Yet, when Gil asked if he was okay, he denied any problem. As they were whispering, Frank pushed ahead and yanked open the next door. There was a crashing sound, and suddenly the sound of gunfire echoed loudly in the narrow space, nearly deafening them.

Gil turned to see that it was Corleski firing. He reached out and shoved the man's arm down.

"Stop it, Jeff. Stop!"

In the stillness following the sudden sound, Gil could see Frank with his shotgun leveled at the door, smoke rising slowly from the barrel, and Monk with a nasty looking little Saturday Night special that had appeared from the same secret place as the flashlight had earlier. The black man hadn't fired, but was holding the gun at ready in one hand, his big wrench in the other. The cause of the first crashing sound appeared to be a stack of ancient metal dinner trays that had cascaded to the floor when Frank opened the door of what now was revealed as a storage closet. Inside, a broken shelf unit seemed to be the reason the trays were set to fall at the first opportunity. Now several of the shelves were tilted, punched out of place by bullets from Jeff's wild fusillade, and a large hole in the back wall testified to the power of Frank's shotgun.

Gil wasn't sure whether to laugh or get angry. But as he tried to decide how to react to the chaotic burlesque of moments before, he heard a voice calling from inside the next door.

"Don't shoot," the small voice whimpered. "Please don't shoot! You can't kill us just for this."

It was the voice of a woman. It sounded familiar. Gil stepped forward, gun at ready, and turned the doorknob, opening the door just an inch or two. He stepped back and motioned to Frank, who stood against the wall and shoved the door open with a foot, while Gil held his weapon in firing position. There was a little squeal of fear from inside the room. He edged forward until he could see a group of three people inside, a man and two women. They weren't doctors.

"Oh damn!"

"What?" Frank asked, tentatively lowering his weapon, as he saw Gil drop his.

"It's the goddamn animal-lovers."

"No shit?"

Regina Allistaire, the leader of the small SAKRED group wasn't acting much like a leader, shaking and whining in a corner behind the other two. Her followers looked dazed. The man was holding a small crowbar, which he dropped quickly when he saw Gil staring at it and realized it might look like he was holding a weapon. The tool's purpose was clear when the detective scanned the room. Several files had been pilfered, the crowbar apparently used to pry them open. The second woman held out a sheaf of papers, like she was turning over jewels she had heisted. At this point Dr. Peters had stepped into the room, and had the papers pushed toward her. She took them out of the woman's trembling hands as Gil spoke.

"We ought to cuff you, and take you in right now," he shouted. "I'd manacle you to the pipes until we're ready to go back, but this place is a lot more dangerous than you could possibly realize. So you are to consider yourselves under arrest, and proceed as quickly as you can to the exit. Tomorrow morning at 10:00 AM sharp, you are to present yourselves at the Thirteenth Precinct, NYPD, where Detective Corleski will decide what to do with you. But right now, just lay down everything you have in your possession that doesn't belong to you, and get your crazy asses out of here."

The wide-eyed SAKRED group members at first looked confused. Then the man and woman in front started inching toward the door, finally moving quickly out and down the passage. Regina Allistair, seeing that she was about to be left behind with the pack of armed men, trotted after them, moaning quietly.

"I can't believe this!" Michele blurted out.

"Aww, I've seen crazier nuts than those wimps," Frank said.

"No, not them . . . these papers."

"What about them?" Gil asked.

"Well, they're original copies of medical school exams, medical board exams, stuff like that."

She walked over to the cabinets and examined the drawers.

"These were sealed by Ted Jamison's order, but he should never have had access to this kind of thing in the first place. Some of them are from the Corellos Medical School in the Falklands where he worked for a while."

"Are they current?"

"No, but I can tell that they aren't copies released after the fact, either. They have seals and everything, so they were the originals from these particular years. I see dates that cover a period around when I completed medical school."

"Who are your contemporaries here?"

"Well, I guess that would be . . . maybe Roncali and Wesley. I suppose Peotre . . . I mean Pretaska, could have been in school then, too."

"Where did they do their medical training?"

"I don't know about all of them, but Roncali was . . . oh shit, yes. Both he and Wesley went to Corellos. Maybe the others did too, I wouldn't be surprised."

"And maybe we know how Jamison recruited some support."

"It's hard to believe. I mean, fixed medical exams?"

"Any harder to believe than killing homeless folks in some kind of experiment, or threatening a nuclear dusting?"

"No, I guess you're right. I just have this kind of childish faith in the medical profession to maintain its integrity. I know there are some idiots who make it into the ranks, but I hate to think that the whole process got subverted."

"Yeah, I've lost a few myths, too."

"Speaking of myths," Frank announced, "Here's a

whole file cabinet labeled 'Magnes.' Isn't that the project those guys were supposed to be working on?"

"Damn. I wish we had time to check it out, but it's too late for that now. Does 'Magnes' mean anything to anybody?"

Michelle answered, "If I remember correctly, Magnes was a shepherd or something, and his staff got sucked against a rock, which turned out to be lodestone. That's why we have the word 'magnet.'"

"Is there any relationship between magnetism and radiation?" Gil asked.

"A relationship, yes. What exactly it is, nobody can say," Michele answered. "Someday, scientists hope to have a so-called 'unified theory' that will explain them both, but for now it's still something of a mystery."

"So no connections?"

"Well, yes, theoretically. The only practical one I can think of right now, is that the Radiology/Nuclear Medicine Department includes both radiation and the MRI technology."

"MRI—isn't that kind of a fancy X-ray, like a CAT scan?"

"Well, it isn't really X-ray at all, but it serves a similar function. It stands for Magnetic Resonance Imaging, and has to do with the 'spin' produced in certain cell structures by a strong magnetic field."

"So what now?" Frank interjected. "We gonna have a class on doctor stuff, or are we gonna get these guys?"

"Well, it's more technology than 'doctor stuff,'" Michele protested.

"Yeah, but all this fits with Jamison's kind of doctor, doesn't it?"

"Physics, bio-engineering, technology . . . that's him alright," Michele agreed. "Sometimes I've wondered if he would have preferred a hospital with nothing but machines and computers."

"If he carries out the threats he put in that letter," Gil replied, "that might be all that would survive."

"So where do we go now?" Jeff asked tersely.

"This area of the tunnels is being used regularly, and it isn't those animal rights folks using 'em. This office is full of Jamison's stuff, things he didn't want anybody to know about. If I were him, I would keep that close to my other stuff. I think we may be close to Magnes, whatever it is. What did you say Magnes means, Doc?"

"Magnes is a name in a myth about the discovery of magnetic materials, but it comes from the same root word as 'Magnitude,' or 'Magnificent.' It has to do with size or greatness."

"Well, I gotta say . . . I don't think this thing is real great, but something tells me it's pretty damn big."

Forty-three

Magnes could not die!

Dr. J was enraged. After all the years of struggle and truly herculean effort; after overcoming monstrous obstacles as well as mastering difficult and demanding disciplines; after maintaining elaborate masquerades, and accumulating through immense force of will the resources necessary to bring the Magnes Project to fruition; after all this the entire project was in danger of being lost. Everything could be for nothing because these fools counted the lives of worthless derelicts more important than that of a great mind.

His present day antagonists were just like his father had been. Again, as so many times before, a stark image came to mind of his last attempt at parental recognition. Despite repeated rejections over the years, Jamison had encountered his father one last time on the week that he had received his Ph.D. degree. His father was a crumbling wreck, kept alive by constant mechanical support. The bitter man's wealth had shrunken to a fraction of its former size, not that James expected any inheritance. All he wanted was a modicum of recognition, an iota of respect. Always before, he assumed that education would be the key. If he could gain a doctorate, he would finally get the man's grudging respect. He was let into the old man's chambers, after an impassioned plea to the house staff convinced them to admit him against orders. The restriction to "family visitors only" was intended to exclude the illegitimate son. The fact that he now introduced himself as "Doctor" seemed to make a difference to the servants.

A hospital bed was set up in the master bedroom, with all the necessary medical equipment to maintain the arrogant patriarch's processes despite his inability to carry on life functions independently.

"Who is it?" croaked the frail figure on the bed.

His son walked closer.

"It's me, father . . . James, your son."

"Get out of here," the old man managed to wheeze, "You aren't my son. I have no son!"

"Yes you do, father. And now I am a doctor, too."

". . . A doctor? Wha . . . what kind of doctor?"

"I just received my Ph.D. in . . ."

"Ph . . . You're no doctor! You call that stupid excuse for a degree a reason to call yourself a DOCTOR?"

Despite his fragile state, the old man managed to shout at the trembling figure before him.

"You're no doctor! You're an idiot. And don't think you'll get a penny when I die. You aren't even mentioned in my will. You're just a bastard. If abortion wasn't illegal back then, you'd never have been born to give people trouble. You aren't my son. You're a piece of scum that should have ended up on the office floor."

James grabbed the frail man by his nightshirt, pulling him close to his face. But words failed him. As he held the man who refused to be his father, trembling with a helpless mix of anger and shame, the fearless old reprobate managed a final insult. He worked his jaw, like he was searching for a word, then spit into his son's face.

Jamison shivered with the memory, shaking his head to bring himself back to the present. The present situation had triggered the recollection, carrying the same sense of powerlessness and rejection. No matter what he did, it wouldn't count. They would sacrifice his genius for the sake of street scum and arrogant MD's that were hardly more than trained chimpanzees. They didn't know it, but they were rejecting the hope of mankind. He was the son of a new age of technology and they were dismissing him.

Now, on top of everything, this little group of fools had the arrogance to keep on coming after him. Despite his warning, despite the demonstration of his power, they didn't have the sense to back off. He decided that would prove to be a fatal error. Following his father's terrible insult, Jamison had injected the man with a fatal dose of insulin. The old despot had stared him down, even as he pushed the syringe into the I.V. tubing, but he had died. And these adversaries would die as well. The video cameras didn't track beyond the area of his archive room, so he wouldn't be able to watch their end, but just a little further down the corridor was a sector perfectly suited to become their final resting place, an eternal sarcophagus of stone and concrete. All he had to do was to wait until they passed beyond the range of the last camera. At their average speed of walking, which he had confirmed by timing them again, they would be perfectly situated approximately four and one half minutes from now, so that his next explosive charge would entomb them forever.

For a moment he allowed himself a small draught of hope. If he stopped them there, he might not have to detonate the third and fourth charges that were set to destroy the wonderful machines and magnificent apparatus of his experiments. But then he plunged into soul darkness again, as he realized the pursuit would not end merely because he terminated this group. Others would come. He had no choice, but to destroy the interlopers along with his priceless work. If all he cared about were saving his apparatus, he could leave the lab alone, but then others might benefit from his loss. He would not allow that. He had sacrificed too much in his life. They would not steal this too.

He was becoming certain that ultimately, he would have to explode the final two devices, along with the radioactive material surrounding them. At one time he would have hesitated to release such devastation, but now he knew that it was probably better that way. Better that the earth be cleansed, if it could not receive his gifts. Human filth would be affected, but the technology would remain. After the last man died, computers would still sit unmarred, the servo-mechanisms would continue to operate, the broadcast media standing ready for new masters to use them. If the new controllers did not do better, they would also end up as dust, and the machines would still go on, generation after generation . . . until eventually they found someone once again as worthy of them as he had been.

He sat across from the security monitors, a glazed look in his eyes, the remote detonator cradled in his hands. He watched as the group of would-be captors moved from the archive room, down the tunnel and out of sight. He stared down at his watch and counted off the minutes.

Monk continued to "walk point" ahead of the others, though Gil now kept position close behind. After a series of turns, the tunnel straightened. The dim light only allowed vision to penetrate a few yards ahead, to the next hanging bulb and its limited aura of light. Weems turned to Gil and asked a question.

"What say we move a little faster?"

"Faster? That could be dangerous, Monk, if there are any side shafts. It could make us vulnerable to ambush."

"Hey, I'm a vet, too. I don't know all of these here tunnels, but I knows there's nothing along this one for a ways. It just goes straight, with no side tunnels. Nobody can ambush us if they've got no place to come from. If this is as important as you say, maybe we could double time it—at least down to the next section."

"I guess you're right," Gil agreed. He hoped nobody was expecting his little group at all, but the less time they used, the less chance of any more nasty shocks.

"Come on everybody, we're gonna try to make up some time," he called to those behind and set off with Monk at a trot.

The decision was a life-saving one. The group of cops and hospital staff had only jogged along for a few minutes when Weems stopped short.

"Oops," was all he had time to say. Before anyone had a chance to ask what he meant, there was a tremendous thunderclap, and they were all thrown in a heap on the dirty floor. It was minutes before Gil could make out anything. Even then it was with his ears, fingers, and nose, rather than his eyes, because they were now in total darkness. But this blackness wasn't like the gentle dark of nighttime in the city, diluted by countless small sources of light, however dim. This almost felt like black oil, viscous, slippery, and pervasive. Maybe it was just a trick of the mind, but the dark seemed to have weight, pushing in at his eyes and face. He could taste dust swirling in the air, and smell a sour mixture of ozone, burned explosive, chalky concrete, and clay dust. At first he couldn't hear anything over the ringing in his ears. Then gradually he began to make out a high keening moan coming from a point a few feet away.

"Who is it? Are you hurt?" he asked, reaching out into the darkness. His hands contacted with a soft body. Unintentionally, his hand touched what he suddenly realized was a woman's breast. It could only be Michele. He pulled his hand away, but not before noticing the heaving of her chest, and the trembling of her body.

"Dammit, talk to me," he insisted, "are you hurt?"

"No-o-o, I, I don't think so. But its so . . . DARK!" She wailed, then started to moan again.

Gil was tempted to slap her, but decided that the best course was just to wait. This was a hell of a woman, he reminded himself. She could probably get herself together without his help. His confidence was justified, as she soon quieted, and despite a gulp or gasp here and there, told him that she was feeling better.

"What . . . about the . . . others?" she asked.

"No problem here," the big voice of Monk spoke from ahead of them, the sound helping them orient themselves.

"Just getting my breath," came Jeff's puffing voice almost at the same instant as Frank spoke from a nearby point.

"Yeah, nothing worse than some bumps and bruises, I think. As long as you don't count St. Anthony's bell choir in my ears."

"It looks like nobody is badly hurt, then?" Gil asked.

"That's the good news," came Frank's wry announcement.

"What's the . . . bad news?" Jeff whispered haltingly.

"We may be trapped down here."

There was a sharp intake of air from Michele's direction.

"I think the passage is completely caved-in behind us," Frank explained.

"But we can still work our way out by going forward, can't we?" Jeff asked nervously.

"You wanta tell 'em, Monk?" Frank said, "or should I?"

"You saw?"

"Yeah, I saw, alright. And if the rest of you didn't see, you just might have heard our famous and highly skilled

Indian tracker utter a rather unsettling word just before the lights went out. How did you put it, Monk? I believe it was something like 'OOPS!' wasn't it?"

"Awright, wise ass, I never said I knew all these here tunnels. Anybody can make a mistake."

"What? What are you saying?" Michele's asked, shakily.

"What he's saying," Frank continued, "is that just before we got the tunnel sealed off behind us, our trustworthy guide led us right into a dead-end."

"Where's my flash?" Monk said, ignoring the sarcasm. There was a scrabbling sound, then a beam of light shot out. The beam swept over the group, who were covered in a layer of chalky dust that had settled on them from the blast.

"Shee-it," he cracked, "I never seen nobody look so white!"

The light moved from person to person, until it was clear that there were no major injuries.

"Let's see what we're up against," Gil told him.

"Here, you take it, I don't have the heart."

The flashlight moved from Monk to Gil, who directed the beam toward the end of the passage, revealing that it was choked with slabs of broken concrete and rock. The light swiveled around in the other direction, the circle of light illuminating an unbroken brick wall. Everywhere the beam probed there was nothing but solid surface. They were trapped.

"Shit," Monk swore, "I think I've even been here before. Damned if this ain't the same place I found that necklace.

"Well, thank God none of us were hurt."

"After you're finished giving thanks," Monk's voice suggested wryly, "Hows about you ask him for more than an hour's worth of air, 'cause I don't figure we've got much more than that."

* * *

Michele Peters was beginning to wonder if hell could be any worse than what she was going through. She had been proud of her control during the journey into the recesses of the hospital center's nether regions, even when it meant long sections of shadowy tunnel and at least one segment in the darkness. The detective had been a lot of help, and unlike earlier, when she had run from her fear, she had managed to operate adequately this time. Or at least she had managed up until the explosion.

The blast had done more than rattle her composure. For a while it blew away every vestige of control, leaving her at mercy to the dark fantasies and terrors she had kept at bay up until then. Sitting there, numb from the explosion, disoriented, and completely removed from even the most fractional light source, she felt herself reliving her childhood desperation. She wasn't an adult anymore, she was a six-year-old child huddling in the corner of an airless closet, waiting to be beaten.

When a flashlight finally slashed into the darkness, Michele wanted to grab it, and hold it, like a parched person reaches for water. It was partially her exhaustion that kept her from acting on the impulse, partially her need to stay still and keep her arms folded close, as if somehow she could physically hold her fragile emotions together.

It was even more difficult to remain calm, when she heard the situation they were in. It was too much like her nightmarish memories and fantasies. How could anything be worse? Trapped in the dark, deep underground, with suffocation only minutes away?

Perhaps it was only a trick of emotions, but she already seemed to notice a thickness to the air, a need to breathe harder to get enough oxygen. She coughed, pulled her knees up to her chest, and laid her head on her arms. The small chamber was silent now, each person coming to terms with the idea that these were likely to be his or her last moments. She felt for Beach in the darkness, and scooted over the few inches to him. He put his arm around her and they leaned against each other. She was glad he didn't say anything. It was kind of late for words.

Forty-four

"There's not much question she would have been dead very quickly. Even if you figured out what was going on, we might not have had time to save her."

Carl Troop was speaking in his office several stories above the place where the pursuit team of volunteers were sealed. Standing before him was Darby Waterly, who had just explained his narrow escape from killing a patient. Woozy, but slowly regaining consciousness, was the woman who had been set up for death. Troop immediately recognized her as the detective that had gone undercover earlier.

"You're Detective Joseph, aren't you?"

"Uhh . . . huh. But Helen is fine."

One arm was in an aircast, and she sat in a wheelchair. Her head was heavily bandaged on one side.

"Yes, Helen. Well, a lot has happened since you decided to play bag lady."

He gave a quick run down of what he knew, including the plan of the small group that set out to find Jamison. He was going to suggest that Helen go get some rest, when the building shook, a dull rumble vibrated through the floor, and the lights went out. In seconds, it became obvious that Al had the back-up generators working again, because the few lights on the emergency circuit glowed yellow, then brightened enough for them to see clearly in the room. Carl Troop voiced his discouragement.

"Oh no. Not again!"

In moments his telephone rang, getting off only one ring before he grabbed up the receiver. He started to yell into the instrument, but heard something in reply that made him speak more quietly. He slowly lowered the handset into its cradle.

"It was another explosion. This one was mostly underground, in the tunnel system."

"The tunnel system? But isn't that . . . ?"

"Yes, I'm afraid it is. It's the area where your fellow officers were located. And one of my doctors. I don't think they had much of a chance."

"Are you saying they're dead?"

"I'm not saying anything for a while. I've been talking too much and not doing enough. Especially when it comes to Michele."

Troop pivoted and yanked open the door. Waterly grabbed Helen's wheelchair and set off after Troop's retreating figure.

As a physician, Michele was more aware than anyone that the air was running out. She felt her chest heaving, and could feel Gil's respirations speeding up as their systems tried to expel the excess CO_2 that was building up in their bodies. Her medical training had taught her that the breathing response was not triggered by a lack of oxygen, but by the CO_2 build-up in the blood. Even poisonous carbon monoxide didn't produce the same effect, despite the fact that it bound to blood cells in a way that replaced oxygen. So a person would go on breathing pretty normally, as they died from oxygen starvation, as long as they kept breathing out any accumulated carbon dioxide. That gave her a thought.

She pulled free from Gil and stood. Despite her short stature, she was able to reach the low ceiling with outstretched hands. The others had often ducked along the way to keep from banging their skulls overhead. She ran her fingers over the surface, especially feeling the pipes and conduits.

"What gives?" Gil asked, sensing her purposefulness.

"Here," she finally said. "Monk, have you still got that big wrench with you?"

"Yes'm. What's up?"

"Shine the light up here. Do you think you can break into this pipe?"

The flashlight revealed her touching a tube among the maze running across the ceiling.

"The hot one here."

"This is a strange time to be wantin' a hot shower," Frank wisecracked.

"It's not a water line," she explained, "it's too big for that. It has to be a steam line. You'll have to be careful or you'll get scalded, Monk."

"I ain't sure I wouldn't rather die in a cool tunnel than get boiled to death," he commented.

"No, just break it near the end here, by the rubble. The steam has to travel that direction, toward the main building doesn't it?"

"Yes'm. So I guess you're right about where to break the line. Steam should shoot out away from us into the dirt. But what for?"

"Do you know what steam is?" she asked.

"Don't play games with me now, lady," he objected. "Of course I know. How you think I passed my license exam?"

"It's just water vapor, isn't it?" Gil asked.

"Which is made up of old H_2O and air, right?" Monk quickly put in.

"AIR!" Frank and Jeff shouted almost in unison.

"How will adding air help, if we don't get rid of the carbon dioxide?" Gil asked, as if he had read her earlier thoughts.

"Let me show off," Monk jumped in.

"Be my guest, Mr. Weems."

"Okay, this here's pretty much a closed system." He didn't wait for a response before continuing. "So opening this pipe is going to add pressure. If they's any leakage at all, I guess the pressure is going to push the bad air out any opening it can find. For instance through the part of the pipe that goes on from here. The part that takes the steam into the building."

"So, if it works, we direct the steam down to the floor, and the CO_2-laden air will be forced out through the other side of the line where it was attached," Michele completed his thought. "Setting up a circulation of sorts."

Breaking the pipe turned out to be more difficult than it sounded. Even two men hanging their weight on the large wrench pried between the pipe and ceiling, only resulted in a bent tube and more chalky dust, as the wrench dug into the soft plaster ceiling.

"Hold on a minute," Monk stopped the grunting effort. "How long do you think this hole we're in is? I put it at about ten feet or so. What do you think?"

"Yeah, that's pretty close, I'd say," Gil agreed.

"Okay, so this type of pipe don't come in lengths more'n twelve feet. That end goes into the wall, but the other end is in the junk from the big bang. Should be a joint someplace in another foot or two."

There was a scrabbling sound, as those nearest the rubble began pulling and digging away the dirt and rock, lifting the larger pieces and handing them to the others, in the light of the dimming flashlight. Michele was now sure that the air was getting bad, as they had to take turns at the digging, each person tiring quickly.

"Yes, there's a joint!" Jeff blurted out in a tight, high-pitched croak. He didn't sound good to Gil.

In a few more minutes they had cleared away enough dirt and rocks so that the connection was exposed. It was joined with a pressure flange and nut. Monk set the wrench and turned slowly until there was a thin scream, and a tiny bit of steam began escaping the loosened fitting. Then he pulled off his shirt and tied one sleeve to the end of the handle. He was able to pull the handle around a half-turn while standing back several feet, then reset the wrench, repeating the operation to make each half-turn. The scream slowly changed to a loud hiss. Clouds of vapor filled the chamber as it mixed with the cool tunnel atmosphere. Despite the light of the flashlight, Monk completely disappeared from view.

Eventually, over the loud hissing, they heard a new metallic creaking, and a yell. The sound of the shooting steam changed, like it was hitting a solid surface. Then that changed too, and the noise level dropped slightly, becoming more like the sound of a hose shoved into a hole, hissing and burbling. The steam became less dense, and when Gil directed light toward the sound, they saw that Monk had managed to bend the pipe down by hanging his weight on it. Now the steam was shooting into a hole its thrust had dug in the rubble. Monk sat against the wall, chest heaving. As the beam of light passed over him, one arm showed a bright red color.

"You've been burned," Michele pointed out.

She quickly went to his side, and began first aid as best she could without medicine or equipment, covering the burn with a piece of wet cloth. That seemed to help, and the man was soon breathing easier, despite the moist air that now filled the chamber with thick heat.

"You got a way with you," he said in soft tone. "I'm glad we brought you along instead of some useless paperpusher."

Michele didn't mention that she was an administrator, even if she was one who did plenty of hands-on medicine. Not that it mattered much now. Despite the temporary respite, they wouldn't survive long in this environment. In fact, she knew, the very steam that was prolonging their lives, would work against them in the long run. The small chamber already felt as hot as an athletic club steam room, and a body could only tolerate such high temperatures for limited periods of time. She decided not to tell the rest of the trapped group that they might have escaped suffocation, only to get slowly cooked to death. If they had any chance of survival a positive attitude would improve the possibilities. If only she could do something about her own outlook!

As the light moved around the room, Gil missed very little. He had tied a handkerchief around his head to keep the condensing steam and sweat that dripped from his forehead out of his eyes. He saw Monk's arm, and got a quick sense of the status of each of the others. He was most worried about Corleski. Jeff hadn't said anything, but he looked to Gil like he was near the edge. His yell before had been that of a person without much left to draw on. In silence now, the detective from the 13th Precinct sat against a wall, a slight tremor shaking his body. There was a wide-eyed look that Gil had seen in the young conscripts assigned to his unit in Vietnam. Once he had seen it in a kid from Fort Worth and minutes later the kid had jumped up and ran directly into a clearly marked mine field. They had to pick him up in pieces afterward. Another time, he had seen it in a cherry lieutenant, who had to be medivaced out in a fairly good imitation of a straight jacket. The look was not a good thing to see. Especially in tight quarters, where there wasn't room for anyone to go too flaky without a serious effect on the others. Jeff, unfortunately, also had a gun, and had already demonstrated a quick trigger finger.

"Jeff?" He tried to get the man's attention. He knew that hostage negotiators and crisis teams had strategies for this kind of thing. All he could remember was that it was supposed to be better if you keep a person talking.

"Jeff . . . you okay?"

There was no answer. Gil started to move toward the man, when a voice, high and filled with tension warned him.

"Get away. Leave me alone."

In retrospect, Gil wondered if he should have done what Corleski asked, but he wasn't used to this kind of situation and gave it another try.

"C'mon, Jeff. Talk to me. What's going on?"

"I said LEAVE ME ALONE!" came the strained reply. But more frightening than the voice was the next sound Gil heard. There was a sound, like a snap being undone, then a sliding swish of hardness and leather, like a gun being drawn from a holster, followed by a loud "chicka-chick" that could only be the slide of an automatic pistol being cocked.

"What the hell is going on?" Frank blurted, recognizing the sound immediately. He had been the latest guardian of the light, and now it flashed in the darkness. The beam briefly illuminated the figure of Corleski, who was frozen in the circle of light, with the barrel of his weapon placed in his own mouth.

"Don't do it, Jeff," Frank called. Corleski didn't pull the trigger immediately, but he pulled the pistol from his mouth and turned it toward the light. Suddenly there was a muzzle flash, and loud report of the weapon being fired. The singing of a ricochet followed, as the bullet bounced off hard brick and stone walls.

"Shit!" Frank exclaimed, dropping the light, which rolled away to shine on a terrified Dr. Peters.

Gil leapt forward, diving low in the direction of Jeff's legs, in case he fired again. He caught the man's shins against his left shoulder, his hands connecting with arms extended in a firing position. He felt Jeff go down, another shot echoing with deafening volume in the small area. Once on top of the other detective, Gil felt all resistance go out of the man, and he was able to easily remove the weapon from a slack hand.

"Frank, are you hit?"

"Jeezus, no. But that was damned close. I almost got the ricochet in my ass, too."

"Anybody else?" Gil asked, and the others indicated that they were alright.

"Speaking of ricochets, Frank . . . did you hear one on the second shot?" he asked his partner. "I was a little distracted at the time."

"Hell, I don't know," Terranova replied. "I guess I don't remember one. Why?"

Instead of answering, Beach stuck Corleski's weapon in his belt and moved to the flashlight, which lay on the floor, its light distinctly dimmer now. Monk came over to watch Corleski, who now had curled up in a fetal ball and was whispering something that sounded like a rosary prayer. Gil swung the light around and swept the area systematically, concentrating on the ceiling and walls. On the opposite brick wall he searched until he found a scarred gouge where one bullet had dug a mark in its bouncing path. He moved to the side wall, and after a few moments of examination, seemed to find what he was looking for.

"It was a long shot, but I was right. The second bullet hit here and didn't carom off."

"So?" Frank asked. "What's the idea? What difference does it make now if it's buried in the wall instead of bouncing?"

"It isn't buried either. It went right through."

". . . through? You mean . . . ?"

"Yes, part of this wall is hollow. This isn't real brick, it's just facing."

"Damn, how thick you think it is?"

"I don't know, but it's sure to be a lot thinner than a brick wall."

"I smell something odd," Frank said, "do you?"

"I don't know, maybe. With all this steam and sweat, I guess we must smell pretty ripe at this point."

"No, it isn't that. Smells like something dead."

"Bullet put a hole in the wall. Could be somepin' on th' other side," Monk offered.

"Well, if we don't get through, there's gonna be something dead on this side of the wall pretty soon," Gil replied.

Weems held out his large wrench. "How's about I take a coupla smacks at it wif this?"

"Hold on," Gil cautioned. "Didn't you say this is where you found the medallion?"

"Yes. Looks like it to me."

Beach slowly moved the light over the side wall, holding it close as the brightness had diminished along with the battery charge.

"Whatta ya got, man?"

"Put it together . . . rigged explosives, evidence of missing people, a fake wall. This isn't some forgotten, out of the way dead-end, it's been used on a regular basis. My hunch is that there's access here. Jamison or one of his friends comes here often enough to have a useable exit."

Gil felt around the edges of the wall section, pushed against it, and then tried applying pressure to the side to see if it would slide. He was pushing on individual brick shapes, to see if one of them could be a secret release, when Michele spoke.

"Did you try pushing up, like it was a roll-top desk?"

Beach did as she suggested, and there was movement.

A gap appeared at the place where the wall met the floor. Monk joined in grabbing under the edge and lifting, which raised the segment further. A terrible stench immediately wafted through the opening. It was an odor Beach had smelled before—in battlefields where the dead had remained, rotting in the sun. He looked into the opening, then clicked off the light.

"Oh God," Michele Peters gasped. "That smells like . . ."

"Yes. There's bodies in there."

"Bodies? As in plural?" Frank asked.

"Yes, I saw at least two. But we don't have much battery life left in this thing. I think we'd better conserve it as much as possible."

"Wha . . . what do you . . . suggest?" Michele asked, a tremble in her voice.

"Well, if this brick wall isn't a complete dead-end, the tunnel should extend beyond it on the other side. If we form a line . . . a hand on the belt of the person in front, we can move along the right side of this room we found, and feel for an opening. It makes sense that there would be a door or something along that side, if the tunnel doesn't end here."

"That's a lot of ifs, isn't it?"

"Got any other suggestions?"

When no one came up with any alternatives, Gil told Monk to get Jeff, and they felt around until they had formed a line. Gil was leading, with Michele grasping at his belt. Behind her was Frank, his left hand hooked onto her waistband. Monk pushed Jeff into the next place, and stayed behind him, bringing up the rear. Corleski didn't say anything, but cooperated, grabbing Frank's hanging shirttail, and holding on. Slowly they began inching along, through the opening, feeling the wall with free hands. Between the terrible smell of death, the darkness, and their desperate situation, the tension was almost unbearable. Then a little sing-song voice sounded. It was Frank.

"Ya dooo the hokey pokey, and ya turn yourself around . . ."

There were chuckles and puffs of exhaled tension from most of the bedraggled group. Gil was thankful for his partner's oddball sense of humor. Even Michele managed to get off a one-liner through chattering teeth.

"He's just happy 'cause he's got a hand in my pants."

The group became silent as they felt their way along the wall. Jeff's first words were an exclamation.

"Holy Jesus!" as he pulled back.

Gil switched on the light and directed it back to reveal Jeff who was looking down at his feet. The weakening circle of yellow illuminated the cause of his outburst. It was a decomposing human limb. The light showed it was connected to a corpse spread out on the dirty floor, puffed up and swollen from putrefaction. The body was next to a dirty mattress, and what appeared to be dozens of pornographic magazines lying about, opened to cheap, but explicit photos. There was a lamp, but when Gil snapped the switch, nothing happened, confirming that there was no power in this area.

"Somebody's been living here. And I think he has some very nasty hobbies."

He turned off the flashlight, but then clicked it back on to check something he had caught in the corner of his vision. It was a white laboratory jacket, hanging from a hook by the mattress. On the jacket was a name tag.

"Anybody know a guy named Merkel in Radiology, Bernard Merkel?"

"Yes, he's a big guy, kind of strange. They call him Buzz. I never liked the way he looks at me," Michele replied.

"Looks like your instincts are good."

Just then there was a tapping sound.

"What's that?"

"It's just me," Frank explained. "I'm checking the wall for another door . . . see if anything sounds hollow."

The group was brought back to their predicament and resumed the line they had formed earlier. Soon there were various taps and knocks sounding along the wall. As they edged along, someone called out.

"Listen!"

Among the hard taps and thuds, there was now a more resonant hollow sound. It came from near the head of the line.

"Yeah, I think I've got something," Gil's voice sounded clearly in the silence, followed by two more knocks. This time, he tried pushing up immediately, and the panel once again slid up into the ceiling. Coolness washed over them.

"Ahhh, it may be old rotten tunnel air to you," Frank sighed, "but it smells wonderful to me."

The new opening did provide some relief from the pungent odor, and meant a new supply of oxygen. But just as important, as soon as they stepped through the door, Gil realized that he was seeing more than darkness. Without the aid of the flashlight, he could make out a small area ahead that was not so dark. It wasn't exactly light, just a dim sense of where the passage was less dark than the surrounding walls. But to see even that much, meant there had to be reflected illumination from somewhere. He felt Michele's hand grip tighter at his belt. Frank kept up his comic relief.

"No clichés, now. If anybody says they see a light at the end of the tunnel, I might deck 'em."

Forty-five

Jamison had almost struck Pretaska. The Serbian was becoming a definite liability. It was time for offensive action, and the handsome fraud only wanted to retreat. Jamison left him and went to check the explosives. He leaned down by the apparatus and examined the third charge. It was secure. It triggered the feedback loop to brighten one of the last two boxes on the detonator's lighted display. Despite his careful planning, the group of hunters was still moving forward. Buzz had heard the discharge of weapons and come upon them in the dark. Unseen he had managed to slip away, to inform Dr. J that they were still alive and progressing toward the laboratory, only a few hundred feet away now.

He made sure that the mechanism was still armed before moving out a side passage, to a place of safety. His smile was no longer pasted in place. Now he wore a grim expression of determination and cold anger.

A short distance away, the group was feeling more like survivors than pursuers, and had stopped for a rest before moving on. Michele wanted to go to the light immediately, but Gil convinced her to wait since they didn't know what was ahead, and needed to approach that unknown with their bodies rested. The presence of even a dim light had already made her less anxious.

"I . . . I'm sorry," Jeff Corleski choked out his words. "I wasn't myself back there. I'm okay now. You can give me back my weapon. You might need me."

"You weren't right from the time we came down in the elevator," Gil responded. "Why should we trust you now?"

"Okay, I understand. I'd probably feel the same way. But there's more to it than you think."

"Like what?"

"Dammit, I was juiced. I . . . I was scared of coming down here . . . scared shitless, if you must know. So . . . so I took something."

"You what!"

"Yeah, I know it was stupid. And believe me, if I get out of this without losing my badge, I'll never do it again. That's why it was so weird, I've never tried any of that stuff before, but I had this box of pills . . ."

"What were they?" Michele asked.

"I don't know . . . some kind of speed, I guess. Whatever they were, I wasn't ready for it. I took three or four of 'em."

"Jeezus!"

"Yeah . . . I know. After a while I just kinda freaked out. I'm feeling a lot better now. And I mean it, I'm really sorry. I know it was a dumb thing to do. But I'm okay now, and you won't have to worry about me."

"Shit man," Frank said, "It's ME I've been worried about. One a those slugs you aimed my way nearly took my nose off. I'm an Italian, man. I don't want no nose job, or my relatives wouldn't let me play Bocce no more."

As usual, Frank's banter lowered the tension level.

"Okay," Gil relented, pulling Jeff's pistol out of his belt and passing it back to him. "But I'm not waiting for you to pull that trigger. If you even look tense, I'm taking it."

"Thanks Beach. You won't regret it."

Gil wondered if Corleski's prediction would be true. He couldn't help thinking it sounded like the proverbial famous last words.

"That's the last we heard."

Al Pearson, chief engineer, was describing the events leading up to the last explosion. He and several others, including Dr. Carl Troop, were gathered in an area of sub-basement where the blast had caved in a section of tunnel. They stood gathered above the hole, where several yards of the floor had collapsed into the passage below.

"Well, we obviously aren't gonna get through that pile of debris," Troop commented. "Where's another access?"

"Don't know as there is one, doc. Those tunnels aren't regular lines of traffic. Folks aren't supposed to use this section at all. We don't even have real accurate pictures of where they all go. Some of 'em are from old buildings demolished long ago. New ones were built right on top. Sometimes the tunnels were in the way, sometimes not. Maybe some old timer on staff might have an idea, but I been working here for fifteen years, and I wouldn't have the slightest idea if there's another way into this one."

"Okay, so get me an old-timer. And in the meantime, we move down fifty feet or so and break in beyond where it collapsed.

"Ahhh, well, that's a little easier said than done, doc. First off, we don't know how far the cave-in extends. Just because this is the only section that fell through the floor don't mean the roof didn't drop a ton of rock in places. Could be the tunnel's jammed up fifty feet, or a hundred feet further on. Second problem is the breaking through. You're standing on solid concrete, laced with reinforcing steel, and overlaid with marble blocks."

The engineer stamped on the solid surface to underline his point. The sound was flat and without give.

"Underneath all that, as you can see from the cave-in, is a layer of dirt and solid rock, mostly rock, and then the structure of the tunnel itself, which varies from simple concrete walls, to reinforced steel, layers of pipe, and whatever. You don't just 'break in' to something like that."

"Okay, Al. I hear what you're saying. But we aren't going to stand here and do nothing. There's got to be a way to figure out where the cave-in ends. And we're gonna find it and get those people out."

"What makes you think they aren't caught underneath the pile of rubble?"

"Maybe they are. I don't know. But if they survived, it was because they were beyond the cave-in. We have to go with the only possible chance they had. If we're wrong, we haven't lost anything but time and money and sweat. But if they lived through that blast, they're gonna need our help one way or another."

Forty-six

They had survived the other explosion, but there was no way Dr. J was going to let them get free of this one. This time there would be no escape. Two tiny box shapes still blinked on the LED display in Jamison's hand. One was wired to the charges in the laboratory, the other to the nuclear storage closet. He was becoming resigned to the necessity of detonating both—there weren't many options left to him. But he wanted to make sure that his pursuers understood what they had ruined before they were annihilated. If he had to die in the purging, he could handle that. But before he and the Magnes Project ceased to exist, he wanted them to know that they were destroying the great hope of mankind. And he wanted them to regret their choice.

Jamison didn't intend to give them a chance for repentance, but he wanted them to know fear and despair, terror and hopelessness. He wanted them to feel as powerless as he had felt before his father. As it had been done to him, he wanted to rebuke and scorn them. He would spit on them before he died, as he had been spit upon. It was not necessary to do it physically. He could spit on them symbolically.

The light the group saw from a distance was coming through a small gap between a plywood cover and the opening to a different kind of passage. When they entered, they found it clean, well-lighted and lined with a facing that gave Michele the impression they were walking through a space station rather than a subterranean chamber. Shiny brackets and new modern couplings held large cables in place. Since the corridor was bright, the lab obviously had access to power through different lines than the rest of the tunnel. She thought of the problems with the emergency power system, and how Richard Schwenker had died trying to find the cause of energy being drained from the system.

She looked ahead at Gil and Frank working their way ahead as a team. They moved with the sureness and silent communication of a well-practiced maneuver. The two men took turns moving forward, one dashing to the next protected spot, while the other held his gun at ready to cover the advance. It looked like something out of a war movie. Jeff followed a few steps behind the other detectives, while she stayed farther back, with Monk bringing up the end, walking backward. "Guarding our rear," he called it. Although she knew he had a gun somewhere, Weems kept it out of sight for now, and wielded only the heavy wrench that had already served so many purposes. She was concerned about his scalded arm, and hoped they could get him decent burn treatment soon. Though he didn't say anything, she was sure it must be very painful.

There was something comforting about being surrounded by four men with guns, all protecting her. It was so elemental, so primal, so . . . so . . . so wrong!

"Hold it!" she announced, so loudly the sound seemed to echo in the enclosed space of the passage.

"What?" the men stopped and looked nervously around to see what had prompted the outburst.

"I want a weapon."

"You want a what?"

"I want a weapon. There are five of us here, and I'm the only one without something to protect myself."

"I don't think you could hardly lift this wrench," Monk laughed. "Now you know I have a piece, too. You want to take that away from me, Miz Doctor? I thought you doctor folks didn't hold with guns and such."

"Well, I don't know about other doctors, but this one doesn't remember signing up to be medical corpsman for this group. And I don't intend to be helpless, either."

"Okay, okay," Frank held up a hand, "we get the picture. But if you think I'm handing over my weapon, you obviously don't realize the intimate relationship I have with this piece of hardware. I call it Linda, 'cause it reminds me of my ex-wife, hard as steel, cold enough to give you shivers, and ready to kill if you get in her way at the wrong time."

"Very funny. But I'm serious. I refuse to remain defenseless."

"That's the last thing I would use to describe you," Gil remarked dryly, "but if you know how to fire it, I have something you can use."

He reached down and lifted up his pants leg where a small holster was strapped to his left ankle. From it he took a small gun that looked shiny and lethal.

"They call it a pocket pistol, but don't let that fool you. It packs a wallop, and has enough rounds to do the job. Should be about the right size for your hand. I don't know if it's big enough for your pride."

"Suddenly everybody's a comedian," she retorted, as she took the pistol. With a practiced air, she hefted the weapon, examined the barrel, and worked the cocking mechanism. Holding the weapon in a two-handed grip, she held it out in the stiff-armed stance of an experienced handler.

"This isn't the first time you've used one of those,"

Jeff commented. "What were you, champion marksman of your medical school?"

He spoke sarcastically, but Michele answered directly. "Markswoman, it you please. And it was college. I was on the target shooting team."

"There seems a certain irony about a pre-med student training to use lethal firearms, don't you think?" Frank suggested. "Or is that why you did it? Kind of a rebel, aren't you?"

"Could be. Mostly I did it just for the hell of it."

She slipped the piece into the pocket of her lab coat, and gave a satisfied nod of her head. It would be ready if she needed it, but she didn't have to wave it around.

The team spread out into their previous positions, with Gil and Frank at the front. The two men had just reached the end of the corridor which opened into a large room filled with machinery, when there was a whirring sound, and a steel-barred gate slid out of the ceiling. It almost caught Beach on the back, but with a flash of reflex action he dropped to his haunches and leapt forward. There was a clatter of metal on metal, as in his dive he lost hold of his weapon.

Frank was far enough forward to be clear of the falling steel. Jeff was caught on the other side. The suddenness of the development startled Michele enough to take two steps backward. That was all that kept her from being trapped by a second gate. Instead, it swung into place in front of her, effectively isolating Corleski and jailing him in a small area of corridor. When he realized his predicament, Jeff turned pale. He began walking the enclosure like a big caged cat, his feet making a dull clanging sound on what appeared to be a large metal plate covering the floor.

"Keep an eye out to the front and rear," Gil warned the others. "This could be a diversion."

Frank and Monk turned back to watch avenues of approach, nervously glancing over their shoulders periodically to see Jeff's predicament. Michele searched the walls for a switch or control that might retract the barred obstacles. She saw none, but noticed a series of dull flat circles over Jeff's area, each about two feet in diameter, recessed into a metal plate similar to the one on which he was standing.

A strange humming sound began, accompanied by an electronic squeal. At the same time the round inserts lost their dull color and began to show a rosy glow. Michele sensed no heat, but her head began to tingle, and she could see Jeff's hair standing on end, as if charged with static electricity. The man looked so strange, wide-eyed and with a corona of wild hair, that it would have seemed like a cartoon, if the fear in his eyes had not been so clearly real.

When the first gate dropped, Michele thought it might be an accident. Perhaps they had accidentally triggered some automatic device or security system. She continued to hold out that possibility until the second gate appeared. Now she had an awful feeling. Someone, perhaps Jamison, was setting in motion a device that was going to kill Jeff. It might kill them all. Whoever was responsible had probably intended to catch several of them in the enclosure. Only luck and quick reflexes had prevented others from joining Jeff in the lethal area he now occupied. Michele suspected that it was like a gas chamber . . . an electronic extermination zone.

"Do something!" Corleski cried.

"Don't panic, Jeff," Gil cautioned. "We'll get you out of there. You're gonna be okay."

Michele wondered if Beach believed that, or was only trying to calm the trapped man. Nobody wanted Corleski returning to the crazy behavior of earlier. Jeff must have realized that.

"Don't patronize me, Beach. I'm not gonna flip out.

I told you it was the drugs before. But you gotta get me outta here. I'm feeling all hot and cold, my head's killing me, and my heart's pounding outta my chest. You don't do something quick, you won't hafta worry about me going crazy, 'cause I'm gonna be a dead man."

The words were spoken through gritted teeth, his hands pressed against temples throbbing so hard that, from yards away, Michele could see his temporal artery pulsing. His skin was starting to take on a ruddy color, and Michele shivered, remembering the condition of Old Joe's body. Had this been the old derelict's fate? Or were there worse tortures beyond this killing machine?

The other detectives seemed immobilized. Monk Weems started banging on the bars of the near gate with his big wrench, but produced nothing other than more noise to meld with the whine and hum of the infernal device that was killing Jeff Corleski before their eyes.

One of the Bellevue freight elevators was large enough that the workmen had managed to roll in a small backhoe. On a second trip they fit in a mini-bulldozer, designed to work in small spaces. The backhoe was usually used to break up concrete walks, dig ditches, and scoop out storm drain catch basins. Now it was slamming away at the floor of the basement, a hundred feet or so from the point of collapse, like a huge mechanical woodpecker. While a certain amount of guesswork was still involved, they had a fairly good idea of where to dig.

A contact at Con Edison had loaned them an electronic device to analyze the integrity of huge conduits, cooling towers, and core components. The piece of equipment could spot structural defects through several feet of intervening masonry, and soon indicated the point at which debris no longer filled the tunnel below.

The work was slow, but by alternately attaching a

heavy steel demolition awl to the backhoe arm, then a digging bucket, the workmen were loosening and removing layer after layer of concrete, rock, and dirt. The biggest concern had been steel reinforcing rods, imbedded in the floor to provide stability. But apparently these were deteriorated from many decades of seeping ground moisture, breaking up more easily than the engineers had predicted at the outset of the excavation.

Earlier, the area had been teeming with personnel. NYPD Rapid Action Team members milled about in bulky gear, carrying automatic weapons. A team from the Atomic Energy Commission was trying to look invisible, while dozens of reporters and media personalities clamored for access. Medical personnel were standing by, civil defense volunteers were helping uniformed Bellevue cops with crowd control, and several politicians along with their retinues were trying to find ways of getting their picture taken, or "deep concern" quoted.

When word of a possible nuclear incident got out, the situation changed rapidly. The AEC team suddenly became more visible, while the reporters were courteously escorted to a distant "Information Center," khaki-clad troops took the place of police officers on the street, and the politicians quickly found reasons to "coordinate" efforts from faraway offices.

Fire marshals appeared throughout the medical center, and along with Bellevue security staff, began directing a massive evacuation. Not everyone was well enough to move. In the Intensive Care Units, volunteers remained with the most critical patients, trying to think of other things than the possibility that the nurses tending the patients might not live much longer than their charges.

Dr. J wasn't able to directly observe the irradiation process. Cameras couldn't operate anywhere near the intense electronic field being created. Originally he had designed the apparatus in order to sterilize the skin surface on subjects for Project Magnes. Only when the device had proved too powerful and terminated one of them, did he realize its potential as a weapon. Now he could cleanse more than microbes. He could sterilize all life from the chamber, including human vermin.

He didn't expect to catch all of them. But those who weren't trapped in the killing radiation zone would have time to contemplate their fate and his control over their puny existences. It was a way to spit in their faces. Soon he would use that power to blow them to fragments along with the Magnes Project laboratory. But first he would continue the demonstration of his power. Jamison reached out to the large dial controlling the field generator. He spun it to its maximum setting, and watched as a meter needle inched up into the red zone. The hum and whine increased in intensity, the pitch climbing to a high scream.

The background noise reached the level of an aching squeal, which was joined by a human scream from the man being penetrated by millions of subatomic particles. Jeff fell to his knees, bony joints making a sickening bang on the metal plate forming the floor. Weems kept banging vainly on the barred gate with his wrench, Terranova ran back and forth on the other side, helplessly looking for something to do.

Gil Beach looked down at his pistol, which had been dislodged when he jumped for safety. He wasn't anxious to reach through the bars for it, to even put one arm in the field of whatever was hurting Jeff. But it gave him an idea.

"Those circular things overhead," he pointed upward. "See if they'll stand up to a shot."

"Stand back!" Frank yelled, and hefted the shotgun he had brought along.

There was a booming report, a burst of smoke and fire, and grapeshot rattled all over the enclosure, raining down like hail. In the clearing smoke one of the circular devices started flashing and shooting sparks. But the glow seemed to intensify rather than diminish. Frank let go another blast at the spot, and more sparks flew, grapeshot again showering the floor. This time, the grid seemed more damaged and began to darken.

"It's working, you got it!"

"Yeah, except there's a couple dozen of those things up there, and I've only got a few rounds for this shotgun. At two shells apiece, I won't take out half of 'em before I run out."

"Jeff won't last that long anyway," Gil said quietly, facing away so the caged man wouldn't hear.

There was not much chance of Corleski hearing anyway. Small trails of blood were trickling from his ears and nose. Rocking on his haunches it was hard to tell if Jeff was still screaming, as the shriek of the machinery effectively drowned out any noise he might be making.

On the opposite side of the chamber, Gil saw Michele staring high up at the side wall. Then he saw it too . . . a tiny blinking light, like a sensor, or the battery life indicator on a smoke alarm. He hadn't seen it before, when he carefully scanned every corner, so the light must have just begun blinking. That could be just part of the infernal killing cycle of this thing . . . or it could be some kind of malfunction indicator. Michele looked at him and shouted over the whine.

"It might be part of the control system. If we can take it out, maybe it will cause a shut-down!"

Gil indicated the direction to Frank, and told him to try to blast it. Unfortunately, the angle was too sharp. The shotgun barrel couldn't fit between the bars at an angle that provided a good shot. Frank slid the whole weapon between two bars, and tried holding it on the other side of the gate to fire. His first attempt missed by a wide margin, and the kick of the gun knocked it from his grip. The shotgun clattered to the floor beside Gil's weapon in the radiation zone. Frank stumbled backward, affected not only by the jolt of his gun, but also the emissions that washed over him when he was so close.

Gil reached out to keep his partner from falling. He was beginning to lose hope when he was startled by the sound of another shot. He looked back at the chamber to see Michele on the other side, with the gun he had loaned her braced against a metal bar. A second shot rang out, and chips of material flew from the vicinity of the small blinking light. He couldn't tell if the chips were coming from the device, from the wall, or were merely bullet fragments, but he could tell she had sighted-in well. If the radiation was getting to her, she wasn't letting it deter her aim. She held a steady shooting posture and fired again. She wasn't lying about the target shooting.

Her third shot had more effect. There was a puff of smoke and flame, a spitting shower of electrical sparks, and the light winked out. Simultaneously, the maddening whine started to descend in pitch, the painful level of noise began to decrease. Gil glanced up and saw the overhead circles losing color. He didn't wait any longer, and grabbed at the gate, trying to lift it. This time there was give to the barred metal section. Frank joined him, and together they lifted the gate several feet. Gil put his back under the lower edge and held it in place, while Frank grabbed a gurney cart standing nearby and wedged it under the gate to prevent it from sliding down. In seconds they had Jeff out of the chamber and sitting against a side wall.

Monk had gotten the other gate open as well. He and

Michele dashed across the killing space to join the others, dodging sparks along the way from the bullet-riddled equipment. Michele examined Corleski, while the others did a quick inventory of their ordinance. Despite looking very sick and hurt, Jeff kept muttering apologies.

"I screwed up again, didn't I? Damn, I'm sorry I'm such a screw up. God, I feel so sick . . . should just shoot me, and be done with it."

"Take it easy," Michele tried to calm the man, who was rocking and moving his head in anguish, both physical and emotional. "You aren't thinking straight from that thing zapping you for so long. Don't give up, Jeff. We need you."

Corleski stopped groaning for a moment. Looking at the woman in front of him, he seemed to hear what she was saying. Tears formed in his eyes and skidded down his face, as he broke into sobs and dropped his head on his arms. After a few moments the sobbing stopped, and they were able to get him on his feet so they could move on.

"You definitely have got a way," Frank said quietly to Michele.

She didn't reply, but looked thoughtful. Before they left the corridor, Gil shared a warning.

"Jamison knows we're here, and had this little surprise waiting. There's no reason to believe it's the only one. We have to be more aware than we have ever been. I should have seen that last one coming."

"I guess we were so glad to get out of that cave-in, we didn't think to watch for a trap," Monk said.

"We have to assume that we have an adversary here, who doesn't intend for us to get to him," Michele added.

"I wish that was all," Gil mumbled.

"What do you mean?"

"If that is all it was, I'd say let the bastard go for now. We could get help and take him eventually. But I don't think he's going to give us that choice. That little booby trap there, that human-sized microwave, wasn't just a delaying tactic."

"Which means?"

"Which means I think we have to assume that he's not planning on letting us out of here alive."

Forty-seven

Excavation was slowed when the backhoe nearly toppled into the hole it was digging. The machine slid halfway into the depression, forcing the operator to scramble quickly from his perch to safety. Fortunately, the small bulldozer that they planned to drive into the tunnel when an opening was created was standing by. That machine had a powerwinch, which allowed them to attach a cable to the backhoe and crank it back into place. But more time was lost.

The breakthrough happened without warning or fanfare. A hole about four-feet square opened in the side of the excavation, with relatively clear tunnel showing beyond it. There was a nervous moment, when they saw movement at the mouth of the opening and dozens of armed personnel drew guns and cocked weapons. To a chorus of metallic clicks and snaps, a grisly face, stubbled with gray whiskers appeared in the hole. A disheveled tramp stumbled out, blinking at the light, smelling like a dump, and holding an empty wine bottle in one hand.

"Don't shoot, I'm goin', I'm goin'," he protested. "Damn! Just tryin' to get a little rest, that's all. Don't need to shoot a man just for holing-up to get warm. Damn!"

At that point a police inspector started barking orders, and his heavily armed Rapid Action Team officers forced everyone out of the room, except a small unit left to guard the opening.

"Wait a minute!" Carl Troop tried to protest, "we can't stop now!" But he was forced out with the rest. There was a brief shouting match between the inspector, a Bellevue police captain, and a National Guard lieutenant colonel concerning who had authority in the situation, but the police RAT unit moved so quickly that the area was cleared before the others had a chance to complete their arguments. The National Guard officer bellowed a threat, before following the others to a conference room two floors above, where a lively meeting convened.

The AEC/NRC team was there, as were two mayoral assistants, Bellevue's chief executive officer, medical director, and risk management head. Two National Guard officers strutted about, while receiving nasty glares from NYPD personnel which included the chief of police, chief of detectives, and head of special operations, as well as the inspector and two deputies. The hospital director of security was also inside the room, while his officers guarded the entrance.

Dr. Troop was not allowed into the meeting, and was forced to wait in the hallway with an assortment of secondary officials, including a burly red-complexioned man in a police dress uniform that seemed to indicate a high ranking officer.

"Damn politicos are gonna argue in there till my men are dead meat," he mumbled, striding back and forth with the flat-footed wide gait of a street cop that had worked his way up through the ranks.

"My name is Troop . . . Carl Troop. I'm acting assistant medical director here at Bellevue."

Troop held out a hand. The big police officer didn't return the handshake at first, looking at the doctor suspiciously.

"I've got somebody down there too," Carl added. "I don't give a damn about politics, but I care about those people."

That seemed to register with the other man, who then put out his own hand.

"Bob Mabry. Deputy inspector. Used to be unit commander at the Ninth Precinct before they kicked me upstairs. I used to do real police work. Beach was under my command. So was Terranova for a little while, but I've known Beach since Academy days."

"If you have that kind of rank now, why aren't you inside with the others?"

"Coulda been. Didn't want to. Can't stomach that stuff. I'm not a politician, and my Irish dander gets up at all the bullshit. I was almost ready to hop on that bulldozer myself. I drove a rig like that for my dad when I was a kid. Sometimes I wonder if I shouldn't of stayed in construction. All this political garbage drives me nuts. If I thought I could accomplish anything in there, I might try anyway, but those assholes are just gonna yell at each other for an hour and get nowhere."

"The team down below might not have an hour."

"That's what I'm afraid of."

The two men looked at each other sharply. They held each other's gaze for a moment, in silent communication and recognition.

"It'd be a crime if they died while all that was going on," Troop added, still staring intently at the other man.

"It's the job of the police to make sure crimes aren't committed . . ."

The deputy inspector gave a slight tilt of his head toward the adjacent hallway. Troop nodded and moved away from the group clustered outside the conference room, down the corridor, and through an exit door. Mabry followed a minute later.

After Jeff was able to move on, the team began moving forward out of the tunnel and into the large room filled with elaborate machinery. When Gil reached the area, he encountered a sense of unreality that was coupled with a vague feeling of dread. He felt like he was walking among monstrous guillotines and elaborate torture racks.

Dr. Peters pointed out large donut-shaped devices that seemed like diagnostic equipment, but with strange attachments clearly of different design. She explained that what looked like an MRI set-up had dangerous looking additions, lead-shielded protrusions, and unlikely looking modifications. Every piece of equipment was distorted by elaborate add-ons, often marked with foreign labels, warning signs, or international radiation symbols. Seemingly endless lengths of dark rubber-coated cables and tubes hung about like loops of black intestine or impossibly long reptilian forms.

"Those weird additions," Michele marveled, "They're growing out of the machines like . . . like . . . technological tumors."

They stared at the elaborate apparatus, star explorers stumbling upon an alien spacecraft. Gil had just turned to check the way they had come, when there was a "pfutt-pfutt" sound and he felt his left leg slammed out from under him. He wasn't confused or immobilized by the sudden blow. For Gil it was a familiar feeling. He had been in Vietnam. He had been on the city streets. He had been shot before.

The first bullet hit low and from the side, catching him at the ankle and throwing him to the floor with the force of the slug. The second bullet might have found his abdomen, if the first hadn't knocked him down. Instead it merely grazed his side as he fell. He didn't lie still, but went with the force of the blow, immediately going into a sideways roll. A third spitting noise sounded, and in the place his head had occupied a moment before a puff of dust and zinging ricochet marked the path of another bullet. By that time he was already prone behind a large control panel, pulling his weapon as he shouted urgently for the others to take cover.

Frank yanked Michele behind a small wall-like partition, dropping his shotgun in the process. Jeff was scrunched up behind the table of the radiation device, and Monk Weems was partially protected by a large spool of cable. The shots seemed to be coming from a point farther ahead, where a large hatch-like door opened onto a continuation of the tunnel. A muzzle flash from behind the metal frame confirmed the location of the shooter.

Gil knew that silencers only work optimally for a limited number of firings, so he was not surprised that the sound was now more of a "Whap" as the suppressor's effectiveness decreased with use. The gunner's aim, however, had not deteriorated. Monk gave a jerk and an exclamation of pain, as a slug caught his exposed arm. Gil fired off a series of shots, the noise echoing in the underground hall. Bullets didn't seem to have much effect. The next shot from the doorway demonstrated that the partition providing cover for Frank and Michele was no real protection, because the bullet punched a hole right through what now appeared to be simple sheetrock panels. Michele gave a small shriek as a slug perforated the wall only inches from her face, showering her with a burst of chalky dust.

She gasped again when Frank dropped to the ground, but he was only getting low for safety. He grinned at her reaction, and reached up to pull her down, too. Meanwhile his eyes searched the area, looking for better cover. The partition offered no real shield from the gunfire, only making the two less visible to the shooter.

Gil felt his ankle throbbing, but there didn't seem to be any blood. He pulled up his trouser leg and saw that he had been lucky. The slug had hit the ankle holster where he had kept the pistol Michele now carried. There was a deep gash in the leather, and it looked as if his ankle was starting to swell, but it was probably more a sprain than a bullet wound. He would be limping, but probably suffer no lasting effect. His side was sticky with blood, but that too was a minor wound. Now that he only had one weapon, he decided to check his remaining ammunition.

Meanwhile, Monk apparently recognized the vulnerability of his and the others' situations.

"Lay down cover," he shouted, "I'm gonna get that fuck!"

Gil had just removed the clip from his gun to check how many bullets remained. Before he could tell Monk to wait, the man was on his feet and running toward the sniper's position in the classical zig-zag of armed services training.

"Jeff, give him cover!" Gil yelled, pushing a bullet into place between steel springs, jamming the clip back into his gun and flipping off the safety. The whole operation didn't take more than five or six seconds.

Those few seconds were too many. No covering fire came from Jeff's position. He never raised his weapon, shivering and shaking behind the temporary shield of the table. Frank wasn't able to get around Michele quickly, and his shotgun was out of reach. With no gunfire to avoid, the shooter revealed himself, stepping out of hiding long enough to level his weapon at the charging figure of Weems. It was the hulking form of a large male in a stained white lab coat.

"It's Merkel!" Michele yelled.

The huge man displayed an idiotic, yet evil smile, as he sighted down the barrel of his weapon. Curiously, Monk never fired his pistol, though he had it in one hand, wrench in the other. Confronted with Merkel's weapon, the engineer seemed to slow briefly, as if aware of the inevitable, but then charged on, a raging roar erupting from him, as he launched himself at the man anyway.

Two bullets slammed into Weems's chest, stopping the big man in his tracks. Huge bloody holes appeared in his back, and he dropped to his knees, then fell backward, legs bent the wrong way under his body. As if lost in the experience of the killing, Merkel seemed unaware of the others, and walked forward to the doubled-up form of Weems. With a sickening grin still pasted on his face, Merkel aimed the pistol at Monk's head.

By this time, Gil had gotten his weapon into firing position as well, and squeezed off a series of five shots. Three of them slammed into the killer, knocking him back a step with each impact. Merkel's sick grin changed to an expression of amazement, then dismay. Now Frank rolled out from behind the bullet punctured partition, grabbed the shotgun and settled on his elbows, weapon propped in firing position. He pulled the Weatherby's trigger and a blast lifted Merkel's dying body into the air, flinging it back against the wall to sink slowly to the floor in a pool of blood.

Michele had the small pistol in her hand, but didn't fire. Gil wasn't surprised. Despite her familiarity with weapons, he suspected that her physician's attitude would make it very difficult to kill a human being.

As soon as the firing stopped, Michele ran to Monk's crumpled form, shoving the small pistol into her belt. She placed a hand by his throat, checking his carotid artery for a pulse. It was weak and thready. The man's eyes fluttered half open, but she could see that nothing available here was going to help him. Blood pulsed from severed arteries in his chest. The massive trauma was more than anyone could be expected to survive unless perhaps a surgical team were available on the spot, complete with a fully outfitted operating suite. She swore at the irony of this brave man dying within a few floors of the surgical facility where he might have had a chance for survival. She disregarded modesty to slip off her cotton blouse, wad it into a ball and use it to staunch the flow of blood. It was no more than a delaying tactic at best. He was dying before her eyes.

"Why did you do that?" she asked him, though not really expecting an answer. But the mortally wounded man choked out a whisper.

". . . Somebody hadda do it . . . didn't they? Any minute he was gonna find you behind that . . . tissue paper wall. But I flushed him out, didn't I?"

Michele swallowed thickly before responding, "But why didn't you shoot back at him?"

"With that thing? That was just for show, doc. That's why . . . I didn't give it . . . to you . . . before . . ."

His face grimaced, and then went slack. Michele found no pulse at his wrist, and didn't detect anything at the carotid artery either. His heaving chest had slowed and stopped. Now she watched as his pupils dilated.

Frank and Gil approached. She reached out to close Monk's eyes, looked up at them, and shook her head. Terranova reached down and picked up Weems' gun.

"I'll be damned!"

"What?"

"It's not a real gun. It's a damn starter's pistol."

"He knew that when he charged the shooter," Gil noted quietly, shaking his head in amazement.

"He was either stupid or one hell of a brave son-of-a-bitch," Frank said.

"He wasn't stupid," Michele said quietly. "You can bet your life on that."

"I guess we just did."

Jeff walked hesitantly up to the group. Sheepishly he avoided looking directly at anyone. No one said anything to him . . . it wasn't necessary. Tight jaws and silence said enough. Gil busied himself straightening Monk's legs out on the floor. He was limping from the bullet that had hit his ankle. Michele walked over to the doorway where Merkel had been hidden, calling back to tell the others she had found a cart there that they could use to carry Weems's body. Frank grabbed Monk's shoulders and Gil took his legs, carrying him through the opening to lay his bloody form on the cart. Michele covered him with a drape that had been folded underneath.

In retrospect, Gil wondered why they didn't bring the cart to the body, instead of going to the extra effort of carrying Weems's dead weight by hand. Maybe it was a kind of tribute to carry the courageous man in their arms, maybe they just wanted to do something—act quickly instead of waiting for the cart, or maybe they wanted to distance themselves from the doleful figure of Corleski. If it was the latter, it didn't accomplish much, because Jeff tagged along, like a stray animal. For whatever reason, they were gathered around Monk's corpse in the adjacent tunnel when a tremendous explosion erupted.

The next to last little box winked out on the LED display of Dr. J's detonator, leaving a dull black circle with the letters "det" for detonated beside it. Now there were three black circles. He sighed. Only one more to go, and that would be the one that sealed his own fate as well. Not that he would hesitate. What was commitment, if it was not ultimate? When the blast came a few minutes later, he was close enough to the explosion to be sprinkled with dust from the ceiling. The overhead lights dimmed and blinked out, leaving only small emergency battery-powered bulbs operating. Clouds of dust and smoke rolled down the corridor, forcing him to step back into the laboratory control room, which was situated a few yards down the corridor from the nuclear storage closet. There wasn't anyplace else to go. This part of the tunnel system was a dead end. If any of his pursuers survived the most recent explosion, they would find him here. *Dead end* seemed a particularly appropriate term.

He was breathing heavily now, and sweat ran down his temples. He sat down in one of the upholstered chairs before the control console. Far off, he heard the crackle and arcing of electrical equipment shorting out. Red warning lights winked on and off across the control panels. He placed the detonator in front of him and waited. Very faintly, he thought he also heard a woman's scream.

Dr. Michele Peters was blind.

In the total darkness she heard someone screaming, and as her hearing came back realized it was her own voice. There was no nightmare that had prepared her for this. Even in her worst fantasies, she had only needed to find her way to the light, out of the darkness. Now there was nowhere to go. The darkness was her own.

"Gil? Frank?" she called, but there was no answer.

Her side hurt, and she realized she was covered with debris. Something heavy and hard was pushing against her. She put out a hand to feel the shape, which seemed to be a large chunk of concrete. It shifted a little as she pulled away, but didn't crush her, as her fear imagined it would. Dirt and rubble was on her shoulders and in her hair. She felt like her body had been through a wringer. There were sore spots everywhere. But nothing mattered as much as the fact that she couldn't see. For a moment she was back in the closet again, a desperate child. But deep within, she found something else. It was a source of strength, that told her she was a survivor. She had lived through childhood abuse, professional discrimination, and direct attempts to take her life. Maybe she could survive again.

Michele's eyes stung and watered, and she could feel gritty particles under her eyelids that must have been dirt driven there by the force of the explosion. She also noticed the sticky warmth of blood seeping from a wound in her hair, and wondered briefly if her blindness was from the trauma to her eyes, or one to her skull. She supposed that she should stay put, but couldn't help being spooked by the sound of crackling electricity and vibrations that shook more sprinkles of dirt on her head.

She lost her composure when her hand contacted a human leg. When she encountered another human body a few feet away, she panicked entirely. Her brain shouted to her to get out of there, and she began desperately crawling away from the bodies on hands and knees, searching ahead by feel.

A few yards further on, her panic began to subside a bit, and she slowed. She reached down inside herself and found that strong place again. *Survive!* It said to her. *You must survive!* Nearby someone was moaning quietly. Feeling about with her hands, she found a human form that moved slightly—another member of the team, but he either wouldn't or couldn't answer her. She felt over the figure, jumping back when the man screamed in pain. It sounded like Jeff. That meant that the bodies she had felt earlier were those of Frank and Gil. If she was going to get out of here, she couldn't count on any help. She was on her own. She shivered, gulped back tears, and moved on . . . inch by inch in her personal hell of darkness.

The first bodies Dr. Peters had felt, were not those of Frank and Gil. In her panic, she had forgotten about Monk, whose corpse ended up next to her in the jumbled aftermath of the blast. The other body was one of the homeless men that often hid out in the tunnels. He had been sleeping off a drinking binge in a dark corner of the corridor, and was caught in the blast. The two detectives were on the opposite side of a pile of rubble that had collapsed from the ceiling. Frank had a severely sprained or broken left wrist and numerous cuts and scrapes. He still had his gun, but he was down to a couple of shells, and he had lost his Glock pistol in the blast as well. Gil had some question about whether his partner was in condition to do much anyway. Frank's right hand was okay, but he normally shot with his left. In the flickering light cast by piles of flaming material, he looked a wreck.

Meanwhile, Beach had a severely bruised shoulder and a broken finger on his left hand, these in addition to the gimpy ankle from before. Despite the pain, they were both able to move, but there didn't seem any place to go. The blast had turned the laboratory into an inferno of smoke, fire, and electrical sparks.

"There isn't any way out, back that direction," Gil said, as much to himself as to Frank.

"Looks like we aren't goin' anywhere. I guess we finally ran out of luck, old friend. What the hell, at least I can get some rest before I buy the farm."

Although he spoke as if he were joking, Gil didn't like the man's tone underneath.

"Forget it. We're getting out of here."

"What are we supposed to do, dig our way out?"

"You got it."

"You shitting me?"

"Look, Frank, it isn't just your sorry ass that's involved here, or mine either. There's a couple of other people who might need us. That pile of dirt might be thick, or it might be a few inches. I could borrow your corny sense of humor and say I'm dying to find out, but I don't plan on dying, and I don't plan on letting you sit here and suffocate either. Did you forget about Helen, or what?"

Painfully, Gil moved to the pile of rubble and began clawing away at the dirt. Soon Frank laboriously moved up beside him and began pulling rocks out of the way with his good hand.

Jamison looked out the window of the control room to see a figure through the clearing dust, far down the corridor crawling along on hands and knees, feeling the ground ahead cautiously. Though hard to distinguish from this distance, it looked like a woman. He was afraid it was another of the scum, the vagrants and bums that he often encountered in the underground corridors, looking for places to hide and infest. Then he saw she was only partially clothed. Her frame was young and well-formed, skin clear. Yes, it must be that irritating woman, Peters. So there was one survivor. For the moment.

Instead of heading straight for the control room, the woman came to an opening in the side wall, felt the corner, and turned into the intersecting passage. That corridor led toward the nuclear storage closet. There was no indication that she could see where she was going. Jamison smiled.

He went to the console and saw that the storage area machinery was still operational. That part of his facility was completely automated, so no one had to handle radioactive materials directly. With the press of a button, he opened the doors, so the woman would not meet any resistance in her path. She was heading straight for the disposal pit, a deep well into which various wastes were deposited, radioactive and human. Up until now it had not received the living, but it looked like that was about to change. Dr. J pushed another button on the console, and hydraulic systems were activated, sliding a heavy

DARK MEDICINE 313

lead alloy cover off the top of the pit into its fitted recess. There was a beveled pitch to the lip of the deep shaft, which had been coated with industrial lubricant to allow smooth operation of the servo mechanisms that normally made deposits into the murky pool below. Every part of the design made it easy for things to slide into the shaft. There were no safety measures installed for the unlikely event of a person stumbling into the funnel-like opening. But if it had been designed as a trap, it couldn't have been planned much better. The woman proceeded blindly, straight for the hole's gaping mouth.

Forty-eight

Beach had selected a good place to dig—at the side of the tunnel instead of the center where the majority of the rock and dirt had dropped. He and Terranova had been laboring for only a few minutes when Gil pulled at a piece of old timber, which slid out of place leaving a small hole to the other side. The success gave them new energy, and soon there was an opening large enough to wriggle through. Emergency lights powered by batteries were still operating, and dimly lit Monk's lower torso, jutting out of the rubble. They decided to leave the body for now, in the interest of quickly finding Michele. Even in the shadowy light, they could see the marks of hands and knees in the dirt, trailing off ahead. They weren't sure who it was, until they noticed the prone form of Jeff, lying a few yards ahead. He was caked with dirt and blood, but was breathing evenly, as if asleep. Since he didn't move at their approach, they decided to let him stay as he was, and come back for him later. They followed the scrapes and hand prints in the dirt. At a point further on, a new set of marks appeared. They looked like a man's shoe-prints.

"Who the hell is that?" Frank wondered out loud.

"I don't know, but they follow the same route. I'd guess someone was following her."

"Could be. They look like a man's shoes. If he's following, it must be back a ways, or she'd see him, right?"

"Depends on what kind of shape she's in. She must be hurt," Gil guessed, "or she wouldn't be crawling."

"I don't see any blood."

"There are a lot of ways to be hurt that don't bleed."

Michele's eyes were on fire. She could barely keep from clawing at them, despite knowing that would be a dangerous thing to do, potentially adding more damage to whatever injury had already taken place. The only light she saw was a phantom pulsing flash of pain, as her head throbbed sickeningly.

She had been following walls up until this point, but now her hands felt some kind of track on the floor. She moved along this path, hoping that it would eventually lead to a way out, or at least a central place of activity, where she could get help. She shivered from the damp cold of the subterranean tunnel, wishing she were wearing something more than a brassiere and slacks. The pants now had holes worn in the knees, and her hands were raw from feeling along the rough surfaces. Tears streamed down her face, mostly from the pain and irritation in her eyes, but partly also as a result of her gut-wrenching fear.

Imagination was playing havoc with her emotions. She imagined rabies-laden rats and other vermin waiting to bite her outstretched hands, sudden holes gaping before her, over which she would fall to her death, madmen stalking her a few feet beyond her reach, live electrical wires lying in her path. Not all of her fantasies were false, but she didn't know that. Her rational, scientific mind kept countering her emotional terror, telling her that no such horrors actually awaited in the darkness. However, this was one of the rare occasions when her intellect was wrong. Someone actually was watching her progress from only a short distance away. And a pit waited just ahead, as awful as any her fantasies might have created.

She jerked reflexively when she felt something touch her. It felt like cold metal sliding across her back.

"Who is it? What are you doing?" she cried out uselessly.

There was a deep and evil laugh. It sounded familiar, but not enough to identify who was tormenting her. Michele felt at her belt for the gun Gil had loaned to her, gasping when she found that it was gone. Somewhere in the last explosion or her crawling obstacle course, it had fallen out. Having the small weapon had been a source of security to counter her terrible sense of helplessness and vulnerability. Now she didn't even have that.

Something sharp scratched across her shoulder. There was a pull and snap, as her bra strap was severed. She grabbed to hold the damaged garment in place. She heard herself moaning in helpless terror. Another scratch burned her other shoulder, as she felt the other strap snap loose.

Michele scrabbled around now, in blind terror, trying to hold up her bra while crawling away from the blade and the awful laugh. She hardly noticed when the track she was following began to slope downward. Her retreat took her away from her attacker, who, for some reason, did not follow. She was unaware that he held back to avoid sliding with her into the horror ahead.

A dark cauldron of lethal fluid waited in a deep shaft a few yards away, fairly vibrating with the activity of its contents. In the belly of this primordial beast lay the remains of other humans, whose fragile flesh now rotted and cooked into a fetid stew of radiated sewage, surrounding still active nuclear materials that gave it a semblance of protean life. The beast's mouth was ready for one more.

Dr. J watched as Pretaska toyed with the woman. It was almost a disappointment when he stepped back from her, laughing. The woman was crawling right into the maw of the depository shaft. Jamison watched in morbid fascination as she scrabbled toward her death. He leaned forward in his chair, as he saw her pass the slippery lip of the funnel where she would be unable to retreat up the incline. If Pretaska had joined her in her fatal slide, it would have been no great loss. He had outlived his usefulness to Dr. J.

But at least the woman was taken care of. She was already past the point of no return. If somehow she managed to stop, it would only delay the inevitable. And if it was necessary to speed up the process, a motorized lorry was in position to be activated. From a position outside the storage area, the mechanical hauler would move along the track to the disposal pit where it would dump its load and push the woman into the pit ahead of it. All he had to do was pull a small lever on the console, and the cart would move along its track, carrying Peters to her fate.

He nearly had a cardiac arrest when a hand touched his shoulder. Spinning around, he was about to grab for the detonator to press the final doom button when he realized the hand belonged to Pretaska. He had been so engrossed in the woman's fate, he hadn't noticed the man entering his lair.

"Peotre!"

"Yes, Ted, it's me. We have to get out of here, right away. I've been avoiding the police, but we have to get out. I think this whole place is going to go up."

"Yes, it is."

"You say that so calmly. You know it's going to blow? You want it to?"

Jamison merely nodded his head.

"Then let's get the hell out of here, or we'll go up too!"

Once again Jamison nodded his head.

"What? You want us to die here? You're gonna blow us up along with everybody else?"

This time there was no response. Jamison just stared back at the flustered radiologist.

"No. No way. You aren't taking me with you on your little self-destructive trip."

"I'm afraid you have no choice."

"That's what you think, love. This guy isn't prepared to commit suicide for anybody."

Out of his lab coat pocket, Pretaska pulled a small pistol.

"I've been following Peters for a while now. This dropped out of her belt. I don't think she even noticed. As you probably observed, she seems to be blind. But I'm not! I know when the party is over. And I'm getting out. Now step away from that doomsday thing, before I have to shoot you."

"You wouldn't really shoot me, Peotre. We're colleagues, fellow professionals, friends."

"Don't flatter yourself, Jamison. I did what I had to do. And that's what I'm gonna keep on doing."

Jamison turned red with rage.

"If you would betray me, surely you won't betray your oath as a physician."

"What, the Hippocratic oath? Be serious. You've been reminding me for years that the only reason I'm an M.D. is because you pulled a fast one. You call me a *phony doctor,* a counterfeit. And now you expect me to let you blow me up because I'm so devoted to that philosophical garbage? Nice try, but no prize, sport."

Jamison appraised Pretaska, trying to gauge his seriousness of purpose. He decided to test the situation and started to make a move toward the place where the detonator lay. There was the clicking sound of a gun being cocked. Jamison stopped and dropped his outstretched hand.

"I'm not afraid to die," he growled at Peotre. "But if you kill me, they will not be chastened or understand my power. If I stop now, they will have won. Surely you understand. You were a part of Magnes. I must purge this place and these enemies. Be a man and let me have the detonator."

"Oh, *be a man* he says! Right. Like you were so anxious to see me that way up until now. Forget it, sweetheart. You'll have to find somebody else to play with you in your little mad scientist routine."

Pretaska waved with the barrel of the shiny little gun, indicating that Jamison should move over to the other side of the room. The older man complied, but when Pretaska turned to go for the detonator, Jamison grabbed a heavy coffee mug from the shelf and ran at his protege. He smashed the large cup on Pretaska's head, driving him to the floor, where they fell together in a pile. The gun discharged as they fell, the bullet hitting Jamison in his upper thigh. Shrieking in pain and rage, he pummeled Pretaska viciously, finally dislodging the weapon. He pushed away, and still lying on the floor, held out the gun and pointed at the other man's chest. Pretaska had pulled out the razor-edged knife he had used to torment Peters, but let it drop into his lap as he saw how useless it was against the gun. He had a funny look on his face. Perhaps he sensed that there were no options left. But out of character, he didn't negotiate or plead, manipulate or lie. Instead, as Jamison bent down to take away the knife, Pretaska spit in his face.

It was the definitive humiliation for the would-be doctor, who rose painfully to his feet, supporting himself on one side with his hand on the console, and fired at Pretaska. It wasn't the radiologist's face he saw now, but the face of his father. He kept pulling the trigger repeatedly, but only one more bullet plowed into the man, before the six-shot magazine was emptied, and the firing pin clicked on an empty chamber.

Pretaska still groaned and moved, despite the two bullets, but Jamison turned away. He stepped to the console and picked up the detonator, wincing at the pain in his thigh. As he grasped it, he looked out through the windows to see the woman, now only a few feet from the dump pit, struggling to hold herself in place, but unable to gain purchase. If his own situation was not deteriorating so rapidly, he might have waited, watching her vain efforts as long as necessary until she fell into the shaft. But he felt a renewed urgency, and decided to speed the process. He reached out to a row of four buttons on the control board and pushed the first one.

A small motor hummed to life, and the waste hauler began moving down its track toward the pit and the stranded woman. As it passed the control room, Jamison pushed another of the four buttons to stop it for a moment, dragged Pretaska out the door, and, teeth gritting in pain, lifted his former colleague over the side, to roll him into the bin of the hauler. Pretaska moaned as his body thudded onto the floor of container. Jamison looked down at the man who had led him on, then deceived and deserted him. He spit on the bloody form. Then he limped back into the control room, stabbed at a button, and watched the motorized cart move on, carrying one betrayer to a final meeting with another, and their joint meeting with destiny.

Blood was all over. Some was from Pretaska, some from his own thigh wound. Jamison tried wipe his hands on his lab coat, but the dark red fluid was everywhere, smearing stickily on everything he touched, including the detonator. The one remaining symbol on the display blinked redly, its cyclops eye bloodshot and tired. The circuits within waited for his command.

Michele's hands were slipping on the slick surface, and she felt a terrible sense of foreboding. On the other hand, she was beginning to perceive some sense of light. Though she still had no real clarity, there was now a foggy contrast that indicated some gradual return of her sight. She kept blinking, letting the tears wash away the dirt and foreign material. But it was her sense of smell rather than clearing vision that warned her of danger.

A fetid odor wafted into her nostrils from somewhere close ahead. She was already near shock from anxiety, but this added element suggested new frightening possibilities. Michele had smelled putrefaction before. She had known the sweet cloying smell of decaying human flesh, and could not mistake it for anything else. She knew ahead was a place where bodies were decomposing—it was more than one cadaver could emit. Nothing else could produce that overpowering stench. Still unable to see too well, she couldn't clearly distinguish what lay ahead, but there appeared to be a large dark area in front of her—an opening, perhaps, in a wide circle of shiny metal, or perhaps it was a pool of liquid at the center of the cone-shaped funnel.

She had no traction on the slippery surface beneath her, and felt herself starting to slide at a downward angle toward the darkness. Her hands and feet scrambled uselessly, trying to stop the forward movement. She squeezed her eyelids together several times, and felt some lessening of the gritty pain. This seemed to help her vision too, as tears carried away the irritants. Physical pain was replaced, however, by emotional distress, when she saw the path ahead more clearly. Though her vision was still foggy, she could now make out the lip of the shaft a few feet away, and the blackness revealed itself as a deep pit from which drifted that deadly odor. She realized that she was caught on some kind of well-oiled track, running down one side of a bowl-like depression that ended in an open pit. The track was acting like a greasy slide that she couldn't avoid descending. Then there was a series of sounds. First she heard two or three sharp reports, like shots, then moments later, a rattling sound from behind her. She turned her head to see a dark shape coming toward her, perhaps a heavy cart, like those used in mines to carry ore.

As her sliding progress took her to the edge of the pit, her feet caught two small projecting flanges, one on each side. They were probably end blocks that caught the cart and stopped it from rolling all the way over the edge. Likewise, her downward slide came to a halt at the lip of the shaft, as she caught the blocks with her toes. But her legs were not made of steel. They trembled with the effort of holding her in place. Soon, she knew, her body would only be in the way of the heavy equipment, as it slammed into those same stops.

Michele couldn't decide which way to look. Before her, she stared into a deep chasm of stinking death, while behind her, a machine approached that would soon dislodge her from her temporary respite. She tore her smarting eyes from the cart bearing down, and stared at the hellish pit, only to pull them back again a moment later. Her future and her end were rapidly becoming one.

For a moment Michele wondered how desirable it was, to have her vision return just at this point. Was it better to view her death coming, or might it have been preferable to never see the approaching horror? Even in this hopeless situation, Michele knew the answer for herself. She preferred knowing. If she had to go, Michele wanted to go with her eyes open. She wanted to go in the light.

* * *

Bo Garfield was awakened by the sound of shots. Though he looked like he was in his sixties, Bo was only forty-two. He had once fought in the jungles of Vietnam, and would never sleep through the sound of gunfire. In fact, the familiar noise triggered a flashback, that only stopped when he found himself almost throttling Squeaker, who was lying next to him on the pile of old clothes and shopping bags.

"Stop it Bo, stop it!" the little man cried. "It's one a them dreams, again. Stop it, it's me, Squeaker!"

The wiry black man paused and got a far away look in his one good eye. Just in time. His grip was like steel from his habit of sitting for hours, squeezing a hand exerciser. After a moment, staring through the walls to a place far far away, he loosened his iron grip and let his hands drop from the neck of his companion. One eye cast about for the source of the shots, his other was covered by a dirty scarf, which was tied around his head at an angle, like a drunken pirate. In the dark alcove, there was little to see, so he began gathering his few belongings and stuffing them into the carry-all bag he kept with him always.

"Where you goin'?" Squeaker asked. "Better stay put. Whatever's goin on out there, it's better we stay outta it."

Bo didn't answer, but he didn't stop packing either. He zipped up the bag and hefted it over his shoulder. As he moved out of the dark alcove, he walked with a strange, halting gait, a permanent symptom of his damaged brain. A moment later, Squeaker followed him into the dim tunnel.

Some of the battery-operated emergency lights were losing their power now, so Gil and Frank found it harder

to follow the tracks in the dirt. But since there seemed
to be no intersecting tunnels, they forged ahead, assuming that Michele must have gone further on the same
route, and hoping they could catch up to her before the
man that seemed to be following her did. They had just
noticed a brighter area ahead, when a cracking noise
sounded once, then twice again. They both recognized it
immediately as the sound of a pistol firing. Gil held his
weapon at ready, as they moved forward toward the
sound. Soon there was a new noise, like the sound of
an electric motor and wheels moving on tracks.

The cart was coming straight for her, now only a few
feet away. Michele cast about desperately for help, but
saw nothing. Her legs were tiring, and she didn't know
how much longer she could perch with only the small
flanges to keep her from sliding. Even without the on-
coming cart, it seemed she would soon fall to a grisly
death.

But a deep instinct for self-preservation refused to let
her give up entirely. That strong place, deep down inside,
would not surrender. She raised into a semi-crouch as
the box-like vehicle came upon her. As she felt the impact of the steel on her knees, knocking her feet from
their precarious perch, she desperately grabbed for something to hold, and managed to throw one arm over the
front side of the cart. Simultaneously the wheels hit the
flange stops, jerking the lorry to a halt. There was little
strength left in her limbs after the ordeal she had suffered, so she didn't have the stamina to hold on strongly.
The sudden braking action was enough to dislodge her
feeble hold. She felt her arm giving way to the weight
of her body.

Yet, as her arm started to slip, there was a strange
development. Something that felt like a hand grabbed

her wrist and held on. The grip was weak, but it held her arm inside the cart at an angle, so that her elbow acted like a hook, holding her in place, hanging from the crook of her own limb. It was painful, but her descent into the pit was halted. The cart sat there, stopped, with Michele hanging from it.

Michele wasn't very religious but now she found herself uttering prayers of desperation, as she waited for some electronic command to tip the cart, dumping Michele and whoever clasped her wrist from inside, into a hellish pit of the unknown.

Forty-nine

When Gil and Frank reached the control room area, they inched their way forward on their bellies. Looking into the cave-like vault where Michele hung over the disposal pit, they quickly saw the situation, but when they started to rise, a figure rose behind the window of the control room, aiming a pistol in their direction. Frank pumped a couple of shots toward the windows which shattered, glass cascading in brittle sheets to the floor.

"That's the last of the shotgun shells," he warned his partner. "I lost my pistol in the last cave-in."

"Okay, I'll cover while you work your way down to Michele," Gil replied, squeezing off two shots.

Frank was able to make the storage vault, out of easy line of fire, and moved to the track that descended one side of the smooth bowl to where Michele was desperately hanging on to a cart balanced on the edge of the pit. He started walking down the incline, but his feet flew out from under him, and he went skidding down the track on his backside, unable to stop until he collided with the rear of the cart. Immense pain shot through his leg, and he saw his knee was bent at a strange angle. *Oh great!* he thought, *As if I wasn't smashed up enough already.*

Hoping it was a dislocation rather than a break, he took a deep breath, shook off the pain, and pulled himself up into the waste hauler, wincing not only from the pain, but from what was inside. Pretaska was not breathing, but his bloody corpse held a death grip on Michele's wrist.

Frank leaned over the edge and grabbed her under the arms. By leaning back, he was able to raise her to where she could use her other hand to help. In a moment they tumbled back into the cart, on top of Pretaska's body. Frank yelled in pain.

"Oh God!" she exclaimed when she saw what they fell on, wrenching her arm from the grip of Pretaska's corpse that still clung to her wrist. "Get me out of here!"

"I'd love to," he replied, "but we aren't going anywhere for the moment. There's no way to get up that incline, unless somebody throws us a rope or runs this rig backwards up the track. Between my wrist and my leg, I know I'm not going anywhere. Right now, Gil's kinda occupied, so we're gonna have to sit tight."

"But this looks like a waste dumper. Any second, it could be activated and dump us into that shaft."

"Maybe. But since it's been sitting here with you hangin' from it for a while, I figure nobody's gonna dump it, or it would already have happened, right?"

Michele didn't reply. Holding her pulled shoulder, covered with dirt and blood, eyes red-rimmed and swollen, she didn't seem to have many resources left. She slumped into a seated position, opposite the corpse and dropped her head, quietly sobbing. Frank put a hand on her shoulder, but said nothing, listening for the sound of action where he had left Gil. They waited.

Studying the situation to make sure he wouldn't have a repeat of the last time he checked his gun, Gil saw nothing that would seem to prevent a brief inventory. He removed the clip and found only two bullets remaining. He wished he still had his second weapon, the Raven auto pistol, but he hadn't seen it since giving it to Michele. That was the bad news. The good news was that no shots had come from the direction of the control room, and perhaps Jamison had little or no ammunition left either. A couple of feints produced no gunfire, which seemed to confirm that guess. He started working forward, when a figure darted out of cover and ran toward the control room door. It was Jamison.

Gil jumped up, and despite his swollen ankle dashed after the man in a gimpy gallop. Jamison appeared to be limping also, so by the time he had reached the room and managed to get the door open, Gil had caught up. The detective dived forward in a tackle that took them into the room and across the floor, where they collided with a table, and were showered with a collection of pencils, coffee mugs, folders, and papers that had been sitting on top of it. Jamison kicked and pummeled at the detective, using the empty gun as a club, which enabled him to dislodge his opponent's grip for a moment. He frantically scrabbled away to the console and managed to pull himself up before Gil got to his feet again. Beach ducked, as the other man threw the empty pistol in his direction.

"Stop! Stop or your friends die!" Jamison screamed, his hand poised over a set of buttons.

Gil paused for a second, assessing the situation.

"These are the controls for the disposal machinery!" Jamison yelled. "All I have to do is push a button and they'll be dumped into a radioactive waste pit."

There was a scratching, tinkling sound, and out of the corner of his eye, Gil saw the bedraggled forms of two derelicts hovering just outside the control room. Another pair of hopeless castaways, somehow living in a dark corner of the underground world. They stood with mouths agape, watching through the shattered window frames, standing on broken glass. One was a thin black man with a scarf tied around his head, angled to cover one eye. The man's head was misshapen and marked with deep scars. The other looked Hispanic, only five feet or so in height, and was grasping the bigger man's ragged coattail. Gil considered how they might help, but couldn't think of a way. They were trapped with everyone else and couldn't be sent to get aid, even if they were willing or not too crazy to understand the need.

"What good would that do?" he asked, not as interested in the answer, as in keeping the crazed man talking.

"Put your gun down, on the floor," Jamison said, "or I'll do it, I really will."

"I believe you, I believe you."

"Take it out by the handle."

"Okay, okay. Don't do anything you'll regret," Gil cautioned, taking out his weapon and laying it on the floor.

"Oh, I've done many things I regret. But they aren't what you think. I regret trusting the wrong people. I regret not eliminating certain thorns in my flesh earlier. I don't regret exterminating scum, like you and Peters and Pretaska."

"Pretaska?"

"Yes, you can't save him either. Not that you have any opportunity. He's already dead."

"But you aren't dead Jamison, and you don't have to be."

"Oh don't patronize me, Beach. I'm a dead man, and so are you. When I detonate my last charge, the whole place goes up, including the nuclear materials in storage. There's more there than you can imagine."

"I know, I saw the NRC guys."

"They don't know the full extent of possible damage either. I have a confidential German connection for materials they've never even suspected."

"You really want to release all that, and kill yourself in the process?"

"I know, you think I'm crazy, don't you? You've read too many comic books. I'm no mad scientist. I don't want to die. I don't want to wipe out half of New York City either. But it's your fault. You are forcing me to do it. Now listen, use your foot to slide the gun over to me."

Gil gave the weapon a push with his foot. Jamison had trouble bending, with the wound in his thigh, but managed to pick up the gun without taking his eyes off Beach, or setting down the detonator. The final red eye pulsed slowly. He held it out, aimed toward Gil, as if it were a gun, like the one in his other hand.

"Look, Jamison, none of that has to happen."

"Oh yes it does. My research is ruined! A little more time and I could have proven my theories. I was on the brink of providing the answer to regeneration. Think of it! Organs that replace themselves without surgery, wounds that heal without skin grafts or prostheses. My work could lead to eternal life."

"Not if you're dead. Put that thing down, and maybe we can find a way for your theories to be carried on . . . DOCTOR Jamison."

Gil knew that Jamison had lost touch with reality, but hoped that he could appeal to the man's warped ego. And sure enough, there was a hint of hesitancy in the man's eyes for the first time. There might be a chance. Just have to keep stroking his ego, that's all.

But before he could think of another line, there was a loud rumbling crash, and clouds of dust billowed from the far end of the tunnel. At first Gil thought it was another cave-in, but then through the murky air he saw the front end of a small bulldozer pushing a pile of debris in front of its blade. He did a double take when he saw the figure in the driver's seat. Though a distance away,

DARK MEDICINE 331

he was sure that he recognized the big man. It was Bob Mabry, his friend, now a deputy inspector.

Hanging on behind the cab was a white-coated figure that looked like Carl Troop. When Jamison saw the machine, and uniforms, his face lost its momentary softness. He turned back to Beach, held out the control and viciously pressed the button.

When nothing happened for a moment, Gil took heart.

"It didn't work," he said.

His brief optimism faded, when Jamison explained.

"There's a built-in delay. You now have three minutes to come to terms with your life . . . and your death."

Michele felt like she was waking up. For some time she had been operating in a fog. Maybe her clouded vision had something to do with it, but the pain, the horror and the shock had their part as well. Despite sitting in a death trap, with the body of Pretaska across from her, waiting to see if she would be tipped into an abyss, she began to find an inner strength beyond anything she had ever known before. She now knew that it was her real self. She was not a person with a strong *spot*, she was a strong *person*. She felt a strange calmness, and busied herself binding Frank's wounds with a section of relatively clean cloth torn from the hem of Pretaska's lab coat. Her mind started operating better, and she leaned over the side of the cart.

"Hey, what are you doing?" Frank protested.

"I don't like sitting here, doing nothing. If this truck has a dumping mechanism, I'd like to jam it. Have you got anything that might work?"

Frank held up Monk's flashlight.

"No juice left, batteries long gone. Would this work?"

"I don't know," she said, taking it. "Hold onto my legs."

Frank held her as she leaned way over the edge. She found what looked like a release lever, and shoved the flashlight into the space, hoping it would prevent the lever from fully disengaging. As she pulled herself back into the waste hauler with Frank's help, she heard a crushing noise, but it wasn't from underneath the cart. It sounded more like a wall collapsing. Then there was the sound of heavy machinery, like a tractor.

"Hold on, Frank. I think the cavalry may have arrived."

"I came to help you, and now you're telling me to hang on."

They smiled at each other. But the smiles turned sour, when there was a clicking sound under the cart, and a ratchet mechanism started to turn.

"Here, take it. I don't need it anymore."

Jamison extended the box toward Gil, while holding the detective at bay with his own pistol. Gil took the controller in numb compliance. He stared at the mechanism, wondering if it would be the last thing he would ever see. The box was sticky with blood. A small display screen blinked redly back at him. He looked at it stupidly, then saw what he was looking at . . . three black circles, dead and unmoving, with tiny letters "det" beside them. One symbol continued to flash. The tiny letters beside it read "act."

"Go ahead and watch," Jamison laughed. "When the message changes from 'act' to 'det,' the charge will go up, and so will we."

Gil didn't know if he wanted to spend his last seconds staring at the mechanism of his own destruction, but long before the three minutes Jamison had described, the display changed. Beside the blinking circle, new letters appeared, so small he could hardly make them out. The letters weren't 'det,' or 'act.' It looked like they said, "fail, retry, abort."

As he stared, Gil quietly whispered the words. Jamison, watching in ghoulish anticipation, realized what was being mouthed, and grabbed the control box out of the detective's hands.

"No, no, no!" he cried, as he punched the button repeatedly.

He stared at the display winking at him, as if in reproof.

"What happened?" he wailed, "what went wrong?"

He shook the device and wet drops flew off. He punched at the button again, but when there was no change in the display, Jamison hurled the detonator at Beach, and ran for the console. He reached for the controls marked "waste hauling system" and stabbed a finger at a row of buttons. Gil hurled himself forward, the force of his dive carrying both him and Jamison over the console, through the empty window frame, and on top of the two staring derelicts.

But he didn't connect with the crazed killer until after the man had punched one of the buttons. Even as they flew through the air, crashing onto bodies, and broken glass, Gil heard a hum and buzz of activated machinery. That was the last he heard for a while, because as they landed, his head hit first, striking the floor with sufficient force to knock him silly. He wasn't out cold, but dazed enough to lose track of his surroundings and let Jamison get free.

Bo didn't know what was going on, except that the two men in the shattered control room seemed to be fighting. Waves of memory washed over him, and the sight of a weapon made him woozy with a recall of war so real it was like a physical blow. His mind struggled to bring together weird combinations of his dreams, memories, and these bizarre sights. All he could understand was that one man looked like a medic, and the other was trying to hurt him. The man in the white coat had to be a doctor, and the other man had a gun. After a few moments, the doctor got it away from him, but then the attacker flew forward, knocking the medic out the window and on top of Bo. As he fell, glass shards sliced painfully into his back and arm.

Squeaker was lying nearby, gasping, the wind knocked out of him. His friend finally quieted, either passed out or dead. It was just like Nam, watching his buddies die. The bad man was sitting up, looking drunk. Bo reached in his bag, took out a can of dog food, and swinging in a wide arc, slammed it into the man's head, who went down again and didn't move.

Then Bo became aware of the blood dripping from his own back and arms. He needed a doctor. His buddy needed one, too.

Dr. Michele Peters also needed help. The bin of the waste hauler in which she sat with Frank and the body of Pretaska started to move and tilt. This time Michele didn't scream or panic. She just waited stoically. The gears ground out a ratchet sound under the cart, which changed to a low whine, and then stopped. Looking over the side, she saw the flashlight case crushed in the release mechanism. It had held.

But the danger wasn't over. There was a clicking sound from the undercarriage and a switch or relay must have re-set, because the whirring motor started, the ratchet sound began, and the metal parts bit down on the mangled flashlight again. If this kept up, it would soon overcome their jamming effort and they would be dumped into the pit. Above, she saw faces appear at the circular lip of the incline. The one that she recognized was Carl Troop. He was just starting for the track.

"Stay back!" she yelled to him. "It's coated with something slick. You'll fall."

"Then we'll get something to you," he called back, looking anxiously about.

He ripped off his lab coat and shirt, tied them together, and yelled at someone out of sight, to give him more clothes. As he was doing this, he also stepped out of his trousers and added them to the clothing rope he was constructing. Suddenly the cart gave another jerk and tilted again. The grinding sound got louder, making her wonder how much longer the flashlight would hold. She felt a tug at her arm, and looked over to see Frank holding out his shirt. She took it with a nod, and after tying it into a loose knot, gave it a toss up the incline toward Carl. It didn't quite make the edge of the lip, but he reached out quickly enough to snag it. She wasn't as accurate with her slacks, which she knotted and threw next. They hit a full six feet short, slowly sliding down the slick surface, past them on the right, to disappear into the dark pit.

"I guess this is sorta like strip poker, ain't it?" Frank wisecracked to ease the tension. "My mom always tol' me to wear clean underwear, just in case of an accident."

With grimaces of pain, he wriggled out of his pants and handed them to Michele. Her aim was better this time, and Carl's makeshift rope was now over half the distance to the cart. But they were running out of clothes.

Only one person was left to strip. With a deep breath, she started stripping Pretaska's cool and bloody corpse. The task was made more difficult, as his body was beginning to stiffen in rigor mortis. Frank began helping as much as he could, with his good hand.

A crunching sound reminded them that very little was holding the cart's bin in place.

"This might sound hard-hearted," Frank started, "but any extra weight in this thing is working against us. We should lighten it up any way we can."

Michele was puzzled, until Terranova directed his eyes toward the body they had just stripped. She stared for a long minute, then nodded agreement. A moment later, they managed to lift Pretaska's body enough to push it over the side of the cart. For a brief instant one arm caught on the edge of the bin and Michele reflexively reached out to catch it. She held the wrist for a second, then let go. It slipped over the side, and then dropped silently into the darkness.

"In a way, he saved my life," she murmured, "when I was hanging like that. Maybe he wasn't such a bad guy after all."

"Is that why you reached out, just now?" Frank asked.

"No, it was just a reflex, really."

"Chances are it was the same with him . . . just a last reflex. And maybe even less virtuous."

"What do you mean?"

"Well, I didn't know him too well, but from what I could tell, he was kinda wrapped up in himself."

"So ?"

"If I had to make a guess, I'd say he only grabbed you, because his last reflex was still to get help for himself."

Michele glanced down toward the pit.

"I guess we'll never know."

"So here we are, an optimist and a pessimist hangin' on the edge of disaster. I suppose you think we're gonna get out of this alive? Didn't you ever hear about that book, *The Naked and the Dead?* Well, we're halfway there."

"Leave it to you to be joking at a time like this," she answered, smiling in spite of herself. "But we aren't completely naked, and we sure as hell aren't dead yet."

As if to kill her optimism, the cart gave another jerk, and a piece of the flashlight's plastic lens popped out and skittered down the incline into the dark shaft.

Troop and Mabry were in their boxers, having contributed everything else to the clothing rope. They made quite a contrast, the young fit doctor standing next to the bloated and pasty old Irishman. But it was Mabry's bulk that was crucial to pulling the others to safety.

Although he carried a gun, Mabry didn't have a chance to pick it up from the floor where he had laid it, when a crazed looking Ted Jamison suddenly appeared, pressing a large, lethal looking pistol to the policeman's head.

"Don't anybody move or I'll blow his brains out," he yelled, eyes bugging out in a crazed look.

"Original line, very clever," Mabry said, sourly, refusing to appear frightened. "Now why don't you put that thing down."

"Oh your lackey already tried that," he spit out the words, "and it didn't work for him either. Shut up and move."

He started shoving the big man toward the opposite wall. He seemed to be heading for a gray metal box on the wall, apparently an electrical supply center or control box.

"I don't know what you did to the waste hauler to keep it from dumping, but every system here has a back-up. When I throw the override switch, the safety stops retract, and the whole cart goes into the pit."

"Well if you think I'm gonna let you kill them just to save my skin, you're even crazier than you look," Mabry's deep voice boomed out, unintimidated. He stopped in his place, not letting the man push him farther forward.

"Dead or not, you can't stop me, anyway," Jamison snapped, and started to squeeze the trigger.

Gil woke slowly, a miniature missile battle going on from one side of his head to the other. He automatically checked for his gun, and found it gone. Next to him lay a still form. He didn't recognize the small man, except he knew it wasn't Jamison. When he raised to a sitting position, he still couldn't see Mabry and Jamison who had moved out of his line of vision. He only saw Troop, curiously clothed in nothing but his underwear. With his foggy brain throbbing and stabbing him with bolts of pain, he couldn't figure out the reasons for that, nor did he have time. He knew Michele and Frank could be dumped to their death at any moment.

He stood shakily, to lean back through the window, over the control console. Reaching upside down, he made out the words labeling the waste hauling system, but there were only numbers attached to the four buttons arranged below the label—one through four. One of them must have activated the mechanism, so one of them probably would turn it off. But which one? If he pressed the wrong button, he might send Michele and his partner to their death. He stared at the controls, trying to think of some logical arrangement, some order that might reveal itself. The only one he could think of, was that the first button, was likely to be the "on" control. Since "on" and "off" were frequently the same switch in other machines he had operated, he hoped it might also be the "off" control. He took a deep breath and pushed the button. Nothing happened. The hum and grinding continued. That left three possibilities. He thought for a minute before making his next choice. He closed his eyes as he pushed it down.

Michele stared at the scene being played out before her, and felt a slight change in the position of the cart that made her wonder if the flashlight was finally giving way. Even if the jamming obstacle didn't fail, Jamison had taken control of the situation with a gun to the policeman's head. The madman had also just threatened to throw a switch that would send the entire cart into the pit. As she scanned the room, Michele also noted squarish shaped packages of some gray material located at intervals around the room, and joined by wires that led to the control box. Maybe Jamison was planning even more destruction than he threatened. Nevertheless, she refused to panic. She was through with that kind of reaction. If death was to come, she would accept it with dignity and courage. No one would take that from her.

As she looked up at the action going on above her, she saw Carl, who had been desperately working to effect a rescue, and wryly wondered why she had never before thought romantically of him. He was kind, ethical, intelligent, and nice-looking in a regular sort of way. And now two more things were clear. He was a pretty damn brave guy, and he cared enough about her to risk his life. She felt as if she was gaining a whole new vision of things, along with her returning eyesight. Unfortunately, she realized as the cart shook the new vision might go to black almost as soon as it began.

As she watched the scene, a new player appeared, a thin gangly black man with a deformed cranium, his face distorted by massive scarring, a dirty scarf tied around his head.

"Medic, medic!" he was shouting, as he moved toward Jamison and the big cop.

"Get back, you filth," Jamison warned, waving a large gun that looked like the one Beach had carried.

"Medic, medic," the man continued to call, as if he hadn't heard Jamison at all. "I'm wounded doc, and my buddy's hit. Call the Medivac!"

The derelict's back was soaked in blood, and he had a dull unfocused stare that looked like he was in a trance. Although she wasn't a psychiatrist, she knew enough to see that the man was not in his right mind. She guessed that he was a victim of Post Traumatic Stress Disorder. In such cases, certain "triggers" could put them emotionally right back into the stressful situation that had overwhelmed them in the past. Chances are he wasn't even here. Emotionally he was in some jungle clearing looking for a medic and a chopper to take him out of the fighting. Although, in fact, he was walking right toward a loaded gun, and an enemy in friend's clothing.

"I'm warning you," Jamison called, moving the gun away from Mabry's head to train it on the approaching man. "Get back, or I'll shoot."

"Shot . . . yes, I think he's shot . . . need a medic. Help me doc," the man lunged forward, as the gun fired with a booming report.

Despite the close range, the first shot missed the man entirely, but the second slug plowed into the right side of man's upper chest, stopping his forward progress and spinning him around. In an attempt to keep his balance, his feet slipped over the edge of the incline. He fell awkwardly with his arms up over the lip, legs and body extending down toward the pit. As he flailed his arms, he managed to get a hand on Jamison's pants leg. With a grip hardened by years of exercise, he held on like a vise.

Mabry took this opportunity to turn and slam a meaty arm down on Jamison's gun hand. There was a cracking sound, and the gunman screamed in pain, as the big pistol clattered to the floor. With the derelict hanging from his leg, Jamison fell heavily and was pulled over to the edge, the weight of the wounded man dragging him toward the slippery incline.

"Medic, medic," the derelict continued to call weakly, as Jamison beat desperately at the grip on his leg with one hand, the other hanging uselessly at his side.

Jamison couldn't dislodge the man's padlock hold and was slowly pulled over the edge. Mabry reached out to help, but Jamison's hands were still coated in blood and his fingers slipped wetly out of the policeman's grip.

The sound of the cart mechanism suddenly stopped, and for a moment there was absolute quiet, everyone staring at the two men locked together, as they slowly slid downward. They passed a few feet to the side of the cart track, where Frank and Michele could only watch helplessly as the pair slid past. As he disappeared into the dark mouth of the disposal pit, Jamison uttered a prolonged cry of despair, the scream stopping abruptly a moment later.

The following silence was eerie, and was broken only when the cart motor once again came to life. This time, the vehicle gave a jerk and started retreating up the track toward safety.

"Thank God!" Michele exclaimed.

"Allll Right!" Carl yelled.

They untied several pieces of clothing from the makeshift rope as the cart climbed to safety. When it reached the lip of the incline, they were partially dressed, and Gil had found the control box on the wall to cut the power, stopping the container's movement. He waved Mabry over to show him that there was also a separate detonator for the last set of explosives.

Michele tumbled out, into the arms of Carl Troop. The hug of relief lasted a long time, and soon evolved into an embrace of a more romantic nature.

"Enough already," Frank griped from his seat in the cart. "Knock it off, you two, before I run you in on a morals charge."

The embracing couple separated, laughing. For the first time in a long while, Michele was smiling, and a dimple appeared in her cheek. Troop slipped a wrinkled lab coat over her shoulders. Hand in hand, they walked over to the cart, and started to help Frank out. As they did, there was a cracking noise, as half a crushed flashlight popped out on the floor, and the cart's bin pivoted, dumping Frank onto the hard surface.

"Ouch!" he yelled, then looked around until he saw Gil. "Took you long enough," he groused.

"Well, there were four buttons. I hadda guess which one would bring you up, and which one would dump you over the edge."

"It's a good thing you guessed right."

"Who said I guessed right?"

"Huh?"

"Actually, I made a mistake. I was going for the one that would dump you, so I wouldn't have to listen to your awful jokes and whining all the time."

Fifty

The buzz of conversation died down at the Bellevue Hospital Center Board Meeting, as the chairman rose to speak. This was one of the quarterly meetings open to the entire hospital community, and almost a hundred chairs were filled, set up facing the board members who were seated behind two large tables put together.

It had been three weeks since the terrible events that had almost demolished a large part of the hospital and nearly made the whole borough of Manhattan uninhabitable. Waste disposal technicians from the NRC were still at work in the subbasement. They had carted off the stored nuclear material, but were taking longer to deal with the waste pit. After some discussion, there was agreement that little could be done to recover the bodies deposited there. They would remain radioactively contaminated for many years, and would have to be disposed of, or sealed over, along with the rest of the contaminated waste. A bronze plaque had been planned to mark the sight, and an anonymous donor offered to pay for a new ultrasound unit as an additional memorial to the victims. Those who ought to know believed the benefactor was Dr. Ira Wachman.

The elderly medical director had finally resigned, acknowledging his poor handling of recent crises, as well as his failure to uncover some of the terrible operations instigated by Jamison. One of the main agenda items for this board meeting was to make a new appointment. Another was to express appreciation to the Ninth Precinct officers who had been so helpful in uncovering the situation and preventing even worse consequences.

Gil and Frank sat uncomfortably, waiting for the meeting to start. Helen sat next to Frank, one hand entwined with his, the other still in a cast. None of them would have wanted the open acknowledgement, but the precinct commander had insisted that they accept it on behalf of the Ninth. Beach suspected it was also a slap in the face of the Thirteenth Precinct, whose boundaries actually included the hospital center.

Jeff Corleski had quietly put in for retirement, his wounds enough justification for leaving active duty. No one discussed his role in the underground events or laid blame. It would have accomplished nothing. When the SAKRED members presented themselves for arrest, no one at the Thirteenth Precinct knew why they were there, but after they offered a guilty explanation and apology, they were allowed to go with a slap on the wrist. A couple of doctors with questionable credentials and implications in the recent events were not so fortunate. The small group that awaited trial included Sal Roncali.

Representatives of the Ninth Precinct and Bellevue Hospital Center took pains to thank the Thirteenth for their cooperation. Captain Thomas accepted their words with stoicism. Since everyone knew it had been a bad show, it was like grinding a knife in a wound to thank him. But that's politics.

Finally the meeting began. The Board's agenda started with a review of the follow-up to recent events. There had been press briefings and public hearings prior to this meeting, so a lot of the hue and cry had already died down, but an official statement had to be included in the quarterly report. Wieman, a circuit court judge who also served as chairman of the board gave a summary of the Board's response and a statement of their judgement.

He expressed regret for all that had happened and assured a thorough prosecution of those responsible, as well as a complete investigation of administrative decisions and supervision to identify how such things could have ever been allowed to occur. Steps had already been taken to reorganize and revitalize the management philosophy and strategies. He made a point of reminding the audience that one mentally ill administrator and a handful of criminal cohorts, however, represented a tiny fraction of the twelve hundred physicians and one hundred thirty-seven members of the administrative staff that carried on the fine tradition of Bellevue. He vowed a renewed commitment to the ideals that made the Hospital Center great. He managed to convey the sense that BHC had weathered controversy and crisis throughout its more than two-and-a-half century history, and it would rise out of this dark incident too. Gil found himself almost feeling the history and tradition of the great hospital as he listened to the Chairman's words. Bellevue was so much more than anyone who worked there, and always would be.

After describing other specific changes and thoughtfully answering a number of questions from the audience, Judge Wieman then continued an agenda designed to move from negative to more positive matters. It was time to put the problems aside, to recognize and thank the people who had helped uncover the problems and "risked their lives to bring the responsible parties to justice."

Frank and Gil shifted uncomfortably at the praise from Wieman. Helen smiled. As soon as he had finished thanking them, the three detectives began to head for the door, embarrassed by the applause that followed. But Carl Troop kept them from leaving.

"You might want to hear this next thing," he said, winking.

". . . a truly great hospital center," Wieman was orating. "And in that tradition, it is only right that we should select a new medical director that embodies such qualities."

"You know what's coming?" Gil whispered.

Troop nodded. His proud grin made Gil guess that Carl expected to be the one named. But the grin got even bigger, when another name was announced.

"After great deliberation," Judge Wieman was saying, "we decided that we could find no person of greater skill, strength and character than our own, Dr. Michele Peters."

There was a rolling wave of applause, and one by one, people rose to their feet for a standing ovation. One of the first to stand was the venerable figure of Dr. Dwight Rutger Junghans. Dr. Peters, who was seated in the audience, dabbed at her eyes with a tissue, but smiled broadly, a dimple forming in her rosy cheeks. She sat straight, and held herself proudly, though one hand absently twisted a lock of hair. She had invited Gil's wife to attend the meeting, as they had become fast friends, and Pilar patted her maternally on the hand. When she didn't rise, or step to the front, the clapping quieted, and people sat down again. After the audience and board members were seated, the chairman resumed speaking.

"Ladies and gentlemen, that was our intention. And on behalf of the Board and community, the offer was made. But I am sorry to say, Dr. Peters has chosen not to accept the appointment."

There was an audible gasp from the audience. Wieman held up his hand, in a gesture that suggested that everyone should wait before over-reacting.

"We regret her decision, but understand that she has personal goals she intends to pursue that will continue to put her at the forefront of compassionate medicine. We were hesitant to detail the information about her selection at all, lest the person finally chosen as our medical director be seen as somehow a less 'desirable second choice' selection.

"We were blessed, however, with another candidate of equal stature, who not only brings a wonderful combination of skills to the post, but also a remarkable humility that insisted we share our selection process, and the recognition it represents for Dr. Peters."

There was a smattering of applause, while Wieman shuttled through papers in front of him, delaying until it was quiet.

"I take great pleasure," he continued, "in announcing the new medical director of Bellevue Hospital Center. We are happy to have selected a physician of demonstrated administrative skills, as well as a doctor known for his kindness and compassion. I present to you, the former acting assistant medical director, and our new medical director, Dr. Carl William Troop!"

Another round of applause sounded. Dr. Troop stood, and moved to the front of the room. He stood silently at the lectern until the room quieted. Then he spoke in a voice choked with emotion.

"Thank you. Thank you Judge Wieman, members of the Board, and my friends. Thank you for your expression of confidence in my leadership, and thank you for the opportunity to continue serving this unique and wonderful institution. I am gratified to accept the position, and will do my utmost to justify your trust.

"As for the selection process, I appreciate the Board's tact, but would never have a problem being seen as second choice to someone as outstanding as Dr. Peters. I am humbled by her character and abilities. I share with her a commitment to expanding the opportunities of leadership of the medical system to women. In that vein,

I am pleased to tell you that the Board has accepted the suggestion of Dr. Peters and myself to appoint as my assistant medical director the well-qualified director of our Oncology Department, Dr. Joyce Castro."

There were murmurs of surprise and approval at this announcement. As Castro rose and walked to the lectern, scattered clapping swelled to heavy applause. She briefly acknowledged the appointment and thanked everyone, especially Michele Peters.

"And don't you worry about Dr. Peters," she concluded. "She has other plans. The City Health Department has finally responded to the many and varied needs of New York City's homeless population by creating a special department to oversee new initiatives and improved clinical services for these brothers and sisters of ours. For a long time this has been a great concern and interest of Dr. Peters, and we are happy for her as she accepts the Mayor's appointment to serve as medical director of that office."

After more applause, Castro continued.

"Dr. Peters assures me that this is what she prefers. She told me that the Mayor guaranteed her an administrative director who would take care of the politics, while she was freed up to do actual clinical supervision and instruction. As I assume the post of assistant medical director, I look forward to learning more about the ins and outs of political realities, but I'm not sure that she hasn't gotten the better deal here."

There were chuckles from some of those present who were knowledgeable in the ways of hospital politics.

"Although we will be sorry to see her leave Bellevue, we expect that she will have many reasons to remain in close contact with our institution."

Gil noticed a little smile on Dr. Castro's face, as she said this last statement, and scattered chuckles from some of the people in the audience. Judge Wieman announced there would be a break in the meeting before addressing other items on the agenda. This allowed people to crowd around Troop and Castro with their congratulations. Peters was mobbed as well, but in a few minutes the crowd diminished around her, and Gil was able to step over to where she stood smiling. Pilar moved to his side and slipped an arm around his waist. He put his arm around her and gave a squeeze.

"Hi ya, Darlin'. I'm glad you're taking such good care of the doc, here."

Then he turned to Michele.

"I was surprised that you didn't accept the top job," he said quietly.

"I finally realized that I had confused what I wanted to see, with what I wanted to be," she replied. "I still want to see a woman in the top position, but having Joyce as the assistant is a step in the right direction."

"And you?"

"As for me, I don't need to prove much anymore, Gil. But I do need some very human things, like family and fulfillment. I believe that my fulfillment has to involve real medicine and action on the part of some of the human discards in our society. Somebody has to try to change the way we discount people, and treat them like objects. Technology is great, but it has to be coupled with humane medicine, or it is more of a destructive force than a healing one."

"And how about the family part?"

"I don't expect that to be a problem."

She had a funny look on her face, as she said this.

"Excuse me for getting personal, but am I missing something here? I kinda thought you and Carl had hit it off together. Doesn't this mean you won't be seeing him as often?"

"Nope," she said with a little grin.

Gil continued to be puzzled by her reaction, until he

noticed Pilar glancing down at the doctor's hand. There was a flash of light from her finger. Then he saw the ring. It held a large diamond. He stared at it, and saw her blush.

"Carl and you?"

She nodded, beaming.

As they stood there, another figure joined them. It was Darby Waterly.

"Hi Michele."

"Hi Tray," she replied with a genuine smile. "Have you met Pilar Beach? I think you know Dr. Waterly, don't you Gil? I've asked him to come with me to the new office."

Gil nodded, and shook Waterly's hand. After congratulating Michele, the other doctor moved on. Gil looked at Michele with a slightly questioning eyebrow.

"I know, I used to think he was inept. But that was a combination of my prejudice and the Emergency Medicine bias toward speed. When he caught the error that almost cost Helen her life, I realized that he was the kind of doctor we needed in my new mission. The homeless and destitute don't need speed as much as to be treated like human beings. Darby is the best at that. He'll be an asset."

Before Gil had a chance to say anything the public address system emitted a chime. A faceless voice sounded loudly out of the speakers.

"Code Ninety-nine, Code Ninety-nine," it announced. "Location One West."

"That's the Emergency Department!" Michele said.

Without another word, she ran from the room. Gil mumbled quietly to himself, as Pilar excused herself to find the women's room. Frank stepped over and commented, "Bad sign, partner . . . talking to yourself. What're you mumbling about?"

"Oh, nothing," he grinned. "I was just thinking about priests and doctors."

"Yeah? . . . Okay?"

"It isn't anything important. Just the way I think about them. First I thought they were all perfect. Then I thought maybe they were all frauds."

"Frauds?"

"Yeah, since I found out they're just human."

"And now?"

"I guess I think they're human like the rest of us. But, you know, some humans kinda listen to a higher calling, don't they?"

"Because they run off to emergencies?"

"No . . . not just that. Maybe this doesn't fit all of them, but I think they mostly really care. They'd never think of not going when somebody was in trouble."

"Then I think you could add some folks to your list besides priests and doctors."

"Like who?"

"I suppose a lot of people. But I know a coupla guys like that who happen to be cops."

"Yeah, I guess you're right. Maybe it doesn't have so much to do with the profession. Maybe it has more to do with a kind of person, and maybe they just naturally end up in certain kinds of jobs."

"Yeah, well, if that's true, I think I know what kinda person naturally becomes a cop."

"Oh? Like what?"

"Like somebody that's crazy as a bedbug. Nobody but a lunatic would do this job!"

"Right," Gil agreed smiling. "But then . . ."

They looked at each other, grinned, and shrugged their shoulders almost in unison. Then they turned and walked out of the conference room, softly laughing.

NOWHERE TO RUN ... NOWHERE TO HIDE ...
ZEBRA'S SUSPENSE WILL *GET* YOU —
AND WILL MAKE YOU BEG FOR MORE!

NOWHERE TO HIDE (4035, $4.50)
by Joan Hall Hovey

After Ellen Morgan's younger sister has been brutally murdered, the highly respected psychologist appears on the evening news and dares the killer to come after her. After a flood of leads that go nowhere, it happens. A note slipped under her windshield states, "YOU'RE IT." Ellen has woken the hunter from its lair ... and she is his prey!

SHADOW VENGEANCE (4097, $4.50)
by Wendy Haley

Recently widowed Maris learns that she was adopted. Desperate to find her birth parents, she places "personals" in all the Texas newspapers. She receives a horrible response: "You weren't wanted then, and you aren't wanted now." Not to be daunted, her search for her birth mother — and her only chance to save her dangerously ill child — brings her closer and closer to the truth ... and to death!

RUN FOR YOUR LIFE (4193, $4.50)
by Ann Brahms

Annik Miller is being stalked by Gibson Spencer, a man she once loved. When Annik inherits a wilderness cabin in Maine, she finally feels free from his constant threats. But then, a note under her windshield wiper, and shadowy form, and a horrific nighttime attack tell Annik that she is still the object of this lovesick madman's obsession ...

EDGE OF TERROR (4224, $4.50)
by Michael Hammonds

Jessie thought that moving to the peaceful Blue Ridge Mountains would help her recover from her bitter divorce. But instead of providing the tranquility she desires, they cast a shadow of terror. There is a madman out there — and he knows where Jessie lives — and what she has seen ...

NOWHERE TO RUN (4132, $4.50)
by Pat Warren

Socialite Carly Weston leads a charmed life. Then her father, a celebrated prosecutor, is murdered at the hands of a vengeance-seeking killer. Now he is after Carly ... watching and waiting and planning. And Carly is running for her life from a crazed murderer who's become judge, jury — and executioner!

Available wherever paperbacks are sold, or order direct from the Publisher. Send cover price plus 50¢ per copy for mailing and handling to Penguin USA, P.O. Box 999, c/o Dept. 17109, Bergenfield, NJ 07621. Residents of New York and Tennessee must include sales tax. DO NOT SEND CASH.